THE DAUGHTER OF THE SEA AND THE SKY

DAVID LITWACK

THE DAUGHTER OF THE SEA AND THE SKY
Copyright © 2014 David Litwack

All rights reserved. No part of this book may be used or reproduced in any manner whatsoever, without written permission, except in the case of brief quotations embedded in articles and reviews. For more information, please contact publisher at Publisher@EvolvedPub.com.

SECOND EDITION SOFTCOVER
ISBN-10: 1622534247
ISBN-13: 978-1-62253-424-1

Chief Editor: Lane Diamond
Cover & Interior Layout & Design by Mallory Rock

www.EvolvedPub.com
Evolved Publishing LLC
Butler, Wisconsin, USA

The Daughter of the Sea and the Sky is a work of fiction. All names, characters, places, and incidents are the product of the author's imagination, or are used fictitiously. Any resemblance to actual events or persons, living or dead, is entirely coincidental.

Books by David Litwack

Along the Watchtower

The Daughter of the Sea and the Sky

The Time That's Given

The Seekers Series

The Children of Darkness

The Stuff of Stars

The Light of Reason

For Peter and Kevin,
and sons and daughters everywhere.

"There are only two ways to live your life. One is as though nothing is a miracle. The other is as though everything is a miracle."

— Albert Einstein

PROLOGUE

The Minister of Commerce trudged up to the steel hut at the peak of the land bridge, a path he'd climbed a hundred times or more. But never before had it felt so steep.

The land bridge was a patch of red clay kept stripped of vegetation by the two governments, though few plants would have grown there anyway. A black metal barrier topped by jagged spikes surrounded the compound, with the sole access through two gates, one to the east and the other to the west. They called them asylum gates because any refugee who passed through them, even by a hair's breadth, had the right to request asylum from the other side.

At the crest of the hill stood the meeting center, a white and green structure, once shiny and new, now faded almost to gray. Small wonder. It had been built fifty-two years ago as part of the Treaty of Separation. Perhaps the time had come to dismantle it and build a new one, or at least bake on a new layer of paint.

It straddled a negotiated boundary and provided the only contact between the minister's people and the soulless, races that had kept apart—except in time of war—since the Great Sundering. At least that was the story preached by the senkyosei from their pulpits. According to them, Lord Kanakunai, creator of the Spirit, in response to the folly of reason, had sundered the world into two identical landmasses: The Blessed Lands for believers, and The Republic for the soulless. These He separated by a great ocean, leaving only this slender spit of earth at the top, like a windpipe connecting the nodes of the lungs.

But as the senkyosei loved to say, only one side possessed a heart.

The Minister of Commerce's first encounter with the soulless had been as a young bureaucrat coming to evaluate refugees requesting transmigration to The Blessed Lands. Back then, he needed two days to travel to the land bridge and would arrive tired and dusty, a supplicant. Today, he'd come with an entourage, and the trip had taken less than three hours thanks to technology he'd negotiated from the other side—a motorized wagon on a newly paved road. Importing such inventions had been one of his greatest accomplishments and had resulted in a better life for his people, but it had also brought great wealth for many on the other side. Now he was a peer in their eyes, no longer a supplicant.

When he reached the hut, he stood patiently, arms outstretched, as troopers from The Republic patted him down, searching for weapons and, far more dangerous, any form of the written word. His own guardsmen would be doing the same to the soulless on the far side. Once he was cleared, he stepped inside.

Underlings from each race were still fussing over the position of the conference table. He watched the debate as the table was nudged first one way and then another to ensure precise placement over the boundary. The representatives of the soulless measured with their instruments, more needless wonders conceived through the worship of reason. His people took a different approach, eyeballing the line intersecting the floor and then praying they be granted their fair share.

When each side was satisfied, he took his seat and waited. This meeting had been set up at his request and so, by protocol, he'd been the first to enter. After a painful minute, a door on the opposite wall opened and two stout men marched into the room, taking up positions on either side of a padded leather chair. Though unarmed, they appeared more than able to defend themselves without weapons.

As he waited, his mouth went dry and his palms began to sweat. He took a sip of water from a glass on the table, and pulled out a handkerchief from his suit pocket to wipe his hands. He'd met many times with high-ranking officials from The Republic, those responsible for education, culture, or trade, but never before had he met a man who commanded an army.

THE DAUGHTER OF THE SEA AND THE SKY

Moments later the Secretary of the Department of Separation strode into the room, a bear of a man with the carriage of one accustomed to power.

The minister sat up straight and forced himself to look the man in the eye, to try to read his thoughts and more, to see the soul those of his ilk denied.

For this man controlled not only an army, but the fate of all the minister held dear.

CHAPTER 1

A BOAT WHERE NONE SHOULD BE

Helena Brewster sat atop the rocks, five feet above the receding tide, and pretended to read. At least until Jason came jogging along the beach below. She planned to wait until he was a few steps away, then turn the page she wasn't reading and let her eyes drift up to meet his. Perhaps his eyes would find hers, and for the first time since he'd reappeared, he'd stop and stay. But today, he seemed agonizingly late. To fill up the time and tamp down her anticipation, she practiced the motion, turning a page and looking up.

No Jason.

She understood the first day's awkwardness, brought on by their unexpected encounter — they hadn't seen each other in over four years, hadn't been in touch for more than two. But the second day wasn't much better. He'd been out of breath and tongue-tied; she'd still been numb from the funeral. It was the third day before they managed a brief conversation, an exchange of pleasantries unworthy of what had once existed between them.

Today she hoped for more.

THE DAUGHTER OF THE SEA AND THE SKY

She abandoned all pretense of reading and stared out to sea. There, through the fog brooding over the ocean, a boat appeared. *What in the name of reason would a boat be doing here?* Must be her imagination playing games with the fog while she waited for Jason to arrive.

She slowed her breathing as she'd been taught, to control the passions and clear the mind. Then she listened again for the beat of his shoes on the sand. Nothing but the slosh of waves breaking on the shore. She checked the high-water mark beneath her feet, calculating how much the tide would have to recede before exposing enough beach for a runner. Still a few minutes to go.

They'd gone to the same academy, she and Jason, levels one through eight, though it took a while before they became close. She sat near the window, he by the inside wall. She paid attention to the mentor, while Jason stared outside, seemingly building castles in the air. Each year, he managed to get assigned a row closer, and by the time they'd achieved fifth level, he sat next to her and passed notes, asking if he could walk her home after school. When she told him she was concerned they'd get caught, he changed the notes, ending each with the phrase: "Take a chance, Helena."

In the spring of that year, she did.

From then on, he walked her home every afternoon along this very beach, but never beyond this point, too intimidated by the big houses on the cliffs.

That came to an end when their class advanced to secondary school. He'd gone to the communal one in the village, and she to the private one where children of the Polytech faculty studied. Yes, they tried to see each other every day, but she'd become obsessed with grades, trying to please her father, and he'd taken a job at a snack shop after school to save money for university. She'd gone to see him as often as possible, ordering a lemon-flavored drink and visiting during his break. It wasn't much, but they were unconcerned; there'd be time when they were older.

After she moved away—she'd never questioned attending her father's school—they stayed in touch for a while. Jason would drop a note, and she'd respond. Then, somehow, two years of silence ensued.

Now, after all this time, he'd reappeared, jogging by as she grieved along the cliffs, exactly a half hour past high tide. Like a fleeting glimmer in this darkest of summers. Like a miracle.

She shook her head. If her father were alive, he'd chastise her for such a thought. She could hear his voice, that of a true scientist—there were no miracles.

The ripple at the edge of the fog again drew her gaze. For an instant, it took shape, but quickly vanished, a reverse mirage, something solid where only water should be. She squinted, trying to penetrate the haze, and turned away to find something more substantial.

She traced the coastline instead. The land rose southward in a gentle curve toward the tip of Albion Point, and ended at the Knob, which stood like a clenched fist challenging those who sailed the Forbidden Sea. The northern firs that capped the rocky coast were broken here and there by a handful of dwellings. From this distance, they looked like great seabirds nesting.

The fog had shifted with the tide, enough for her to pick out her parents' home, the white one in the center, overlooking them all from the highest cliff. It was where she slept for the time being, where she stayed alone and apart. Only the second floor of the house and the garret above it showed. With the rest blended into fog, the house looked like a phantom rising from nothing. It had felt that way since her father died.

Each of the four days since driving her mother to the farm, she'd come to this spot, always a half hour before high tide. To her left, the long stretch of beach ended at the cliffs. To her right lay an inlet carved into the rocks, where waves crashed with a roar that echoed off the walls. Her father used to call it the thunder hole. Sitting on this bench-shaped rock above it, she could dangle her bare feet in the spray, neither in the water nor out.

Her father had given her a silver anklet for her twelfth birthday, an age when she worried she might be too old to curl up in his lap. He'd claimed that if she sat on the rocks above the thunder hole at high tide, the spray would wet the chain and make the links sparkle. Two days before he died, he reminded her of the anklet and told her when the ocean brought the stars, she should think of him.

Jason, she assumed, came for more rational purposes—the breadth of the beach below, the firmness of sand compacted by the waves—to this spot, their spot, the last easy place to clamber up to the road before the cliffs. Old friends turned strangers, now reunited by the rhythm of the tides.

THE DAUGHTER OF THE SEA AND THE SKY

She glanced back out to sea and caught the beacon of the Light of Reason. The ancient tower stood on a craggy rock in the middle of the bay, ten stories high and always first to peek through the fog. She balanced the book on one knee and scanned lower, down along the horizon.

The mirage burst out and became solid — a boat where none should be.

The sail luffing in the breeze was a clumsy triangle with no arc, holding little air. The front was awkwardly shaped, more tub than prow, and it sailed where boats were banned — a ripe target for the shore patrol. If it had been launched by zealots overcome with missionary zeal, it was too small and ill-fitted, not salvation vessel, but death trap.

And it was drifting toward the rocky coast.

She turned to a new sound — Jason finally arriving on his tidal schedule. Soon he'd slow to a halt, measure his pulse with two fingers on the carotid artery, and gulp half a bottle of fortified water. After checking his time, he'd scramble up the rocks to her perch, flash that boyish grin she remembered so well, and ask how she was doing. She'd smile as she struggled to find words to make up for the years apart. When she failed to say much, he'd mumble some nicety, turn, and jog away down the steps and along the road to the village.

Or that's how it would have gone, if it weren't for the boat.

It drew closer now, gaining speed. The sea breeze had risen with the turn of the tide, and the resulting chop held the boat in its grasp, driving it toward the rocks below the cliff. Even if it were seaworthy, it was doomed.

Jason pulled himself onto the rocks and approached her.

She closed the book and set it down, forgetting to reset the bookmark, and pointed toward the boat. A kingfisher glided along the coastline and dove where she pointed, disappearing into the water.

Jason smiled.

She shook her head and tried to find her voice.

"A boat," she finally said.

Now, Jason saw it as well. The sun glinted off something on its bow as it dipped into a trough. When it rose again, someone clutched the mast — a girl with golden hair.

Jason vaulted back to the beach and beckoned for Helena to follow. She moved to the edge, squatted, and jumped. He caught her by the waist and swung her to the sand.

In those few seconds, the boat crashed against the rocks. The crack of wood splintering rose above the sound of the waves.

The two of them raced into the surf as the girl with the golden hair thrashed about in the water, struggling to avoid jagged debris from the shattered boat. They waded in a few steps, braced against the undertow, and pressed forward again. Three more waves and they reached her.

Jason grabbed the girl just as she began to sink. Despite the buffeting sea, he carried her back to the shore without straining and lay her fragile form on a swath of grass beyond the rocks—a slip of a child no more than nine or ten years old.

Plain cotton pants clung to the girl's legs, and an elaborately embroidered tunic covered her slender frame—the typical garb of the zealots, but other than her clothing, she looked nothing like a zealot. Her skin was light and perfect, unblemished but for a trickle of blood on her arm. Her golden hair hung down to the middle of her back, and her round eyes held the color of the ocean.

Were Helena a believer, she'd have considered this the face of an angel.

Jason offered his bottle, but the girl shied away. Helena cradled the child's head and tilted her chin while he trickled a few drops into her mouth.

The girl licked her cracked lips and opened for more. After she'd drunk her fill, she turned to Helena. Her eyes grabbed and held. "The dream," she said. "It's true. I can see it in your eyes."

Helena felt a sudden urge to distract the girl, to disrupt that penetrating gaze. "Who are you?"

The girl ignored the question, instead resting her hand on Jason's forearm.

His muscles twitched as if he were unsure whether to linger or jerk away.

"Your arm is hot," she said.

"That's because I've been running."

The girl's ocean-blue eyes opened wider. "From what?"

He withdrew his arm and flexed his fingers. "Are you from the Blessed Lands?"

The girl nodded.

"Why would you make such a dangerous voyage alone in such a small boat?"

THE DAUGHTER OF THE SEA AND THE SKY

"I was in no danger," she said.

He waved a hand at the flotsam, still surging in the tide. "But your boat's destroyed, and it took us to save you."

"Yes, I suppose." She looked back out to sea as if expecting to find her boat still afloat. "Then I thank Lord Kanakunai for sparing me and delivering me to kind people who would help."

"But who are you?" Helena said more insistently.

The girl motioned for more to drink, this time grasping the bottle with both hands and emptying it. When she finished, she sat up and lifted her chin like royalty. "I am Kailani, the daughter of the sea and the sky."

Then slowly her lids closed and her body went limp.

Helena looked to Jason. "Dear reason, is she...?

He probed the hollow along the girl's neck with two fingers and found a pulse. "Just exhausted. She's passed out."

From the road behind them, a door slammed and footsteps approached. A uniformed official walked toward the sea, some sort of locator in hand. Halfway there, he stopped to recheck the coordinates. The title inscribed above his shirt pocket read: Examiner, Department of Separation.

"What's happened here?" he called out before he reached them.

"This girl sailed in," Helena said, hardly believing her words. "On a small boat that crashed on the rocks."

"Impossible."

Jason walked him to the edge and showed the wreckage scattered on the beach like matchsticks, already being reclaimed by the sea. "There's what's left of the boat."

"Well, that would explain the size of the blip on the readout. When they're that small, it's usually driftwood or a school of mackerel. Is she alone?"

Jason nodded.

"Odd," the examiner said. "Still, she has to be taken in. That's the law."

Helena knelt by the girl's side. "Can't you see she needs medical attention?"

"Well... that may be, but she's still here illegally."

"She's just a little girl."

"So I see. I'll call for help, but make sure she doesn't go anywhere." The examiner turned and headed back to his patrol car.

When he was out of earshot, Kailani began to stir, mumbling, slurring her words. "Penance... must do penance for the loss of the wind."

Helena brushed away a strand of hair that had fallen across the child's face. "It wasn't the wind, Kailani, it was the chop. No one could've sailed through that, not in such a small boat."

But the girl was dozing again.

Helena glanced at the examiner, who held an earpiece to his ear and fiddled with his communicator.

She leaned in close to the girl and stroked her bare arm. "Kailani, if they ask you questions, don't say anything about penance or dreams. Do you understand?"

The girl faded in and out, and Helena shook her as gently as she could. "Kailani, can you hear me?"

The lids fluttered.

"If they ask why you've come, say just one word—asylum. Can you remember that? Asylum."

Kailani's lips moved to form the word, but she drifted off to sleep as the sound of sirens approached.

***

Jason returned from the road where he'd delivered Kailani to the health services van. He plodded toward her, rubbing his hands together, studying them as if trying to understand how they could've let the girl go.

Helena felt the same.

When he was two steps away, he stopped and faced her with the same smile she remembered when he was a boy.

"The examiner took my statement. He said to wait for him. He wants to speak with you as well." He glanced at the ground and shifted from side to side, his running shoes sloshing with each step. His clothes were still dripping with a salty combination of sea water and sweat.

"I have a towel," she said, "if you want to dry off."

"Thanks. I'll be all right." He scanned the horizon before fixing on her. "He said they'll need to interview us up in the city. You know the department—security above all."

"What will they do with her?"

"The department? Who knows? Figure out why she came, then send her back, I suppose. Unless she keeps talking like that...."

Helena turned from him and stared out to sea. All she could think of was loss—of her father, of the girl she hardly knew. "She's just a child."

If only the boat could arrive again. If only she and Jason could rescue the girl again, but this time whisk her away somewhere safe, shelter her, protect her. That's what was due the daughter of the sea and the sky.

Jason focused on the road. "I should go. I have just enough time to finish my run and get back to work."

"Where do you work?"

He cast a glance over his shoulder. "At the Polytech."

At the Polytechnic Institute, like her father. Thoughts of her father distracted her, and the spell was broken. The girl with eyes the color of the ocean was gone, and Jason took off at a jog toward the village, never looking back.

She turned to watch as a maverick wave, oblivious to the ebb tide, crashed into the thunder hole and slogged back to sea with a groan.

When she glanced back up, she was alone.

Chapter 2

The Department of Separation

Monday morning, Chief Examiner Carlson tried to temper his usual interrogation. He'd never dealt with a refugee this young before. A nine-year-old girl was unlikely to be a threat.

"Are you feeling better today?"

She glared back at him. "Three days ago I was outside on the water. I haven't seen daylight since."

"I know, and I'm sorry, but we have to keep you secure until we determine your status." A trace of disdain in her tone had forced him to apologize even before the interview had begun. "I trust you've been... comfortable?"

The question needed no answer; she seemed anything but comfortable.

The overstuffed chair, designed to be welcoming to the newly arrived, was far too big for her. She slouched in it, unable to find a position where she wasn't constantly slipping down. Her feet kicked about, reaching for the floor. The uniform the department of separation

12

THE DAUGHTER OF THE SEA AND THE SKY

had provided was too big as well—they simply never received refugees this young. The orange sleeves covered her hands, all but the fingertips, and some well-intentioned attendant had kept the rolled-up trousers from falling by tying a pink ribbon around the child's waist.

Carlson glanced past the child to the poster of the Lady of Reason, holding her torch on high and offering hope to the oppressed. He'd often used it as inspiration in challenging situations, though he'd never seen one quite like this before.

"It might be easier if we call each other by name, don't you think? My name is Henry Carlson, but everyone calls me Carlson. What's your name?"

She fiddled with the ribbon, inspecting its bow.

When she finally looked up, he blinked twice, certain he'd seen the ocean in her eyes.

"I am Kailani."

"Very good. Kailani." He wrote the name down phonetically and followed it with scribbles that looked like waves. "And do you have a last name?"

"No. Just Kailani." She tugged at the bow, but it was double-knotted and refused to release.

"Okay, Kailani, then can you at least tell me who your parents are?"

"Why do you have no windows in this room?" Her tone was oddly adult and commanding.

Her very presence, the golden hair and the deep-seeing eyes, made his office feel drab. Sure, the dark wood was worn and faded, but he took pride in his workplace and always kept it orderly. Files were lined up neatly in rows, and on either side of the poster, perfectly spaced, hung portraits of his father and grandfather, their tops level and their frames dust-free. Centered under each was a slightly tarnished plaque engraved with the words: Chief Examiner, Department of Separation. He was third generation, defending the Republic from zealots and offering support to refugees.

He had nothing to be ashamed of. "Many of our offices have windows. Mine does not."

"Why not?"

"Because that's the way it is." He wasn't about to explain seniority to a nine-year-old. "But we were talking about you, Kailani. Do your parents know you've come here?"

13

She pressed down on the chair's arms and lifted her head. The arc of her neck was perfect. "I am the daughter of the sea and the sky."

Carlson made an effort to not roll his eyes. *Why on a Monday morning?*

He reveled in order—folders aligned with the edge of the desk, paper clips paraded in a row. For more than thirty-two years, he'd arrived to work at eight and left at four-thirty. The retirement clock that glowed in the corner was ticking down the time he had left: seven months, six days, three hours, and a diminishing number of minutes and seconds. When it reached zero, he would, like his father and grandfather before him, retire with the Republic at peace, the shores secure, and a solid pension in place.

He forced himself to refocus.

Beyond her odd speech, the girl from the far side of the ocean was nothing like other zealots he'd met. Her skin, though tanned, was naturally fair, not the olive of her countrymen. No dark pupils scowling through almond shaped eyes, and no unruly black curls; instead, long yellow hair hung straight to the small of her back, and she had a face that might adorn banners carried into battle by acolytes.

Could she be a diversion? Could others looking to make trouble have disembarked earlier? Might they be disembarking now? The zealots were not above using a child. In his grandfather's day, soon after the Treaty of Separation, boats would arrive with dozens on board. Some were asylum seekers, others missionaries. Occasionally, armed insurgents had hidden among them.

His father had warned him to be careful to distinguish between them. "The mythmakers are a race of fuzzy thinkers," he said. "None of them have a right to the benefits of the Republic unless they're willing to fully assimilate. When in doubt, ship them out."

"Tell me, Kailani," he said, "did you come here alone?"

"Did you see anyone else in the boat?"

"No." He rearranged the paper clips on his desk from a horizontal row to a vertical column. "But it's hard to believe someone as... young as you could've crossed the ocean by yourself."

"I am alone."

How does she manage to end every sentence as if the interview is over? He persisted. "Did someone send you?"

"Why would they do that?"

"I don't know. That's why I asked. It would be useful, Kailani, if you'd cooperate. You've violated our borders and broken our law. You're in a fair bit of trouble, and I'm trying to help."

THE DAUGHTER OF THE SEA AND THE SKY

She nodded, not disagreeing but not paying much attention, either, and went back to picking at the bow.

He checked his fingers. The tremor that had troubled him since Miriam left had returned. He did his best to control it. "Could you please look at me when I'm speaking to you? I'm curious why you'd undertake such a dangerous voyage alone."

"I'm the daughter of the sea and the sky. I was in no danger."

Blind faith. He'd have to come up with a more effective approach, or—

"Is it true you punish people for believing?" she said.

He lost his train of thought. "We don't—"

"And that you deny Lord Kanakunai and his gift of the Spirit?"

Almost the exact words of Olakai, their so-called prophet, before he launched the fourth holy war. "Why do you deny Kanakunai?" he'd thundered. Twenty years of bloodshed followed, ending only when the Treaty of Separation was signed.

Carlson eyed her more suspiciously. "I see you've been brainwashed by your people. Here in the Republic, we don't reject any idea out of hand, but we won't accept your god merely because you say so. What you call belief is based on myth, yet your people pursue it with a blindfolded certainty."

She slid back in her chair, set her feet onto it, and hugged her knees. "I don't understand," she said, with something less than blindfolded certainty.

He pressed the advantage. "Don't they teach history in the Blessed Lands? This is its lesson—mythmaking muddies the mind and unleashes the passions that lead to violence. The preaching of your faith has led to four wars and unspeakable assaults on our citizens. Thousands of innocents have died. Because of that faith, we're bound to be vigilant about our security, even at the cost of our freedoms. That's why we have a law against preaching. Were you an adult, you'd have just broken that law. But we're a rational people and you are a child, so I'll strike your words from the record. Now once again, Kailani, tell me why you've come to our shores."

"Why does it matter to you?"

"Please don't play games with me." He let his bifocals slip down his nose and glared at her through them. "I may be your only friend."

She tilted her head to one side and stared back as if he were the curiosity. "I was sent by a dream."

15

DAVID LITWACK

"That's interesting. Can you tell me about the dream?"

"I saw the soulless in my dream, people with sad eyes. I came to help."

The soulless. Carlson had heard the term many times before. But this child was different from the other zealots he'd processed, who spat out the term with contempt or sugared it with sentimental pity. He'd need time to observe her. The system offered only three options: grant asylum, send her back, or arrest her as a threat to their way of life. What if none were applicable in this case?

She squirmed about in her seat and glanced up at the corners of the ceiling.

He thought she'd forgotten he was there when she fixed him with her gaze.

"Why are *you* so sad?"

Sad. How dare she pry into his personal life? His problems were his own. She was a child from a backward culture whose values he'd rejected his entire career.

He smacked his palm on the desktop, making her jump. "Enough! This is my interview, not yours. I ask the questions. Why have you come to our shores?"

Her little shoulders quivered and a trace of fear flashed in her eyes—she was, after all, a child.

A moment later, she whispered a single word. "Asylum."

***

Helena called the department the morning after Kailani's arrival, desperate for news, but the official she spoke with was hardly forthcoming.

"This is *not* a patient in a hospital. This is a zealot who entered the Republic illegally. You'll have to wait until she's been processed. The chief examiner will answer your questions when you come in for your debriefing on Tuesday."

So for four long days, Helena waited. Now that Tuesday had arrived, she sat in the reception area outside the chief examiner's office and waited some more. She tried to study her book, hoping to keep her promise to her father, but the words swam on the page. She'd skimmed and re-skimmed the same paragraph for the last ten minutes and absorbed nothing.

She gave up and decided to study the reception area instead, beginning with the ceiling, which needed some paint, with bits of plaster bubbling in places and threatening to fall. The walls were faded tile, possibly once green, but now too dreary to be considered a color.

And what is that smell? She sniffed twice and thought she detected a faint odor of disinfectant. It reminded her of the waiting room where she'd spent so many hours with her father.

***

She'd taken leave from the university so she could accompany him to treatment; her mother had been too distraught to go. On their visits to the hospital, they always had to wait. She distracted herself by analyzing the faces in the waiting room, hoping to learn from others how to cope. She watched the faces as they changed, old faces getting older, and young faces thinking about the old faces getting older and becoming more vulnerable. With nothing else to do, she began to worry about time, about how much her father had left, about what remained for her and how best to use it.

Eventually, they were ushered into the infusion room, a long hall, with blue recliners along either side. Floral curtains hung from tracks on the ceiling, providing some modicum of privacy. Behind each curtain, patients sat with needles in their arms, reading, napping, or listening to music — anything to make the time pass while the chemicals seeped into their veins.

They waited again for Sorin the nurse — her father had taken to calling her Sorin the Savior — to come and connect the tube.

Sorin unwrapped two hot packs and shook them until they were warm enough to place on her father's forearm. "Do you care which arm?"

He shrugged.

"How about where I stick you? Wrist or forearm?"

"Anywhere's fine, as long as the stuff makes it into my veins."

When he'd first been diagnosed and given no chance for a cure, he'd remained reasonable as always, saying he wanted to die in peace and be no burden to his family. But the doctor said he had a growth pressing on his lower spine. As an expert in the field, her father knew the consequences — incontinence, paralysis, and pain. If he desired a peaceful end, he would need treatment.

Helena wondered how he could be so buoyant.

He looked up at the ceiling while the needle went in.

Nurse Sorin kept up a constant chatter as she arranged the tubes. "So, are you retired?"

"Do I look that old?"

"No sir. You look like you could run a long-distance race."

"I did, just three years ago. And I'm not retired. I teach at the Polytech."

Helena glanced up from her book. She couldn't let him get away with the understatement. "He's a tenured professor of physiometry, named best teacher at the Polytechnic Institute five years in a row. Some say he's in line for the Order of Reason."

The nurse wrapped the plastic tube around the pole and flicked it with her finger. "That right? You must be very smart."

"Not as smart as my daughter," he said. "Have I introduced you to Helena? Someday, she'll be a better researcher than me. She'll solve problems I never dreamed of, find cures for diseases like the kind that's killing me."

Helena flushed and looked back at her textbook, but the words had blurred.

***

It had been the same textbook she was staring at now — and the words were no clearer.

The door beside the receptionist's desk opened, and to Helena's surprise Jason emerged. As soon as he saw her, he flashed that boyish smile, stepped in her direction and spoke her name. Her lips parted, and she rose to greet him.

An official-looking man came bustling from behind and wedged himself between them. He placed a hand on Jason's back and nudged him toward the exit, clearly eager to avoid the two of them speaking before he'd interviewed them separately.

"Thank you for coming, Jason. Please contact me if you think of anything else." Only when Jason was out the door did the official turn to her. "And you must be Helena. Come right this way, please."

As he led her into his office, Helena twisted around to peer into the hallway, but Jason was gone again. She had so many questions to ask him. What had he been up to these past few years? What kind of man had he become? Had the dreams of their youth worked out better for him than for her?

But more, she wanted to ask the most unusual of questions: if he'd dreamed the past three nights as she had; if he too was haunted by a girl with golden hair on the prow of a sinking ship.

CHAPTER 3

JASON

Jason Adams stopped between the granite columns that graced the top of the stairs and squinted into the sunlight. The walk back from Carlson's interview had been unsettling, too much like the dream that had troubled his sleep since childhood — like the dream, but in reverse.

In that dream, he'd awake to a muffled keening and follow the sound, first through a chamber lined with granite columns, then down a hallway with ever lower ceilings, until he had to crouch to pass through. Finally, he'd come to a tiny room where a little man stood, smaller than life-size, with a woman kneeling on the dirt floor beside him in prayer.

Some nights, when the moon had poured its pale light through the window of his bedroom, he'd rouse, rub his eyes, and blink up at the ceiling, wondering what the dream meant. By his mid-teens, he knew.

When he was young, maybe four or five, his mother took him to see where his father worked. He remembered granite columns and marble floors with blue-gray swirls that caught and held his eye.

"Is this where my daddy works?"

THE DAUGHTER OF THE SEA AND THE SKY

"No," his mother said. They passed through a hall and down stairs to a smaller room.

"Is this it now?"

"Not yet."

Finally, they'd found his father in a cramped and dusty mailroom, and the younger Jason began to cry.

His father had stopped sorting mail into cubbyholes to comfort him, but his mother began to pray. She was always praying, a family tradition she refused to give up. His father begged her to stop, but she kept on, irrationally invoking some ancient god.

Jason now had few other memories of his mother: how she grew ill a year later and wasted away, how he watched her casket lowered into the ground, how his father clutched him and told him how terrible it was to be alone.

He shook off the mood. Today had been better. The chief examiner's office was nicer than the cell of his dream, the woman in the waiting room from a happier memory.

Helena.

She'd glanced up as he entered, her face open but astonished, as if she'd found the years apart to be a constant surprise — and not always pleasant. He smiled at her the way he used to smile when they'd walked home along the cliffs, and she responded with her usual half grin, one side of her lips curling upward while she tilted her head the other way. A glint in her eyes seemed to say, "You're a silly boy, Jason, but I like you anyway."

He'd stepped toward her, but before he could get near, Carlson had herded him out the door.

Helena. He'd been delighted to see her that first time, sitting on the cliffs at the midpoint of his jog. Though he'd often thought of her, they hadn't spoken in years. Then the letters stopped, too. Which one of them was last to write? Who was first to not respond? He couldn't recall.

Of course he'd heard about her father and knew how much she must be hurting. He wanted to take her in his arms and comfort her, but Now she seemed so distant, barely making eye contact. He hadn't been able to think of what to say.

Now, they shared a gift from the Blessed Lands, the daughter of the sea and the sky. They'd been given a second chance.

He knew at once what to do: wait for her, even if it took the rest of the afternoon. He'd wait outside in the warm air, far from the

21

windowless office. Summer was waning, and he'd take advantage of it while it lasted.

Across the street from the department sat a small restaurant called The Freethinker's Café, with a few tables set out on the sidewalk for the summer, each shaded by a red-and-white umbrella fringed at the edges. A sign hanging over the entrance declared it the ideal place for friends to meet, but it was well past lunchtime and no friends were there. He'd be the only customer.

He wandered over to take up his watch. From this vantage point, he had a clear view of the thirty-two stairs he'd just descended. She'd have to come out that way.

***

An hour later, Jason watched Helena pause between the columns to let her eyes adjust to the glare. When he called out her name, she cupped a hand over her brow and peered toward the sidewalk at the base of the stairs.

He raised his arms over his head. "Over here, across the street!"

She finally noticed and responded with a flip of the fingers, then brushed a strand of hair from her face and started down. She skipped over the first few steps but checked herself, hands flying out like little stabilizers, while he bounded across the street. They converged while she had one step to go.

"I have some time," he said. "I thought we could have a drink and compare notes."

"Notes?"

"About Carlson and the little girl."

"Did you believe him?" She glanced back up the stairs as if expecting the chief examiner to be spying on them. "He asked if there were insurgents lurking in a mother ship, if she carried subversive literature or weapons."

"He asked me that too."

"All I wanted was to find out why she came and what will happen to her. Such a beautiful child."

"I know." He conjured up the two of them rushing into the surf, him carrying the girl to safety. The face with eyes the color of the ocean surfaced in his mind, but he shook it off and focused instead on the face before him—Helena. "So, will you?

THE DAUGHTER OF THE SEA AND THE SKY

Her eyes had adjusted to the sunlight, but she still seemed distracted. "I'm sorry. What were you asking?"

"Will you join me?" He contorted his brow into a rebuked schoolboy face. "Or are you mad at me for not answering your last letter?"

She reached out and stroked his cheek, then tried to smooth the furrows from his brow, just like she used to after he'd had a bad day at school. "And all this time I thought *I* was the sinner."

He took her hand and lowered it to his chest, cradling it in both of his as he'd done so often when they were younger. But something was different now—a tension in her fingers.

After a moment, he let go. "Then we're both equally guilty. Or innocent. Why don't we start fresh?"

The worry on her face evaporated, and she broke into a smile. "Okay."

A few minutes later she was sipping a glass of her usual lemon-flavored drink, trying to keep the ice from touching her teeth, watching him over the rim. Other than telling him what she wanted to drink, she'd said little.

At last, he snuck a hand across the table and took the book from her purse.

She snatched it back before he could see the title. "What are you doing?"

"I've waited all week to see what you're reading."

She closed and opened her hand as if to imply it had never intended to interfere, then slid the book over.

"Tell me," he said, "why do you sit on the cliffs each day at the changing of the tides and read...?" He picked up the book. "*Fundamentals of Physiometry?*"

She wiggled her fingers, motioning for the book back, and he dutifully complied. "It's a textbook. I'm studying for an exam."

"And here I'd been picturing you reading poetry by the sea."

"You were the whimsical one, Jason, always staring at the clouds. I'm a down-to-earth Brewster. We do science." She replaced the book in its pocket and stored the purse beneath her seat.

He balanced on the front legs of his chair and inched a hand closer to hers. "I wasn't staring at the clouds, Helena. I was staring at you."

She gave a dismissive wave, a familiar gesture that reminded him how much he'd missed her, but now he had her attention. Her eyes were on him, unable to look away. They were sadder than he remembered.

He recalled the memorial service from the week before. "I was sorry to hear about your father. He was a great man."

"Thank you," she mumbled. Her mind was very much elsewhere.

He tried to bring her back to the present. "But why that rock and why that time?"

"It's where he used to bring me when I was little. He'd take me there just before high tide. We'd watch the spray and listen for the sound of the waves crashing between the rocks. He called it the thunder hole."

Her voice cracked and she needed a long sip of lemon drink before continuing. "He was a runner, like you. When he was invited to speak at conferences, he'd find exotic places to go for a run. Then he'd come home and tell me stories about them. His favorite spot was where you run, on the beach below the cliffs."

"I didn't hear much," he said. "Just the eulogy in the student newspaper. What happened?"

She started to answer, but her eyes welled up and she needed three breaths to regain control. "The doctors said there was nothing they could do but make him comfortable. Some cells in his body had decided to reproduce too quickly. That's all. No more meaning than that."

She lost her train of thought and began to fiddle with her hair. She removed the silver clip that held it in a ponytail and combed her fingers through once, twice, three times, trying to gather the errant strands in a bunch and reset the clip.

While she worked at it, Jason watched. Up close, he could see how much she'd changed—a grown woman now. Serious. No longer the schoolgirl of his youth. But one thing was the same: an intensity palpable enough to touch.

She looked up and caught him staring.

He nodded, a tilt of the head, enough to say: *Go on, I'm listening.*

She returned the nod. "Four months later, he was gone. He was a great scientist and expected me to be the same, but the last lesson he taught me was that science has its limits." She set the clip back in place, but awkwardly, so hair spilled about her neck.

Jason waited, still trying to fathom the person she'd become. When the silence began to drag, he made a guess. "Will you?"

"Will I what?"

THE DAUGHTER OF THE SEA AND THE SKY

"Become a great scientist like he was?"

Her lips parted, but no words came out. Instead she lowered her head into her hands and massaged her temples with her thumbs.

"Sorry," he said, though he wasn't sure for what. They'd always been able to say anything to each other. He moved closer and placed his palms flat on the table. "I didn't mean to pry. I just want to know more about you than that you study physiometry at high tide. I want to know everything about you, Helena Brewster, all the good and the bad since we were last together."

She fidgeted in her chair and shifted toward the granite façade across the street. Her face took on a pained expression, like someone about to make a confession.

She sighed. "I was in my last semester when he got sick. He made me promise I'd graduate on time, that his death wouldn't delay the career he'd planned for me, but I had to take leave from school to help care for him."

"Where was your mother? Weren't they a famous research team?"

"My mother?" Her voice sounded like surf rolling into the thunder hole; he waited for the crash. "She was brilliant at organizing his lab and his life, but when he needed her most, she couldn't bear to watch him die. So his care fell to me. After the funeral, when I needed her most, she ran up north to a place called Glen Eagle Farm."

"A farm?"

"More like an art colony, a place where people go to get their lives back together, reason be damned. She was such a mess, I suspect she would've transmigrated if it weren't for me. I haven't done much better. The university gave me a waiver until the end of September, but I haven't been able to focus. I bring this book to the cliffs every day, but mostly just stare out to sea."

"And rescue strange little girls from the chop."

She turned back to him. Her failure now out in the open, she seemed more relaxed. "You're the one who rescued her. I just stuttered and watched. Enough about me. Why do you always run at high tide?"

He was surprised at the shift in the conversation, but pleased. "I'm training for the Albion road race next spring. I run on the beach because, like your father, I think it's the best place to run, especially after high tide, when the sand's been compacted by the waves."

"And?"

"And what?"

25

DAVID LITWACK

"I want to know more about you, Jason Adams, than that you run on the beach." She said it with a hint of a smile.

He laughed. "Fair enough. Let's see... no house on the cliffs, just a one-room flat with no view. No world-changing research like your father, but a good engineering job at the Polytech." He took a sip of his own drink. "Enhanced communications."

"Communications? I thought the department controlled that."

"They do, and you know how secretive they can be, but they're starting to loosen up. People like us can only use communicators to talk, but the technology can do much more: send images and printed material. The department restricts it to keep it away from zealots—too efficient a way to spread myths—but researchers at the Polytech argued that controlling communications was inhibiting progress. Reason prevailed."

"Is it what you want to do?"

"It's a good living with a bright future."

"But is it what you want?"

She stared up at him with that same look she gave him when she'd visit at the sandwich shop. The question was the same too: was it what he wanted? He'd place his sandwich-shop cap on her head and watch the way her pony tail spilled out the back. Then he'd patiently explain how his family was different from hers, that if he hoped to go to university, he had to work after school. He'd accomplished a lot had since then—a degree, a professional job—both firsts in his family. More status, more money. More loneliness too.

He tried to smile. "Why do you ask?"

"Remember how we'd talk about what we wanted when we grew up. My path was set: follow in my father's footsteps. Now I'm not sure. But you? It was something different every few months: climb the highest mountain, find a cure for diseases, sail across the ocean and show the zealots the light of reason. From my regimented existence, I could only look on and admire. And envy. You never accepted the way things were. You wanted more. What happened to that Jason?" She found his eyes and waited.

He looked away, inspecting the underside of the umbrella. A breeze blew through the café, making the umbrella sway, knocking over a menu on a nearby table. He got up to retrieve it and set it back in place.

"That Jason grew up." He sat back down and forced another laugh; he was done with his turn. "So back to Mr. Carlson. You remember him." He mimicked the chief examiner's voice. "'Were there explosives strapped to her chest when you found her?'"

Her intensity vanished. "How could he possibly — "

"He's on a mission to protect us from a half-drowned nine-year-old."

An uncomfortable silence followed.

Helena broke it first. "I've dreamed about her the last three nights. Do you find that odd?"

"Not at all. I've never met anyone like her." He glanced up, suddenly wishing the umbrella had a hole in it so he could see through to the sky. "Helena?"

"Yes?"

"We both rescued her. Maybe we should go visit her together. It's an hour's drive from Albion and...."

He waited as she drained the remainder of her drink, then reached across, trying to bridge the gap between them. When his fingers brushed her hand, she pulled it away.

He slid his hand closer, fingers beckoning. "Come with me, Helena. Take a chance."

He followed her hand as it joined the other, unclasping the hair clip and resetting it, this time flawlessly, and fluffing the hair in front so it framed her face.

"Okay," she finally said, then reached back and rested her hand on his.

CHAPTER 4

A DIFFERENT PROMISE

The next afternoon, a matron in a blue uniform led them down a corridor that smelled worse than the reception area, a mix of sweat and cleaning fluid. Helena tried to concentrate, matching her steps to the squeaks of the matron's rubber-soled shoes. *Please don't let this be where they're keeping her.* When the matron pulled a jangling ring of keys from her pocket, Helena's shoulders slumped. She glanced at Jason. The color had drained from his face, and he walked stiffly with his arms tight to his sides. They passed seven evenly spaced doors, all with reinforced metal at their edges.

At the eighth door on the right, the matron slipped a key into the lock and released it. The door swung open.

"Five minutes," she said, and began to close the door behind them.

Jason thrust a foot out to block it. "Only five minutes?"

The matron glared at his shoe until he removed it. "I'm sorry, sir. I don't make the rules."

The door slammed shut, followed by a click as the bolt snapped back into place. Helena felt her lungs constrict.

The Daughter of the Sea and the Sky

The sterile room contained nothing but the basics: a bed, a desk lit by a gooseneck lamp, a straight-backed wooden chair, and a small bureau with two drawers. A fluorescent light buzzed overhead, and like Carlson's office, there were no windows.

Kailani lay on her side atop the narrow cot, knees curled up to her chest, facing the yellow cinder block wall. She wore an orange prison uniform several sizes too big. Though Helena was certain she'd heard them enter—a shudder of the shoulders gave her away—she kept staring at the wall.

Jason spoke first. "Kailani?"

She hugged her knees tighter and refused to answer.

Helena tried next. "It's Jason and Helena, the ones who brought you ashore when your boat crashed."

The child stirred and turned toward them. Her face was like a flower that had bloomed a few days earlier and now, denied the sunlight, had begun to wilt. Yet when she recognized the visitors, she brightened. She swung her feet to the floor, stood up, and took a step toward them.

"Why are they keeping me here?" she said. "Is this my punishment?"

"Not at all," Helena said. "Why should you be punished?"

An odd look came over her, as if she could see things far away—a prophet preparing to prophesy—but she said nothing.

Jason squatted down to make his height less imposing. "Kailani, remember the drink I gave you?"

She nodded.

"I could bring more if you'd like."

"And sweets too," Helena said, "the next time we visit."

Kailani's eyes narrowed. The faraway look was gone. "Does that mean...?"

Jason touched her shoulder. "Go ahead, Kailani. Ask. We're here to help."

She stared at him, and then turned to Helena, who could feel the question coming like a cold wind.

"Does that mean I have to stay here? I can hardly breathe in here—no air, no light. It's like a tomb."

"Kailani, listen to me," Jason said. "No one wants to hurt you. It's just that they haven't figured out what to do with you yet. I promise we'll...."

Helena could see him struggling between what promise he should make and what he'd be able to deliver.

"We'll talk to Mr. Carlson," she said, "and get him to change things." She waved her arms to encompass the dingy room. "Something nicer."

"Will I be able to see the ocean?"

"I don't think so. We're far from the ocean."

"Or water?"

"I'm afraid not." Helena's next words burst out before she had time to appreciate what they meant. "We'll find a way to get you out of here."

The girl came closer and waited for Helena to kneel alongside Jason, then draped an arm around each of their necks. Her little hands clutched them for a long time.

The knock on the door seemed to shake the room. Before the matron could enter, Kailani stepped back, leaving the two of them kneeling before her.

"You saved me from the sea, Jason and Helena. Now, with the grace of Kanakunai, you'll save me from this windowless room."

It was more pronouncement than request.

She reached for Helena's hand and placed it over her own heart. "Promise you'll come back and take me away from here."

The door opened and the matron entered, signaling it was time to leave.

Jason stood and backed away slowly, trying to buy a few more seconds.

Helena followed, never taking her eyes off Kailani. She swallowed hard—she wasn't good at keeping promises. "I promise."

The door closed between them, lodging in its frame with a thud.

***

Carlson was on a secure call with the district commander when the door swung open. His assistant bustled into his office with a yellow note card in hand, the agreed procedure when she needed to interrupt. He glanced at the card: Helena Brewster and Jason Adams were waiting outside, demanding to see him.

He placed a hand over his communicator and raised an index finger. "A minute, please."

He ended the call with the requisite courtesy, and gestured for his assistant to escort the couple in.

THE DAUGHTER OF THE SEA AND THE SKY

The two young people approached his desk and waited for him to acknowledge their presence. He made a point of reshuffling the papers in a file—a means of establishing his authority.

"What may I do for you?" he finally said.

Helena Brewster seemed about to lose control. "How could you treat her like this? She's done nothing wrong."

"I understand—in fact, share—your concern, but your statement is not reasonable. The first job of the department is to protect our citizens, yet we bend over backwards to welcome refugees. She could've filed an application for transmigration. Even if she were fleeing from the zealots, the land bridge would have been a better choice than the sea. She chose neither option, breaching our borders by boat instead. Whether she is nine or ninety, she entered our country clandestinely. That is against the law."

"But—"

"Now, please have a seat and let's discuss this in a reasonable manner."

Helena remained standing, gripping the back of a visitor chair so tightly, her knuckles whitened.

Carlson cast a pleading look at Jason, who managed to convince her to sit. Then he settled into a chair beside her.

"There, that's better," Carlson said. "I assure you, we all want to help Kailani, but the department has procedures that smart, well-meaning people have prescribed in detail over many years. I'm bound to work within them, and with all respect, so are you."

Helena's white-knuckle grip had shifted from the back of the chair to its arms, but when she spoke, her tone had softened. "She's just a child."

"I know. This is a most unusual case, but the department offers me only three options: deport, assimilate or incarcerate. I can't send her back since she won't tell me anything about herself. I won't toss her out onto the streets. Beyond being too young to fend for herself, she's shown no inclination to assimilate. It's obvious she's an unlikely criminal. Thus, all I can do is shelter her until... we figure out what to do."

Helena took a deep breath. "And how long will that take?"

"I'm in the process of researching it. It may take months before her case gets on the docket at the land bridge. Even then... let's just say the zealots aren't good at sharing information."

31

"If there's no information," Jason said, "then what?"

Carlson held out his hands. "Eventually, she'll go before a tribunal, and they'll decide what to do with her. I'd prefer to delay that as long as possible, give her more time to learn our ways. You've heard the way she talks. Every time she opens her mouth, she breaks our laws. I shudder to think what a tribunal would do."

"Aren't you being overly harsh, Mr. Carlson?"

"Overly harsh? Those of your generation are too young to remember. You complain we're too secretive, too invasive, but after the war ended, when zealots flocked to our shores and innocents began to die, people screamed for us to take harsher measures. You may not like our ways, but for thirty years, they've kept our shores safe from attack. Here at the department, the Republic's security is our highest priority, well beyond the understandable concern for a single zealot child."

Helena slid to the edge of her seat and glared at him. "So that's it, Mr. Carlson, the response of the rational world? Let her rot in that cell?"

It would be irrational to respond in kind. He pulled a handkerchief out from his pocket and dabbed his brow, just as he'd done the day Miriam abandoned him, after they'd shared bitter words.

"I know you see me as a cold-hearted bureaucrat," he said, "but I'm not unfeeling. I have a daughter of my own. It's just that the system leaves me no alternative."

They didn't know him. He cared about people and worked hard to mitigate the harm his bureaucracy could cause. He still loved his daughter, even though she'd locked him out of her life for the past six months since Miriam left, locked him out as if her mother's leaving was his fault.

He was breathing harder than the situation warranted, and took a cleansing breath, letting it slowly in and out. Then again and again. *Meditation is not a religious ritual. It's a calming practice to clear one's mind of unreasonable thoughts.*

He waited as Helena's face cycled through anger, confusion, and resignation. She released her grip on the arms of the chair and slumped back.

Jason didn't give up so easily. "You said you're sympathetic, Mr. Carlson. Isn't there anything we can do in the meantime?"

Carlson stared at his guests — two intense young people. Like all young people, they believed every problem in the world revolved around them. They thought badly of him, but he knew better.

THE DAUGHTER OF THE SEA AND THE SKY

He picked up a pencil and scanned the desk as if searching for a form that would solve the problem. He tapped the eraser on the desktop, and looked past his guests to the portraits of his father and grandfather. He thought of Miriam, racing out the door with a half-packed suitcase in hand. He envisioned his daughter when she was nine.

Then it came to him. *What about a furlough?*

Filing for a furlough would certainly trigger the attention of the tribunal, but what if he granted one off the record? It would be a serious breach of protocol, but not a violation of rules. He'd have to shred all paperwork, so the security officer wouldn't discover what he'd done in the monthly audit. The last thing he needed this close to retirement was a black mark on his record.

"I might be able to arrange a furlough," he said, "a day you can take her out for an excursion. I wish I had a better option, but that's the best I can do."

"When?" The two spoke at the same time.

"Let's see." He pulled the calendar on his desk toward him. "She's due for a health check tomorrow. How about Friday?"

Both nodded.

Jason stood and extended a hand. "Thank you, Mr. Carlson. We'll be back for her on Friday."

CHAPTER 5

THE NATURE OF THE SPIRIT

Helena awoke on Friday morning eager to start the day. It would bring not only reprieve for Kailani, but a respite from the big house on the cliffs. And Jason would be with her.

After showering and dressing, she peeked through a crack in the curtains to see if he'd arrived. To her delight, he was waiting in the driveway with the motor running.

On the hour-long ride to the city, Jason talked about his new job, how his team had merged a comm link with a text processor to create something called the encomm, an enhanced communicator that let universities around the country share research.

"Your father was one of the best researchers in the Republic," he said.

"Maybe the best." She smiled.

"How much more could he have accomplished if he were able to discuss his ideas with colleagues at other universities, every day, as if they were sitting right next to him?"

"Is that possible?"

THE DAUGHTER OF THE SEA AND THE SKY

"Possible and more. Our latest project will add photograms to documents — voice, data, photograms, and documents, shared as if you were in the same room. Encomm will someday change the world."

She eyed her childhood friend while he beamed at the road ahead as if the future lay beyond the next curve. Maybe this *was* the kind of adventure the younger Jason had been searching for.

Helena had little to say about her own circumstance. She mostly listened until the city limits came into view, and then their conversation turned to Kailani. Who was she? Why had she come? What would the day with her be like?

At the department, they signed the requisite paperwork, swearing allegiance to the Republic, and accepting responsibility for the child under penalty of incarceration for the crime of collusion with the enemy. That is, if she should escape or they should fail to return her. Then they waited while the matron fetched her.

Kailani burst into the waiting area, thrilled to be free from her cell, but she became most excited when she caught sight of Jason's car. She bounced on tiptoes and clapped her hands, telling them she'd ridden in what she called a motorized wagon only twice before. She thought Jason must be very important to own one.

Once underway, their first order of business was to buy her something to wear; she couldn't very well wander around Albion Point in prison garb.

At the outskirts of the village, Helena asked Jason to stop at a clothing store, where she bought the girl a pair of tan shorts and a flowered blouse. It was the first time either of them had seen her properly dressed and dry. She was enchanting, mesmerizing, no longer a felon but a golden child alight with innocence.

Kailani reveled in her new clothing, preening in the store mirror until Helena reminded her that the ocean awaited.

By the time they arrived at Albion Point, Helena was ready for lunch, but Kailani refused to eat until she'd been to the shore.

Helena and Jason had discussed where to take her. Returning to the cliffs where the boat had crashed seemed ill-advised, and Helena didn't feel comfortable bringing the girl to her parents' home. Both quickly agreed on the perfect place — the Knob.

Helena described it to Kailani along the way. "The Knob stands on a jut of land sticking out into the bay. At its end, it rises up to this rock dome high above the water. I think you'll like it — a place to rest and reflect."

35

Kailani gaped at her as if she'd explained the ocean had turned from blue to red while she was in her cell. "It sounds like a place of the Spirit. Why would the soulless care about something like that?"

Much as she hated to admit it, Helena could see Carlson's point. Talk like this could get Kailani in trouble. "Well, maybe we're not as soulless as you think. Maybe we just use different words. Like you, we care about beautiful things, and we try to help each other. Otherwise the Knob wouldn't even exist."

"I don't understand."

"The path to it would've been washed away long ago by time and tides. The giant boulders that protect it have to be maintained. The equipment that sets them in place is paid for by a donation left to the town by the Knob's late owner, Cornelia Eldridge. The townsfolk help too, raising money from an annual road race and other such events, as well as volunteering their time. As a child, I'd go to the Knob every spring with my classmates to help clean up damage done by winter storms. You'll be glad once you see it."

The moment Kailani was out of the car, the smell of salt water seemed to energize her, replacing her need to ask questions. They took the path between two stone pillars, past the plaque giving tribute to Cornelia Eldridge, and entered the woods. Kailani skipped along, hopping from stone to stone, jumping over roots and fallen branches.

In five minutes they emerged from the woods. A narrow causeway followed an exposed ridge that curved around to its end, with the final rise to the Knob constantly in view. The land dropped off dramatically on either side, armored with sloped boulders, protecting the path from erosion. As if to prove their necessity, a gusty wind blew from the north, driving whitecaps that pounded the rocks. The causeway terminated at a dozen stairs flanked by scrub pines on either side.

Kailani raced ahead to the steps, golden hair flashing about her shoulders.

"She's like a sunbeam," Helena said. "How can we let her go back to that cell?"

"What else can we do? Penalty of collusion, you know."

"If we could convince her to assimilate—"

"Hard to do, Helena. She was raised that way."

"She has a mind. She's seems bright, and she's too young for brainwashing to be permanent. All she needs is time, teaching, a place with lots of support."

THE DAUGHTER OF THE SEA AND THE SKY

"The way she talks—"

"A place where we could hide her away without breaking the law."

Helena pictured her mother's farm in the distant north, not far from the land bridge, an art colony where some less-than-rational people plied their craft removed from the oh-so-reasonable world. What harm could Kailani do there?

"Like the farm," she said, thinking aloud. "It'd be perfect for her. A child from the Blessed Lands? Instead of being offended, my mother and the others would hang on her every word. If only...." She turned and caught Jason staring. "Is something wrong?"

"Nothing. It's just that for a second I caught a glimpse of that girl I used to know, the one who sat by the window and cared so much. It's nice to see her again." He reached out for her, palm up.

Growing up, she thought of her mother's hand as palm down, restraining. *Don't go there, Helena. Stay near me.* Jason's hand had always been different, beckoning. *Come along, Helena, let's explore.*

She took his hand.

Kailani had stopped at the bottom of the stairs and was waiting for them to catch up. When they were a few paces away, she rushed toward them. With a squeal of joy, she squeezed between them, grasped each of their hands, and led them up at a respectful pace.

Helena glanced down at the little hand in hers, then across to the other hand lost in Jason's. The three of them climbed the steps to the Knob as she and her parents had done years before. Finally, she looked at Jason.

He smiled as if he'd been watching her the whole time.

At the top, the scrub spread in a half circle, which sheltered the rock dome from the wind but opened up where it faced the sea. Several visitors strolled about, taking in the views of the ocean to the north and east and of the harbor to the west. Most nodded as they passed but stayed silent. If anyone spoke, they did so in whispers.

In the center, a young couple walked with their baby daughter toddling between them, secured by a grip on each parent's hand. When she lunged for the ground, the mother lowered her to all fours, and she began to crawl. After a moment, she glanced up and smiled at her parents—mostly to be sure they were watching—then raised her butt and rose to a wobbly freestanding position. She teetered, unsure whether to attempt her first step. She tried three times before conceding and plopping back down.

Helena's own knees wobbled and she spread her arms for balance, as if the child's failure had been her own.

There was a tug at her thumb. She looked down to see Kailani patting her hand.

"Don't worry, Helena," the girl said. "She'll walk the next time she tries. You may not believe it, but it's the nature of the Spirit to rise up and walk on our own."

Helena stared at her. "How do you know these things, Kailani?"

"My mother, the sky, told me." She became thoughtful, her eyes misting. She looked to the broad expanse of ocean and sky, both so achingly blue the horizon between them virtually disappeared, and stared out as if trying to see all the way to her homeland. "She told me when the wind first arose and tried to walk."

***

Jason was reluctant to leave the Knob, afraid to let the moment go, but it was mid-afternoon and even Kailani was hungry.

He drove the short distance to Albion Village and parked near the shore to ease the transition. From there they walked the last few blocks, past stacked shell fish traps and fishing nets hung out to dry, until the smell of the sea gave way to the more civilized aromas of the town.

A seaside resort, Albion Point teemed with tourists in the summer, but it was also a university town, dominated by the Polytech. The combination drove demand for high-end restaurants, but also quaint cafés, stores filled with ocean kitsch—colorful buoys, harpoons and other relics once used by real fisherman—but also bookstores and pubs.

As they strolled down the main street, Kailani's chin drooped to her chest and her eyes focused on the cracks in the pavement. She seemed to smile only when in sight of the ocean.

She perked up when they wandered beneath the maroon awning with the drawing of the steaming kettle that marked the entrance to Molly's Tea Shop. She gaped through the window at the pyramid of cookies, and the cakes and pies lined up in a row. She beamed as she inhaled the scent of baked goods wafting through the open doorway.

"I think we've found our place," Jason said.

Inside, a hostess told them to sit anywhere. As they headed for a table in the corner, Kailani dawdled over to the pastry display.

The waitress behind the counter, a round woman who looked as if she enjoyed sampling her own wares, smiled at her. "Would you like a slice of cake or pie?"

Kailani checked with Helena. "May I?"

"You should have lunch before—"

"Of course you may," Jason said. Anything to cheer up that sad face.

The discussion became animated as Kailani and Helena considered their options, finally selecting the lemon burst tort and a slice of the seven-layer chocolate cake. Then they settled down to the challenge of choosing tea from the five-page menu.

Tea pervaded the place, with tins of every shape and size lining the shelves, along with an assortment of tea services. Paintings on the walls told the story of the tea trade's history, with images of five-masted schooners pulling into port with their precious cargo, giving lie to the mythmaker's claim that the races had been created apart. Ancient charts showed sailing routes from the lands to the east, before the world was divided.

Jason and Helena ordered the Island Essence, described in the menu as having a big, fruity, berry flavor. Kailani picked the Lady Catherine's blend for no other reason than she liked the way it sounded. The tea came in pots wrapped in flowered cozies, each with its own unique design. The waitress turned over a small hourglass that stood in the center of the table and told them to let the tea steep until the time was up.

Kailani stared at the hourglass. "What's that for?"

"It measures time," Jason said. "When all the sand has run through to the bottom, our tea will be ready."

Kailani studied the sand until half the grains had passed through the narrow neck.

"Is that what time looks like? Can I touch it and see how it feels?"

Jason fumbled for a reply. Kailani could be a little too otherworldly for his engineer's temperament. "It's sealed and can't be opened. Besides, those are just grains of sand, the same as you'd find on the beach. Someone's measured how long it takes for that much sand to pass through the neck."

"If I turn it upside down, will the time start over?"

Jason sighed. "Time's a concept we have no control over. It only goes in one direction, forward, and always at the same rate."

DAVID LITWACK

Kailani stared at the hourglass. "Then why does it have to be measured?"

Jason pictured himself running, with an hourglass strapped to his wrist in place of a sport watch. *Why must time be measured? To know how fast you're running. To make sure life doesn't pass you by.*

Helena rescued him by removing a cozy and pouring Kailani a cup of tea, even though the sand had not run out. "Careful now, it's hot."

Kailani took the cup in both hands, her fingers too small to lift it with just one. She lifted it to her nose, sniffed, and her eyes lit up.

They drank their tea, ate their cakes and pies, and ordered seconds. The afternoon passed easily and their spirits lightened—until Jason checked the time. The department was an hour's drive away, and he'd promised Carlson to have Kailani returned by five.

"Kailani," he said, "we'll have to leave soon. Would you like a piece of cake to bring back with you?"

"Back where?"

"To the department."

The room grew still, with no sound except the clink of cups on saucers, now unnaturally loud. Jason watched Kailani. He was sure she'd heard him, but she went on drinking like a kitten licking milk. He took a last sip of his own tea. It had gone cold now and had a bitter taste. He turned to Helena for help, but she looked as if she were the one being sent back.

Finally, he spoke. "Didn't Mr. Carlson explain that we were only taking you out for the day?"

Kailani shook her head so hard, the long hair swished about her shoulders and a strand fell across her eyes. "I don't want to go back. Why can't I stay here with you?"

Jason brushed her hair aside. "It's just for now. Someday, you won't have to go back."

"And how long will that be?"

"I don't know."

"Will it be a long time?"

"I wish I knew."

She ventured a hand across the table, tipped the hourglass upside down, and stared as the sand flowed through its narrow neck.

"That must be," she said, "why people measure time."

CHAPTER 6

THE BLESSED LANDS

The Minister of Commerce struggled up the stairs to the sandstone arch marking the entrance to the marketplace. With the sun at its zenith, he'd find no relief until he reached the shadowed alleyways of the suq.

As he paused to wipe his brow with a well-used handkerchief, he drew the scrutiny of a guardsman, who clicked his heels together and made a formal bow. "Excellency."

He offered a half nod.

The guardsman stiffened. "Are you sure that you're in the right place, Excellency?"

"I'm sure." He'd been through this before.

His white suit and leather shoes marked him as a modernizer, and of a different class than those who frequented the market. He'd stood out everywhere he'd searched. Being accosted by guardsmen was uncomfortable and embarrassing, but he hadn't let it dissuade him from his mission.

The guardsman held out his hand. "Your papers, please?"

The minister reached into his jacket and produced his identification papers in a waterproof pouch. He watched the man's eyes to see which way his soul was inclined—supporter or critic. He was a symbol of change, and change polarized people.

The guardsman unfolded the papers, glancing up while he read them as if to make sure the minister was still there. His eyes told the story. A supporter.

When he finished, he made a second, deeper bow. "Forgive me for not recognizing you, Excellency. Men who come here dressed as you are usually up to no good—smugglers and such." He tucked the papers into the pouch and handed them back. "Please, sir, you should know this marketplace is far from the corridors of power. You must be aware you have enemies."

The minister put the papers away, and dragged the handkerchief across his face one last time before pocketing it as well. "I am, but I have urgent business that won't be deterred by such concerns."

The guardsman stared toward the harbor, squinting at the flashes of sunlight off the waves. "Sir, I'm not permitted to leave my post, but if you'd wait an hour until I'm off duty, it would be my honor to accompany you."

The minister did his best to smile, a gesture he'd used so little these past months. "Thank you for the offer, but your presence would only complicate my task. I'll be careful."

"Please do, sir. You're doing wonderful work for our people. There are those of us who pray you'll become the next Supreme Leader."

With this, the man straightened, gave an informal salute and stepped aside.

***

While little sunlight penetrated the alleys of the suq, the press of warm bodies more than offset the cooling shade. The minister, possessing a bulky frame, did not glide easily through crowds. He was constantly bumped and jostled, forcing him to keep one hand on his papers and wallet.

It was late afternoon. How many shops had he searched that day? How many villages and towns had he visited this past month? The stubbornness that had brought him so much success sustained him, along with a desperate faith that he was only one clue away.

THE DAUGHTER OF THE SEA AND THE SKY

He chose his next target, a shop for apparel and sundries. Pushcarts bracketed the doorway, stacked high with the loose-fitting smocks favored by his more traditional countrymen. Overhead, bright-colored headscarves hung from an awning and swayed in the breeze created by bustling passersby. A young man with thick eyebrows slouched in a seat by the door.

The minister entered.

In the far corner, an old man sat on a rocking chair and sipped coffee the color of tar from a tiny cup. He glanced up, almost surprised to see a patron, but as soon as he took in the minister's features, his expression darkened—a critic. He set down his cup, pressed hard on the arms of his chair, and rose on unsteady knees.

Once upright, he extended a bony finger at the minister. "You." The palsy in his hand sent tremors through his body. "You have brought a curse on our land with your soulless ways."

The young man who'd been sitting by the door rushed in and positioned himself between the minister and the old man. "Be at peace, Father. I thought the Holy Book teaches hospitality to guests."

"This is no guest. This is the devil." The old man spat three times on the dirt floor.

His son pressed his palms together in front of his chest and bowed. "Forgive him, Excellency. His eyesight is poor, and he's mistaken you for someone else."

The old man tried to shove his son aside. "It's you who are blind. Can't you see who this is?" He turned and fumbled through a stack of government bulletins on the table behind him. Finding what he was seeking, he waved a crumpled page in front of the young man.

The son took the paper and glanced from the imprint on the front to his new guest. His eyes narrowed. Without further argument, he grasped the minister by the arm and led him outside to the front of the shop.

When they were out of earshot from the old man, he bowed again and smiled. "Forgive my father, sir. He's of the old school. Those of my generation understand what you've done, how you're bringing us a better life. Now what may I do to make up for my father's behavior?"

A better life.

When the Supreme Leader came to power thirty years before, he preached the value of happiness in this world as well as the next. Since the Great Separation, the blessed had stagnated. Through too strict an

43

interpretation of dogma, they'd fallen behind the soulless in things that mattered to people's lives—medicine, transportation, communication. Quietly, the Supreme Leader reached out through back channels provided in the treaty, seeking expertise from his former enemy.

He'd established modern, more secular institutes of learning, and identified the most gifted children to train in a pragmatic mix of the spiritual and physical. The minister was among the first so educated. Hardworking and practical, unburdened by ideology, he rose quickly through the hierarchy. As a mid-level official, he negotiated an agreement with the soulless, allowing his country to import the knowledge to build self-powered wagons. Then he used it to start an industry that quickly flourished, producing motorized carts that let farmers more easily bring their produce to market. He was promoted to the newly created position of Minister of Commerce—a hitherto unthinkable role—where he introduced more aggressive reforms, becoming a legend among modernizers.

But now, all his accomplishments were like a handful of sand.

He reached into his pocket and pulled out the waterproof pouch, then withdrew the well-worn parchment with the portrait so lovingly drawn by the Poetess. As he unfolded it, he turned it toward the man.

"Can you tell me," the minister said, trying to sound official while hoping for a miracle, "have you seen this girl?"

CHAPTER 7

AN EPISODE OF IRRATIONALITY

It was mid-September and Helena could feel the summer passing. Afternoons along the cliffs were still warm, but the evenings brought an offshore breeze that chilled rather than refreshed, and every day the sun set a few minutes earlier.

She trudged down the corridor to Kailani's cell, a walk she'd come to dread more with each visit. At least the circumstances had improved; Carlson had managed to bend the rules enough for Helena to be declared a family friend, a status that allowed for longer and more frequent visits. She went as often as possible — at least four days a week.

She and Jason met for dinner most nights, but he made the trip to visit Kailani only on weekends. His weekdays were consumed by his new project, developing the communicator that would change the world.

It was odd. When they were younger, he'd been the unfocused one, filled with whimsy and preposterous dreams, while she'd been grounded, committed to the goal her father had set for her. Now, the grown-up Jason knew what he wanted from life and had a plan to

DAVID LITWACK

achieve it, and Helena was adrift. She'd abandoned all pretense of studying and rarely opened the textbook anymore. With only two weeks left until the exam, the chances of keeping that promise to her father were slim. What interested her — no, obsessed her — was Kailani.

When she reached the locked door that led to the row of cells, she smiled a greeting to the matron, who'd become more accommodating since Helena's new legal designation. Yet something was different today.

The matron thrust out her jaw and wrapped her arms tightly about her chest. "Morning, Ms. Brewster. May I have a word?"

Helena fell back a step and nodded.

"I'll have to limit you to ten minutes today."

"Is something wrong?"

"Mr. Carlson needs to speak with you."

"Do you know what it's about?"

"No, ma'am, I'm just the messenger."

She led Helena down the hallway, then hesitated at Kailani's door. As she turned back to Helena, her stern demeanor softened.

"I can understand how you feel, Ms. Brewster. I've been doing this for twenty-two years and never met anyone like her. I hope you can help." The matron unlocked the door. "I'll knock when ten minutes are up."

Kailani sat on the bed with her legs dangling, ankles crossed, and hands folded in her lap like a model student. But this was no schoolhouse, and she was no student. Her gaze was cheerless and blank.

"Hello, Kailani."

"Helena." She looked up, her smile more tenuous than usual. "It's been two days since I saw you last. I'm getting better at counting days. I have a calendar now."

She gestured toward the wall where an oversized calendar had been stuck above the bed, featuring a picture of an ocean view at sunset. Beneath it were the words *Albion Point Board of Trade*.

"That's lovely," Helena said. "Where did you get it?"

"Mr. Carlson brought it, so I could see the ocean."

"That was thoughtful of him."

"He brings sweets too, every day — ever since I told him about Molly's."

On recent visits, Kailani would jump up when Helena arrived, giving her a squeeze of the hand or, on good days, a full hug. Now she was listless, waiting for Helena to fill the gap between them.

THE DAUGHTER OF THE SEA AND THE SKY

Helena settled at the end of the bed and edged closer. "I won't be able to take you out today. I'm sorry, but I just found out Mr. Carlson needs to see me."

"I know." Kailani uncrossed her ankles and kicked her feet. "I heard thunder outside. Is it raining?"

"Drizzling, but threatening."

"Then I guess I don't mind staying in."

Helena struggled to find something to say, and then she noticed that each of the last two days on the calendar had been crossed out with an angry X.

"What are those marks for?"

"Mr. Carlson taught me how to measure time."

"But what is it you're measuring?"

Kailani looked away. "I can't tell you. Mr. Carlson told me not to."

Damn. Helena checked her watch—seven minutes to go.

Kailani scanned the far wall, as if searching for a loose cinder block that might offer an escape.

Helena cast around for a way to regain her attention. "What's it like in the Blessed Lands? Is there ocean everywhere?"

"Only by the shore."

"Is that where you and your family live?"

Kailani's mouth opened, but no words came out. Instead, she blinked and looked away.

Helena tried again. "Does the terrain look like here?"

"It's flatter. Not so many hills."

"And the buildings?"

"Not as tall. Red tile roofs."

"And the trees?"

"Not as many. Too dry. Not many flowers, either. It's more brown than green."

Time to take a chance. "And what are your parents like?"

The girl sat up and raised her chin. "I am the daughter of the sea and the sky."

Helena found herself strangely sympathizing with Carlson. "You understand there's no way they can send you home without knowing who your parents are."

"I can't go home until I've done penance."

"Penance?" Helena blurted out before she could stop herself. "You think staying in this cell is penance?"

47

"My Lord Kanakunai has sent me for a purpose."

"What purpose? To be locked in here for months on end? Because that's what will happen if you never tell us anything."

Kailani's lower lip trembled. "Why can't I stay with you?"

Helena watched those ocean-blue eyes well up and fought to keep her own eyes dry. She drew Kailani closer and pressed the child's head to her breast, then chanted as she rocked. "I wish you could. I wish you could."

When they separated, Helena grasped her by the arms and leaned in until their foreheads nearly touched. "I don't know what it's like in the Blessed Lands, but here in the Republic we run our lives by laws — reasonable laws. The law that's keeping you here may seem harsh, but it was made to protect us after a terrible war, one that ended before my parents were born. That law was never intended for someone like you, though, so we have to wait until a tribunal decides what to do. Do you understand?"

Kailani glanced up to the fluorescent light, then behind her to the picture of the ocean on the calendar. After a moment, she turned back to Helena. When their eyes met, it seemed as if the child had seen into her soul and found the pain.

"And what are *your* parents like, Helena?"

Helena let go and stepped away, afraid to show her face until sure she was under control. After three breaths, she turned back to Kailani. "My father was a great scientist, a man of knowledge. I grew up with him and my mother in one of the houses on the cliffs near where your boat came in."

Kailani brightened. "Why wouldn't your law let me go live in the house on the cliffs with you and your mother and father? I wouldn't be any trouble, and I could see the ocean every day."

"My father and mother don't live there anymore. He died recently, and she moved away. She couldn't bear living in that house with its memories. And I'm not sure the authorities want you wandering about town."

"You don't think he'd have liked me?"

She sighed. What would her father have thought of Kailani? He'd have liked her, of course, because he was a kind and decent man, but he was also a man of science, suspicious of absolute faith. *Absolute faith constrains the mind,* he used to say, *and stifles new ideas.*

"He'd like you, Kailani, but he'd consider you a distraction to me. You see, before he died, I promised him that I'd study hard and become a scientist like him. Unfortunately, I'm not doing a very good job of it."

THE DAUGHTER OF THE SEA AND THE SKY

Kailani came over and pulled until Helena was close enough to feel the warmth of the nine-year-old's breath on her cheeks.

"Your father's spirit lives on," she whispered. "The sky says the spirit in each of us never dies. If you speak to him, he'll answer."

Helena gaped at her. "You can't really believe that?"

"The sky said if I tried hard enough, I could speak to the wind, though the wind has never answered me. That's why I have to do penance. But you've done nothing wrong. You just need to listen harder. Try under the stars, and he'll speak to you."

There it was — absolute faith, what had been lost with the Treaty of Separation.

Kailani released her grip, went back to the bed, and plopped down. "Where did your mother go?"

Helena was grateful for the change in subject. "Up north, to a place called Glen Eagle Farm."

"That's a pretty name. What's it like? Have you been there?"

"Only once, when I took her there. It's an artist colony, very beautiful, all green, with rolling hills and mountains in the distance."

"Is there ocean?"

"No ocean. It's inland, far from the sea." Upon seeing Kailani's disappointment, she added, "But there's lots of bubbling streams. I think you'd like it."

"Is your mother happy there?"

"I'm not sure."

"Haven't you asked her?"

"We haven't talked much since my father died."

Kailani focused on her hands, taking time to form the question. Finally, she looked up. "Does she blame you for your father's death?"

"No, of course not."

"Then why doesn't she talk to you?"

The cinder block walls seemed suddenly to close in. The air became thick, and Helena had an urge to charge the door and pound on it until she was let out. *What must it be like to be locked in here for days on end?*

When she gave no answer, Kailani crooked a finger, inviting her closer, and spoke in the same hushed tone as before. "You should talk to your mother, Helena. The two of you share the Spirit."

Share the Spirit? Then why had her mother fled, leaving her only daughter alone with her grief?

There was a knock and the door opened; time was up. Helena was almost relieved.

"Sorry to interrupt, Ms. Brewster. The chief examiner's waiting."

Helena got halfway across the room before Kailani rushed after her. "I don't mind if there's no ocean."

"What?"

"Glen Eagle Farm. Maybe the law will let me go there to be with you and your mother."

"I can't—"

"And Jason. If you and Jason were with me, I wouldn't need the ocean. It would be enough."

The matron cleared her throat.

Helena rested a hand on Kailani's cheek, long enough to let its warmth linger. Then she followed the matron out the door.

***

Helena waited while Carlson flipped through a folder on his desktop. She craned her neck to read the tab; all it said was "Kailani."

Impatience got the better of her. "What's going on, Mr. Carlson? What's happened?"

He let his glasses slip down his nose, and looked at her over them. "The tribunal had a preliminary interview with Kailani. They've set a date for her hearing."

"When?"

"The fifth of April." He set the folder on its edge and tapped it twice so the papers lined up inside.

"That's more than six months." She imagined Carlson sneaking sweets into Kailani and tried to temper her tone. "You can't leave her here for that long."

"I know."

The way he said it sent a shiver down her spine. "There's something more, isn't there?"

He started to fiddle with his paper clips, then stopped and stared straight at her. "Next week, she's to be transferred to the Deerfield Correctional Facility for Juveniles."

"A correctional facility? But she's done nothing wrong."

"You weren't at the interview. She told them she came to our shores in the name of her god to show us the way of the Spirit. That's almost the

THE DAUGHTER OF THE SEA AND THE SKY

word-for-word legal definition of proselytizing. Understand this is a compassionate ruling—normally the justices would have ruled for incarceration. When she returns in April, she'll need to convince the tribunal she's changed. If we can't find out where she's come from, and she still refuses to assimilate, the tribunal will have only one choice left."

"But why a correctional facility? She'll be in with young criminals. She'll be eaten alive."

"Not just criminals. There'll be other questionable refugees from her homeland. She'll be safe there—they do maintain order. She needs to be in a place where she can adjust to a life of reason rather than the way she was raised. The correctional facility is a relearning center. At least there, she'll have a chance."

"Do you really believe she's a threat to anybody?"

Carlson shook his head. "A threat to individuals? No, of course not. But to our society? Let me ask you this, Helena. You've seen the effect Kailani has on people. Do you really believe there aren't some who might exploit her to their own ends?"

Helena began to argue, then shook her head. Though she hated what he was saying, it carried a ring of truth. Was that why Kailani had fled her homeland? Was that why she was so secretive now?

"How far away is Deerfield, Mr. Carlson?"

"A full day's drive, I'm afraid. It's the nearest place we could find to take someone so young. I'm sorry, Helena. We've both become attached to her."

Helena brought a thumb to her teeth, tapped twice, and bit down hard. She looked at Carlson across her knuckles. "Is the decision irreversible?"

"It could be changed, but there really isn't an alternative. As we've both agreed, she can't stay here."

Helena blinked, hoping he'd look away, but his gaze never wavered, as if he expected her to speak next. Was she ready to say what she wanted to?

She swallowed hard. "What if... I were willing to take her? What if I could offer a more benign place where she could learn our ways without being exposed to society?"

Carlson released his gaze.

Is that the hint of a smile at the corner of his lips?

"I was hoping you'd ask. Frankly, I'd much rather see her with you than in an institution, but it won't be easy. In the past three

51

weeks, I've made accommodations for you. This is different. If she's caught causing trouble, it could blow up in our faces, moving up the asylum hearing, or worse, biasing it toward incarceration. If I'm to circumvent the correctional facility, the tribunal will need something better, both for the child and for our society. Something more... reasonable."

"What does that mean?"

"I asked the justices about this, and they said there are three non-negotiable terms. First, she must be released into the care of a mature and responsible citizen of the Republic—I immediately thought of you. Second, she should be able to learn not only our ways but some skill, so she can someday be useful to society. Third, and most problematic, she must be isolated from centers of population to prevent her from preaching in public while she assimilates. Any violation of these terms during the trial period will result in rescission of the stay and immediate incarceration."

A vision came into Helena's mind of rolling green hills and bubbling brooks. She sucked in a stream of air and let it out slowly, then licked her lips to bring moisture. "What if I could provide that?"

Carlson slid his glasses back up the bridge of his nose, and then brought his hands together, making a steeple of his forefingers. His magnified eyes stared into hers, eyes too watery for a bureaucrat.

It seemed forever before he responded. "You're serious about this?"

She nodded.

"Fully committed?"

"I... think so." She said the words too loudly, hoping to hide the tremor in her voice.

Carlson followed with a detailed line of questions.

She did her best to answer but found it hard to focus. The blood thudding in her temples kept obscuring his words.

***

The thwacking of the wipers pounded inside Helena's head. Shortly after she had merged onto the highway, the sky darkened and the drizzle that had cursed the day turned into a downpour. Rain streamed across the windscreen, forcing her to squint to see the road.

A single thought reverberated in rhythm with the wipers: *What have I done?*

The Daughter of the Sea and the Sky

Her father would have called it an episode of irrationality, but after he was gone, she'd been the rational one, trying to hold her mother together. All her mother could do was rail against the Soulless Land for denying her husband an eternal spirit. She'd threatened to transmigrate to the Blessed Lands, but in the end considered Helena—if she transmigrated, they'd never see each other again. Now, she meditated two hours a day and spent the rest of her time sewing and making jewelry.

Carlson had insisted Kailani be kept busy and learn a skill, and though Helena hated asking, she needed her mother's help to get them into the farm. Her mother would almost certainly take to the girl from the Blessed Lands, help with her care, and teach her a craft. Yes, her mother and the farm would be the first part of the solution.

Jason was the second.

Kailani's plight may have given her purpose, but finding Jason again had brought much more—the hope of being happy someday. Could she convince him to abandon his great mission for a while and come to the farm? It was precisely the kind of preposterous adventure he'd once dreamed of. This time, would *he* take the chance?

Finally, she considered the promise to her father.

For seven semesters she'd fought to live up to his expectations, doing well enough to have a shot at highest honors, but highest honors were now out of reach, and simple graduation seemed increasingly unlikely. More telling, she no longer cared.

The downpour became heavier, as if someone had turned the spigot to full. Water coursed along the glass in a blinding stream. She flicked at the wiper control but turned the knob the wrong way, and the wipers stopped mid-windscreen. In a panic, she hit the brake, hoping no one was behind her, and then fumbled with the control until the wipers resumed.

She slowed her breathing, as every citizen in the Republic had been taught, to calm her passions and see the situation through the clear lens of reason. If they brought Kailani to the farm, she would fail to graduate. Worse, she'd never go back to the path her father had laid out for her. She'd break the promise made that day in the brightly lit room.

How bright it had been, inappropriate for someone who was dying.

***

Helena sat by his bedside, one hand resting on her father's arm, staring at the pain meds dripping into his vein.

Seemingly asleep, he let out a wheeze. She doubted he knew she was there, until his eyes opened and locked on hers.

"Promise me, Helena," he said in a weak voice. "Promise you'll finish and go on to fulfill your potential. To be a greater scientist than me."

She grasped his hand.

His eyes clouded, but he returned the pressure, now gulping for air.

"I'll try," she whispered.

"Promise," he said, more gasp than speech.

"I promise."

His grip slackened, and he was gone.

CHAPTER 8

CHOICES

In the wee hours of the morning, Helena dreamed the door to her bedroom opened, as it had opened so often when she was little. Some nights her father would work late at the lab and not come home until long after she'd gone to bed. He'd tiptoe to her door and nudge it open a crack to check on her, but the door squeaked just enough that she always knew he was there.

This dream was different. The moment the door opened she flung off the covers and swung her feet to the floor, expecting her father. Instead, a girl stood in the doorway, her face hidden in scrim, her tiny arm extended and beckoning.

"Follow me," she said. "I'll take you to him."

When Helena awoke from the dream, the room had brightened—not the brightness of daylight but the faint gray of predawn. A chill settled on her and she realized she'd kicked the covers off. She reached for them, tugged them to her chin, and pressed her eyes shut again, but there'd be no more sleep that morning.

They'd moved to the house on the cliffs when she was six, one of her earliest memories. Her father had taken a tenured professorship at the prestigious Polytechnic Institute, a big step up and a significant increase in pay. For Helena, the change was even greater. Their former home in the city had been a gloomy place, an old house that moaned with a strange cacophony of shudders and creaks. Her bedroom pulsed with dark eaves, and spider webs shadowed the corners. A ghostly cypress blocked the sun from her window, and its branches scratched the glass like bird claws whenever the wind blew. Many a night, her father would have to come in and talk her to sleep, explaining that ghosts were myths and that she'd learn to see things more clearly as she grew older.

When they moved to Albion Point, it had been a revelation. The house was open and airy, and sunlight streamed through the windows. And of course, there was the ocean.

Now, despite the sun and the sea, this house, like the old one, seemed pervaded by gloom.

She finally got up and rattled around the house, pacing from room to room and organizing things that needed no organizing. She tidied the magazines littering the coffee table in the living room, and fluffed the throw pillows on the sofa before setting them back, corners up and overlapping. She wound the big clock in the hall, turning the key only twice before the spring drew tight. Then she came to the shrine.

The shrine was her name for the display of photograms she'd arranged on the dining room buffet after she'd cleared away her mother's collection of knickknacks. The photos—her and her father on the beach, at the lab, on the cliffs—needed no tidying.

She checked the clock: too early to find Jason, so she opened the buffet drawer and began to flip through old pictures. A third of the way through the pile, she came upon one of her family at the Knob. Her mother looked much younger then, her hair not yet turned gray, but there was something else. While the young Helena was focused on the stairs of the Knob, her mother was watching her with a look of.... She had no words for it, but it made her throat tighten.

Now they hardly talked.

She took the picture from the pile, dusted its frame, and set it in the center of the shrine. It seemed to belong there. Did her mother deserve it? No, but for Kailani's sake, it was time to forgive.

Finally, sunlight came streaming through the lace curtains. The work day would soon begin. She dressed quickly and hurried off to campus.

THE DAUGHTER OF THE SEA AND THE SKY

She took a shortcut through the new science complex that had housed her parents' lab—new because she'd watched it being built when she was little. Her father had presided over the dedication when the red cedars that lined the walkway were first planted. Now, as she raced up the hill, their mature branches swayed in the end-of-summer breeze.

How have they grown so tall?

This was her first time back on campus since her father's memorial service, and her path seemed constantly blocked by family friends eager to offer condolences.

"I'm sorry, Helena. You father was an amazing man."

"Best pure researcher I ever knew. What a loss for the field."

And the question she dreaded most. "So, how are your studies coming?"

She smiled and shrugged off the comments, trying to be polite, and moved on as quickly as manners allowed until she reached the engineering quadrangle.

Engineering had been unfamiliar territory to her theoretical scientist father, a confusing warren of offices and partitioned workspaces that almost looked like a factory. She accosted anyone whose attention she could catch, and asked for Jason Adams. After several tries, she found him in a cubicle, hunched over a device that looked like a text processor with an oversized screen stuck on top. She hovered, waiting for him to notice her, but he was too engrossed in his work.

Finally, she came up from behind and tapped him on the shoulder.

He turned. "Helena, how nice to see you." His face said otherwise.

"Do you have a minute?"

"I wish. The revision goes live tonight, the one with the photograms, but it's still not working. I need every second."

"It's Kailani. They're moving her to a correctional facility."

Without further prodding, he abandoned his work, grasped her by the elbow, and led her down the hall into a glass-enclosed conference room. "A correctional facility? Why would they do that?"

"It's the tribunal. If she doesn't assimilate, they'll have to lock her away. They're sending her to be re-educated—Deerfield, I think it's called, several hours from here. I couldn't sleep last night. For reason's sake, Jason, a correctional facility where they send zealots and criminals!"

She was talking too fast. As a child, she'd always talked too fast when upset. Her mother used to say, "Slow down, Helena. Count to three when you're worked up. If you talk too fast, you'll say something you regret."

She counted to three now. "I have a plan to stop it. Carlson supports it." She paused to assess Jason's reaction.

He was staring at her like he used to in the classroom from two aisles away, pupils wide, lips parted.

At me and not the clouds. She took an extra breath and spoke each word deliberately. "It could get complicated."

He took her by the arms and steadied her. He always seemed to be steadying her. "Sounds too important to discuss in a rush, and I have no time now."

"You won't be angry with me?"

"Why would I be angry?"

The vent above her head kicked in, blowing cold air down the back of her neck. Its hum joined the drowsy drone of communication devices around her, a dull and hollow sound. Not the time or place to explain.

"Can we meet for dinner?" she said.

He snuck a glance outside the conference room. Two men in blazers wandered down the aisle toward them, deep in conversation. "I won't be done by then. There's a problem scanning images—the header's being garbled. It could be a late night."

"Come to my house no matter how late it is. I'll wait."

He nodded, opened the door, and pointed her toward the exit. Then he raced off before his colleagues could turn the corner, and vanished amidst the warren of cubicles.

***

The clouds on the horizon had long since turned from red to pink to purple, then scattered to be replaced by a host of blinking stars. For the first time in a week, the night had stayed warm, so despite the late hour, Helena decided to wait outside. Yellow beams streamed across the lawn from every window of the house, and she added candles along the path to brighten Jason's way.

She waited on one of the wooden plank chairs spread across the yard, her head tipped back, gazing at the stars. When the crunch of footsteps on gravel approached, she jumped up and swung open the gate in the picket fence.

The Daughter of the Sea and the Sky

"Beautiful night, isn't it?" Jason said.

"It is. How did your project go?"

He rolled his eyes and grinned. "You should see it, Helena—images as crisp as the originals, transmitted halfway across the country. It will change the world."

She tried to smile—she knew how much it meant to him—but her smile quickly faded.

"Is it that bad?"

She released a sigh as he settled next to her. "Maybe. I offered to take her until the tribunal."

"And Carlson's gone along?"

"Yes," she said, "with some conditions."

"Well, it'll be nice to visit her here without the hour's drive."

She shook her head. "That's the thing. Carlson won't let her stay near the city—too much chance of getting in trouble. He wants someplace supportive but remote."

"Like where?"

"Like my mother's farm. Kailani would have a safe area to roam around, lots of activities, plenty of caring people to look after her, but no nearby population she could accidentally proselytize. My mother will help, hopefully teach her a craft. There's no ocean, but it's beautiful. Kailani has already said she'd like to go there. I discussed it with Carlson, and he's agreed."

She paused, counting the surges from the surf below, three in and three out.

"How far is this farm?" Jason said, as the fourth surge began to break.

"About a four-hour drive."

His face contorted as if he'd eaten something sour. "That's a long way for a weekend visit."

She reached across and covered his hand with hers. "I don't want you to visit. I want you to come with us."

He pulled his hand away. "What?"

She stood and edged toward the cliffs, keeping her back to him. "It was the only way I could think to save her."

He came up behind her, his breathing quick and sharp, but he didn't respond.

She turned to face him. "You're angry with me."

"I'm not angry."

"I didn't plan this."

"It's not in my plans, either."

"Please... don't be mad."

"I'm not mad, just... disappointed." His voice dropped so low, she could hardly hear his next words over the surf. "We're finally together after all this time, and I thought—"

"We have the opportunity to save a child."

"But to give up everything for a little girl I hardly know...."

She felt as if her ribs were constricting, squeezing the air from her lungs. How could she let Kailani go to the reformatory?

"I won't go without you," she said. "You and I have been given a second chance. We may not get another."

He edged closer and grasped her bare arms. The warmth of his touch eased the goose bumps that had formed despite the warm night. "What about the promise you made to your father? If you leave, you won't be able to graduate."

"I know, but I made a promise to Kailani too. She's alive, and my father's gone. Besides, I was never going to finish school."

He stared at her—the look of a stranger, the look of a friend, the look of something more. It seemed forever before he spoke. "When did you decide?"

She took time to order her thoughts.

Behind her, the beacon atop the Tower of Reason whirred through its eight-second cycle, sweeping across the water and grazing the rocky cliffs before disappearing again. As if in response, a full moon cleared the roof of the house and cast a more permanent path of gold on the ocean.

In its pale glow, Helena felt an odd and unexpected clarity.

"I decided," she said, "before he died, before I ever made the promise."

***

She and Jason talked about other things for a long time—his project, how much the job meant to him, the visit she'd had that day with Kailani and the little she'd learned. She painted a word picture for him of the farm, with its eccentric artists and rolling green hills. She insisted she wouldn't go without him, but there'd be no decision that night.

Instead, they reminisced about their last night together, before she'd gone off to university. It was a night like this, with a moon as full and bright.

She said she'd forgotten how beautiful the ocean could be in the moonlight, and he said maybe it only shone like that for them—when they were together. She said she wished he'd said that the last time, before they drifted apart.

When words ran out, they came close together and embraced. They held on, neither wanting to be the first to let go, clinging to each other as if to ward off the unknown. Finally, he pulled gently away. The hour was late, and he had work tomorrow. He kissed her and headed off down the path.

Helena watched until his outline nearly vanished against the pale cliffs, not taking her eyes off him until his dark shape had disappeared around the bend.

The yard of her childhood home was awash with moonlight now, cold and lucid, strong enough to cast a shadow beside her and lay sparkles on the tips of the waves. As she blew out the candles and prepared to go inside, a voice in her head made her pause, a whisper telling her to look up at the stars.

Try under the stars, and he'll speak to you.

She stretched her mind beyond its rational limits, trying to see the universe through Kailani's eyes, to touch her father's spirit and ask forgiveness. Feeling weak-kneed, she sat on the ground, reaching out with either hand to steady herself.

She held her breath and listened for a response.

She heard the squawk of a sleepy gull, the ebb and flow of the sea, the sough of the wind through the stand of birches that bordered the house, and the creaking of their branches. But she could sense no spirit in the wind.

When she released her breath, the air came out in a rush, as if she'd been drowning in loss.

When she was a teen, maybe thirteen or fourteen, her father had taken her out on their boat to a nearby lake, a sheltered place with calm but deep water. She'd always been a good swimmer but was afraid of staying underwater for long—something to do with the darkness and a sense of being alone.

Her father had insisted she overcome that fear.

***

He dropped a line and measured to the bottom—thirty feet—then ordered her to dive down and bring up a fistful of silt. He calculated how many seconds it would take to go down and return, and assured her she'd have breath to spare.

She dropped over the side and descended no more than a body length before bobbing back to the surface, gasping as if she'd been under forever.

He said it would be all right and to try again, reminding her to kick her feet straight up and point her toes to the sky.

She took a bite of air and flipped her legs up, keeping her knees together and pointing her toes. There was a rush of water, a change in temperature, pressure on her eardrums. Kicking hard, she descended this time until she struck something solid. The rest was a haze: grabbing a handful of silt, flipping around and groping for the dim light above, seeing the blur of a familiar face, bursting through the surface, the wet silt oozing through her fingers.

Her father applauded wildly.

***

Now, there was no one to correct her form, no one to say it would be all right, no one to tell her what choice to make.

She rose to her knees and brushed the blades of grass from her palms, noticing as she did so that her hands were shaking. A different voice in her head whispered—a terrible, cold voice. *He's gone.* Tears prickled the corners of her eyes; she blinked them back.

She was on her own.

CHAPTER 9

BITTERSWEET

Two days before Kailani's transfer date, Jason joined Helena for the final furlough. He hoped the time together would help him to decide.

He was loathe to abandon Kailani to her fate, but hated to take leave from his job when it was going so well. He racked his brains until he came up with a solution—use the new technology to work from the farm. After all, wasn't that exactly what it was designed for?

"Absolutely not," his supervisor had said. "The project's too critical. We need a hundred percent effort from all our engineers."

Jason pleaded his case, swearing he'd keep up with his workload. He badgered until his supervisor offered an alternative.

"We're hiring testers to work remotely. You can have that job, but it'll mean a demotion and a cut in pay—a step backward in your career, at least until you return. Take a couple of days to think it over."

Jason remained undecided, torn between loyalty to his project and a desire to help Kailani. What would Helena think of him if he said no? The choice made him light-headed, as if he were balanced on a knife-edge above a mist-filled gorge. He was afraid to pick a side, fearing the slightest sway in either direction might lead to a plunge into the unknown.

He recalled the first time Helena had gone away—late summer, before she headed off to university.

***

His father asked him to carve out a few hours to visit the cemetery as the anniversary of his mother's death approached, but he was busy with the start of school by then. His father urged him to commemorate the day. He resisted—too much to do, lots of work at the sandwich shop, saying goodbye to Helena—but he finally agreed.

They went the next morning. His father shuffled to the grave to place a ragged set of roses he'd purchased at a discount store. When he knelt and bowed his head, he seemed to shrivel, curling up on himself like a dry leaf in winter.

That night, as Jason mopped the floor of the sandwich shop, it came to him that the path he was on led down the ever-diminishing corridors of his dream. He dropped the mop on the spot, went home, and started to pack. When his father came in to ask what he was doing, Jason said he was moving out. He needed fresh air, a fresh start, to be on his own, away from the home where he'd been raised.

He called Helena and begged her to come see him, telling her to make whatever excuse she must to get away, then grabbed two blankets and met her at the entrance to the Knob. There, he used a propane lantern to navigate the path in the dark, until they found their way up the stairs and to the bench overlooking the sea.

They stayed until sunrise. He told her about the harsh words he'd said to his father, and how he wanted more from life. They made a vow to each other to be true to their youthful ideals. When they clutched each other in a goodbye embrace, neither was willing to let go. In his heart, he knew why.

Both understood how uncertain the future could be.

***

Youthful ideals. Was this where they'd led him now?

While awaiting his decision, Helena had forged ahead with the plan, persuading her mother to make arrangements for their arrival at Glen

THE DAUGHTER OF THE SEA AND THE SKY

Eagle Farm. She had Carlson prepare two sets of paperwork: Kailani's release until the hearing, and a transfer manifest to the reformatory, as if the girl were a piece of freight. The choice was up to him.

On the drive south, Jason kept glancing into the rearview mirror to observe Kailani. For much of the ride she'd been sullen and still, gazing out the window as the landscape passed by. But when he checked on her next, her eyes were locked on his.

"Why don't you come with Helena," she said, "every time she visits?"

He smiled. "I have a job. I don't have as much time off as Helena. If I did, I'd love to visit you more."

Kailani shimmied over and filled the gap between the front seats.

"Not me, Jason. I meant, why don't you want to be with Helena more? You like each other, don't you?"

"Of course we do."

"That's good." She shifted back to the window and pressed her nose against the glass, humming for a few seconds in rhythm with the tires before speaking again. "The sky says each of us has a trace of the Spirit inside. Sometimes, one person can touch that Spirit in another. It was that way when the sea met the sky, and it's that way with the two of you. The sky says I'm good at sensing the Spirit in people. I can tell."

A trace of the Spirit. More irrational ramblings from the Blessed Lands—each person carrying around a bit of some magical force, and having the bits touch like a pair of live wires to make a spark. And yet.... He glanced at Helena. She tilted her head toward him and smiled. His face grew warm.

He looked back at the road in time to catch the familiar green sign. "Look, Kailani. Albion Point. We'll be at the ocean soon."

Kailani huffed steam on the window to make it fog, then rubbed it clear with her hand.

When she didn't respond, he called out. "Aren't you glad to be back at the ocean?"

After a pause, she answered, "No."

He checked in the rearview mirror. "Why not?"

"Because I know this will be my last time."

***

The awkwardness that had descended in the car lingered on the beach. Jason encouraged Kailani to play in the waves, but she declined, instead

DAVID LITWACK

dragging her feet through the sand with head bowed. They stayed only fifteen minutes. When he asked what he could do to cheer her up, she suggested they find sweets for this, their final outing. Jason quickly agreed, and Helena proposed the perfect place: Uncle Bill's.

"What's Uncle Bill's?" Kailani said.

"A candy store like no other," Helena said. "And you'll soon see why."

"Can't you tell me now?"

"It's one of my favorite places, where my father used to take me to buy candy as a reward."

"A reward for what?"

"For getting a good review in academy. He'd give me one chocolate for each perfect grade."

"And tell Kailani," Jason said, "how many chocolates you earned?"

Helena winked at Kailani. "All of them."

Before going into Uncle Bill's, they paused to watch the taffy pull that whirred in the store window. Several pounds of sugary candy hung on a hook, while two steel arms twisted it in slow overlapping circles.

"What is it?" Kailani said, mesmerized by the spinning arms.

"Saltwater taffy," Jason said. "After it's cooked, it needs to be pulled to make it thin enough to cut into bite-sized pieces."

"It's a funny motion, like a dance. May I try some?"

"Of course."

He took her by the hand to lead her inside, but before crossing the threshold, she pulled away. "Will I have to go back after this?"

Jason squatted down and grasped her by the shoulders. "We'll have a little time to sit on a bench and eat our candy, but after that, we'll have to return you to the department. Do you understand?"

She nodded and stepped inside.

The first order of business was to buy taffy. Kailani toured the bins, each crammed with candy in brightly colored wrappers. She picked a dozen pieces and plopped them into a white paper bag.

After Jason paid, he held the bag open to let her choose.

She closed her eyes and pulled one out. "How do I open it?"

"I'm a saltwater taffy expert," Jason said as he took the piece from her. "Watch."

He grasped the twist on either end and pulled. The glob of taffy spun around until it lay exposed, stuck to one side of the waxy paper.

He offered it up with both hands. "Go ahead. Lick it right off the paper."

THE DAUGHTER OF THE SEA AND THE SKY

Kailani licked and gave a weak smile.

"There's more candy over here." Helena urged them on to the back of the store.

Kailani took the bag and studied the remaining pieces. "I think I'll just eat my candy and watch the taffy pull."

Over by the window, the taffy machine chugged, separated from customers by a polished mahogany bar. Kailani drifted over to it, sliding a finger along as she passed. She settled on a wooden stool, folded her arms on the bar, and rested her chin on them.

Jason backed away, keeping an eye on her until he felt a touch on his hand. Helena's fingers prodded his, which had tensed into a fist. She pried them loose, and he let their fingers intertwine.

"She'll be all right," Helena said. "Come see. Remember these? My favorites." She led him to a glass case that contained stacks of soft butter caramels.

When he offered to buy some, her face lit up in a way he'd hoped Kailani's would. He brought the candy to a counter with an old-fashioned cash register and waited for the clerk to ring it up.

When he turned to hand the caramels to Helena, his smile vanished. "Where's Kailani?"

The stool was empty. The white paper bag lay on the floor, pieces of taffy spilling out around it.

He scanned the corners of the store, then rushed outdoors with Helena close behind. They glanced north toward Molly's and south toward the sea. Kailani was gone.

"She only knows the way to the beach," he said too loudly. "She must've gone there."

They dashed through the village and past the harbor, not stopping until they reached the breakwater that protected the beach from storms. There, below them, Kailani strolled at the edge of the waves, shuffling her feet and singing to herself. She'd abandoned her shoes midway on the sand.

Helena started for the stairs, but Jason stretched out an arm to block her.

"Let me," he said.

It was late in the season, too cold for swimming, and the beach was nearly deserted. A fisherman stood hip-deep in rubber boots, reeling in his fly. Further along, halfway to the old pier, a man in a straw hat searched the sand for lost coins, a sifter in one hand and a metal sensor in the other. With his ears blocked by headphones, he hardly noticed as Jason passed.

Jason tried to approach Kailani without alarming her, but when a startled gull squawked and flew off in a hail of feathers, she turned. Their eyes met. She froze for an instant, then took off at a sprint.

He ran after her. No way could she outrun him, but when he drew too close, she turned from the beach and hopped onto the pier. He followed, and slowed when she reached the end. He did his best to tread softly, but his steps, much heavier than hers, clattered on the tar-stained boards.

She glanced at him over her shoulder, and then without hesitation leapt over the end of the pier and into the sea.

He hissed a curse and followed her in.

Cold water closed over his head. He bobbed to the surface and got his bearings. Then he saw her, two bare arms and a bolt of hair in the trough of a wave. He kicked hard and stroked, trying to reach her before she sank. She squirmed as he grabbed her, but he held on, one arm wrapped about her chest, and her head resting on his shoulder so it lifted gently with the waves.

As he paddled back to shore, he pressed his cheek to hers and whispered in her ear. "We'll help you, Kailani. We won't let it happen."

She was hysterical, irrational. What could they have done to her in the Blessed Lands to drive her to such extremes?

He collapsed on the beach, grasping the girl with both arms. For now, she was safe. He lay there with the coarse sand caked onto his wet skin, trying to regain control of his breathing, as he would after a long run. As Helena rushed toward them, an odd longing came over him, different from the desire for a better job or a faster time in a road race — a more profound yearning to care about someone so much that he'd offer his life for them.

***

The drive back to the city was somber and silent — Kailani said not a word. The trip home was little better.

Jason refused to discuss what had happened, not yet, not in the car. By the time they arrived, it was almost twilight. He parked near his flat so he and Helena could walk to her house along the cliffs.

They stopped by the thunder hole, where Kailani's boat had crashed a month before. A late September breeze pushed waves across

THE DAUGHTER OF THE SEA AND THE SKY

the bay to land as surf breaking gently on the shore. Dusk approached on the tide.

Helena gazed out to sea, and he came up behind and rested a hand on her shoulder. She trembled beneath the fabric of her blouse. After too long a moment, she reached back and covered his hand with hers, and the trembling stopped. She turned and buried her face in his chest, and when he lowered his lips and let them brush the tip of her ear, the trembling returned.

A flash of orange distracted them, as a ladybug landed on Helena's bare arm, just below the sleeve. Both of them stared, bemused as its shell sparkled in the remnant of sunlight. Jason reached out to brush it away, but Helena's look warned him off.

She held her arm motionless. "Leave it," she whispered. "My father always said ladybugs were good luck." She watched as the insect began its pilgrimage down her arm.

Jason waited, knowing her, knowing that the most important things took time for her to say.

She finally spoke, never taking her eyes off the bug. "He was a scientist who believed there was a solution for everything if you worked hard enough, but he'd never harm a ladybug. Once, when I caught a firefly in a jar, he made me let it go, saying it was wrong to keep it. When I cried, not wanting to release it, he promised to make it up to me. The next day, he brought a poster from a gift shop in the village, a picture of a girl releasing a firefly from a jar. Her arm was outstretched with a tiny landing spot open between her thumb and forefinger, like she expected it to return. At the bottom, it read, 'My first firefly, but he got away.'"

The ladybug continued its journey along her arm, oblivious to the audience.

"Fireflies and ladybugs," she said. "And a silver anklet that made stars in the waves. He didn't believe in myths, but he thought his daughter was magic. She'd grow up to solve all the problems that had confounded him."

She glanced up at Jason and touched his cheek with the fingertips of her free hand. "I never should've asked you to come to the farm. I had no right."

He shook his head. "You were right to ask."

She returned her attention to the ladybug and, as if sensing her focus, it froze in place.

69

Jason stared past her. To the east, the beacon atop the Tower of Reason flashed and fell dark. Eight seconds later its beam reappeared, paving a roadway of light on the water before vanishing again. The tower had been built ages ago as a lighthouse to guide sailors ashore. When boats were banned, some had argued it should be torn down, but the department decided it was easier to apprehend illegals on shore than after their boat had sunk on the reefs—a reasonable plan.

Jason suspected they kept it because everyone liked the way it looked. *So much for reason.*

Now he wondered about his own reasoning. He counted *one, two, three*, hoping to see what the next beam of light might reveal—another boat perhaps, a second vessel from the Blessed Lands, maybe Kailani's family come to fetch her home.

Nothing but sea.

He tipped his head back and looked up, squinting until the stars blurred in the spangled sky, wondering if people's souls—his mother's, Helena's father's—ended up there or sunk down into the earth with their bones. The universe contracted and a sense of loss flooded over him, as though he stood again at the edge of the dirt hole, watching his mother lowered into the ground.

He shook it off and let a new and more powerful sensation overwhelm him, a sense that he and Helena were the first human beings who had ever lived, the first who had felt this way for each other, the first to discover love.

How much they'd changed in the years apart. He used to be the adventuresome one, always ready to take off on a quest. She'd been the steady one, the north pole of his compass, making the most practical choices. Now....

What Helena asked of him was foolhardy, but at this moment, he was sure of only one thing. He'd never leave her again.

"I'll go," he said.

"Jason—"

"My supervisor's agreed. A feature of the encomm—the ability to work remotely—I'll be its first test site."

"Are you sure?"

The bug started crawling again, past her elbow and onto her forearm.

"Don't ask," he said. "I might change my mind."

THE DAUGHTER OF THE SEA AND THE SKY

The ladybug reached the back of her hand. She raised it high and gave a flick of the wrist. Speckled wings sprouted from what had appeared to be a hard shell and the ladybug flew off.

As Helena watched it go, Jason placed a hand on her face and traced her cheekbone down to her chin with his thumb. She rose up on her toes and kissed him.

Then they walked arm in arm to the big house on the cliffs, their footfalls crunching softly on the gravel path.

CHAPTER 10

A MOST UNUSUAL CASE

Carlson hurried past the locked doors with an uncharacteristic spring in his step. In his hands he balanced a paper plate decorated with drawings of balloons and fringed noisemakers, with the words "Happy Birthday" at the bottom. On the plate was an oversized slice of vanilla cake, a corner piece with a pink-sugar flower on top. When he came to the eighth door on the right, he stopped and noticed some frosting had come off on his finger. He licked it clean, then straightened and knocked, even though the door was locked from the outside and he held the key. It was proper manners.

A forlorn voice responded. "Come in."

The girl hunched on a corner of the bed, arms wrapped about her as if she were cold.

"I've brought you something, Kailani."

"What is it?"

"A birthday cake."

"It's not my birthday."

"I didn't think it was, although I wasn't sure, since you never tell me anything about yourself. It's the birthday of someone here in the

THE DAUGHTER OF THE SEA AND THE SKY

office, and I was able to smuggle out a piece of cake for you." He held out the plate. "It's the best kind, a corner piece."

She shook her head. "I'm not hungry."

"Oh." He had counted on a celebration, but this was not a good start. He began to take a cleansing breath but stopped himself; meditation was to calm the passions, to let reason rule. This seemed an occasion to let his passions flow.

Kailani interrupted his thoughts. "Mr. Carlson?"

"Yes?"

"Is it time?"

"Oh no, not at all. Not until tomorrow. And I have some good—"

"What will it be like there, Mr. Carlson? Will I be in a room like this, with no windows and a locked door?"

Carlson smiled and felt not lightheaded but light all over—like when he'd signed the release order, flaring out the bottom of the "y" in Henry and gleefully looping the top of the "l" in Carlson.

"I have some good news for you, Kailani. The plan has changed. You're not going there anymore."

"Then I'll be staying here?" Her expression brightened a bit. "Does that mean Jason and Helena can still visit?"

"There'll be no need. You'll be leaving tomorrow to go to a new home and—"

She looked more hopeful. "Will it have windows?"

"I'm sure it will."

"And ocean?"

"No ocean, but there'll be bubbling brooks and mountains and plenty of trees."

She got off the bed and took a step toward him. "Where am I going? Please tell me."

"To a place up north and far away." He was grinning like a fool. "A place called Glen Eagle Farm."

Kailani's smile blossomed and grew. She pressed her palms together in front of her chest and bounced in place. "Will I be going with Jason and Helena?"

"Why, of course, but there's one condition."

The bouncing stopped. "What is it?"

"That it's something you want to do. By regulation—according to our rules—I need to ask you. Do you want to go with them, Kailani?"

73

She beamed. "Oh, yes, Mr. Carlson. Yes, yes, yes."
Then she lowered her eyes.
"What is it, Kailani?"
"I think I'll have that piece of cake now."

Chapter 11

A Seedy Café

A hot wind blew across the harbor, raising whitecaps on the sea. The Minister of Commerce pulled the map from his pocket and crossed off the latest town. Soon, there'd be no towns left to search.

He paused by the waterfront and scanned the docks, listening to the rattle of rigging against masts and the sloshing of boats as they tugged against their moorings. He sniffed the air as if trying to scent a clue, but all that reached his nostrils was the stench of petrol floating in rainbows on the water, and carcasses left by the gulls.

To the right of the docks lay a boardwalk, crammed with shops built so close together, only a child could slip between them. They included a nautical supply store, a kiosk for bait and fishing tackle, a food mart, and a seedy café of the sort frequented by sailors in their few hours ashore. It was late in the day, and though exhausted, he decided to check one last location. He'd return in the morning for the rest.

He chose the café.

He trudged across the boardwalk, trying to keep some semblance of dignity, but his leather shoes clattered awkwardly on the worn boards. At the café, he hesitated, taking in the newest smells—old cooking oil, stale sweat, and alcohol. He took a last gulp of fresh air and pushed open the door.

Only two tables were occupied, and those by fisherman too drunk to notice his presence. A man with a shaved head and a big belly stood behind the counter and nodded as he entered. The barkeep seemed unsurprised by his well-heeled appearance.

The minister stepped to the counter, too tired to be anything but direct. "I'm looking for a girl."

The man leered. "You've come to the right place, Excellency."

He closed his eyes for a moment and sighed. Help might come from even the vilest of sources. "No. A specific girl. This one." He produced the drawing and turned it toward the man.

The man stared at it. "A lovely child, but a bit young for you, if you don't mind my saying."

The minister snapped, darting his beefy hand across the counter and dragging the man's face close to his own.

"Not in that way, you fool. This one has run off." He released the barkeep, who backed away, pressing his hands together in front of his chest and making the traditional bow.

"Forgive me, Excellency. I misunderstood."

"Well, have you seen her?"

He struggled to temper his tone. How many times had he asked this question? How many days had passed since he'd last seen the poetess? He sent messages saying he was well, but true to his word, gave no report of his progress.

She'd replied in sparse phrases: *Glad you're well, stay safe*.

He worried she might not survive.

Back when he was a junior bureaucrat, his job had been to screen candidates from the Soulless Land seeking salvation. Transmigration had become less common in the generations since the signing of the treaty, and tended to be mostly one way. Few of his countrymen wanted to transmigrate now that the Supreme Leader's reforms had taken root. A growing economy offered citizens a quality of life not much different from that across the sea.

Yet life in the Soulless Land remained unsettled. The denial of the Spirit left a hole in the hearts of its people.

And so they came to the Blessed Lands. Many were not seekers of the Spirit but failures at living: children of the privileged unable

THE DAUGHTER OF THE SEA AND THE SKY

to find a niche in life, fugitives from the law, or those devastated by tragedy. When they'd given up hope, they sought to transmigrate. His job was not to heal the soul-sick but to identify those who could contribute. The Supreme Leader's emerging society had no place for the unproductive. Two out of three were sent back.

He'd found the job to be more distasteful than rewarding, the rejection stamp always heavy in his hand.

Then the poetess arrived.

She was from one of the finest families in the Soulless Land—a child of wealth and privilege, of culture and education—but something was missing in her heart, a void where faith should have been. She'd requested transmigration for all the right reasons.

They were as different as could be: he was thick-boned and swarthy; she was delicate and fair. He had black hair and almond-shaped eyes like his countrymen; her eyes were round and framed by locks of gold. He was practical, grounded in his work and on a mission to provide a better life for his people; she was a poetess who spoke in metaphors and had thoughts that threatened to make her float away.

Despite all that, somehow, she'd touched the Spirit that dwelled in his heart.

The barkeep eyed him warily, no doubt suspecting he was police. No wonder. Despite new rules and better training, some remained heavy-handed in enforcing dogma—why they were called zealots, and the reason he searched alone.

When the barkeep had nothing to say, the minister turned and headed for the door.

Before he could cross the threshold, the man called him back. "Excellency, I can help."

The minister turned, the muscles in his arms tensing. "Don't play with me."

"But I've seen her, Excellency, the golden child with eyes like the ocean."

The minister froze. "When?"

"Three, maybe four weeks ago."

"Where?"

"She came into my café."

"Why would she do that?"

"She was looking for a boat."

The minister withdrew his handkerchief and wiped the sweat from his brow. "Are you certain it was her?"

"Excellency," the barkeep said. "If you've met this girl, you know. This is not a child one easily forgets."

CHAPTER 12

THE NORTHERN KINGDOM

Helena gazed at the mountain stream that ran alongside the road. The ride had passed quickly, and they were now less than an hour from the farm. She turned toward Jason, needing to watch him as he watched the road ahead. Her own personal fog was beginning to clear, and she almost dared peek past the present to see what the future might bring. If only —

Cries of distress rang out from the back, and she jerked around to see Kailani clawing at the fabric of her seat in a swimming motion and gasping for air.

Helena unbuckled her safety belt, reached behind, and stroked the child's arm. "Wake up, Kailani. You're having a dream."

"Should I pull over?" Jason said, checking in the rearview mirror.

"No, she'll be okay."

Kailani rubbed the sleep from her eyes, and then stretched until her fingertips brushed the padded roof overhead.

"What were you dreaming?" Helena said.

"Where are we?"

DAVID LITWACK

Jason pointed to a blue sign up ahead. "That says we're entering the Northern Kingdom."

Helena smiled at Kailani. "How come you're always asking questions, but you never answer any of ours?"

"It was a dream, Helena, nothing more." She slid forward and stared out the front window. "Is it really a kingdom?"

"It's just a name," Jason said. "Not a kingdom, but it's northern all right, almost as far as you can go before coming to the fenced-off zone around the land bridge."

"Then why do they call it a kingdom?"

"I don't know. It's an old name, maybe a kingdom of nature."

Kailani slid over to the window and cried out with delight when she spotted the stream running alongside the road.

"Water! Where does it come from?"

Jason tossed a glance at Helena. They'd agreed to take turns responding to Kailani's endless questions, and now was her turn.

She'd been no different at that age, always asking questions. Her mother got annoyed, but her father answered them all, one after the other: the moon controlled the ebb and flow of the tides; the rocks on the breakwater were to keep the beach from eroding in storms; the constellation in the summer sky was called the Great Archer and the three stars in a row were his belt; when you died, you went to sleep.

"It comes down from the mountains when it rains," she said, "or when the snow melts. Aren't there streams like this in the Blessed Lands?"

"Just ocean, and water in wells." Kailani crinkled her nose. "What's snow?"

"It's rain that freezes when it gets cold and comes down in white flakes. I guess there's no snow in the Blessed Lands, either."

"No. It never gets cold. But I remember now." She brightened. "The sky once told me about white water that floats down from above and makes the land glisten."

"And what does the sea say about snow?" Jason said.

"The sea has never seen snow. The sea is too busy helping the Supreme Leader create a better world."

"Ah-hah. At least we know the sea has a job."

"I didn't say—" Kailani put a hand over her mouth.

"Am I right?" Jason said, ignoring Helena's glare.

"No. You wouldn't understand."

THE DAUGHTER OF THE SEA AND THE SKY

"Don't be so sure." Helena reached back to touch her.

Kailani pulled away. She took a quick breath, as if she were about to say something but swallowed her words. Her posture stiffened.

When she finally spoke, her voice was more adult than child. "Why do you deny the Spirit here?"

"What makes you ask that?"

"It's what the senkyosei say."

"What's a senkyosei?"

"It means one who preaches the Spirit. What word do you use for that?"

Helena looked at Jason, who came to her rescue.

"We have no such word. It's against our law to preach."

"Then you *do* deny the Spirit."

"No, we don't. We can believe whatever we wish, but we're taught to think rationally."

"Then why can't you preach?"

How could Helena explain it to this child who'd been raised in a different world? Should she tell her the stories they'd learned in school about the smuggled-in fanatics who gathered followers and led them into madness? Should she describe the suicide bombings that killed and maimed so many?

She took a deep breath and chose her words carefully. "The prohibition against preaching is to keep people from organizing into groups to impose their beliefs on others."

"Maybe," Kailani said, "that's why you're so alone."

Helena squirmed in her seat and worried how such talk would be received at the farm. Glen Eagle was an art colony, not a religious retreat, though she'd heard some members had mythmaker tendencies—a problem if the department found out. An eccentric commune in the northern woods was fine, but they'd frown on a group of would-be zealots, even this far away.

She set aside her concerns.

Kailani was finished with her questions for now, focusing instead on the unfamiliar landscape. She folded one arm on the window's edge, rested her chin on it and watched the world go by.

They passed the remains of corn fields, brown stalks stripped of their ears, left to be tilled under next spring. They drove by hillsides slanting down from the road into tree-filled glens, where spring water ran and dappled cows went to drink. They came to a lake where a stand of white birches bordered the shoreline, like those that framed the Brewster home but a hundred times more. Sunlight played off their paper-thin bark, making them shine.

At one point, Jason rolled to a stop on the shoulder. He touched a finger to his lips and gestured across a clearing to the edge of the woods. At first, Helena couldn't understand, but then she saw them — a doe and two speckled fawns. For all his practicality, Jason had stopped for a family of deer, something her father might have done.

Kailani, who was the last to spot them, let out a gasp and spoke in a reverential whisper. "They're beautiful."

The doe turned and stared at them. No one in the car moved; none dared twitch. Finally, the doe made up her mind: danger. She nudged the fawns toward the woods, and all three took off with a bound. Jason waited until they were out of sight before easing back onto the pavement.

Later, they passed a diamond-shaped sign with a drawing of a moose. Kailani noticed it and asked what it was. Helena tried to answer first, anticipating the more difficult question to follow, but Jason was quicker.

"It's a moose, like the deer we saw, but bigger. And the males have antlers." When he sensed she wasn't following, he added, "Horns on their heads, like the branches of a tree. That's what you see on that sign."

"But why is its picture there?"

A tilt of Jason's head declared it Helena's turn. She caught a hint of a smirk at the corners of his mouth.

"It's a warning to motorists," she said. "Sometimes, the moose run out onto the road unexpectedly."

"And what happens?"

"Drivers do their best to avoid them," Jason said. "But sometimes they hit them by accident."

"And then?"

He took pity on Helena and responded, even though it was her turn. "And then they're killed. Sometimes the drivers too."

Hoping to soften the blow, Helena added, "It's not on purpose, Kailani. It's just a part of nature."

Kailani went quiet for the next ten minutes, and Helena had almost forgotten the moose-crossing sign when the child spoke up again.

"It's not on purpose," she said. "Death is a part of the Spirit too."

The Daughter of the Sea and the Sky

Helena gaped at Kailani, trying to find words to pose her own question. "Did... that sign remind you of something?"

"No."

"Is there something you'd like to tell us?"

"No." She slumped against the window and mumbled into it. "No deer, no moose, no snow. Nothing like this at all."

Then Kailani's attention lapsed, returning to the stream.

Soon, the unending miles of forest and farms changed. An occasional cottage began to appear, and then houses clustered together along the roadside, a precursor to the village of Northweald.

The road curved around a green guarded by a statue of a weary soldier, sabre at his side, returning from some forgotten war. A gazebo stood in the center, a place for band concerts on summer evenings. At the edge of the green sat the town hall, its white steeple poking into the blue-green background of balsam and spruce that covered the surrounding hillside.

Jason swung round to the far side of the green, and seconds later, they were there. Northweald contained a dozen stores crowded into a single block—art galleries and a craft cooperative, a sandwich shop that featured homemade ice cream, a post office, a gift shop, and opposite each other in the center, the two largest buildings: Hal's Sporting Goods Mart and the Northweald Emporium.

Helena considered asking Jason to stop at the Emporium. When she brought her mother to the farm, they'd stopped there to check out the rows of handmade quilts and the plastic case with slabs of fudge. A wholesome smell had permeated the store—fresh fabrics and penny candy, baked goods and pine incense. Now she longed to bring Kailani there, but she blocked out the thought.

Time for that later. This was no visit. This was the next phase of her life.

A mile north of town, she directed Jason to take a sharp right onto an unmarked dirt road. The winding road climbed, snaking back and forth over a ridge and across a stream. No one said anything. Even Kailani had no questions. There was no sound save the pinging of pebbles on the underside of the car, the whining of gears, and the rattling of loose planks as they crossed over three narrow bridges.

Shortly, they descended into a flat valley, where the road ended. A hand-carved sign, framed in birch limbs read *Glen Eagle Farm*.

Jason coasted to a stop and set the brake in a dirt lot at the edge of a lawn. The farm's great house stood at its far side, guarded by an arc of oaks a hundred years old or more, its façade fronted by a wraparound porch with white columns supporting the roof.

A manicured garden framed the porch stairs on either side, with a vibrant mix of purple asters surrounded by yellow and pink mums. At the corner nearest them stood a waist-high statue of a girl with a sunbonnet, holding out a basket of flowers in greeting.

A man waited between the statue and the garden. He was slightly built, almost frail, with what might have been a young face except for crow's feet at the corners of his eyes and a prominent wattle below his chin. His ears seemed too big, or rather they may have been the right size when he was younger but stubbornly stayed the same as the rest of his face shrunk. His smile spread easily, nearly reaching to his earlobes.

He grasped a walking staff that rose a foot above his head. Carved into it where the handgrip would normally be were four preposterous faces, each with a different expression. As the guests approached, he caught Kailani staring at the faces in the staff. With a wink, he spun it around like a wizard, while his free arm stretched wide in welcome.

"Who's that?" Kailani whispered to Helena.

"That is Sebastian, the Supreme Leader of Glen Eagle Farm."

CHAPTER 13

SEBASTIAN

Sebastian waited for the car to roll to a stop. The bridge that formed the gateway to the farm needed some work, but in the meantime, while he scratched for funds to repair it, the clatter of loose boards served a useful purpose: alerting him to arriving guests. He liked going outside to watch them before they realized they were being observed.

The three newcomers emerged from the car. Even if he hadn't met Martha Brewster's daughter once before, she'd be easy to pick out. Her hair color was different—Martha had gone gray—but they shared the same prominent cheekbones and astonished eyes, and their bearing reflected the same lingering grief. The daughter seemed like all young people who came to the farm—beautiful and sad.

Then there was the young man. Martha had said little about him, only that he was tall, fit—a distance runner, apparently—and worked at the Polytech, where she and her late husband had spent their careers. He looked normal enough, perhaps too normal for this little community of craftsmen, artists, and lost souls.

And finally, the girl from the Blessed Lands.

DAVID LITWACK

Martha had told him nothing more than that she loved the ocean, had a sweet tooth, and was extraordinary. He'd learned over the years to maintain a level of detachment with those who came to the farm. All had stories, most special in their own way, but this little one was different. She reminded him at once of a spring day in his youth and the deepest sorrows of his life. No doubt the residents of the farm would like her, but some might... embrace her too much. He'd have to keep an eye on her.

He stepped forward and broadened his smile. It was no act. He loved his job.

"Welcome, welcome, Helena, Jason, and little Kailani. Welcome to Glen Eagle Farm. I trust you've had a comfortable drive."

Helena turned to face Jason. Their eyes met — a knowing glance.

If it were dark, Sebastian suspected he might have seen sparks.

Helena urged Jason forward. "Jason, this is Sebastian, the managing director of the farm."

Jason nodded politely and extended a hand, which Sebastian pressed in both of his, more a hand clutch than a shake. The young man's grip was firm. When Sebastian hugged Helena, he could feel tension in her shoulders and made a note to find out where that came from. Then he squatted on creaky knees and reached out to the little girl.

She held back, her cheek pressed into Helena's hip, her eyes never leaving his staff.

"Do you like my walking staff, Kailani? It was a gift from one of the many artists who've passed through here. The four faces signify sadness, joy, anger, and surprise. I try to keep my hand over the angry one. And some claim the happy one looks just like me. What do you think?"

She edged closer and touched the staff, letting her fingertips linger over the sad face. He invited her to hold it, but she shook her head and backed away.

He tugged on the staff to pull himself upright. "Why don't we all go to my office? I have some tea brewing and I bet I can come up with some candy for you." He smiled at Kailani. "A little bird told me you have a sweet tooth."

Once they were settled in his office, he got down to business.

"While your cabins are being set up, I'll take you on a tour to get you acquainted with the farm. You've come at a good time of year. Soon

THE DAUGHTER OF THE SEA AND THE SKY

the leaves will turn and the woods will be aglow at sunset." He turned to Kailani. "I hear you love the ocean. I'm sorry we have no coastline here, but if you're an early riser, you can hike up a nearby hill and catch the valley below hidden in mist. With a bit of imagination, it'll look like the ocean on a foggy day."

She remained sunk into her seat but gave him a wan smile.

"Before I show you the grounds, I need to find out more about my new members, to get to know you better so I can determine how we can serve each other's needs."

Kailani spun around to Helena. An elusive fear had crept into her eyes. "You said there'd be no more questions here."

"It's just a few," he said, trying to mimic the happy face on his walking staff. "It'll take no time at all."

Helena reached over and brushed aside a strand of hair that had tumbled across the little girl's eyes. "Don't worry. Everything will be fine." She turned to Jason. "Would you please take her outside for a few minutes? I'd like to visit with Sebastian alone."

Sebastian waited until the two were gone and the door to his office was closed. "I'm sorry to have upset the little girl. Is she always this skittish?" When Helena kept staring at her fingernails, he bent his head, trying to slip beneath her gaze. "What did I do wrong?"

Helena looked up, eyes pleading. "Couldn't you skip the interview? She was incarcerated at the department for over a month, interrogated several times. She's afraid it might be the same here."

"Ah." Sebastian shuffled over to the built-in cabinet that filled his bay window, and poured a cup of tea for each of them from his favorite teapot. He'd found it a year ago while browsing the antique store in town. Artists at the farm, who tended toward modernism, made fun of it as too baroque, but something about it had caught his fancy—perhaps the puffs of clouds set in blue with the rosy-cheeked cherubs nestled on top.

After bringing the teacups to the desk, he returned to the cabinet for Lizzie's bell. He slipped his index finger through the oval that formed its handle and gave it a shake.

The ring startled Helena. "What's that for?"

"This is Lizzie's bell. Everyone on the farm knows it. I use it to mark all sorts of occasions—a ritual, they might call it, where Kailani comes from. In this case, I rang it to commemorate our first cup of tea together. I've been ringing it for each new member since I came here."

"May I see it?"

87

DAVID LITWACK

"Of course."

She took the bell, let her fingers glide along the scalloped edges of its handle, and studied the etchings on its surface.

He'd stared at them many times himself, trying to decipher their meaning. Sometimes, he'd found flowers mingled with serpents, others the runes of a long-lost language or the writhing of lost souls. At times he believed it was magic, though he kept that thought to himself.

"Why is it called Lizzie's bell?" she said.

"You'll find I like to tell stories, Helena, but the story of this bell is one I don't share easily. Perhaps when we know each other better."

He accepted the bell back and laid it to rest in its usual spot, then waited until she'd taken her first sip. There was something soothing about tea.

"I trust you don't view me as an examiner," he said, "and this farm is certainly not the department of separation, but it does need to be managed. We mostly get people who have some wound that needs healing, though occasionally someone comes for the wrong reason. It's my job to understand how each arrival fits in so nothing will upset our little world. That's all."

She leaned forward, placing a hand on his desk, her lips stretched into a thin line. "Couldn't you make an exception for Kailani?"

He reached across and patted her hand. "I'll tell you what, Helena. Why don't you and I talk? We'll see if you know enough about the others to satisfy my curiosity."

After she nodded, he opened the top drawer of his desk, pulled out his supply of tissues, and placed the box within her reach.

When she looked perplexed, he said, "Just in case," then gave an extra bob of his brows.

She finally smiled.

***

Helena began to relax. Her mother had spoken fondly of Sebastian, and now she could see why. She accepted the tissue box and gave a little laugh. "It *has* been a difficult summer."

"So I've heard. I was saddened to hear about your father."

"Thank you." She slid back in her chair and sat upright, as if interviewing for a job. "There, I'm ready. What would you like to know?"

He lifted the teacup and let it hover between the saucer and his mouth. "I've been managing the farm now for twelve years. I've learned

THE DAUGHTER OF THE SEA AND THE SKY

most people come here with a gap in their heart. If I were a believer, I'd say a gap in their soul. My job is to help fill that gap with work, with an art or a craft they love, or with relationships they form here. Whatever's needed." He paused to take a sip.

A gap in her heart. She had a gap, and he clearly knew it.

"When I was younger," he said, "I managed big construction projects — industrial and commercial developments, highways, the occasional bridge or dam. Now I manage Glen Eagle Farm. It's not that different. A good manager gets to know the people he's with, assigns them appropriate work, and leaves nothing to chance. I just need to understand how each of you fits into our community. Let's start with you. What is it you like to do, Helena Brewster? What skills do you have? What inspires you?"

"There's not much to say about me except what I learned in university — nothing useful to the farm unless there's an interest in physiometry."

"Your mother said much the same when she got here. Yet in the past weeks, she's developed a knack for crafting jewelry — already sold a few pieces at the co-op in town. She's even learned to sew and now makes clothing for some of the others. Maybe you should apprentice to her and learn a craft or two."

Learn from her mother — something unavailable to her as a child.

"Yes, of course," Helena said, though she guessed Sebastian could see right through her.

Next she described Kailani's story. The two of them would need to work together and stay close. She reminded him of her status as Kailani's legal guardian, designated as such by the tribunal until the asylum hearing.

Sebastian finished scribbling on a small yellow pad and looked up. "And Jason?"

"What about Jason?"

"I understand you've known each other since childhood."

The corner of Helena's mouth curled into a half smile. She tilted her head to one side and pictured her and Jason as children, strolling hand in hand along the cliffs. "That's right. He used to walk me home from school every day."

"And how do you think he can contribute to the farm?"

"Oh no," she said. "It's not like that. He didn't come here to be a farm member, but to support me and Kailani. He has a job at the Polytechnic Institute and needs to work on it while he's here."

89

Sebastian tapped his pencil on the desktop three times and set it down. "Then we have a problem. Glen Eagle Farm's not a guest house. It's a commune that depends on the productivity of its members to survive. Everyone is expected to contribute."

Helena stared past Sebastian's right shoulder. On the wall behind him hung a painting of the great house in winter. Below it on a narrow table sat a flowerpot with an orchid growing in it. A cluster of three shiny leaves filled the pot and a single long stem sprouted from them, exploding at its top into a spray of blossoms. Each blossom had four white petals arranged in a whirl around a center of violet. If she squinted just right, the blushes of violet on the side petals became eyes and the center took on the look of a purple mouth with an orange tongue sticking out at her.

"Jason's on an important project," she said, "something that will make life better for everyone. All he needs is a desk and a comm link, and he can work remotely with his colleagues. He won't be any bother."

"He still needs a cabin, a place to sleep. And he'll consume our food."

"What if I worked extra hours?"

"I'm sorry, Helena, but it's a hard and fast rule. The goods we produce here aren't quite enough to pay the bills. We get some support from the generosity of the Friends of Glen Eagle Farm, former members and others who appreciate what we do, but even with that we barely get by. Everyone must contribute."

Helena grimaced and sucked air in through her teeth. She and Jason had only just rediscovered each other. He was her glimmer, the hope of healing the gap in her heart. She wouldn't stay without him, but that meant Kailani would....

"Please, Sebastian. There must be a way."

He reached across and nudged the tissue box closer.

Only then did she realize her eyes had begun to tear. She blinked twice, took a tissue and dabbed at them, then crumpled the tissue and fumbled for a place to dispose of it.

Sebastian took it from her and with a flourish of the wrist tossed it into a wastebasket. "I'll tell you what, Helena. Let me talk with him, and I'll see what I can do. If there's a way to make it work, I'll find it. Now, before we start the tour, do you have any questions for me?"

She shook her head without looking at Sebastian. Instead, her eyes flitted about the room: in the painting, the snow blanketed the roof of

THE DAUGHTER OF THE SEA AND THE SKY

the great house; on the teapot, the cherubs nestled on their cloud; Lizzie's bell rested in its place; and the face on the orchid had reappeared.

She could almost hear it laughing.

***

When Helena swung open the screen door, she was met by the afternoon sun filtering through the trees. The dappling of light and shadow confounded her vision and her eyes needed a few seconds to adjust. Once they did, she needed additional time to sort out the scene before her.

Her mother sat on the top step of the porch with Kailani by her side. In the space between them lay a box filled with semiprecious stones—the raw materials for her mother's new avocation. She grasped an amethyst between her thumb and forefinger and held it up so waves of purple rippled across the delighted child's face.

Jason looked on, beaming.

When not in the lab, her mother had always worn the unofficial Polytech uniform—pressed slacks and a stylish but conservative blouse. Now, a wrinkled housedress drooped to her ankles, covering the tops of well-worn shoes caked with the remains of a muddy day at the farm. Her chestnut hair had reverted to gray and hung unkempt to her shoulders. Most surprising, her mother was playing with Kailani. Playing in a way she'd never played with Helena.

Helena let the screen door close with a bang. "Hello, Mother, I see you've met Jason and Kailani."

Her mother held up a hand, indicating she must finish telling the tale of the stone. Moments later the story ended, and she restored the stone to the felt compartment reserved for it in the box.

"Hello, Helena," she said without looking up, fumbling for the next stone, a sliver of amber. "Yes, Kailani and I have met. She's everything you said and more. Give us a moment, dear. I promised to show her the amber next, and then the tiger's eye. I didn't think you'd be out this soon. Sebastian can go on sometimes."

Only when the final stone had been put away did her mother get up, brush the dust from her housedress, and focus on Helena. She grasped her warmly by the arms and pulled, but Helena stiffened, leaving some distance between them.

91

Her mother stepped closer to fill the gap and gave her a peck on the cheek. "It's wonderful to finally meet your friends, and I'm glad to see you too. You look well."

Look well? Her mother had been playing with rocks on a farm while she grieved for her father. "You look well too, Mother. I'm surprised."

"Well, let's say I've had time to think on the farm, to meditate on the nature of things, and I've found a certain peace."

Helena caught Jason eyeing her. She could read the question forming in his mind. After all she'd told him about Martha Brewster, he'd discovered a saint.

"I wish I could say the same," she said.

Her mother patted her arm. "Give it a while, dear. People are so driven these days. They don't take time until it's too late."

She pressed her lips together, afraid the thoughts simmering in her mind would boil over.

Jason came up beside her and slid his hand up and down the small of her back, massaging lightly.

The great house door swung open, and Sebastian burst into the silence. He glanced from one to the other, then rubbed his hands together as if preparing for work. "Good. I see everyone's met. Are you all ready for the tour?"

When no one else answered, Jason said, "Yes."

Helena glared at her mother before following Sebastian down the stairs.

CHAPTER 14

GLEN EAGLE FARMS

"My first project," Sebastian said, waving his staff at the barn. "It's where all the work gets done. It was in tough shape when I got here, but I knew the farm's future depended on it."

Jason gazed up at the clapboards tapering to the peak of the gambrel roof and the eagle-shaped wind vane swaying above them. When he looked back, Sebastian seemed to have fixed on him as the one most likely to care.

"We reinforced the frame, replacing the rotted sills and the main carrier beam with steel, and punched a big addition out the back. Then we coated the whole thing with so much red paint, it outshines the other buildings to this day."

"He won't admit it," Martha Brewster said, grasping Jason's arm to get his attention, "but there'd be no barn without him. The farm was nearly bankrupt before he got here, and he rescued it by using his own savings."

"Ignore her, Jason. Those are old stories." He nonetheless seemed pleased they were still being told.

The inside of the barn was more impressive. The front opened into a high-ceiling dining area, exposed to skylights. Behind it was a stainless steel kitchen, where food was prepared, preserved, and packaged.

"We sell vegetables in season from a stand on the highway," Sebastian said, "but year-round we sell jams, baked goods, maple syrup, and almost anything coated in maple sugar. Not every member's creative. If they have neither aptitude nor desire to do crafts, they tap trees, peel apples, or prepare food for sale—whatever helps with the running of the farm. Everyone contributes."

Jason wondered about Sebastian, a man who seemed capable of more. Why had he ended up rescuing a broken-down farm? And how had they ever functioned without him?

Next, they moved on to the two-story addition, which housed a dozen studios, all with large windows in the southern wall. Sebastian explained that they used the first floor for crafts requiring heavier equipment, such as woodworking, sculpture, ceramics, and stoneware. The airy loft contained rooms for the more delicate arts like painting, flower arranging, jewelry making, and quilting.

Kailani skipped from studio to studio, fascinated by every project. As she passed, each artisan set down their work and smiled.

In the third room, a silversmith with safety goggles pounded a metal blank into foil with a flat wooden mallet, striking the sheet until it became paper-thin. Then he switched to an even smaller mallet and tapped with the pointed end, making overlapping circles in the silver until they resembled fish scales. As Kailani stared wide-eyed, he wrapped the foil around a wire frame so it became a fish with no eyes.

When Sebastian tried to move her along, she said, "But the fish will be blind."

"I assure you, Kailani, my friend here has always found eyes for his fish, and is likely to do so again, whether you're watching or not."

As Jason approached the next room, a wave of heat hit him from a small oven.

A tiny woman sat on a stool by the fire, holding a metal rod with a piece of molten glass at its end. When Kailani stepped closer, curious as always, the woman turned. Her face was almost birdlike, with no chin and bulging eyes, made more prominent by the glow from the flame.

Without a word, she motioned for Kailani to sit on a nearby chair and withdrew the molten glass. After rolling it on a metal bowl to give

THE DAUGHTER OF THE SEA AND THE SKY

it shape, she poked with a pair of tongs and prodded here and there until a head, a tail, and four legs appeared. Then with a final tap she gave it eyes and held it up for Kailani to see.

"A horse," the girl said.

The woman nodded.

Kailani cocked her head to one side. "But can you make it a unicorn?"

Martha looked on amused, but Helena seemed bothered. She rested a hand on Kailani's shoulder.

"There's no such thing as unicorns," she said. "It's a myth, even in the Blessed Lands."

Ignoring Helena, the glassblower placed the horse back into the oven. She gave it two quick turns, withdrew it, and with a single pluck at the horse's forehead, a horn appeared.

"See." Kailani beamed at Helena. "There are unicorns if you believe."

Martha winked, but Jason noted Helena wasn't smiling. The gloom that descended on the great house steps had followed her on the tour. She'd been wandering around in a daze, glaring whenever her mother said a kind word to Kailani.

After leaving the barn, they followed a dirt road to a pergola, its roof laced with vines, some still bearing late summer roses. On either side hung wind chimes of every shape and size.

"I encourage each artist to create a unique chime," Sebastian said. "With only one condition: it has to harmonize with the others so when the wind blows there'll be no discord."

At the far end of the pergola, a crescent of two-unit cabins was arrayed around the sprawling branches of an impressive beech tree.

"Come see our sentinel tree, Kailani." Sebastian reached out for her, but she shied away.

"Go on, Kailani," Martha said. "Sebastian doesn't bite."

Helena shoved in front, blocking her mother's way. "It's all right if she doesn't want to go."

"I was just trying to—"

"It's none of your business."

Kailani froze, caught between them until Jason stepped in and led her to the tree.

She glanced up at the branches. "A sentinel tree? Why's it called that?"

95

"A long time ago," Sebastian said, "someone noticed how it stood guard over our cabins, and gave it that name. I'll bet you have nothing like it in the Blessed Lands."

"No," she said. "It's so... big."

"Plenty of rain helps. But wait till you see it at night. Spotlights shining through the branches make it look magical."

Next came a tour of the cabins. All were the same: small, clean, and well kept, with a clerestory to let in light. In good weather, the high window could be opened using a pole with a latch hook on top. Each unit had a door with a slide bolt to ensure privacy. Jason and Helena were assigned the unit adjoining Kailani's, so they would share a common wall.

Kailani took her time surveying her room. She bounced on the bed, opened and closed each drawer of the bureau, and gazed up at the branches visible through the clerestory. Then she shuffled to the door and checked for a lock. When she saw there was none on the outside, confirming it was no prison, she rushed into Helena's arms.

Sebastian waited until they separated. "And now, little lady, are you ready to find more of the farm's surprises?"

"What kind of surprises?"

He reached out and tapped her nose. "If I told you, they wouldn't be surprises. The farm's crisscrossed with paths, some you'd never find without a guide. I'm busy today, but I can spare a half hour to get you going. I'll show you the easiest to find." He tried again to take Kailani's hand.

Again, she held back, grabbing onto Jason instead. Together, they followed Sebastian to the far side of the sentinel tree. There, hidden in the folds of its trunk, hung a cylinder suspended from a teak yoke—a foot wide and taller than Kailani, made of bronze an inch thick. Dragons and other fantastic creatures had been etched into its surface. A wooden striker hung at its side, attached by a leather thong.

"This," Sebastian announced, "is the most valuable artwork on the farm, a donation from a friend. It's more than a thousand years old and probably came from your part of the world, a temple bell that may have once been used to call your monks to prayer."

Kailani reached for the striker. "May I ring it?"

"Oh no. We ring it only to call people to meals or in the unlikely event of an emergency. But if you're gentle, you may touch it."

Sebastian hovered nearby as Kailani let her fingertips glide over the engravings, a high priestess trying to unravel its mysteries. He gave her

THE DAUGHTER OF THE SEA AND THE SKY

a few seconds and urged her to move on, as if anxious to find more surprises before he ran out of time.

Behind the cabins, a well-maintained path stretched into the distance, far enough that Jason could see himself running there early in the morning. After a hundred yards, a side trail opened onto a clearing, in the center of which stood a life-sized statue of a woman. A flower pot lay at her feet and in it grew a single white dahlia. The woman bore a clay urn, tilted as if watering the flower. A bird sat on her shoulder supervising the task.

"What do you think, Kailani?" Sebastian said.

The girl looked at the woman's eyes, at the urn, and at the flower. "The urn's gone dry. There's no water."

"It's a piece of art, Kailani, an image." He turned to the adults. "It's a sculpture by Serena, our most famous alumni. She came here after her marriage fell apart, but has since moved on and made quite a name for herself. She exhibits all over the country. This statue is one of two works she donated to the farm."

Kailani seemed to have no interest in the résumé of the artist, and wandered over to touch the flower petal. "But the flower's real. How does it grow?"

"Don't worry. I assign a farm member to water it."

She smiled. "Then there must be water nearby."

"Yes, there's water, as you'll soon discover."

"But, Mr. Sebastian, why is that bird on her shoulder?"

"That bird's a golden eagle, one of many that have adopted this place as their home over the years and given the farm its name. No one has ever found where they nest, but you can often spot them at dusk gliding on the wind. If you're lucky, you might find one of their feathers. The ancients who lived here believed eagle feathers possessed magic, and would offer them to members of other tribes as a sign of friendship."

"Have you ever found an eagle feather, Mr. Sebastian?"

"Of course, but I've had a long time to look. If I find another one—" He held out his hands as if cradling a feather. "—I'll offer it to you, welcoming you to our land."

From then on, Kailani ran ahead, checking the ground for feathers and craning her neck to catch eagles in flight, though it was still midafternoon.

As they rounded a bend, she faltered and shrank back. "I found something, Mr. Sebastian, a strange man."

"Don't worry, Kailani. We only have a few ogres in these woods, but just in case, let's you and I go together."

He offered his hand and this time she accepted. Sebastian inched ahead as if he really believed there might be an ogre.

"Ah-hah!" he cried. "It's only our all-purpose handyman, Benjamin, cleaning out the path to Grandmother Storyteller. Hello, Benjamin."

A man knelt with his head bowed as if praying, his gloved hands lost among the flowers embellishing the entrance. He was slighter than Sebastian but much younger, and gaunt, with a beak of a nose and hair cropped so close it was hard to determine its color.

He stood and nodded to Sebastian, then to Martha, who returned the gesture with something deeper, more like a bow. His button-like eyes studied the newcomers, flitting from one to the other until they lit on Kailani. His lips twitched, revealing small, pointy teeth that reminded Jason of a weasel.

"Recruiting them young these days, Sebastian?" Benjamin said.

Jason felt Kailani press into him, tucking her head beneath his arm. He rested a hand on her shoulder.

"This is Kailani," Sebastian said. "She's come to us from the Blessed Lands."

Benjamin offered a thin smile, but his eyes refused to participate, and he moved on to greet Helena.

Kailani whispered to Jason, "The sea says to beware of people like that. They watch you but see only themselves."

Jason understood what made her speak that way. Benjamin was an odd-looking man, with a bony face, eyes set too close, and a sliver of cartilage for a nose. Yet despite her upbringing in the Blessed Lands, Kailani couldn't see into his soul.

"Behave yourself," he whispered back, "and be polite."

After all had been introduced, Sebastian encouraged them to continue along the path, and Benjamin followed. As they advanced deeper into the woods, the sound of running water greeted them. They soon came upon the source, a stream tumbling into a hollow in a rock ledge, forming a pool.

Presiding over the pool like its mistress was a second statue, an earth mother, larger than life. She squatted on a rock that rested in the shallows. Black braids flowed down her breasts from behind a clay shawl draped over her head, and her huge thighs were made of

THE DAUGHTER OF THE SEA AND THE SKY

boulders with tiny images of children frolicking on them. Under one arm, she held an urn tipped toward the pool, but unlike the first statue, water poured from it.

Kailani circled the pool, seemingly relishing the music of the water. At last she stopped and stared at the statue, then turned to the others as if she were the tour guide. "The mother's protecting her children from falling into the water."

The adults looked at each other bemused. A sign beside the pool told a more straightforward story. The statue was titled Grandmother Storyteller, celebrating the tradition of oral history common among the ancients, but not one of them corrected Kailani.

Jason finally broke the silence. "Serena seems to have an affinity for water jugs. I wonder why."

Sebastian began to explain, but Kailani interrupted, speaking to Jason as if he were the child. "The sea says water is the source of life."

Jason gave a nervous laugh.

"It's true," she said. "You need to believe, and you too, Helena. You should be more open to the elders' wisdom."

"And what other wisdom do they have for us?" Jason said.

"The sky says the stars are the source of dreams. You must have life and dreams to find your way."

Sebastian let out a chortle, and Martha smiled.

Helena's gloom lifted long enough to let her beam at Kailani.

A tingling at the nape of his neck caused Jason to turn. Behind them, Benjamin showed a more profound reaction, his mouth dropped open and his eyes glazed. It was, Jason realized, a look of awe.

***

After Grandmother Storyteller, Sebastian begged off but urged them to keep exploring in the hour before dinner. As he headed back, he insisted Benjamin return to work as well.

Once on their own, they proceeded at a more leisurely pace. Kailani went ahead with Helena's mother, while Jason stayed behind with Helena.

He turned to her once they were alone. "What's wrong?"

"Why'd you take her side?"

"Your mother? She was just trying to be nice to Kailani."

"You don't know her like I do."

99

When he tried to comfort her, she turned away, but when he reached for her hand, she let him grasp it. She squeezed, acknowledging his touch, and he held on.

There was an excited squeal ahead, and they picked up their pace, not wanting to miss the latest surprise as seen through Kailani's eyes. Another trail led to a circular maze, its paths marked by stones, with a knee-high rock pile at its center. A wooden sign by the entrance bore instructions:

The Labyrinth is an ancient meditation path
Once within, release your concerns and quiet your mind
At the center, be open to what the moment offers
As you leave, review and reflect

Kailani needed no instruction. She cried out, "A labyrinth," and raced in to play.

Helena pulled away from Jason and scurried to catch up.

The winding course sometimes took them nearer the center, and other times to dead ends. The two of them dashed around, retracing their steps as needed. Once at the center, Kailani celebrated with Helena around the rock pile.

When she was finished, Kailani skipped to the exit, pausing neither to review nor reflect. She rushed into Jason's arms.

"What made you so happy?" he said as he spun her around.

"In the Blessed Lands, I used to play in a labyrinth with the wind. Now, in this labyrinth, I could feel her Spirit again."

***

For a long stretch there were no more surprises, but eventually Jason discovered a new path into the woods. Its access was marked by a boulder with a single word chiseled into its surface: Reflection.

They ambled along single file until the path ended at a clearing. In the distance, the land dropped off to a split-rail fence, and beyond that, to a real farm with a few horses grazing. In the middle of the clearing stood a structure that seemed to have been partially built and abandoned.

A dozen saplings had been planted in a circle. These tapered to some eight feet overhead, where their tops were lashed together. Ragged strips of cloth filled the gaps between, creating a curtain-like effect. A wider opening formed the entrance.

The Daughter of the Sea and the Sky

Inside lay a pile of sticks, a mock campfire with no sign of charring or ash. Jason had to duck to avoid a ragtag collection of objects suspended overhead by twine: beads and bags, a white water bottle, a foam cup with writing on its surface, and a silk purse that jingled with coins inside.

And there were notes. Jason touched one, so crinkled he could hardly make out the words—a crude attempt at poetry. He grasped another written on dog-eared stationery. The farm's cheery logo contrasted with sad words.

His cheek brushed against the spinning foam cup. He steadied it between his thumb and forefinger.

"Read it, Jason." Helena said. "It's too high for the rest of us."

He raised a brow, but did as he was asked.

"I miss mornings with you. I miss days and nights together. I miss the sound of your voice, your gentle touch. You were the love of my life and always will be."

When he looked back, Helena was staring.

She said, "Sebastian told me people come to the farm because of a gap in their heart. That must be why they leave things, to describe their gap." She spun around, touching a note here and there as if trying to take them all in at once. "I wonder if that was a failed love, or someone who died. Go ahead, Jason, read another."

Jason glanced at Kailani.

She'd raised her hands to her head and was pressing her temples with her thumbs as if trying to read her own secret thoughts. The joy of the labyrinth had vanished.

"I don't think—"

"Please, Jason, one more."

He searched through them, hoping to find an innocuous one, but Helena had made her choice.

"This one," she said.

The note hung directly overhead, written not on a cup or farm stationery but on flowery notepaper. The writer had formed the letters in bold, as if to make sure they could be read.

Jason swung it toward him. "'Last March was Stephanie's birthday. She would have been four years old. I was surprised the day was so difficult. We never celebrated her birthday before because she was too young to understand the marking of time. It meant nothing to her. But this year it meant everything to me. I fell apart and have yet to pull myself together.

DAVID LITWACK

"'Grief is not a broken arm; it doesn't heal in weeks. There's no cast to bind it, and if there were, the heart would not be made whole again in such a short time. After she died, I cried for—'"

Jason stopped at a rush of air and turned to see Kailani disappear through the shelter opening.

Outside, a horse neighed in the distance as the girl from the Blessed Lands stood at the edge of the clearing with her back to them, her shoulders heaving as she sobbed. Helena and her mother left his side and went to comfort her.

Jason found himself frozen in place, drawing in quick breaths as though he'd been running for miles. As he watched the drama play out before him, he was struck by a thought: they knew so little about the Blessed Lands, and even less about Kailani. After watching her fret about a tin fish's eyes and beg for a unicorn, commune with the statues and romp through the labyrinth, and now grieve for the loss of a child she never knew, he was certain of one thing: she needed something different from assimilation and the pursuit of reason. She didn't belong here, at the farm or in this land. She belonged in a place far away, where the wind and the sea and the sky could speak to her.

A new sound arrived on the breeze, the clanging of the dinner bell. With it a new purpose came to Jason, a more worthwhile goal: to discover why Kailani had left the Blessed Lands, and to find a way to send her home.

CHAPTER 15

A BOAT GONE MISSING

"Are you sure it was stolen?" the Minister of Commerce said.

The harbormaster browsed a report on a clipboard. "Yes, Excellency, the details are right here. In the middle of the night three weeks ago—not the finest boat in the harbor, a modest sloop, part of a fleet of four used for fishing and recreation."

"Was anything else missing?"

The harbormaster turned to a second page and studied it before answering. "A few petty thefts the night before—charts, food, water jugs—but oddly, no locks were broken. Police on the scene believed the thief slipped between buildings, through cracks in the walls and holes at the foundation where the dirt had been worn away."

The minister's thoughts flashed to the lost one, to waves washing over her still, small body. His mind recoiled. "Was the boat seaworthy?"

"Oh yes, sir, old but well maintained. I know the owner, and he has a consistent safety record. He was most upset by its loss."

"Do you have any idea...." He paused to pick his words. "Why would someone would take such things?"

DAVID LITWACK

The man flipped through more pages until nothing was left but the brown backing of the clipboard. "I'm sorry, sir. It would be speculation." Then wilting under the minister's stare, he cleared his throat. "It's as if someone was trying to escape across the sea, a risky way to transmigrate. As if they were trying to avoid the authorities."

Speculation, but the minister knew the missing girl's heart and the brooding that had possessed her. He shifted his gaze to the epaulets on the harbormaster's shoulders, and then past them to the charts on the wall. His eye caught a tiny speck, the offshore island that had been his childhood home, and where he had returned with the poetess to raise their family.

How happy they'd been, but sometimes life took on the truth of myth. Each year, on the winter solstice, the islanders would hold the festival of the turtle demon. The story went that on that one day, the demon would emerge from the sea and slog across the island in search of a human sacrifice. He moved too slowly, however, and the islanders would retreat to a hilltop far inland, far enough that he could never reach them before sunset. There they would roast a pig and hold a feast until dark, when it was safe to return.

When she was young, the curious child wondered if the turtle demon ever caught his prey, or if he was destined to always wander aimlessly before returning to the depths. The answer, according to legend, was that the demon could find a victim only if their faith was weak, if they'd given up hope. Only such a person would go willingly into the sea.

Not this child; this golden child would never lose hope. She'd gone to sea for a different purpose.

He looked back at the harbormaster, pressed his palms together in front of his chest, and made a slight bow, befitting their respective ranks. "Thank you. You've been helpful. I have one last request. I want to speak to the owner of the stolen boat."

He'd found his next clue. Now he'd follow it wherever it might lead, to the edge of the forbidden sea and, if necessary, beyond.

Chapter 16

Benjamin

The next day was the last of September, and Sebastian could no longer deny their predicament. He thumbed through a stack of overdue bills that by themselves would exceed the budget. The pile beneath them—purchase requisitions awaiting his approval—would only make matters worse. For the past year, he'd been draining what was left of his savings to make up the difference, but now that source had disappeared, and his natural optimism waned.

On the walk from his cabin that morning, a raw wind had forced him to hunch his shoulders and draw his collar up around his neck. Though the leaves had not yet turned, winter came early in the Northern Kingdom and would not be far behind.

He worried most about the old generator.

Benjamin did his best to maintain it but insisted it was a losing battle. "I can lap the valves again, but that isn't going to cure the piston slap, and I've already pulled the shims from the bearings. It's only a matter of time before it beats itself into scrap. It needs to be replaced, or one of these winters the power will go out and we'll all freeze."

105

DAVID LITWACK

Sebastian had Benjamin send out a special newsletter pleading for donations.

> To: *Friends of Glen Eagle Farm*
> From: *Sebastian*
> Subject: *Ye Old Generator*
>
> *Dearest friends,*
>
> *Winter is coming to the Northern Kingdom and we need your help. Glen Eagle Farm requires a capital outlay we can ill afford, to buy a new generator to keep us warm when the snow falls. Here at the farm, we nourish the creative mind, but creativity only soars when the body is healthy, well fed, and warm. Please help.*

The response was meager, and mostly silence ensued.

He'd always thrived on challenges, managing even the largest projects on time and under budget, but when Lizzie fell ill, she became his only project. Instead of managing construction, he managed her decline, trying to make the remaining time bearable for her, knowing he was destined to fail. When she was gone and he found himself alone after forty-one years of marriage, nothing seemed to matter. Friends urged him to get back to the office, to use work as therapy, but his heart hadn't been in it.

He'd felt as he had as a young man returning from the war, emerging down the gangplank of the troop carrier into the midst of a bustling city. He resented those around him who had no idea what he'd been through — their constant efforts to filch a little more money from each other, their quest to find a better restaurant or speedier car, their need to dream their insignificant dreams.

Foolish people. After the war they trespassed on his madness. After Lizzie died they encroached on his grief. He went through the motions for a few months and then gave up.

A friend whose sister had gone to the farm had recommended it as a place where he might get his life back together. When he arrived, he found it in shambles and had volunteered to help. The farm soon became his new project, one he could manage from start to finish, one that mattered.

Now he worried it wouldn't survive.

When he heard the knock at the door, he welcomed the distraction — Jason dropping by for his interview.

The Daughter of the Sea and the Sky

"Come in," Sebastian said.

The young man strode into his office carrying a bulky black case in one hand as if it were lighter than air. The young were like that, flowing through the physical world, flinging their bodies at life.

He'd been that way too, flinging his body at the war, the last battle with the zealots before the Treaty of Separation brought peace. Now he moved more cautiously, afraid to fall and break a hip, but he flung himself at things in a different way. Emptying his bank account was an irrational act, leaving no safety net for his future, yet he'd gladly do it again.

This young man probably had misgivings about spending so much time away from the office.

"Good morning, Jason." His upbeat greeting was only a little bit forced. "I trust you slept well."

Jason beamed, his face fresh and flushed. "Yes, I did. Better than I have in some time."

"The farm can do that to you. I think it's the mountain air. Have a seat."

As Jason settled in, Sebastian flipped the stack of bills over onto their blank back sides. "You look like you just finished a run."

"I did. I jogged down to the reflection shelter and cut through the woods to that dirt road by the horse farm. Then I followed it all the way to the highway. Great place for a run."

"An early morning jaunt through the woods." He stared out the bay window, envisioning a path from an earlier time. "Did you see their tracks?"

"Whose tracks?"

"The animals—their little footprints on the ground. I used to go for a sunrise walk myself before my knees started acting up. As a city boy, I loved finding the tracks they left in the dew, letting me know they'd passed this way."

The young man gaped at him as if he were an addled old man.

Best to return to business. "Maybe later, after you've slowed down. Now, I understand you expect to work for the Polytechnic Institute while you're here."

"If you let me. All I need is a quiet place with a desk, a chair, and a comm link." He patted the black case. "This will do the rest."

"So Helena tells me. Some kind of experimental communications, isn't it?"

DAVID LITWACK

"That's right. The latest technology. I'll be able to share documents, data, and photograms almost as if I were there."

"Sounds impressive, Jason, but it gives *me* a problem. I have a hard and fast rule. No one stays at the farm without contributing. To do otherwise would be unfair to our other members. I've never made an exception, and I don't intend to start now."

Jason lowered his eyes and studied his hands.

Sebastian waited, giving him time.

Finally, the young man looked up and met Sebastian's gaze. "Helena mentioned your rule, and I've given it some thought. I'm willing to do whatever it takes to stay, Polytech work at night or early in the morning, and in between, rake leaves, mop the kitchen floor, wash dishes. Anything you ask."

Sebastian placed his elbows on the desk, made a platform with his hands, and rested his chin on them. "I was hoping you'd say that. Here's what I'd like you to do. Most of our members are artisans or culinary people and are absolved from the upkeep of the farm. In fact, most of the maintenance and administrative work is done by a single person, and he could use a second pair or hands. Would you be willing to help him?"

"Who's that?"

"You've already met him. Our jack-of-all-trades, Benjamin."

Sebastian watched Jason closely as he spoke, and caught an expected hint of a grimace, quickly controlled. A bad sign; the two would have to work together.

"Oh, I know. Benjamin's unusual," he said, "but he's a hard worker and has done everything I've ever asked of him. Just do what he tells you, and you'll get along fine. Will you give it a try?"

Jason shifted to the edge of his seat and leaned in. "And in exchange, you'll provide me a place to do my work in the off hours?"

"I've already asked Benjamin to set up space for you in his office. It'll be tight for the two of you, but—"

"I'll take it."

Sebastian unfolded his hands, stretched the right one across the desk, and held it firm until the young man grasped it and gave it a shake.

***

Jason followed Sebastian down a creaky corridor, while the managing director once again gave a tour. "The great house was built over three hundred years ago when settlers first braved the north country—a farming family, I think, by the name of Macintyre. A descendant of theirs still lives in Northweald and runs the Emporium. It was modest at first, just the foyer and my office, but they expanded it like a patchwork quilt, a new wing for each generation. The old girl's cranky at times and a burden to heat, but we do our best to maintain her."

He stopped near the end, just before a back door opened onto a small porch. "On the right is a common room our members use to make calls to friends and family. On the left is your new home, where Benjamin works when he's not maintaining the grounds."

Jason peered inside—the space wasn't much larger than his cubicle at the Polytech, only big enough to hold two chairs and a table. On the table sat an older model text processor attached to a printer, and a hand-cranked mimeograph machine with an ink-fed drum. The usual office supplies clustered around these—reams of paper, a jar with plastic pens, a paper-cutter, envelopes, a sponge for sealing them, a roll of stamps, packing tape, and scissors.

"Now," Sebastian said, "where did Benjamin go?"

The man Jason had met by Grandmother Storyteller poked his head out from underneath the desk, a screwdriver in his hand.

"Ah, there you are," Sebastian said. "Look who I've brought."

Benjamin crawled out from under the table, scrambled to his feet, and made a cursory bow. A furrow formed at the corners of his mouth, exposing the tips of his teeth, apparently his version of smiling.

Jason nodded, trying to be friendly, but the man barely made eye contact.

"Good news, Benjamin," Sebastian said. "Jason has agreed to use your handiwork in the off hours in exchange for being your helper in between."

Jason caught a nearly imperceptible movement as the man's posture stiffened and the pointed teeth were tucked away.

Sebastian paid no mind. "I assume you'll take advantage of him in the best possible way."

Another small bow.

"Wonderful. Then I'll leave the two of you to your work. I have plenty to do myself."

When Sebastian was gone, Jason extended a hand to Benjamin, smiled, and said, "I look forward to working with you."

No response. His hand hovered unmet in midair until he withdrew it.

DAVID LITWACK

Jason tried to draw him out. "Do you prefer to be called Benjamin, or is it Ben or Benji?"

"It's Ben-ja-min."

"Okay, Benjamin it is."

"I have always been called Benjamin, not Ben or Benji. My mother called me Benjamin. My father called me Benjamin. Everyone calls me Benjamin."

Jason pictured a boy being teased during recess—"Ben-ja-min, Ben-ja-min"—in schoolyard sing-song, and wondered how many fights that had caused.

"Well, Benjamin...." Jason tried to banish the sing-song from his head. "You maintain the farm's equipment as well as the grounds?"

"I'm not one of those prima donna artists," Benjamin said. "I do whatever Sebastian asks of me."

"Like what?"

"Weed the flowerbeds, arrange the stones that line the paths, send out newsletters to the friends of the farm." He glanced up, perhaps to see if Jason was impressed. "And I hunt in season to provide food."

"Really. What do you hunt?"

"I'll bag a couple of bucks a year," he said, "and a few does too. It saves Sebastian money, and everyone loves fresh venison."

"Are you a good hunter?"

"Better than I am a handyman. I learned all the tricks as a child—how to stalk my prey, how to position downwind with the sun at my back and, most importantly, how to hit what I aim at." He shuffled to the window and pointed. "See that top window of the barn?"

Jason looked out and nodded.

"That's the quilting room. From there I could pick off a squirrel dashing across the front lawn."

"Is that so?"

"That's so, Jason." His lips twitched, and the points of his teeth showed again. "Take it to the bank. I'd hit it every time."

***

Jason found Benjamin to be hard working and intelligent, but eccentric, a self-absorbed man with a braying laugh that often burst out at inappropriate times. The two would never be friends but might make passable colleagues, at least for his stay at the farm.

THE DAUGHTER OF THE SEA AND THE SKY

Benjamin had learned all he knew about machine repair from reference manuals that sat on a shelf above the work table. He spent the bulk of his time on that and grounds maintenance. But he was most proud of his role as overseer of the Friends of Glen Eagle Farm.

"I publish a newsletter once a month," he said, "more often if something special's going on. I write the articles, format the pages, and paste in pictures of the artwork we hope they'll buy. Then I run off the copies and fold them, address the envelopes and stuff them, stick on the stamps, and take them to the post office in town. We had fewer than forty friends when I started. Now it's up to two hundred fifty-seven. In the spring and the fall, we hold a reception for them so they can see the fruits of their generosity.

"But it's never enough for Sebastian. He wants more friends to sustain the farm. I recruit them when I find time, especially from universities like yours, but lately, nothing seems to move the numbers."

"Have you tried advertising?"

Benjamin straightened. Though a slight man, he seemed to grow a few inches. "This is Glen Eagle Farm, Jason, a special place. It's not some country fair."

A few months seemed suddenly like a long time. Jason thought it best to change the subject, and pointed to the small white box mounted on the wall above the desk. "Is the comm link live?"

"I hope so, but I just installed it and haven't had a chance to test it yet. Sebastian only told me about you this morning. Fetch me my tool box." He gestured to a metal box on the floor.

"No need," Jason said. "I can test it from this."

He opened the black case and pulled out a plastic box not much bigger than Benjamin's text processor, but with a larger screen embedded in its front and a more complex keyboard folding out below. A black cable snaked out from its back.

After laying the device gently on the desktop, he borrowed Benjamin's screwdriver and attached the cable to the comm link. With the flick of a switch, the screen sprang to life and words appeared:

Welcome to the Polytechnic Institute Network
Please Sign On

Jason's hands hovered over the keyboard, and he typed *Jason-Adams*. When the system prompted for a password, he slid the pointer

111

DAVID LITWACK

over to the appropriate field, but when he caught Benjamin peering over his shoulder, he paused to turn a dial and darken the screen. Only then did he finish typing.

"What was that all about?" Benjamin said.

"Security. I had to enter my password."

He brightened the screen again and typed:

To [William-Jackson@Polytechnic-Institute]. Hi, Bill.

Benjamin placed the flat of his hands on the desktop and let his weight rest on them. "What are you doing now?"

"Letting my colleague know I'm connected. I've tied into the network and am linking our machines."

He waited, and after a few seconds new words scrolled down the screen, though Jason had typed no more.

Benjamin pressed down harder until his knuckles turned white. "How did you do that?"

"I didn't. That's Bill Jackson back at Albion Point replying to my message."

Benjamin's eyes grew wider as he realized what he was seeing.

Jason couldn't resist, and typed:

Bill, send me a document.

Moments later, a document rippled across the screen, the tenets of the Republic, the standard treatise about pursuing a rational life for the benefit of all. Embedded in the text was the ubiquitous image from the land bridge, the statue of the Lady of Reason with her torch held high. Jason heard a quick intake of breath behind him.

"How did that picture get into the document?" Benjamin said.

In answer, Jason pulled a second device from his case, this one appearing like a sleeker version of Benjamin's printer. With a twist of a screw, he connected it to the encomm. Then he glanced about the room.

On a bookshelf behind Benjamin lay a pile of old farm newsletters. He grabbed one, pausing to admire its cover, and then fed it into a slot in the new device.

He pressed a button and a motor whirred. Light leaked from the edges of the newsletter. Gradually, a photogram displayed in layers on the encomm's screen. It showed the great house in autumn with the mountains behind. Green pastures and trees filled the valleys, brightly colored foliage graced the slopes, and snow covered the summits.

Jason typed:

Check this out, Bill. My new home.

112

THE DAUGHTER OF THE SEA AND THE SKY

After a moment, new words appeared on the screen:
Document received. Lucky you, Jason. Looks great.
Jason turned, expecting to find Benjamin impressed. Instead he caught him staring at the encomm like a man making plans.

***

Late that night, Benjamin paced the confines of his cabin and let his mind race. He didn't like Jason and had no desire to work with him. This so-called man of reason talked down at him like his father used to. *'You're a Thorndike, Benjamin, not a damn peasant. It's time you became reasonable, abandon your foolish notions, and make something of your life.'*

He'd make something of his life, all right, but something worthwhile, something more meaningful and lasting than money or power. He'd had some success but was limited by his remote location; spreading the word was difficult. He had to sneak the special mailings in a few at a time to keep Sebastian from noticing the increase in postage.

Then came Kailani, as if sent by Lord Kanakunai himself, a golden child full of faith and blessed with a spirit bright enough to enlighten the soulless.

Now an even greater gift had arrived — Jason, the man of reason, and the miracle device his reason had produced. Jason possessed resources Benjamin lacked, resources he could use to further the cause.

He'd do as Sebastian asked — take Jason under his wing, work him hard and make him earn his keep. At the same time, he'd learn new ways to attract more believers. Once he'd been shown how, he'd sneak in late at night, after a worn-out Jason had gone to bed, and take advantage of the device.

He shoved the cot aside and yanked off the loose board he'd cut away to create a hiding place, knowing someday they'd come to search his room. From inside the wall he withdrew a scroll that held the list of names, a list that was still too small.

The irony of it: a nonbeliever would show him the way. He felt a stab of remorse. *Is this the way to paradise?* He tossed the scroll into the air and caught it, then put it back into its hole.

A *nonbeliever* would show him the way. No matter. The Lord worked in mysterious ways. The end would justify the means.

113

CHAPTER 17

THE SPIRIT OF THE WIND

Helena strolled alongside Kailani, holding her hand and swinging it in rhythm with their stride. The day was perfect for their outing, the air crisp and clear. Both kept checking the tree line on their right, searching for the marker Sebastian had described. Kailani could barely contain her excitement, and Helena was much the same.

Jason prowled ahead. Of the three, only he had yet to adapt to the slower pace of the farm. While she and Kailani were making jewelry, he'd been slaving away at the menial tasks Benjamin assigned him, all the while still putting in long hours for the Polytech. It left scant time for sleep and no time for them to be together. He never complained, but his shoulders seemed to slump more each day.

After a week, Helena intervened, insisting Sebastian give him time off. He'd earned a break and the chance to do something with her and Kailani. She asked Sebastian for a suggestion, some surprise they'd yet to encounter.

THE DAUGHTER OF THE SEA AND THE SKY

He'd recommended a spot on the farm's high point of land, a place called the Spirit Hill. From the top they'd be able to look out over the valley and watch the sun set before dinner.

About a twenty-minute walk from the cabins, she found exactly what Sebastian had described—a side path, narrower and not as well maintained as the others, its entrance marked only by two knee-high boulders. Without Sebastian's directions, she'd have wandered right past it.

"Over here, Jason." She tightened her grip on Kailani to keep her from racing ahead, and let Jason take the lead.

Fifty yards in, the trail dropped into a hollow where rain had pooled, leaving the ground mossy and moist. Across from them, where the soil firmed again, stood a knee-high statue of a man stripped to the waist, holding his arms outstretched to the heavens. As Kailani mimicked the pose, Helena guessed why Sebastian had placed the artwork far from the main path—too much like a man praying.

Just past the statue, the trail turned into a series of switchbacks, winding back and forth but still steep enough to challenge their breathing. Helena plodded along behind Kailani, while Jason led the way.

After fifteen minutes, the scrub pine thinned and the sky broke through the branches. A minute later, they reached the summit.

Their attention was immediately drawn to a massive stone bench carved into a boulder that dominated the rear of a clearing. Some artisan had chiseled seats for three into a recessed center, surrounded by broad arms fashioned into ornate scrolls. The crest of the boulder arched overhead, topped by the sculpted face of a lion, who seemed to lord over the clearing like its protector. The overall effect was more cradle than bench.

Kailani knelt in the center and gazed into the lion's eyes, until she noticed a trough tapering across the back of the bench. Inside the trough she found a smattering of odds and ends, a hairpin, a locket and other items, but mostly a collection of stones.

"What are those?" she said, fingering the more interesting pieces.

"Sebastian explained it to me," Helena said, glad at last to have a straightforward answer to one of the girl's endless questions. "It's a tradition for people to leave a token to mark their journey."

"Why would they do that? The climb wasn't so hard."

"Not that kind of journey. The journey that brought them to the farm."

DAVID LITWACK

Kailani considered a moment. "Oh. You mean a journey of the Spirit, like at the Reflection shelter or the labyrinth."

"Sort of," Helena said. "According to Sebastian, people go to Reflection to express their problem and to the labyrinth to contemplate it. They come to the Spirit Hill when they've overcome it. Once the bench was finished, they began placing whatever they had with them in the trough, but the high winds up here kept blowing things away. After a while, they started to secure them with stones. Later on, the tradition became to leave just a single stone."

Kailani replaced the pieces she'd taken, careful to lay them where she'd found them. Then she hopped off the bench and combed through the dirt until she found three stones, two large and one small. She placed them on a clear spot at the center of the trough, stepped back, and studied them. Finally, she shook her head and scooped them back up.

"What was that all about?" Helena said.

"I thought...."

"It's okay, Kailani. Go ahead."

"That I'd leave a stone for myself and the sea and the sky, but it's not yet time. My journey isn't complete." She knelt to return the stones to the ground.

"Wait," Helena said. "Give them to me."

"Why?"

"What if I place one for each of us instead, for you and me and Jason?"

She reached out for them, but Kailani pulled back. After weighing the stones in the palm of her hand, she tossed them away.

Before Helena could question her further, Kailani turned, drew in a sharp breath and pointed to the west. "Look."

All three had been preoccupied with the stones and hadn't noticed the sight behind them. At the front of the clearing, the land dropped off so sharply the tops of the trees lay below their feet. The notch in the woods exposed a layered vista, with bright green foothills close by, darker mountains beyond, and even greater mountains fading into a vague horizon, and then distant clouds that might be another range, merging into the sky.

As they nestled together on the bench to admire the view, Jason turned to Kailani, who was seated between him and Helena. "Bet you can see as much sky here as you can at the ocean."

"Nearly as much. It *is* a place of the Spirit." She turned to Jason. "Where have you been? We hardly see you anymore."

116

THE DAUGHTER OF THE SEA AND THE SKY

"I've been working to help Sebastian. I hear you've been working too."

"Not work, Jason. We've been making jewelry with Miz Martha."

"Do you like it?"

"I like it a lot, but I don't think Helena does."

"She's exaggerating," Helena said, wondering how she could have considered placing a stone in the trough. She'd overcome nothing so far. "I love learning from... Miz Martha."

Kailani turned to face Jason. "You spend too much time with your work. You need to spend more time with Helena. She smiles more when you're around."

Blood rushed to Helena's face as Jason laughed.

"Well, you're right, and that's what I'll try to do—find time for you and Helena." He reached across and took Helena's hand.

The orb of the sun had swelled, demanding their attention. As they watched it drift toward the horizon, the sound of footsteps crunching along the path startled them. They turned to the opening in the trees where the trail cut through.

An out-of-breath group of climbers burst into the clearing, relieved to have reached the top. All but one wore white robes that hung loosely over their clothing and down to their ankles. Diaphanous white shawls covered the tops of their heads and flowed down their shoulders, and each carried a pink blossom cradled at the waist.

The exception was a small figure who seemed to be their leader. He wore a brown robe and carried a bamboo flute, hung from a leather cord slung around his shoulder. A hood covered his head and nearly obscured his face, but his dusty boots and pointy-toothed sneer gave him away.

It was Benjamin.

The others organized themselves in two rows behind him at the edge of the overlook—shorter ones in front, taller in back. Helena recognized most of them, farm members she'd seen before, but an odd one, the slightest of the group, hung back in the glare of the setting sun. Helena was unable to make out the face.

"Hello, Benjamin," Jason said. "Have you come to join us to watch the sunset?"

"We're not tourists," he said. "We don't come here for the view."

"So why do you come?"

Benjamin scowled. "Someone like you would never understand."

117

To Helena's surprise, Kailani hopped off the bench and approached him. "Then you can tell me, Mister Benjamin, and Jason and Helena can listen."

Benjamin beheld the eager child, and his eyes softened. "Yes, of course. You'd know."

He came forward, closing the distance between them by half, then signaled for two of the others to join him. They took positions at either side.

"It's the call at twilight," Benjamin said. "A tradition from the Blessed Lands. We sound it in the evening to summon the spirit of the wind."

Helena heard an intake of air and noticed Kailani's shoulders quiver.

Benjamin waited for her to speak.

"I've heard of this," the girl said. "Summoning the spirit of the wind, though whenever I've tried, I failed. Perhaps you could teach me."

Benjamin's face turned ashen, and he looked like he might drop to his knees. "It's an old tradition, maybe different from what you've seen. We... may not perform it right. It almost never brings the wind."

"This farm is special," Kailani said. "I can feel the Spirit in this place. Maybe your summons will succeed when we're all together."

After a moment's hesitation, Benjamin turned to the sun, now fat and orange, a half disk sinking into the horizon, and signaled for the others to turn as well. He swung the flute around and steadied his fingers, then covered three of the five holes, brought the slant-cut blowing edge to his lips, and began to play. The flute possessed a haunting sound, surprisingly rich for so simple an instrument.

Helena felt a tug on her hand as Jason pulled her back, separating them from the odd ritual. Benjamin's pilgrims gazed out at the reddening sky as if expecting to see music floating on the air.

When Benjamin finished, the acolyte to his right took a bell from his pocket and rang it three times. Helena recognized the scalloped handle and strange markings — Lizzie's bell. When the clapper struck, the tone reverberated across the hillside and lingered.

As it began to dissipate, a squawk rang out overhead. *Skree. Skree.*

Kailani looked up and pointed to two eagles gliding on the wind.

Benjamin lowered the flute and gaped at the child. "Do you know these ancient ways because you come from the Blessed Lands?"

118

"Oh no," she said. "I know them because I'm the daughter of the sea and the sky." She glanced back at Helena, a smile of satisfaction on her face.

As Helena nodded in approval, she caught the figure at the rear of the formation peek around to get a better look, and stifled a gasp.

The slight form behind the others was her mother.

CHAPTER 18

THE DAUGHTER'S TALE

Benjamin settled in front of the new device, still warm from use, and stroked its plastic sides. He'd crouched outside in the trees for hours, waiting for Jason to turn off the office light and go to bed, and it was now well past midnight.

Leaving the office dark, he toggled the switch on and the apparatus came alive, with the glow from its screen and the hum of its fan, so much like his text processor but so different. This one could send words and photograms in a way Sebastian would never see.

Once the welcome message came into focus, he typed "Jason-Adams." The prompt to enter the password challenged him in the dark. His fingers hovered over the keyboard as he strained to recall the code. Jason always darkened the screen when he logged on, but Benjamin had been able to decipher the start of the password by observing the keystrokes. Of the eleven letters, he'd caught only the first three: TAK. Were they the beginning of a phrase or a random sequence? He fumbled with combinations well into the night. At the darkest hour, when the moon was down and no shred of the dawn had yet appeared, he gave up.

THE DAUGHTER OF THE SEA AND THE SKY

He'd have to send a mailing the old-fashioned way, a risky choice, but this message was sent from the Lord, and he was compelled to obey. He turned off the device, making sure to leave no sign it had been touched, and went back to the text processor.

Half an hour later, he'd composed a draft. He was poised to print but hesitated; best to review.

The title read: "A Refugee from the Blessed Lands Summons the Wind."

He drummed the desktop with his fingers, dragged the pointer across the first words, turning them blue, and typed. It now read: "Kailani Summons the Wind." He gnawed on his fingernails, then deleted the word "Kailani."

Did he dare?

He began typing again, and nodded with satisfaction when he was done. The title now read: "The Daughter of the Sea and the Sky Summons the Wind."

After skimming the new draft for errors and double-checking the spelling, he printed the newsletter, loaded the hand-cranked copier with paper, and ran off two hundred and fifty seven copies—one missive for each friend of the farm.

Then, lest Jason discover him there, he fled the office before dawn.

***

The next morning, a bleary-eyed Benjamin staggered into the office with a stack of papers under his arm and found his young assistant glaring at him.

He slapped the stack on the desk, printed side down. "What are you staring at?"

"What's the matter, Benjamin? Rough night after your party on the hill?"

Jason was a fool. What did he know of the passion that drove a believer to go without sleep? "Don't concern yourself with things you don't understand. Here on the farm we have more freedom than in the city to live and believe as we choose. And we have lots of work to do. Today, we send out a newsletter."

Benjamin handed him a stack of envelopes, a pen, and a list of names.

"Address these. I'll fold the newsletters, stuff the envelopes, and seal them."

121

DAVID LITWACK

He hoped Jason would find the task tedious. Sure enough, after scrawling an address on the first several envelopes, Jason set down the pen and flexed his fingers.

"You do this every month?"

"Sometimes more often."

"I have a better way."

"How?" Benjamin forced his tired mind to stay alert. He didn't want to miss a detail.

"Lots of these people are affiliated with universities and would be on the network. We could enter most of the list once and cut the work way down."

Benjamin shifted his weight to the balls of his feet. "Show me."

His cocky assistant turned to the enhanced communicator and logged on, as usual careful to conceal the password. Once connected, he brought up a list of names, picked a few from Benjamin's roster, and searched.

He found a match within seconds. "Here's one. And another. We could create a broadcast list, cross them off your paper, and never have to send them mailings again."

Buoyed by his faith and encouraged by Jason's pride, Benjamin decided to take a chance. "But what if you're not here? I'd need the password."

He saw at once he'd pushed too far.

Jason's eyes narrowed. "Just what's in these newsletters?"

Benjamin turned away in a huff. "If you don't think I can be trusted, then I'll do the rest myself. Go earn Sebastian's food. The flower bed in front of the great house needs weeding."

As he resumed his folding, Jason surprised him by grabbing for a newsletter. Benjamin pulled the stack away.

Jason snatched one of the sealed envelopes instead, ripped it open, and pulled out its contents. As he read, his face flushed. "Kailani! You can't send this out."

Benjamin flicked out his hand to take back the newsletter, but the younger man was quicker. "Give it back, Jason. Sebastian said to do as you're told."

Jason stood, towering over him. "We'll see about that."

He spun on his heels and raced out the door.

***

Sebastian sat in his high-backed chair and listened while Jason and Benjamin argued.

122

THE DAUGHTER OF THE SEA AND THE SKY

"Such a story," Benjamin said. "A girl from the Blessed Lands seeking refuge at the farm."

"She's on probation," Jason countered. "A story like this could land her in a correctional facility."

"Because of a few friends of the farm? You're being unreasonable."

"She's none of their business."

"Her summoning the wind would inspire them."

"Kailani needs kindness, not the glare of strangers. Don't use her to promote the farm."

Benjamin shoved in front of Jason. "You see her through your own lens. You may be seeing too little."

"Don't tell me what Kailani is. I know her better than you."

Sebastian glanced from one to the other and back again. Jason was sensible and well balanced, whereas Benjamin was unpredictable—he'd tried to sneak through reckless newsletters before. As a good manager, Sebastian's first priority had always been to shield the farm from harm, but this time, most of all, he needed to protect the little girl with the sad eyes.

He smiled at Jason. "Thank you for bringing this to my attention. Now please, go on about your chores. Benjamin and I need to talk."

***

The chill in the craft studio cut Helena deep. Kailani hummed as she worked, but Helena said not a word. After an hour of listening to the echo of tools clattering on the workbench, she set down the half-formed necklace she'd been fumbling with.

"I need a break," she said. "Let's take a walk."

"Where are we going?" Kailani asked.

"Not you, just me and Miz Martha. How about you go visit the glassblower?"

"You mean the unicorn lady?"

"That's right." Helena turned to her mother and spoke in clipped tones. "I'll take her. You meet me outside."

Kailani didn't need to be asked twice. At the glassblowing studio, she gave Helena a hug and went to see her new friend.

Once back outside, Helena lingered in the doorway of the barn. On the path ahead, her mother gazed up at the tree tops with the expression of a woman trying to think pleasant thoughts but failing.

123

"We need to talk," Helena said.

Her mother turned to her with her newfound look of serenity. "What is it, dear? Tired of jewelry making already?"

Helena clomped down the stairs and along the dirt path until she stood two paces away. "Don't pretend. I know you're not that obtuse."

"I don't—"

"What were you doing on the Spirit Hill last night?"

"Oh that," she said. "It's just a few harmless rituals."

"A few? What else do they do?"

"Only a couple, actually." Her mother fiddled with her hair, trying to stuff the ragged ends behind her ears. "There's the evening call to the wind that you saw, and a brief morning prayer at Grandmother Storyteller. I don't always go, but I try to join them a few times a week." When Helena continued to glare, she added, "It doesn't mean anything, just a few symbols that make me feel better."

"What are they, some kind of crazy cult?"

Her mother lifted her chin. "We're not a cult, Helena. We're Lemurians."

"What are Lemurians?"

Her mother glanced up at the peak of the barn as if overcome by an urge to check the direction of the wind vane. When she turned back to Helena, she needed an extra breath before answering. "Lemurians believe the world was once undivided, a single continent called Lemuria. It was a place of the spirit and the arts, but a reckless faction came along, seduced by the pursuit of knowledge, and tried to control nature. As a result of their experiments, the continent was split in two: one land for those who worship reason, and the other a refuge for the blessed."

"Are you serious? You can't possibly believe—"

"Whether I believe it or not doesn't matter, only what it symbolizes. Benjamin asks us to focus on the way of the blessed rather than the soulless. The rituals remind us to pause, to sense the Spirit in the wind, and to remember that water is the source of life."

"So Benjamin's your teacher now?"

"I don't recall needing your permission for what I do. Why are you carrying on so?"

"Because you're talking nonsense. You and Dad taught me to believe what the mind can explain and prove, not what's just... made up."

THE DAUGHTER OF THE SEA AND THE SKY

Her mother stepped closer, her serenity gone. "That's right. He believed in science—make a hypothesis and test it. We'd work on an experiment for weeks, and when one succeeded, we'd go to dinner and celebrate over a bottle of wine. But where is he now?"

"But you're mythmaking, creating an arbitrary story with no grounding in—"

"Aren't you listening?" Her mother's voice rose. "Where is he now?"

"He's gone. He doesn't exist anymore."

"Is that the best you can conceive of?"

She stared at her mother, hoping she'd provide a better answer, but she stayed stubbornly silent. Finally, her mother wandered past her to the small landing at the back of the great house and settled on the steps, smoothing her dress across her lap and down to her ankles.

"Come sit with me, dear." When Helena didn't move, she tilted her head and beckoned.

Helena edged closer but couldn't bring herself to sit. She hovered nearby, while her mother crouched on the stoop, seeming older than she remembered... and more frail.

She softened her tone. "So you've become a believer now?"

"Oh, I don't know. Being with them just makes me feel better." Her mother brushed the porch floor with her fingertips, making patterns in the dust. "When I first came here, I was running away with nothing to live for. Benjamin helped me. He teaches that it's better to affirm life than to deny it. To affirm the...." Her voice trailed off as if she'd just realized to whom she was speaking.

Helena remembered one of her father's favorite quotes from a writer long gone. He'd displayed it prominently on the wall of his lab: "Faith is a myth, and beliefs shift like mists on the shore; words, once pronounced, die; and the memory of yesterday is as shadowy as the hope of tomorrow."

"To affirm what?" she said, more desperate this time.

"I'm not asking you to adopt these beliefs, Helena, only to respect them. Benjamin teaches that too many of us run around trying to accumulate money, reputation, and recognition, but none of that matters. Life itself is gift enough, and we should be grateful for the time we have. Since nothing else is certain, we should be willing to accept a power greater than ourselves." She paused and took a long breath. "Please sit."

Please sit. The words took her back to the white room.

***

"Please sit," the technician said.

Helena took the chair in the corner while her father was prepared for a bone scan.

The technician laid him down on a plastic slab, his feet bound and his arms wrapped to his side. A camera hung overhead, and at the end of the slab was a round tunnel.

The technician turned a screen toward Helena. "The camera will scan his body. You can follow if you like. You'll see his feet appear first and then proceed to the head. This clock in the corner will count down—twenty minutes."

The technician pressed a button and left them alone.

Seconds ticked off the clock as the slab inched her father's body beneath the camera. After a minute, white lines appeared on the screen outlining her father's feet, then extended as the slab progressed.

Her father had been told not to move, but he remained so still she had to check if he was breathing. The line doll on the screen continued to be drawn as the timer ticked down: 12:43, 12:42, 12:41—a digital hourglass, measuring what was left of his life.

Before his torso entered the tunnel, he spoke, his voice distant in the white room. "Helena, are you there?"

"I'm right here."

"Do you know why your mother never comes with us?"

"No, I don't."

A pause. The machine whirred on.

"Is it because she's angry with me?"

"Angry?" Helena said, fighting to hide her own anger. "Why would she be angry?"

Finally, as he was about to vanish into the tunnel, he said, "It's all right, Helena. You can be my guardian angel instead."

Her hands wanted to fly out to her sides, but she froze them in place, feeling like she had to remain as still as him.

His guardian angel? How can she ever live up to his expectations?

***

And now, too late, her mother thought *she'd* become a guardian angel, protecting both Helena and Kailani. No. She hadn't earned it.

THE DAUGHTER OF THE SEA AND THE SKY

Faith is a myth.

"Where was your faith," she said, "when my father lay dying? You have no more answers now than when you abandoned me to run off to the farm—nothing but the ramblings of that odd little man."

"I'm... so sorry, Helena. Please, come sit."

She turned her back and stomped off to the barn. At least there she could produce something she could touch and feel, something of substance, something real.

***

Benjamin crept through the night mist, down the service road to the back entrance of the great house. Unable to sleep, he'd spent half the night praying, purging his anger at Sebastian—Sebastian, whom he'd helped at every turn. This was Jason's fault; he'd turned the managing director against him.

Never mind. None of them know my purpose, and my purpose is all that matters.

For years he'd struggled to bring the message to the soulless, but few had heeded his call. He was not gifted in a way that others followed, and he preached only a vague recollection of the words. During his brief stay in the Blessed Lands, while in their holding cell, a pious guard had offered him the Holy Book to read for comfort. When it became clear they'd send him back to the soulless, he begged for a chance to take the scripture with him, but the Treaty of Separation forbade it, not even allowing him to take notes.

While waiting in vain for his appeal to be heard, he memorized as much as he could. He tried so hard, barely sleeping for three nights, but his imperfect memory had failed him.

Then, a perverse fate had placed him in this outpost in the north country, far from the centers of population where he might find converts. He'd volunteered to do the newsletters so he could use them to spread the word, but Sebastian combed through each article and censored what he could say. He stayed in touch with his most loyal followers by communicator, but he had so little time to have a conversation alone, and not many of them were willing to forgo sleep like him.

Now everything had changed. The child from the Blessed Lands had come. She'd learned the scripture all her life, had lived it, and

127

beyond the scripture, she had the gift—the Spirit shone through her. If others could hear her, they'd understand and believe. And by the grace of the Lord, she'd brought Jason and a way to bypass Sebastian's restrictions.

Sebastian had forbidden him from attempting such a story again, and he was bound to obey, but through the device Jason had brought to the farm, he could send messages without Sebastian's knowledge. Yes, he'd need to work in the middle of the night. No matter. His purpose was more important than sleep.

Now he just needed the password.

He stumbled into the office and fumbled for the power switch. A pale light emerged from the screen, flickering off his hands as they groped for the keyboard.

After he'd entered Jason's name, the white box challenged him again. He positioned the pointer and typed. T. A. K. What was the rest? He closed his eyes and prayed for a vision. He prayed harder than ever before, relaxing his fingers as if to let the Spirit guide them.

Then an answer came and he struck eight more keys. The box now contained eleven letters. Taki Shimana, the town in the Blessed Lands where he'd been imprisoned. It had to be.

He pressed enter, and the screen flickered a response:

Access denied.

He tipped his head back and glared at the unseen heavens. He was not yet worthy and would need more time. The miracle would have to wait.

CHAPTER 19

DUST IN A SUNBEAM

The second Thursday of October, 8 p.m. — time for the farm's monthly town meeting. Helena flowed with the crowd from the cluster of cabins toward the barn. In the past two days, the foliage had exploded with color, a final celebration before yielding to winter, but as the leaves turned, the air had assumed a sharper bite. She drew her sweater tighter about her shoulders and hoped it would be warm enough on the way back.

She studied the faces around her. With members wandering in and out of the dining room during meals, she'd never seen everyone together. So many people, so many stories. Did they all have gaps in their hearts?

Her scientist father used to say people were like dust particles in a sunbeam, mingling in a multitude of ways, sometimes reacting positively, and at other times doing damage for no reason at all until their energy was spent. She'd learned differently. People were unlike dust particles because they knew what was happening to them.

A step ahead, Kailani skipped along with the crowd despite the firm grip Miz Martha kept on her. In her free hand, she grasped the eagle feather Sebastian had found, absentmindedly stroking its soft edge against her cheek.

"More members than I expected," Helena said. "Quite a congregation."

"Not a congregation, dear. A town meeting. If we called it a congregation, we'd have the department all over us. Now remember, if you want to speak up, be careful what you say. People here can be easily offended, and there are some who'll argue your ears off. Frankly, unless you feel strongly about something, I'd keep quiet." She wagged a finger at Kailani. "That especially means you, young lady. You're not to speak up at all."

As soon as they entered the barn, Helena scanned the room for Jason. He'd gone back to his office after dinner as usual, with a promise to join them later. Tables had been pushed aside, and rows of seats now faced two lecterns at the front of the room, one for Sebastian and the other presumably for speakers. She rose on her tiptoes to see over the crowd. To her relief, Jason waved from the aisle and pointed to four empty chairs, and she waved back.

Her mother kept going in the opposite direction.

Helena pushed through the crowd, bumping into people and apologizing as she went until she caught up. "Jason's over there. He saved seats for us."

"But I always sit with my friends."

"And I always sit with Jason."

Her mother ignored her and headed for a block of seats guarded by Benjamin, with the Lemurians already occupying half of them.

"I don't think Kailani should be sitting with them."

"Really, Helena, you make them sound like criminals. Just because they see things differently from you doesn't mean they're bad people. They're fascinated by Kailani. She'll be fine with them."

More members poured through the double doors, forcing Helena farther from Jason. As her mother dragged Kailani toward the Lemurians, she was jostled by strangers.

Sebastian had begun to gavel the assembly to order. No time to argue.

Helena squatted close to the child so she'd be able to hear amid the hubbub. "Will you be okay with Miz Martha? I'd like to go sit with Jason for a while."

Kailani took on a dreamy look as if she were searching another world for an answer. When her focus returned, she responded with confidence. "You go with Jason. You belong with him. I'll take care of Miz Martha. We'll be together soon."

Helana gave her a squeeze and threaded her way through the crowd to Jason.

"Where's Kailani?" he said.

"My mother insisted they sit with Benjamin and his bunch."

Jason scrunched up his nose and glared across the room, but before he could comment, Sebastian pounded the gavel three times and called the meeting to order.

Several hands shot up. As each speaker was recognized, they stepped to the second lectern and spoke with passion on a variety of issues, from the scarcity of carrots on the lunch menu to the need for a fourth communicator in the common room—apparently the wait had become too long, more than an hour during prime time.

Benjamin kept raising his hand, and Sebastian kept ignoring him—a form of punishment perhaps for that misguided newsletter. After everyone else had their say and the little man's hand was still raised, Sebastian had no choice but to recognize him. A collective groan met his ascent to the podium. Once in front of the group, standing beside Sebastian, Benjamin took a few seconds to organize a sheaf of notes before speaking.

"My fellow members," he began in his nasal whine. "Glen Eagle Farm has become home to us all, a home we love because it provides succor for our deepest needs, needs our society has chosen to ignore. That's why we have an obligation to promote our accomplishments in order to strengthen the farm."

There was a smattering of applause from the Lemurians.

Benjamin waited until the room quieted down before resuming. "We make a mistake if we don't take advantage of the wonderful stories we have to tell, stories that humanize us. Just as we're free to express ourselves in art, we should be free to publish what we want in our newsletters. For the good of the community, we should reject all forms of censorship."

Helena jumped to her feet. "That's not right."

Sebastian intervened. "I'm sorry, Helena. This is your first meeting. Rules of order require someone with a comment to raise their hand and be recognized."

She remained standing but raised her hand.

Sebastian turned to Benjamin, urging him to continue, but Benjamin made his annoying little bow instead. "Let the young lady speak. I yield the floor to her."

Once all eyes were on Helena, she became flustered. "We shouldn't.... The greater good can't be *good* if it takes advantage of a child." She paused to reconsider her words. "We shouldn't...."

Jason was suddenly at her side.

"Freedom of expression applies," he said, "only if it doesn't infringe on the rights of others. I'm sorry to disagree, Benjamin, but you're mistaken on this issue."

Mutterings clashed as the crowd split both ways, but most seemed to agree with Jason.

When Benjamin tried to shout over them, Sebastian gaveled the crowd to silence. "It seems the majority disagree with you, Benjamin."

"I call for a vote," Benjamin said.

"I think you'd lose, but no vote is necessary. Our bylaws protect the rights of the individual. As always, thank you for your point of view. Now please take a seat. You too, Helena and Jason."

Sebastian asked for a motion to adjourn, and a minute later the meeting concluded without further incident.

As Helena waited for the crowd to disperse, she turned to Jason. "I made a fool of myself, didn't I?"

"More hero than fool. We both need to look out for Kailani."

He was being kind, but she felt better—until she scanned the room. Her mother, apparently offended by the proceedings, had vanished... along with Kailani.

***

Helena waited with Jason for the barn to empty, having no desire to mingle. When they finally left, the moon shone brightly on a clear path. She and Jason walked along hand in hand, saying little.

After they passed through the pergola, she stopped beneath the sentinel tree and glanced up. Moonlight and spotlight conspired into an unearthly glow that made the branches shimmer like ghosts when they swayed. It made her queasy and she had to look away, back to Jason, who'd never taken his eyes off her.

"Is there anything I can do?" he said.

She shook her head. "I just need to sleep it off."

As she started toward their cabin, still keeping an eye on the tree, she tripped over a loose stone and stumbled.

Jason immediately caught her and propped her up.

THE DAUGHTER OF THE SEA AND THE SKY

She turned to him. "I always seem to be off balance lately, and you always seem to be catching me."

She moved to pull away, but he clasped her a moment longer, pressing his face to her neck. He kissed the soft skin above her collarbone, then her forehead, her eyes, her nose.

She lifted her chin and pressed her lips to his, letting them linger.

They began to walk again, but this time he kept an arm around her waist.

When they reached the cabin, she hesitated. "I feel like such a bother to you."

"A bother?"

"Talking you into coming here and then being out of sorts."

"I'd rather be with you than away from you, in or out of sorts."

He tried to draw her closer, but uneasiness settled over her, as if the weeks of mourning had all at once taken their toll. She pulled away. "Go ahead without me. I need some fresh air, a chance to clear my head."

"Will you be all right?"

She nodded and gave him a last kiss, insisting she'd be fine. When he'd left, she wandered back to the pergola, settled on a stone bench, and sat there for a while, listening to the stirring of the chimes.

She allowed herself to drift backward in time, visiting the small places that held painful memories. A hint of her father's voice echoed in her mind, and for an instant, she could feel her child's hand lost in his. Then the feeling vanished. She raised her hand to the moonlight and swore she could see through it, as if her flesh no longer had substance.

She closed her eyes and hummed to the song of the chimes, trying to drive all thought from her mind. A gust of wind lashed her cheeks, forcing her to wrap her arms around herself and rub for warmth, but the rubbing brought neither warmth nor solace. When the goose bumps refused to go away, she rose to join Jason inside, but as she turned, someone startled her from the shadows.

"What do *you* want?" Her voice trembled.

Benjamin started toward her, but stopped, as if concerned he'd frightened her. "I wanted to express my sympathy for your loss. Your mother told me about your father. I'm sorry."

Helena mumbled a 'thank you' but wished he'd go away.

Instead, he came closer and spoke in a hushed tone. "There's meaning in this world, Helena, despite what they say. Everything has a purpose."

133

"Really? Then tell me the purpose of my father's death."

"Not all purposes are revealed to us."

"That's just an excuse." She glared at him. "There was no reason for him to die like that."

"How do you know? Is life so clear to you?" He gave her time to respond, and seemed to continue only when he sensed her uncertainty. "Of course not. We see as through a glass dimly. We know nothing for sure."

She dismissed him with a wave and stood to return to the cabin.

He leapt around her, nimbler than she'd imagined, and blocked her way. "Did you see them tonight? All different but all the same. They fear the same, hate the same, love the same. Do you know why? Because the Spirit dwells in each of them. But some want more, want to be better than others. They dream their selfish dreams, pretending their accomplishments will matter, yet in the long run, the only thing that matters is the Spirit."

She felt blood rush to her cheeks, burning in the cold night air. "You're a fraud, Benjamin, a charlatan. You fooled my mother, but you can't fool me. I don't believe in your myths, and I don't believe in your Spirit."

He closed his eyes and bowed his head. "Then I'll pray for you." He slipped around her and crept back to the pergola, but he stopped at its mouth and turned. "I know you're bitter at your loss, but tell me: why do you cherish the memory of your father? Why does his passing pain you so?"

"That's none of your business."

"Why, Helena?"

Suddenly she saw Benjamin differently. His eyes no longer seemed small and close, but dark and piercing. She tried to leave, but his look held her frozen, immobile.

"Why, Helena?" His voice grew softer. "Why?" When she still refused to answer, he released his gaze and looked up through the slats in the roof of the pergola and beyond. Then he turned back, those eyes sharper than ever, locking with hers. "Could it be you shared the Spirit? And can you believe that Spirit you shared is gone forever? No, Helena. Despite your skepticism, it lives on and will never die. If you allow the Spirit to fill your heart, there can be no room for despair."

With that, he turned and walked away.

Helena surprised herself by calling him back. "If his spirit survived, why can't I reach him?"

THE DAUGHTER OF THE SEA AND THE SKY

He paused beneath the canopy of the beech tree and stared at his boot tops for what seemed a long time. "Perhaps you're unwilling to take a chance."

"You sound like Jason."

His demeanor changed, the lofty tone dampened for the moment. A sneer crossed his lips. "In what possible way could I sound like Jason?"

"His favorite saying. Take a chance, Helena. It's how he convinced me to let him walk me home from school."

A tremor rocked Benjamin, making his shoulders shudder. For a brief moment, he wavered, but then his eyes brightened as if he'd just communed with the Spirit.

His lofty tone returned. "Jason was right. We need to be open to possibilities or we'll miss the miracles in our lives. Your father's passing has left a gap in your heart, but maybe in his death, he's also left the means to fill that gap, not just in *your* heart but in the hearts of others."

"What's that supposed to mean?"

He shifted to one side so his face was lit by the beam of a spotlight. His arms spread wide. "The child. Did you think it was an accident she came in your hour of need to the spot where you sat by the shore? Do you think it was an accident you brought her here to the farm?"

Panic rose as she envisioned the boat emerging from the fog, crashing on the cliffs, and Jason coming back into her life. A coincidence or something more? Her feelings flew in all directions, a centrifugal whirl of emotion.

Benjamin seemed to sense her weakness. "Yes, Helena, it was meant to be, part of a divine plan. In the darkness left by your father's passing, the golden child appears from the Blessed Lands with a message for us all. Amidst all this sorrow, there is hope."

Then he retreated beyond the circle of light that surrounded the sentinel tree, and was gone.

Helena waited a moment, blinking at the great tree as if expecting him to reappear, then resumed her trudge to the cabin. She stopped at the first step, clutching the log railing. After a moment, she headed instead to the common bathroom that lay between the cabins. Inside, she checked the stalls to be sure she was alone, then went to the row of sinks, selected one at the end, and stared at her reflection in the mirror. The naked bulb above cast an odd glare, seeming to surround her hair with a corona. She turned on the cold water, cold as the streams that flowed through the farm.

Water is life.

She cupped both hands under the faucet until they were nearly numb, and splashed her face. When she looked up again, the light blurred. In its haze, she could picture Benjamin in the spotlight, his eyes raised to the heavens with a look she at last recognized—a look of hope.

A hope she'd never known.

***

Benjamin dashed through the darkness to the great house. With the moon cloaked by a cloud, he had difficulty keeping to the path and nearly stumbled on a tree root, but nothing would slow him down.

A miracle at last.

In his hour of near despair, the merciful Lord Kanakunai had spoken to him through the lips of a nonbeliever. When she said the phrase, he could see the first three letters burning in the air behind her... and he knew.

He opened the back door to the great house an inch at a time, trying to mute the creaking. With each inch, he felt as if he were prying open a portal to a new world. In the office, he slid the chair so close to the desk his belt touched its edge. Though the blackest hour of night had come and the moon was gone, he left the room dark and relied only on the light from the device.

The welcome screen took forever to appear. When it did, he entered Jason's name.

Now the test. Am I worthy?

He typed the first three letters and, after a brief prayer, finished the phrase—Jason's favorite saying: "Take a chance."

He hit enter and waited; two breaths in, two breaths out.

The screen refreshed, adding a single word:

Connected.

He filled his lungs and let the air out slowly. He'd been granted a miracle, but reminded himself to temper his pride. Yes, he'd send the story of the Daughter summoning the wind, but only to a select few. No sense risking Sebastian's wrath. Not yet.

He pulled out the scroll from his pocket and picked five of his most loyal followers, those who were at universities but not friends of the farm. He'd swear them to secrecy.

He'd fully embrace this miracle, but first he'd verify that Jason's device really worked.

CHAPTER 20

A DISTANT SHORE

The mariner smiled broadly, causing a web to blossom at the corners of his eyes. He waved a hand across the boats like a father introducing his children. "Here they are, Excellency. One, two, three. Not the finest boats in the harbor, but they've provided a good living for me and my family for forty years. I do what I love. Though I care most about my wife, near behind her is the sea." He knotted his brows and wagged a finger. "You won't tell her I said that, will you?"

The minister shook his head and forced a weak smile, but he had no appetite for small talk. He reached across and pressed down on the bow of the nearest boat as if to gauge its buoyancy. "What do you remember from the time the boat was stolen?"

"Remember, Excellency? That I was in shock. With all the finer boats in the harbor, why mine? I'm not a rich man, and the boat is irreplaceable. Forty years to get to four. It was like losing a child."

"But did you see anything unusual in the days before?"

"Unusual, Excellency? The winds were strong from the southeast, the days hot and sunny, but as you know, that's not unusual in our land. Now if it had rained, that I'd remember."

"What about suspicious activity?"

The man glanced at the nearest boat and began absent mindedly checking the knot of the mooring line. "Hmmm... no sir."

"Or strangers?"

He considered a moment and shook his head.

Frustrated, the minister shifted his attention to the third boat.

The mariner blurted out, "There was one—a little girl, fair-skinned with hair of gold. I suppose you'd call that unusual in our land."

The minister maintained his mask, but could feel his heart against his ribs as it swelled with blood, preparing for each urgent beat. "A little girl, you say. What did she want?"

"She asked to sit inside each boat, to go for a ride on the waves while they were moored. A strange request but harmless enough. She was just a child." He must have noticed a twinge in the minister's expression. "An innocent request, Excellency, don't you think?"

"The boat that was stolen," the minister said. "How did it compare to these?"

The man lifted his chin. "It was the oldest and not the prettiest, but it had the broadest beam and deepest keel. Any experienced seaman would know it to be the most seaworthy of the lot."

The minister reached into his pocket and withdrew a metal case with cards in it. He handed one to the man. "You've been a great help. Send a message to the location on this card, and I'll see to it that you're compensated for the loss of your boat."

The web around the man's eyes crinkled upward. He grasped the minister's hand and made to kiss it—an outdated tradition—but caught himself.

Instead, he took the card with both hands and bowed. "I'm most grateful, Excellency. If there's anything I might do for you, please ask and I'll find a way."

If only it were that easy.

The minister now knew she'd stolen a boat and supplies. She'd always been curious about her mother's homeland, and foolhardy though it might be, she had the imagination and will to undertake such a voyage.

"There's one last thing, master seaman."

The man made a deeper bow. "Anything, Excellency."

"Have you sailed far from these shores?"

"Of course. I've gone to sea for weeks at a time, following the schools of cod."

THE DAUGHTER OF THE SEA AND THE SKY

"How far to the west could a boat like that sail?"

"To the west, Excellency? The west is easy. The currents and winds favor that direction. But no experienced sailor would go that far, because the trip back would be too hard. Better tack to the south."

"But if one was determined to go west, how far?"

A look of understanding crossed the mariner's face. He nodded slowly, then more quickly. "It wouldn't be easy, but with a few days of fair winds and a stubbornness of will? All the way."

"All the way?"

"To the Soulless Land."

The minister stared out, trying to see beyond the horizon to what he'd always known as the land of lost souls. The sun hung low in the west and brightened a path along the waves, a golden passageway for a golden child. Great white herring gulls squawked and wheeled in circles overhead, celebrating the sunset, oblivious to her fate.

How the poetess loved the ocean. After the girl was born, she begged him to move back to the island where he'd grown up. They were happy for a time. The poetess taught the child to weave orchids into leis, so those leaving the island could toss them into the sea—an offering to the gods for their safe return. He taught her to sail. When the time came for guests to leave, they would all gather on their boat and follow the ferry, the child at the helm. As they approached the mouth of the harbor, she'd turn the tiller over to him, stand on the gunwales, and dive off as a sign of farewell. She'd grown up with the sea.

Now, she'd been clever enough to steal food in small quantities, not enough to force a search for a thief. She'd taken water containers, a compass, and charts. The elements were in her favor, and she had an instinct for the wind.

Was it time to tell the poetess?

At first, they'd waited and prayed. The security service had done its best, searching until the trail grew cold.

He'd watched as the poetess began to disintegrate before his eyes, her skin becoming translucent, as if her essence was fading away. She sat in their mountain retreat and sank into sadness. Her poems became heavy and dark.

His response had been different.

***

The will inside that would not accept despair compelled him to act. Yet he was afraid to leave the poetess alone.

One evening, as they sat on the lanai, he told her his plan. She stared out at the valley below as the last rays of the sun turned the desert red, and he waited, understanding she'd need time to accept his departure. He continued to wait as the great red ball sank beneath the horizon, leaving the desert gray and releasing a cooling breeze from the mountains behind them.

"I'd go with you," she finally said, "but I'd do more harm than good. I couldn't bear to learn she, too, has been lost."

The minister reached out for her, but she stiffened. He pulled until she went limp against him, and warm tears moistened his bare arm. He knew better than to speak. She had more to say.

When they parted, she gazed up at him, uncharacteristically fierce. "Find her. I know she's alive. Search by the ocean, near our former home."

He nodded. "If I go, will you be all right?" The dark of night had arrived and with it the desert chill. He could feel bumps on her skin.

She turned to go inside but stopped in the doorway. Light streaming from within gave the illusion of a halo around her hair. "Go and I'll pray for your return. But I have no strength for false hope. Tell me nothing until you know for certain — one way or the other."

He was the strong one — he'd survive — but she was fragile, delicate as a desert flower. His strength might yet be his curse; he might survive them all, holding nothing in his hands but sand.

***

Now, he'd wait to tell her, for he'd learned only what was intended, not the result. Likely the girl had drowned. He'd give orders for the shore patrol to search the coast for the debris of a shipwreck or a... small body washed ashore.

What if she'd made landfall on the distant shore? Lines of communication were few. He'd order his staff to monitor messages, to send queries to his contacts on the other side. He prayed that if she'd reached them, the soulless would be kind to her. He'd met some, and they were not as the senkyosei portrayed them in temple sermons — empty shells or demons. They were not so different from him; they loved their children and grieved for their dead.

He closed his eyes to block out the glare, and prayed one last time: *Let her be safe, and let me one day bring her home.*

Enough. He opened his eyes and lifted his head. The beach had emptied; the gulls had fled. The sole sound was a buoy that tolled in the harbor when aroused by a wave. Soon it would be night.

Time to get to work.

CHAPTER 21

A SERPENT IN THE GARDEN

Sleep had brought little comfort to Helena. Bizarre dreams intruded: a boat crashing on the cliffs, herself as the girl in the boat, Benjamin carrying her ashore.

Her anger spread daily like venom in her veins. Each morning, she'd drag herself out of bed and barely muster the strength to bring Kailani to her mother's studio. Once there, the craft offered no antidote to the poison.

By the third day following the town meeting, she'd lost all patience. Their task that morning was to make earrings from teardrop crystal beads.

Her mother had cut four lengths of chain to support the beads that would hang, two from each earring. "And now, Helena, let's see if you've learned enough to attach the chains to the beads. I'll do the first one and you can do the next. Watch closely."

Kailani hovered nearby, fascinated by the process, while Helena observed from behind. Her mother slipped a head pin into a bead, used a pair of chain-nosed pliers to bend the end into a loop, attached it to

142

THE DAUGHTER OF THE SEA AND THE SKY

the chain, and bound it by coiling the pin around itself. It took no more than a few seconds.

She passed a kit—bead, chain, and pin—over to Helena. "Your turn."

"You did that so well. Why don't you finish the rest?"

"Can I try?" Kailani snatched the blue bead and held it up to the light.

"Not yet. Let Helena learn first and then we can both help you."

Helena took bead and pin in hand. They seemed impossibly small. She needed three tries to thread the pin through the hole in the bead, and by that time, her vision had blurred and her fingers were shaking. Her mother handed her the pliers, but as she bent the pin it snapped in two, sending the free end skittering across the workbench.

"You squeezed too hard," her mother said, passing another pin. "Try again, gentler this time."

Helena cradled the pliers and twisted until the pin bent at ninety degrees. One more turn and it formed a loop. She attached the chain, but when she tried to wrap the pin around, it snapped again.

She dropped the half-formed earring and tossed the pliers away.

"Don't worry," her mother said. "It took me a while to learn as well."

"You'll run out of pins."

"I have plenty."

"What if I can't do it?"

"You'll learn. I'll help you."

"Of course you will. You're so good at helping me."

Her mother stiffened. "What's that supposed to mean?"

"Are you two arguing?" Kailani said.

"We're not arguing. Helena and I are just having a discussion."

"How could we be arguing?" Helena said. "Miz Martha never gets upset. She's found an inner peace."

Martha sighed. "That's uncalled for."

Kailani pressed her hands to her ears. "Don't argue. It makes my head hurt."

"She doesn't need to hear us carrying on like this."

"But I want to carry on, Mother. I want to have it out once and for all." She turned to Kailani. "Why don't you go visit Jason? I'm sure he'd love to take a break."

"May I play in the labyrinth instead?"

143

"That sounds like a lovely idea, dear," Miz Martha said.

Helena held her hand up. "You most certainly may not. The labyrinth's in the middle of the woods."

"This isn't wilderness," her mother said. "The farm's perfectly safe and she knows the way. Go ahead, dear, but be sure to come back when you hear the lunch bell."

Before Helena could stop her, Kailani slipped away.

Helena turned on her mother, the venom coming to a boil. "How dare you contradict me? I'm Kailani's legal guardian, not you. And I'm the only one here she can count on."

Her mother looked like she'd been slapped. The mask of calm dissolved for an instant and then re-formed. "I'm sorry I let you down. I'd... do anything to make it up to you. Just tell me what to do."

"How about grieving for my father? How about shedding a single tear?"

"I've shed more tears than you know."

"But never with me."

Her mother wandered over to the workbench and began gathering the loose beads. "No, never with you."

"And why is that?"

"I was... a different person then."

"Different? And now you're better? Someone who can take over and be a mother to Kailani?"

Her mother set down the beads. "I'm sorry I contradicted you, Helena. I thought she needed some distance from—"

"Guess you'd know. You're the expert on abandoning daughters."

The blood drained from her mother's face; the mask was gone.

"What's wrong?" Helena said. "Isn't the Spirit that Benjamin's so fond of strong enough for you?"

Her mother seemed to diminish, shrinking into silence.

Helena glared at her, hoping for a tear to trickle from her eye. Nothing. Yet for an instant, she could almost see it deep inside—not the Spirit, but a pain as deep as her own. She felt her heart strain, trying to reach through the wall formed by her chest, trying to touch the person her mother was.

Her mother stretched out a hand to bridge the gap.

Helena hesitated, unsure how to respond. She'd aimed a viper strike at her mother, and the venom had hit its mark. So why was her own blood burning?

THE DAUGHTER OF THE SEA AND THE SKY

She turned away and stumbled out of the studio.

***

Benjamin was raking leaves by the entrance to the labyrinth, when he heard the rhythmic crunch of footsteps approaching. It was his job to clear debris and reset the stones that lined the border where careless members had disturbed them—one of the many mindless tasks that Sebastian had assigned him. He tolerated the burden without complaint; his faith sustained him.

He looked up, surprised to see Kailani coming towards him alone, and froze in place like one of Serena's statues. The girl's long hair swished as she skipped down the path, humming to herself, oblivious to him and the rest of the world. Now perhaps, the purpose of his indignity would be revealed. All that he'd suffered may have been for this one moment.

When she spotted him, she stopped her humming and performed a half pirouette, coming to a stop in a sideways pose, neither proceeding forward nor taking flight.

He encouraged her, waving with one hand while the other squeezed the handle of the rake so tightly his knuckles throbbed. "It's all right. I was just finishing up. Have you come to play in the labyrinth?"

She nodded shyly.

"Like the labyrinths in the Blessed Lands."

Her eyes widened slightly. "How do you know?"

"I was there once."

"What were you doing there?"

His mind filled with memories—the thrill of arriving in the holy land, the humiliation of being sent back. "I thought that's where I belonged. I'm a believer, like you."

She looked confused, doing a little dance step, first back and then forward. "If you're a believer, why are you living among the soulless?"

"I was meant for a different purpose, to help the soulless change their ways."

She took a step closer. "I came to help the soulless too."

A quiver ran through his body—the girl alone in the labyrinth, and now this. "I knew it. I knew that's why you were sent to me."

"I wasn't sent to you, Mr. Benjamin. I came to do penance."

"Penance for what?"

145

DAVID LITWACK

"I can't tell you. It's a secret between me and the wind."

Penance. A lever on the soul. "Penance can be difficult. Have you completed yours?"

She shuffled her feet and made to go around him to the entrance of the labyrinth. When he blocked her way, she stopped and stared at the ground. As the toe of her shoe dug a hole in the soft dirt, she whispered, "No."

"To follow your penance to its end, you need a guide. Since we're both of the Spirit, perhaps I can show you the way."

"I don't want a guide."

"Have you ever heard...." He tried to pay proper respect to the sacred name. "...of a land called Lemuria?"

She shook her head.

"Lemuria was once a great nation, a single landmass that included both the Republic and the Blessed Lands, but it was split asunder by the sins of the soulless. If we don't help them change their ways, their fate is foretold. All will be destroyed."

Her eyes widened again. "What will be destroyed?"

"All of this, everything you see."

She glanced behind her, beginning to be frightened.

He pressed the advantage. "And every*one* as well."

"Everyone?"

Benjamin took three steps toward her, careful not to startle her into flight, and squatted low so his face was level with her eyes. "Everyone."

"Even Jason and Helena?"

"Especially Jason and Helena, but you can save them."

She drew in a gulp of air. "What would I have to do?"

"There are others like us, believers in this soulless land. Help me draw them together."

The dance step returned. She shifted from side to side, but this time more away than forward. "I don't understand."

"Don't worry, understanding will come later. For now, if you wish to complete your penance, you must do as I ask."

"Do what, Mr. Benjamin?"

"Speak to the people who come to see you."

"What people?"

"The pilgrims. When they come, you must agree to speak with them, no matter what Miz Martha or Jason or Helena say. You may be saving their lives."

146

"What will I say?"

"They'll ask questions. Tell them the answers you learned in the Blessed Lands."

She looked at him more puzzled than before. "What kind of questions?"

"Questions like 'where do we go when we're gone?'"

"How would I know where you go?"

His palms began to sweat, and he squeezed the handle of the rake tighter as if trying to wring out the moisture. "I mean the Spirit. What happens when the Spirit leaves us?"

"Oh, that. The sky told me the answer to that." She scooted around him and pranced through the labyrinth, hopping over the border whenever she pleased to get to the rock pile. When she arrived, she turned, ready to make a pronouncement. "There's no difference between us and the Spirit. Can the wind be different from the Spirit of the wind? When the wind stops blowing, is the wind gone? The Spirit of the wind will always be with us."

Benjamin edged closer, stumbling over stones he'd meticulously set in place. She looked amused, but when he stretched out a hand, her face clouded.

Don't leave. Not now. He dropped to one knee. "Daughter of the Sea and the Sky, don't forsake us. The people of this land need you to lead us to a better way."

She fumbled with the stone that lay at the pinnacle of the rock pile. After a moment, she shook her head. "I don't understand."

"Understanding will come when the pilgrims arrive."

She glanced behind her as if to check if anyone was emerging from the woods, then dissolved into laughter. "You're joking, Mr. Benjamin. No one's coming to see me."

She replaced the rock on the top of pile and, with no regard for the rules of the labyrinth, jumped over the rows of stone and ran off down the path, leaving him standing like a scarecrow, rake in hand.

***

Jason stood in Sebastian's office and rolled his eyes while Benjamin pleaded his case once more.

"I beg you." Benjamin's voice was tight and desperate. "Let me publish it."

DAVID LITWACK

Sebastian had apparently reached his limit, and slapped the flat of his hand on the desk. "Enough! I don't want to hear about this ever again. Write anything you want that promotes our artists, sells our crafts, or solicits donations. We only have a few days left until the reception. Do something to attract a bigger crowd. But for sweet reason's sake, leave Kailani alone. Now get back to work, both of you."

Jason eyed the little man suspiciously, but like everyone else on the farm, he found it impossible to say no to Sebastian. He turned to go and was relieved to see Benjamin follow.

Back at the workshop, he slipped on his work gloves and gathered his tools to head outside.

Benjamin blocked the way. "Sebastian was right, Jason. We have only a few days left." His voice rose uncomfortably. "All of our days are numbered. We're being measured and judged."

"I'm sorry. I don't—"

"There's nothing Sebastian can do to stand in the way of what's preordained. And nothing you can do, either."

He gaped at Benjamin. It had been clear from their first meeting that the man was odd, but now there was something more—something dangerous.

The little man whirled on him. "The world has two choices, as in the past, but this time, the way of the Spirit will prevail."

Jason's mind raced. Sebastian had worked with Benjamin for years; surely he could get along with him for a few months.

Before he could say anything, Benjamin surprised him. "Are you happier than you were before you came to the farm?"

Not a question he'd expected. He pictured himself running along the farm's pathways in the morning. He thought of Kailani, of Helena.

"I suppose...." He wavered, then steadied. "Yes, I am."

"And why is that?"

No need to answer. Sebastian's underling had somehow been transformed, replaced by someone with a more complex mind, one Jason struggled to fathom. Best to let him go, and see where he ended up.

"Shall I tell you why?" Benjamin said at last. "Because all your reason has led you to a hollow life. Here, you've been allowed to thrive. She came into your life and brought you closer to your inner spirit, to the Brewster girl, and to the greater Spirit that surrounds us all. Can you deny it?"

Jason remained silent.

148

Benjamin smiled, the kind of smirk that would have made Jason want to strike him if he'd been a violent man.

"I didn't think so." The smile vanished. "Then why would you deny her to the rest of the world?"

Finally, he could see where Benjamin was heading, but he refused to help him get there. "Kailani is none of your business, and nothing you say will make me help you publish that story."

"Then you haven't learned."

"Learned what?"

"That we're insignificant in the scheme of things." Benjamin tilted his head back and gazed at the ceiling as if he could see to the heavens beyond. "No. The Spirit cannot be constrained. The Spirit will find a way."

Jason had no response, nor was any necessary.

Benjamin's mind had gone elsewhere, to a place he could not imagine. He was no longer Sebastian's loyal handyman but a raving zealot.

***

Benjamin knew she was rare, a mix of charisma and innocence, but like most of her ilk, she had no patience for the mundane details of creating a movement. By contrast, he was unappealing, even repulsive. Few would follow him, yet he possessed the discipline and skills to build a following for her. She was the spark that flashed brightly and burned out. He was the rock on which a movement is built — the perfect apostle.

He logged on to the encomm and created a broadcast list as he'd watched Jason do. Next, he fumbled in his pocket for his scroll of followers, and searched for names that matched. After some experimentation, he managed to find a listing of universities on the network and, within each of these, a directory of subscribers. One by one, he located his disciples and added them to the list. When he finished, he had only an hour left before dawn.

Time to compose the missive.

He entered the subject:

The Daughter and the Spirit.

He prayed for inspiration, and the words came to him. He worked deliberately, afraid his hands would shake. As he typed, the letters burned in the darkness.

Today, as I stood alone in the midst of the woods, I encountered the Daughter of the Sea and the Sky, sent to us from the Blessed Lands by the Lord. She flitted between the trees like a sunbeam and came to me as if guided by a vision. I stood before her dumbfounded.

"I have a message for you," she said, "and for all those who believe."

I bowed my head, unable to look at her directly.

"I am your servant," I said. "What do you wish of me?"

"Say this, Benjamin. The essence of Lemuria lives on in the Blessed Lands. I have come to offer a final chance to the soulless. The Treaty of Separation is null and void. There is no difference between us and the Spirit. Can the wind be different from the Spirit of the wind? When the wind stops blowing, is the wind gone? The Spirit of the wind will always be with us."

My brethren, all who receive this message, tell the others. Flood the farm with your presence, and together we'll build a better world.

When finished, he wiggled the pointer over the word "Send." Before clicking, he raised his index finger and dragged it across his brow. When he held it up to the flickering light, it gleamed with sweat. Instead of drying it, he replaced it over the pointing device and let it hover.

His finger twitched, withdrew, and curled on itself, refusing to commit. He pressed his eyelids shut, trying to see through them all the way to an ancient land. Sebastian and Jason would not stop him. He prayed for a flood of followers, so many that even Sebastian would have to heed the word. He prayed for a deluge.

Click.

He opened his eyes. The missive was sent.

Chapter 22

Embers

Jason rested his cheek against his hand and stared at the encomm screen. He'd managed to talk his supervisor into granting him access to the archives, an immense bank of information available online. So far, an army of graduate students had encoded the last few decades of journals, magazines and newsletters. The dream was to someday have all the knowledge in the world searchable and accessible through the network.

He'd hoped to shed some light on Kailani—who she was and where she'd come from—but so far he'd turned up more propaganda than fact. Too many walls had been built between races.

Worse than that, he'd come across strange messages in his search. Most presented a simple idea simply stated—Lemuria was an ancient land of the Spirit that had been despoiled by the experiments of the soulless. Their efforts to control nature had caused the Great Sundering. The people of the Republic should take heed, learn from the past and turn away from their soulless ways.

More disturbing were stories about a girl with golden hair who had come from the Blessed Lands to spread the word, referred to as the

151

Daughter of the Sea and the Sky. Some carried a grain of truth, complete with dreamy platitudes typical of Kailani, but most offered nothing but myths.

Jason struggled to put the pieces together.

Benjamin was the most likely culprit, but he'd been keeping a close eye on him the past few days. Benjamin hadn't left the farm. No mailings had gone out. How could he be spreading the word? What if the stories came from somewhere else, a secret network of zealots, perhaps even some who had infiltrated the department during Kailani's incarceration?

Much as he hated to admit it, Carlson was right: Kailani was safer as far out of the way as possible.

He recommitted to his research, this time searching for *blessed lands* and *nine-year-old* and *boat*—all three together.

He found one match, the tale of a family of four—father, mother, and two small children. The father had been persecuted for questioning the ruling clerics. He'd been fired from his job, his children harassed and eventually expelled from school, their house vandalized by hateful slogans. Finally, a firebomb was hurled through a window. The four managed to escape with their lives, but their home burned to the ground. Friends scratched together enough to buy them a small boat with provisions, and they set off for a more enlightened life in the Republic. Only the nine-year-old survived.

Jason checked the date: thirty years ago.

He buried his head in his hands. *Enough.* He'd been reluctant to involve the department, but if he hoped to find more about Kailani, he'd need access to their contacts at the land bridge. He addressed an envelope to Chief Examiner Carlson and began to compose a letter.

Mr. Carlson, I need your help. While Kailani is doing well, I'm concerned about some of the reactions she's stirring up at the farm. If only we could find a way to send her home, I know she'd be better off than here. I've exhausted my resources trying to learn more about her, and she still won't tell us anything.

Could you please —

A scuff of boots in the hall outside the office made him stop. He darkened the screen and flipped the letter over. When he swiveled around, he found Benjamin lurking in the doorway.

"What are you doing here so late, Jason?" the little man said in his nasal whine.

THE DAUGHTER OF THE SEA AND THE SKY

"Polytech work."

"Looked like you were writing a letter. Was it about Kailani?"

"That's none of your business."

"Perhaps you'll be more willing to discuss it in the morning." Benjamin spoke the words quietly and turned to leave.

Jason caught up with him, grabbed him by the elbow, and spun him around. He towered over the smaller man, and his free hand was balled into fist. "I don't know what you're up to, but I'm warning you. Leave Kailani alone."

A quiver racked the little man's body as his muscles tensed and released.

Jason wished Benjamin would argue or break into a rage.

Instead, he made his little bow and said, "As you wish." Then he pulled away and slipped out the door.

***

Carlson smiled when he saw the two letters from the Northern Kingdom, more news about his favorite refugee. He opened Helena's first.

She'd promised weekly updates and had been true to her word. Kailani was doing well, she said, better adjusted and happier every day. Taking her to the farm had been the right decision. She was hopeful all would end well with the tribunal.

Then he opened Jason's letter... and sighed deeply.

It seemed Jason saw the world differently. Yes, Kailani was doing well, but he worried how some of the farm members were reacting to her. And though she still refused to tell anything about her past, a lingering sadness made him believe she missed her home. What if a loving family were searching for her? He needed to know. The letter continued:

> Could you please reach out to whatever contacts you might have at the land bridge? Nothing complicated, just a request for information about a missing nine-year-old with blue eyes and blond hair who'd have left the Blessed Lands in midsummer and answers to the name Kailani. I'm certain that if a loving family exists, the request will find its way.

Carlson sighed again. He'd already searched to no avail. The Blessed Lands were less well organized than Jason seemed to believe, and the zealots were more apt to obstruct than to share.

What was the point of stirring the embers? Both Jason and Helena agreed that Kailani was adjusting to her new life, and sending her back

153

went against everything Carlson believed in. He'd heard stories from other refugees about life on the other side—rigid laws, harsh punishments, limits on personal growth.

Such a beautiful child deserved a full life in a free society. Sure, it might be rocky for now, typical for transmigrants, but she was young. She'd adapt.

He flipped through his calendar to the hearing date—the fifth of April—not so far away. He hoped the tribunal would place her permanently with Helena and Jason.

Leave her be until then. At a farm so far removed from the bustle of society, what could go wrong?

He was loath to lie to Jason, so he'd send a message to his representative at the land bridge, a request for information about a missing child—no description, no name, sent with the lowest priority. Their bureaucracy suffered the same inefficiencies as his own. The request would rattle around at the bottom of the organization, eventually to be filed and forgotten.

Chapter 23

The Blessing of the Wind

The perfect weather made this the ideal day for the fall open house, when friends of the farm came to view the results of their generosity. A warm breeze, unusual for this late in the season, sent puffs of clouds gliding across the sky, and the peak foliage spread in full display.

For Helena, the changing of the seasons meant the passage of time, and with the tribunal approaching, time was not her friend.

She found scant minutes to spend with Jason. Benjamin burdened him with work as if doling out punishment, but even if she could have pried him away, she had little time to spare herself.

Sebastian had tasked Helena and her mother with designing harvest centerpieces for the tables at the reception. Starting a few days before, they'd set off with Kailani to search for plump pine cones and brightly colored leaves, those laced with the yellows, oranges, and reds of autumn. Yesterday, they'd sat around a craft bench weaving vines into wreaths and attaching the leaves and cones to the wreaths with glue.

Guests began to arrive by midafternoon, hours ahead of the evening reception, to participate in Sebastian's tour. While they were gone, members of the farm carried tables from the dining room out onto the lawn in front of the great house. Once they'd covered the wood-grain tops with cloth, Helena and her mother set out their decorations. Stacks of plates, wine glasses and napkins followed.

After setting the tables, Helena's mother whisked Kailani back to the cabins to get cleaned up. She'd spent the weeks prior to the open house making the girl a dress along with some ornamental jewelry. Both of them had teased Helena about the new outfit, refusing to let her see it before the reception. Helena marveled at the joy in her mother, the pleasure she took in doing simple things for Kailani.

This far north, so late in the season, nighttime came early. Farm members placed candles in colored lanterns hung from stakes set around the perimeter. Only after they were lit did she realize the sun had set. As night ascended, stars appeared one by one, and then the slimmest arc of the moon, transforming the lawn from a grassy field to a twilit garden.

As if on cue, Sebastian arrived leading a parade into the clearing, and called everyone to order.

"Honored guests," he shouted, holding his hands out in greeting. "I'm pleased to announce we have record attendance this year. This is in no small part due to the efforts of our friends-of-the-farm coordinator, Benjamin Thorndike, and his new assistant, Jason Adams."

Polite applause accompanied an occasional cheer. One woman at the back called out, "Which ones are they, Sebastian?"

The managing director scanned the crowd and pointed. "Over there. Benjamin's the one on the porch steps with the camera, taking your pictures. And you can't miss Jason. He's the tallest here, but just in case, raise your hand, Jason."

Helena watched, bemused, as Jason raised his hand. He seemed embarrassed, but she thought he was enjoying the celebrity.

Once Sebastian completed his welcome, the crowd headed for the food and drink, then milled around sipping apple wine and taking in the scene. Two farm members mounted the steps of the great house and began to play music on a penny whistle and violin, a lilting tune from a time when farmers would gather to celebrate the harvest. A few people came over to meet Benjamin and shake Jason's hand.

Suddenly the chatter changed to hushed whispers.

On the path from the cabins, Kailani pranced along, almost preening as she went. She wore her new dress, a delicate white garment

THE DAUGHTER OF THE SEA AND THE SKY

that seemed made of chiffon and hung loosely from her shoulders to below the knee. They'd cinched the waist with a red ribbon tied in a bow, reminiscent of Kailani's department uniform but far more elaborate. In her hair, a string of aquamarine stars lay softly, and when she entered the circle of light cast by the candles, they sparkled.

Helena's mother trailed behind like a maid-in-waiting.

The throng immediately turned, forming a semicircle awaiting Kailani. Everyone seemed to know of the child from the Blessed Lands.

Helena tried to shield her from the crush of visitors, but Kailani waved her off. "It's my duty to greet them all." And with no hint of shyness, she began to hold court.

Gray-haired widows surrounded Kailani, hanging on her every word, while middle-aged men in tweed jackets tried to look dignified as the nine-year-old answered questions about the universe.

"My husband passed on last year," one woman said. "What do you of the Blessed Lands believe happens when someone is gone?"

"We believe the Spirit is eternal."

"But where does the Spirit go?"

"It doesn't go anywhere. The Spirit remains everywhere at once. Nothing is lost."

"Then may we communicate with a loved one who's gone?"

"If you're deserving. If you've been kind to them—or if not, if they've forgiven you."

After each pronouncement, the audience oohed and aahed.

Helena was proud of Kailani but surprised. While her sullenness had eased in her time on the farm, now she sparkled, soaking in the attention as if it were ocean air.

Helena had become preoccupied with the performance and hardly noticed when her mother came jostling through the crowd. Finally, she burst between a smoking jacket and an exceedingly large woman to reach Kailani.

"Good evening, Kailani." The charm she'd always been able to turn on when teaching class at the Polytech had returned.

"Hello, Miz Martha." Kailani looked a little taken aback by the interruption, but recovered quickly, taking the older woman's hand and beaming at the audience. "This is the lady who made me this dress and these stars." She patted the stars in her hair, careful not to dislodge them.

"I have a question for you, Kailani," Martha said. "Do you have music in the Blessed Lands?"

157

DAVID LITWACK

Kailani nodded yes.

"And do you dance to that music?"

"Sometimes." She looked puzzled.

"Then come. Let's you and I dance."

Without waiting for a response, Helena's mother dragged the little girl away from the crowd to the center of the lawn. Her posture straightened, then she grasped Kailani at the waist and swept her along to the music, as if she were made of the sparkles that reflected off the gems in her hair.

Kailani's audience turned to watch the two dancers, leaving Helena on the outside looking in. The guests across the way turned as well, leaving Jason alone. Their eyes met, and he circled around and came toward her.

"She gathers in the light wherever she goes," he said.

Helena took in the setting—the warm air, the candles in the twilight, Jason next to her. She should be content, but as her mother danced with Kailani, her mood darkened.

Jason took her hand and squeezed as if he'd sensed the change.

She glanced up to reset her thoughts. The puffs of white that dotted the evening sky had merged and swelled, conspiring in ominous clumps, a line moving in from the northeast. In the encroaching darkness, it was hard to tell if it was night arriving or the edge of a storm....

...until a gust turned the tablecloths to sails.

One of the centerpieces blew off and skittered across the lawn with Helena in pursuit. As she set it back in place, Sebastian rushed by and grabbed Jason by the arm.

"I don't like the looks of that sky," Sebastian said. "I'm going to run in and call the weather station. No sense putting out the main course just to move it back inside. Get ready to relocate the tables."

Helena was glad he'd seen the same dark clouds as she had—it wasn't her mood casting gloom upon the sky. She turned back to Jason.

He was staring at her. "What's wrong?"

She laughed an awkward laugh. "You know me. I worry about things."

"Like what?"

She glanced at the backs of the guests who'd formed a circle around her mother and Kailani. "Like how my mother's so content making dresses and jewelry, and now beaming as she dances on the lawn. And how Kailani seems to be drifting away. And...."

THE DAUGHTER OF THE SEA AND THE SKY

She stopped before asking what she had no right to ask; he'd done all of this—came to the farm—for her.

"And what?" Jason said.

"And how you and I get so little time together."

He glanced at the center of the lawn, his height allowing him to watch the dance.

She studied his profile for those few seconds, still the face of the boy she knew so long ago. She hoped they'd never be apart again.

He turned to her, put an arm around her and drew her close. For a moment, everything else disappeared—no farm, no crowd, no reason and no Spirit—and she felt—

Sebastian burst outside and landed on the top step of the porch, swinging Lizzie's bell in a broad arc as he called for quiet. "Ladies and gentlemen, members and honored guests. I just spoke to the weather station and they say there's a nasty squall headed our way. If our strong, young members will take the tables inside, we'll reconvene for dinner under the protection of the great house."

Helena tried to hold on, to keep Jason near, but they were carried away in the rush.

***

By the time everyone crammed into the foyer of the great house, the storm had arrived. Black clouds rushed in, accelerating the night, and the breeze became a gale. For an instant, daylight reappeared in a flash. Three seconds later, a boom shook the house, rattling windows and heralding a downpour.

Everyone shifted to the center of the room and huddled together.

The squall lasted only a few minutes. When it ended, the assembled relaxed and went back to their activities, nibbling hors d'oeuvres as Kailani spouted words of nine-year-old wisdom.

Yet Helena felt as if the clouds had never left. She searched the room in vain for Jason, still engulfed by the crowd. If she could be granted one wish by Kailani's Spirit, she'd be back alone with Jason on the cliffs, or on the Spirit Hill, or at Grandmother Storyteller—just the two of them.

But that moment had passed like the storm.

She felt flushed, needing air, and navigated her way to the front door and out onto the porch. The air on the farm was always clean, but

159

now it smelled freshly washed. She sucked it in and closed her eyes, letting her head clear. When she opened them again, it had grown bright outside, brighter than could be explained by the residual lightning flashing over the distant mountains. She stepped onto the lawn and looked up.

"Is everything all right, Helena?" Her mother must have seen her leave and followed.

Unable to answer, she pointed as she had the day Kailani's boat arrived. Only once before, as a little girl on a family vacation, had she seen such a sight. Curtains of light rippled across the night sky, their folds shimmering in rose-pink and pale-green, sheer as the most delicate fabric. Helena could almost hear their movement, a distant, whispering swish.

"The Northern Lights," her mother said, and dashed back inside to tell everyone.

The assembled filed through the door in ones and twos, onto the porch and down the steps to the lawn still wet from the rain. All had the same response: a look around, a glance up, and a cry of delight... like a child waking on her birthday.

"It's the Northern Lights," Sebastian confirmed as if still giving the tour. "We get them once or twice a year. How wonderful you should be here to see them."

Kailani wandered out of the great house, wondering why her admirers had left. When she saw the lights, she ran to Helena and grasped her around the waist. "What is it?"

Helena stroked her hair. "We call it the Northern Lights."

"But why are there lights in the sky?" She whispered as if concerned her ignorance might disillusion her followers.

Helena could feel her shivering through the fabric of the dress. "You'd be unlikely to see them in the Blessed Lands because they appear only in the far north. It's caused by particles that travel all the way from the sun. When they hit the upper atmosphere, the collisions emit energy in the form of light."

"I don't understand. You're telling me what it is and how it works. I want to know why."

Helena realized she'd been regurgitating her father's explanation from years before. His words echoed in her mind. *'I've explained how it works, Helena. There's no why, just what and how. Take it for what it is and marvel while you can. You may never see it again.'*

She struggled to find better words. "Truth is, Kailani, I don't know. I guess that's why people in the Blessed Lands make myths. A myth I heard as a child said the goddess of the dawn created the Northern Lights, her gift to ease the night. For a few moments in a lifetime, she'd send a wind from the north in the form of pure light to drive away the darkness."

As Kailani listened, her concern abated until, at the end, she brightened. "The wind."

She released Helena and stepped forward. With her white chiffon dress and the sparkles from the aquamarine stars, she looked like an apparition reflecting the lights from above.

People parted, clearing a space for her. Conversation stopped as all eyes turned to the girl at the center of the lawn.

Never taking her eyes from the sky, she raised her arms to the heavens like the statue at the base of the Spirit Hill.

"The Spirit of the wind has forgiven," she said. "It's the Blessing of the Wind."

***

All the guests had gathered on the lawn and were staring at Kailani or looking up at the sky. From the top step of the porch, Benjamin had a clear view of her, and not a soul was watching him.

He raised the camera; one good shot was all he needed. If others could see her in this setting, they'd believe as he believed. The dark night with the yellow rays streaming from the windows and the light from the aurora above would add to the effect. He'd have to check what it looked like on the screen, but he could touch it up, adding a nimbus if necessary.

***

The next morning dawned crisp and cold. The previous night's storm had driven summer from the Northern Kingdom, leaving a pleasant autumn day in its wake.

Jason was too tired to appreciate the change. The reception had run late and the subsequent cleanup even later. Then he'd slept poorly, tossing and turning all night. He dreamed he was sitting in his cubicle at the Polytech working toward a deadline. On the screen appeared a warning from Kailani, but every time he tried to read it, the bulb above his desk would buzz and flash in an otherworldly display of pink and green, obscuring the words. He awoke to find he'd overslept and, in spite of the nice weather, had to forgo his morning run for the first time at the farm.

Now, he sat at the encomm and the words on the screen were perfectly clear, dozens of messages on the university network about the reception the night before. How could the news have spread so fast?

He scrolled, bleary-eyed, and selected a couple at random.

~~~

Posted by: HenryK | Oct 22nd, 5:18 a.m.

Last night, I experienced my first miracle. At the farm's open house, after a storm, we were fortunate to see the Northern Lights. Those of us accustomed to our rational world watch such phenomena dispassionately and analyze. Through the eyes of the girl from the Blessed Lands, I was able to see its true meaning — the blessing of the wind.

~~~

Posted by: BarbaraJ | Oct 22nd, 6:07 a.m.

I awoke after a few hours and have been unable to get back to sleep. I keep thinking about the scene from last night. The Daughter from the Blessed Lands has so inspired me that I will never be the same again.

~~~

So inspired? Jason dragged his fingers through his hair and tried to replay the events of the night before. Long after the Northern Lights had faded to a memory and been replaced by more familiar stars, he'd been loading trash bags onto the farm truck for removal the next morning. Helena had kissed him goodnight hours earlier, and left to take an exhausted Kailani to bed. As he worked to finish the cleanup and join her, the great dark dome of the sky seemed to settle upon him, his own private but infinite universe. With it came a foreshadowing of his mortality, a sense of being alone.

He'd dropped the bags he was carrying and scanned the clearing, hoping Helena had returned. He'd searched the porch of the great

THE DAUGHTER OF THE SEA AND THE SKY

house and the path to the cabins. He scanned the wood line until his eyes teared, trying to catch a glimpse of her through the trees, but all he could see was the moonlight flickering off the wet leaves.

When he returned at last to their cabin, he found her asleep. He kissed her once, twice, on the soft skin at the base of her neck. She rolled over, still asleep, and rested her head on his chest. He lay there, drinking in the rhythm of her breathing, the elixir of life, as he drifted off into dreams. By the time he awoke in the morning, she was gone.

He fought off the memory and focused on the screen. What did these postings mean? He scrolled past a few more, too fast to read, then chose one at random.

~~~

Posted by: NewWorldBeliever | Oct 22nd, 6:32 a.m.

For those of you who need proof the Spirit exists, you should have witnessed what I saw last night. In our oh-so-rational land, we refer to it as a natural phenomenon, but seen through the eyes of a child from the Blessed Lands, it was a miracle. Check out this picture and believe.

~~~

Jason positioned the pointer over the attachment but hesitated. He closed his eyes so tightly that colors flashed beneath the lids, his own personal aurora. Then he opened them and clicked.

A photogram appeared. At its center stood Kailani in her white dress. She stared out, frozen on the screen, her arms raised to the sky and a blue light reflecting off the stars in her hair.

CHAPTER 24

THE ADMIRING HOST

Sebastian understood little about Jason's remarkable device, but he could see the impact on the farm. As stories out in the wider world multiplied, word began to filter in from family and friends. Soon lines formed at the entrance to the common room, waiting for a turn at the communicators, as curious members hoped to learn more.

For the past two days, the farm buzzed with talk of Kailani's newfound fame. Despite all his years as a manager, Sebastian could never predict how people would react. Some puffed out with pride at her celebrity; others thought it appalling.

Jason and Helena were understandably outraged, claiming the chatter might endanger the child's status with the tribunal. Sebastian finally gave in and intervened, suspending Jason's workload long enough to let him deal with the crisis.

Jason had asked for and received clearance from his supervisor to delete the most damaging posts. He'd explained to Sebastian that for the better part of a day, he'd poked around, following the chain of offending messages and removing them until he'd exceeded the

THE DAUGHTER OF THE SEA AND THE SKY

Polytech's reach. Then he changed his password, and began locking up his device in Sebastian's office when not in use. There was nothing more he could do.

To Sebastian, the breach of their sheltered world had been far from disastrous. Kailani seemed oblivious to her image flying over the comm link. Members remained respectful of her privacy, and following the reception, a few more donations had begun to trickle in. He wasn't sure he saw the harm.

Until the morning of the third day.

The porch of the great house was scheduled to be enclosed with plastic insulation for the winter, so he decided to relax on a rocker and take in the still unobstructed view. The clattering of planks on the bridge interrupted his reverie. Moments later, he stepped off the porch to assist a middle-aged woman from an oversized sedan, a complete stranger to him.

"How may I help you, madam?" he said. "Do you need directions?"

The woman glanced around with the look of someone who was lost. "I'm not sure. Can you tell me how to get to Glen Eagle Farm?"

"You don't need to get there." Sebastian tapped the birch wood sign with the tip of his staff. "You're already here."

"Oh." She seemed flustered. "And who are you?"

He made an exaggerated bow. "I, dear lady, am Sebastian, the managing director of the farm. What may I do for you?"

She glanced past him to the peak of the great house roof. Her eyes widened and a worshipful expression crossed her features. "I'm here to see the Daughter of the Sea and the Sky."

Sebastian's brows froze in the down position, and his grin tightened into a thin line. "I'm afraid that's not possible."

"Not possible? Why would that be? Isn't this where she lives?"

"Madam, this is a private residence. We can't have strangers showing up to see one of our members uninvited, especially a child."

The woman stared at him, incredulous, then wandered in a circle as if searching for someone with a better answer. When she returned to the starting point, her breath came in short bursts. "But I've come so far."

"I'm sorry, but the privacy of our members must be respected."

The color drained from her face. She fanned herself with one hand and staggered.

Sebastian caught her by the arm. "Oh dear. Maybe you should come into my office and have some tea before you drive back."

165

With his help, the woman made it inside and collapsed onto a guest chair. When he turned to fetch the teapot with the cherubs, he heard a moan like a wounded animal, followed by uncontrolled sobs. He hastily finished pouring the tea and fetched the ever-ready box with the tissues.

While she alternately sipped tea and blew her nose, he studied her. Great round cheeks accentuated eyes so swollen it was hard to imagine the lids fully covering them. They looked as if they'd been wet for weeks.

Five tissues later, she composed herself enough to speak. "My name is Mary McAllister. I'm sorry, Sebastian, if I've broken your rules. I had so wanted to see her."

"Pleased to meet you, Mary. May I ask why?"

She appeared ready for another outburst, but took hold of herself.

"It's been such a hard year. I lost my son a month ago after a long illness. I have no other family, nowhere to turn for solace. Then a friend forwarded a message to me, the story of that night with the picture of the Daughter. Mary, I said to myself, now there's someone who can help, someone who understands your pain and can offer comfort. It was then I decided to make the six-hour drive to come here."

"I'm sorry for your loss," Sebastian said. "But I'm afraid—"

"I don't mean to cause trouble. I've read about the farm and understand the good you do here. Isn't there any way I could see her?"

Sebastian had seen the effect Kailani had on strangers at the reception. He thought about how far the poor woman had traveled, how distraught she was.

What would be the harm? "Very well, I'll see what I can do, but the best I can offer is a brief visit, no more than a few minutes. Please wait here while I go check."

As he left the office to find Helena, he heard a new round of sobs. He made a mental note to place an order for more tissues the next time the supply truck drove into town.

***

Sebastian watched as Mary McAllister's car drove off, trying to assess his decision.

Helena had been furious with him when he suggested the meeting, insisting Kailani had been exploited enough. He determined to send the woman away, but Kailani piped up and said, "I'll be glad to meet with her," as if it had been the most routine request in the world. Helena stood by helplessly, her last bastion of resistance being to demand she accompany the child at all times.

The three of them had taken a few minutes alone in Sebastian's office to commune with the Spirit. When they called him back in, the look on Mary McAllister's face had eased from desperate to serene. Before leaving, she asked Kailani to bless her. The little girl placed a hand on either side of the woman's round cheeks and kissed her forehead, then exited, dragging an astonished Helena behind her.

Mary McAllister had thanked him profusely, saying it had been worth the trip, then pulled a bankbook from her purse and proceeded to write a money order on the spot. Sebastian had forced himself to fold it and slip it discreetly into his shirt pocket without looking at the number.

Now, as the car vanished around the final curve, he peeled back one corner and read the amount. His hand slipped from his staff, off the angry face and down to the sad one. Rarely had he been handed a donation like this, and never one for such an astonishing sum.

He staggered back to his office and went behind the desk to the painting of the great house in winter, groping under the frame for the latch. The frame swung wide, revealing a small wall safe. Three spins of the dial, pausing at numbers only he knew, and the safe popped open. He deposited the money order inside, not daring to look at it again for fear it might evaporate. Then he locked the safe and reset the frame.

He stepped back and admired the painting—another gift from an artist in pain, another gap in the heart healed. He loved the farm, prided himself on managing it well, on anticipating problems and fixing them, but recent events had confounded him.

Mary McAllister had been helped and so had the farm. Had he exploited the child to do that? What did it all mean?

As he pondered, a new sound came wafting on the breeze—more clattering of planks. He looked out the window, waited and watched, and gasped as two more cars came rumbling across the bridge.

CHAPTER 25

MADNESS

Helena stood to the side as Kailani held court in the anteroom of the great house. The Daughter, as she'd come to be called, sat on the edge of an overstuffed chair offering solace to a pilgrim. She'd fastened the eagle feather from Sebastian in her hair with two aquamarine stones. It fluttered and bobbed as she nodded—strong magic to enhance that which she apparently possessed on her own.

For three days they'd come, with more arriving each day. Kailani insisted on seeing each and every one of them, and Helena could only hover nearby, regent and protector. They came burdened with sorrow or self-pity, and left with a newfound hope—frequently with their wallets lighter.

Helena couldn't fault Sebastian; he'd never encouraged these people to come, nor had he solicited their donations. The funds raised weren't for his personal benefit but for the good of the farm. Yet neither had he opposed the turn of events. With the conferences becoming a fact of farm life, the pragmatist in him took over. He moved some furniture to the anteroom and provided an ample supply of tissues.

For the past few months, Helena's days had dragged, the hours crawling by. Suddenly time seemed to be careening out of control. So many pilgrims, so much sorrow, and all the while Helena's fears mounted—that the chasm gaping between her and her mother would never close, that Kailani would be taken away and incarcerated, that Jason would tire of her gloom and Benjamin's abuse and go back to Albion Point.

That she'd be left utterly, breathlessly alone.

The pilgrim droned on. When he had nothing left to say, Kailani stood, gave him her blessing, and bade him farewell.

As soon as the door had closed, the aura of the Daughter disappeared, leaving only the look of an exhausted nine-year-old.

"Are there more?" she said.

"You don't have to do these," Helena said.

"Yes, I do. It's why I came." She removed the feather and stones from her hair. "Can we get ready for dinner now?"

Helena felt as if she were back underwater, grasping the fistful of silt and groping for the surface; above her, through the vague sunlight, a familiar face.

"You go ahead," she said. "I'll meet you in the barn."

After Kailani left, Helena fluffed the sofa pillows and fetched a fresh box of tissues for what would be an early session the next day. She froze, box in hand, sensing someone in the room. She turned, and there he stood, framed by the arch of the window, lit by the red light of sunset streaming through the curtain.

Jason.

He reached out and touched her bare arm. The tissue box slipped from her fingers and thumped to the floor.

***

Jason could feel her trembling, but she said not a word. He listened for her breathing, her heartbeat, for any hint of what she felt inside.

He held on until the trembling stopped and then led her to the front of the room. "Come sit and tell me what's wrong."

"That's Kailani's chair."

"I'm sure she'd approve."

She sat and he perched on the arm.

"I... feel so confused," she said. "I...."

When she struggled to find words, he finished the sentence for her.

DAVID LITWACK

"...don't understand what's happening."

"I don't know how to stop them. I don't even know if I *want* to stop them. They keep coming."

"Why does she insist on meeting with them?"

"Penance, she says."

"This is Benjamin's fault."

Helena nodded, then shook her head. "My mother takes comfort from him, something I can hardly blame her for."

"He's a zealot."

"Kailani seems to trust him—like a voice from the Blessed Lands. And these people... if these myths mean so little, why do they need them so much. What if we're the ones with closed minds? Sometimes I want to believe too."

Her eyebrows bunched together until a crease appeared between them. When she frowned like that, she looked more like her mother than her father. For an instant, Jason pictured her climbing the Spirit Hill at sunset with a pink blossom cradled in her hands.

He slipped off the arm of the chair and knelt in front of her. "He's dangerous, Helena. Look at what he's done to Kailani, how he's put her at risk."

"Which of us is blameless? You and I brought her to the farm. Sebastian accepts the donations. My mother abandoned me. And I couldn't save my father."

"You can't possibly believe—"

"And now I can't even help Kailani."

Jason studied her for a long moment, then recalled Kailani at the Reflection Shelter and saw it at once. The mirror images—grief and penance. Grief was Kailani's burden; Kailani was Helena's penance.

He grasped her by the hands and looked into her eyes. "You're wrong. You did all you could for your father, and if he could see what you're doing for Kailani, he'd be proud."

She stared at him and squeezed his hands.

He held his breath. *Please let me in.*

"Oh, Jason," she said at last. "I need you."

She slipped off the chair and into his arms.

***

Benjamin knew the routine: after the last pilgrim left, Helena would

THE DAUGHTER OF THE SEA AND THE SKY

send Kailani back to the cabins to change and wash up for dinner. He waited behind the common bathroom, hoping to catch the girl alone.

At last, she came down the path. The skip in her step had vanished, and she walked with her shoulders hunched.

He stepped out of the shadows.

"Mr. Benjamin." She made a small bow. Since the pilgrims had begun to arrive, she'd treated him with more deference—like an elder.

He responded with a bow deeper than hers. "Good evening, Daughter of the Sea and the Sky. I hope you're doing well."

She looked downcast. "Not so well."

"But why? You've been sharing the Spirit with those in need."

"I've done penance like you told me to, but I still can't speak to the wind."

"Absolution is not easily attained. I've been doing penance at the farm for many years, and only recently has the Spirit begun to speak to me. To complete your journey, you must be willing to give more of yourself."

"Like what?"

"Only the Spirit knows. Perhaps if you told me why you need to do penance, I could help you find your way."

She wavered, but only for a moment. "I can't tell you."

"Then your penance will continue."

"But for how long?" she said, more plaintive this time.

He waited, allowing her yearning to grow, and then squatted, his face inches from hers.

"Perhaps," he said, "for the rest of your life."

***

When Kailani was late for dinner, Jason went outside to look for her. He found her shuffling toward the barn, dragging her feet and seeming more distraught than usual. In the distance, he could make out Benjamin's slight form lagging behind.

Before Benjamin could enter the barn, Jason grabbed him and pulled him around the corner, out of sight of the dining room windows.

"Time to stop this madness," he said.

"What are you talking about?"

"These people you've brought here."

"That's absurd, Jason. They're strangers to me."

DAVID LITWACK

"But somehow you made them come."

"Listen to yourself. How could I make them come? I don't control them. Now, let me loose. You're hurting me and I'm sure that's not your intent."

Jason released Benjamin, who stumbled backwards, rubbing his arm where Jason had grabbed him.

"What about all those messages?" he said.

"You think they're all me?"

"I think you somehow started it, and you know how to stop it. And, Benjamin, it needs to stop."

"But why? The Daughter wants to do it, and the pilgrims who come are benefiting. So is the farm. Perhaps it's meant to be."

"Meant to be? All she does is spout sayings from her childhood, and these poor people eat it up. If they want their myths so badly, they should all transmigrate."

Benjamin winced as if he'd been struck. He tried to step around Jason to the entrance of the barn, but Jason blocked his way.

"What disturbs you most?" Benjamin said. "That the pilgrims come with unfulfilled needs and the Daughter satisfies them? Or that you can't explain it without admitting a power greater than us?"

When Jason still refused to let him pass, the little man's eyes flared and he bared his small teeth. "Or do you still not see what she is?"

Jason drew in a quick breath. "What do you think she is?"

Benjamin made him wait as if he had a great secret to share.

"The crossroads of history," he said at last.

"How could she—"

"The crossroads," he repeated, his face now flushed, his voice rising. "A prophet who will change the world." He slipped past Jason, who was too stunned to stop him, but turned before he reached the corner of the barn. "She's the birth of a new way. The way of the Spirit."

"But she's a child!"

"Not just a child. Can't you see how they flock to her? Like bees to honey."

Jason narrowed the gap between them. "So what's the next chapter in this fantastic story of yours?"

"She leads us to salvation. Though like honey, she's sweet but insubstantial—not the rock on which a movement is built. That requires a disciple like me who can sustain it after she's gone."

Jason's blood ran cold. "After she's gone?"

172

THE DAUGHTER OF THE SEA AND THE SKY

"Yes. If you'd been to the Blessed Lands, you'd know. They flare brightly, these prophets, brightly but briefly."

"And why is that?" He clenched his fists until the nails bit into his palms.

"Because most of the time," Benjamin said matter-of-factly, "they're martyred."

***

Jason rushed to the office right after dinner. He'd been too cautious in his letter to Carlson, and needed to be more aggressive.

A thought struck him: what if, as Benjamin claimed, Kailani was some sort of spiritual leader, a high priestess to her people? What if she'd been speaking the truth, that she'd come or been sent to convert the soulless? What if she'd been known differently in her world?

Time for a new approach.

He'd ask Carlson to search again, this time not for Kailani, but for the daughter of the sea and the sky.

CHAPTER 26

BLIND SPOTS

How to begin?

Jason needed to warn Sebastian about Benjamin without sounding like a disgruntled employee. He'd practiced his speech with Helena the prior evening, but now, as he sat before the managing director, the words seemed lacking... effect.

He waited until Sebastian had poured his morning tea and settled into the high-backed chair before blurting it out. "You have a problem at the farm."

Sebastian raised his cup and eyed him through the steam. "And what would that be?"

Images raced through Jason's head, everything since that day he and Helena had rescued Kailani. He'd always been driven by the dream: the grand chamber with the granite floor, the dingy hallway to the mailroom where his father worked. Here, in place of the dingy hallway were millions of trees spread across the mountains, and the sky went on forever. And Helena was with him. He hoped Sebastian wouldn't cast him from the farm.

THE DAUGHTER OF THE SEA AND THE SKY

"Benjamin." He said it louder than he intended.

Sebastian laughed. "Is that all? From the look on your face, I thought the termites were back in the great house."

In his month on the farm, Jason had come to respect Sebastian as much as anyone he'd ever worked with. But everyone had blind spots.

"The man's a zealot, Sebastian, a genuine my-beliefs-are-the-only-way-to-salvation madman. He's obsessed with Kailani. Has he ever given you one of his crazy speeches?"

To his dismay, Sebastian nodded. "Cornered you, has he? Closed the office door and poured forth his strange ideas? You think I haven't heard them too?"

"And it doesn't bother you?"

Sebastian took a sip of tea and set the cup down. "Oh, it bothers me. I'm not a fan of that sort of thinking, but you need to see beyond the speeches. He may be fanatical, but he's also hurting. Did you know he comes from one of the wealthiest families in the country? Got the best education money could buy, but he fought with his family. I don't know what about, but he claims he rejected the material life. At any rate, they disowned him, said if he was so holier-than-thou, he could make his own way in the world. He wandered around for a while, spending the last of what they'd given him, and then he tried to transmigrate."

Jason must have flinched, because Sebastian backtracked.

"That's right. Transmigrate. He went through all the paperwork and got conditionally accepted as one of them, but it didn't last. They kept him bottled up in one of their processing centers and finally rejected him. Said he was unsuitable to be a citizen of the Blessed Lands. Department officials at the land bridge offered him a ride back to the city but he refused. Trekked twenty miles over the mountains with no sleep and nothing but the clothes on his back, until he crossed the highway and stumbled upon that dirt road behind the farm. He showed up here hungry, exhausted, and soul-sick. I took him in because I felt sorry for him."

"And he's stayed all this time?"

"Had nowhere else to go. Everyone comes to the farm looking for something. I understand most of them, but not Benjamin. He says it's spiritual, but I don't know. I do know he's done everything I've ever asked of him. I even trust him with Lizzie's bell for his little rituals."

"What about the photogram, the picture of Kailani? That had to be his doing. You ordered him to leave her alone."

DAVID LITWACK

"Yes, that surprised me, but it was hardly an act of violence. And you have to admit, it's worked out for everyone."

Jason moved closer until his knees pressed against the desk. "And his cult? The Lemurians?"

"You worry too much, my friend. That bunch is just a few gentle souls, utopians following a fantasy — peculiar but harmless."

"Blind faith, believing in myths, is never harmless," Jason said, careful to use the phrase every citizen of the Republic had been taught as a child.

"My dear Jason, there's a thin line between faith and fantasy. Fantasies are benign, a game of the mind. People invent fantasies when they find reality too painful. Then they discuss them with their friends, act them out, and retell the story to anyone who'll listen."

"And how's that different from faith?"

Sebastian's smile vanished. The skin on his face became taut. "Faith is something you impose on others, something you're willing to kill for. I know. Fifty years ago, I fought a war because of faith."

Jason folded his hands on the desk and stared at his knuckles. Fantasy or faith. What if Kailani's arrival had driven Benjamin to cross the line between the two?

Sebastian turned away and stared at the morning light streaming through the bay window, looking as if he were imagining a bedraggled Benjamin arriving again. He waited a few seconds before speaking, as if needing time to formulate his thoughts.

"I'll let you in on a secret, Jason. Some mornings, when I'm here alone, I make myths of my own. I imagine Lizzie's with me, sitting right in that chair. I swear I can smell the perfume she used to wear. I close my eyes and inhale it, and convince myself she's still around. Does that make me a zealot? Of course not. It's just a fantasy that gives me comfort. Would you deny me that?"

Sebastian waited, insisting on an answer.

Jason shook his head.

"Listen, you've come here for good reasons. Helping me keep an eye on Benjamin is just one more. Would you be better off if you left the farm? Would we?"

Sebastian was right; Jason was committed. He'd never leave Helena, and if they left the farm together, what would become of Kailani? Like Benjamin years before, she had nowhere else to go.

The tension in his neck eased. He'd said his piece and was still welcome at the farm. More important, Sebastian had been forewarned.

176

The Daughter of the Sea and the Sky

The managing director smiled as if he'd read his mind, then stood and sent him on his way.

***

Jason emerged from the great house and found Helena waiting on the lawn, bent over the statuette of the girl with the bonnet and the basket of flowers. He caught her picking out browned petals that had long since succumbed to the cold nights.

She'd agreed with his going to Sebastian, but fretted that he'd be banished from the farm. Sebastian didn't tolerate much discord. When she heard his footsteps on the floorboards, she looked up, saw his expression and smiled. Apparently she could tell at once that all was well.

They spent the rest of the morning together, strolling the pathways of the farm, Helena leaving Kailani to Miz Martha and Jason ignoring his job.

When he arrived back at the office, it was nearly lunch. Just enough time to log on and check messages. Recently, the volume had decreased. As Polytech management trusted him more, they bothered him less, and he was gradually losing touch with his few acquaintances. Even the strange postings about Kailani had dwindled.

So he was surprised when an anonymous message appeared— garbled sender, no subject, sent in the wee hours of the morning. He clicked to open it.

I've heard you are seeking information about a missing girl from the Blessed Lands. Beware. There are those who would do her harm.

He stood and checked the corridor, then closed the door, turning the knob slowly so the latch settled into place with hardly a click. He went back to the desk and dragged the pointer over the text, turning the background blue, and reread the words until he'd memorized them.

Then he deleted the message, making sure it was gone without a trace.

CHAPTER 27

A CALL TO ACTION

"This message is two weeks old." The Minister of Commerce tried to temper his annoyance at the official standing before him. Too harsh a response might discourage future revelations. "Why wasn't I shown it until today?"

The official pressed his hands in front of his chest and made a nervous bow. "Too vague, Excellency, with no urgency, sent to the lowest level. Our ministry gets lots of chatter from the soulless, much of it nothing but propaganda. We were afraid to waste your time, but when the second query arrived, I thought—"

The minister waved him to silence. The decision was hard to argue; the message *was* vague—a missing child, no age or gender, no description or time frame. It lacked seriousness, but the way the official's pupils shifted from corner to corner caused a flutter in his stomach. He peeled back the first message, exposing the second.

Another request about a missing child sent to the same clerk, but this one had more details. One caught his eye.

Can it be?

This message offered proof enough to hope again, proof enough to act.

178

THE DAUGHTER OF THE SEA AND THE SKY

He rang the small bell that sat atop his desk, and his aide responded at once.

"Get my chief of staff," he said.

"And the subject, Excellency?"

"The subject?"

"Yes, he always asks the subject. He tries to be prepared."

"Tell him... it's a private matter, but make sure he comes right away." *A private matter, yes, but more vital than any affair of state.*

He scanned the row of portraits on the wall, every Supreme Leader his country had ever known. Some in his country prayed he'd be next. Once he'd have traded everything for that opportunity, but now, this message from some low-level bureaucrat on the far side of the ocean was worth more.

Slowly, he reread the text, touching his fingertips to the words: *the daughter of the sea and the sky.*

It was like touching a dream.

CHAPTER 28

PERIPHERAL VISION

The ceiling sloped downward until Jason had to walk in a crouch. His back ached from bending over, but he was driven onward by a keening sound. He turned the corner into an even more cramped corridor, driving him to his knees. At its end a hinged door opened upward, like the kind people make for their pets. He ducked his head and squeezed through.

At the far wall, a little man sat addressing envelopes with a quill pen and stuffing them into the pigeonholes of a mail cabinet. Beside him, a woman knelt praying. She wore a white robe that hung down to her bare feet. A diaphanous shawl covered her hair and flowed down her shoulders.

The woman looked up and let out a gasp. "Jason, you've come back." It was Helena.

When the little man heard her, he stopped sorting and turned, and his rodent-like features came into focus.

Benjamin.

180

THE DAUGHTER OF THE SEA AND THE SKY

Jason tried to stand but bumped his head on the ceiling with a thunk. An alarm sounded, small and tinny like the room. *Beep, beep, beep.*

***

Jason awoke to find his forehead resting on the keyboard, pressing an invalid key. So much for working late.

He'd been fighting exhaustion after another long day doing Benjamin's chores, but the breeze outside the window had set the leaves rustling, a sound like the surf near Helena's home. Before he knew it, he'd been dragged down into a dream-filled sleep.

He sat up and tried to reorient himself. He'd always taken pride in his job and now, working remotely, he'd raised his expectations even higher. Yet despite his efforts, he struggled to meet the latest deadline. He'd hoped to finish that night, but now had to concede he'd be late.

Might as well give up before I fall asleep again.

He archived his work, packed up the encomm, and switched off the desk lamp. As he headed to Sebastian's office to lock up the device, he noticed a light coming from the common room. He reached around the doorjamb to turn it off.

"Is someone there?" It was Martha Brewster's voice.

He thought to ignore her and leave, but manners compelled him to be polite. He stepped inside. "Oh, hello, Miz Brewster. It's me, Jason. I thought I was the only night owl and was going to turn off the light. You're here late, aren't you?"

The long and narrow room contained a thin table built into its back wall. Three communicators sat on it, with a chair in front of each. Martha Brewster sat in the middle one.

She swiveled around to face him. "Oh, Jason, come in. I had a few calls to make and was just finishing some letters to send off in the morning. I try to wait until after Kailani's asleep. Everyone treats her like an adult, but she's just a child. These conferences take their toll."

Helena complained that her mother had a way of putting her on the defensive at the beginning of every conversation. He could see now what she meant and felt the urge to explain.

"I'm as uncomfortable as you are with what's going on." He took a breath and lowered his voice. "I'm the one who pulled her from the ocean. I know as well as anyone she's just a child."

181

She seemed to relax, and looked at him with the same astonished eyes as Helena. "Please call me Martha. We're both adults, you know. Have a seat. I've been hoping to spend some time with you."

He was tired but couldn't refuse the offer. He pulled up a chair and sat. "So who were you writing to at this late hour, Martha?"

"Oh, I still try to keep up with friends at the Polytech. My husband and I were there for almost twenty years."

"I've heard. Your friends there must be different from the members of the farm."

"Oh yes, quite different."

"In what way?"

She glanced up at the wooden beams of the ceiling and then down to the letter she'd been writing, as if expecting to find an answer there.

"In what way are they different?" She sounded like a teacher about to begin a dissertation. "Well, first of all, researchers are normal. Artists are not."

Jason must have flinched, because she quickly recanted.

"Oh, dear, not like that. I mean it only in the most positive way. Let me try again. Scientists view the world through the center of their pupils, the part that's most focused. Artists are the opposite. They see through peripheral vision, observing shadows and imagining the rest. In the end, each paints a picture as detailed as the other, the scientists using logic and facts, the artist using feelings and instincts. Neither has a monopoly on truth, and each creates their own world and makes it real."

Jason tried to reconcile the teacher at the Polytech with the woman he'd seen on the Spirit Hill, clad in the gown and gossamer shawl, gathering to summon the wind. "Is that why you've taken to worshipping with the Lemurians? To create your own reality out of half-seen shadows?"

Her expression tightened. "If there's comfort to be had from the Spirit, I'll take it. Just as I take comfort from making jewelry and sewing dresses for Kailani. That's all. It's nothing more than that."

"And has Benjamin given you that comfort?"

"You don't like him, do you?"

"I don't trust him. Do you?"

She hesitated, thinking it through. "When he first spoke to me, I was angry with him. I went back to my cabin and screamed into the mirror, 'The Spirit is a myth.' After a while, I made my peace with the

THE DAUGHTER OF THE SEA AND THE SKY

idea that there might be something greater than us. Have you ever lost someone you loved, Jason?"

Thinking of his mother, he nodded. "Yes, but it didn't make me give in to fantasy."

"Well, maybe I'm not as strong as you. I took what comfort I could."

Jason stayed still, staring until she became uneasy and turned back to her letter writing.

"And what about Helena?" he said, gently. "Where was her comfort?"

Her hands froze over the paper. The hum of the heater fan at her feet started up, sounding unnaturally loud.

"I was so distraught," she finally said. "I hardly knew who I was. I couldn't help *myself*, never mind anyone else. Now I'm sorry I left her, terribly sorry. I was wrong."

"Have you told her that?"

She resumed writing, fumbling with the pen—scrawl, scratch out, scrawl again—until she shoved the paper away.

"Tell her? I can't tell her anything right now. When I suggested she try meditation the other day, she nearly bit my head off." As if sensing his dissatisfaction, she turned to him. "She's my only daughter, Jason. She's all I have left. I want her back."

He stared at her, trying to picture her as the mother of a nine-year-old Helena.

"What is it, Jason? Say something."

"You're different from what I thought. I'm learning more on the farm than I did in my time at the Polytech. I guess I still have a ways to go."

Martha Brewster smiled. "As you get older, you'll realize you know less and less. That's another difference between scientists and artists. Scientists think all truth can be found if they work hard enough. Artists know better."

"So we're supposed to be confused?

She laughed, then went silent. When she spoke again, the astonished eyes bore in on him. "There's something I want you to know, Jason. For all my confusion, there's one thing I've learned since you came to the farm— seen for myself, confirmed by empirical evidence." She paused.

He waited, until finally he had to draw it from her. "What is it?"

"The one thing that makes Helena happy."

A question he'd been asking himself since he first saw her on the cliffs. "And that would be...?"

"You, Jason. She wants you."

183

CHAPTER 29

FIRST SNOW

November was a bleak and soggy month in the Northern Kingdom. As it came to a close, the leaves that had adorned the October trees floated to the ground and decayed to form a brownish muck along the farm's pathways.

Helena spent her days scheduling Kailani's pilgrims and chaperoning the resulting meetings, while Jason raked and cleared brush, and did his best to keep up with his Polytech work. With the exception of meals and an after-dinner stroll when the weather permitted, they had little time to be together.

Helena remained unfazed. Winter would come and pass and Jason would be with her. Perhaps by the fifth of April, they'd even find a way to convince the tribunal to let Kailani stay with them.

Meanwhile, her mother cloistered herself in the studio and complained to anyone who'd listen how she hardly saw her daughter or Kailani anymore.

One afternoon, when the audiences had ended early, Helena suggested Kailani go see Miz Martha while she used the time to visit Jason.

THE DAUGHTER OF THE SEA AND THE SKY

"Only if you come too," Kailani said. "Miz Martha needs to see her daughter."

She reluctantly agreed.

In the studio, they set a cut onyx into the prongs of a silver ring. Thankfully, her mother was content to let Kailani help while Helena watched. They finished without incident and had time to spare before dinner. With the days so short, her mother suggested they take advantage of the remaining light to go for a walk.

They revisited Serena's statue of the woman with the golden eagle on her shoulder, and let Kailani commune with Grandmother Storyteller. On their way back to the barn, white flakes began to drift through the air.

Kailani held out her hands and stared at the flakes landing on her palm and fading away. "What is it?"

"It's snow," Helena said. "Remember we told you about snow when we were driving up to the farm?"

"It tingles on my skin. May I taste it?"

Helena glanced at her mother, who responded with a look that said, *you were once much the same way.*

Kailani stuck out her tongue and waited until a few flakes rested on it, then swallowed.

Helena smiled. "So how does it taste?"

"Wet." The girl from the Blessed Lands twirled around as if trying to touch each flake.

Helena watched her catch the falling snow in her hands and on her cheeks, and thought of another winter long ago, when she and Jason where children. Huge clumps of white had floated through the air, snow melted on her tongue and kissed her face with cold, making her cheeks flush. Jason had called—no school that day. He insisted on trudging through the drifts to meet her on the cliffs. The two of them played outside, tossing snowballs at each other, tumbling and rolling in the snow... and reveling in their first touch.

Helena's mother interrupted her reverie. "If you look quickly, when they land on your clothing, you'll see they all have a six-pointed pattern, but each flake has its own design."

Just like her mother to describe the geometry in the flakes. Her father would have said it differently: water high up in the atmosphere forming tiny crystals around a piece of dust, each a unique, lace-like pattern of six-sided fractal art. The crystals would clump together into flakes as they fell, covering the land with snow.

Now that she and Jason had freed Kailani from her cell, the girl would get to see it for the first time.

Kailani froze, studying her right sleeve. When a few flakes landed, her face lit up. "I see." She gave a shiver. "But snow makes you cold."

"Of course it does," Helena's mother said. "It's frozen water, and it reminds us that you, young lady, are not ready for winter."

"What do I have to do?"

"What you have to do is accompany us to town, if you can spare an afternoon away from your admirers, so we can buy you some winter clothes."

"Can't you sew me some, Miz Martha?"

Helena's mother rolled her eyes. "You may be able to perform miracles, Kailani, but as a seamstress, winter coats are beyond my abilities." She turned to Helena. "Why don't you check with Jason and see if you can pry him away from his work long enough to drive us into town? Maybe we could have lunch together. My treat."

"You wouldn't mind?" Helena said.

"Why would I mind? He's such a nice young man. I'd like to get to know him better. And you, my dear, should spend more time with him."

***

At a quarter till noon the next day, the four of them loaded into Jason's car and headed to town. More than a month of dealing with pilgrims had left Helena drained. How good it felt to take a break from their endless tales of woe and spend time with Jason, even if she had to share him.

Now, after finishing lunch at the Northweald sandwich shop, they waited as Kailani spooned her way through a heaping hot-fudge sundae, which she insisted was essential before she could buy a new coat.

Helena watched Jason watching Kailani, and saw the delight he took in her. She pictured him carrying her out of the surf, the sun and seawater making the muscles of his arms gleam. She recalled the look on his face — not just the exhilaration of rescuing a child, but how much he cared.

Kailani had been right; they shared the Spirit.

Her thoughts were interrupted by a conversation from the table behind her, where two middle-aged women sipped coffee and swapped stories.

"My grandfather loved sports," one said, "talked about the local university team constantly. When my dad was growing up, he pushed

THE DAUGHTER OF THE SEA AND THE SKY

him to get in shape and practice so he could earn an athletic scholarship. Dad came to loathe sports and the university as well, but my grandfather tried everything to get him to go there."

"And did he go?" her friend asked.

"He did. And you know what? If he hadn't, he never would have met my mother. They've been inseparable for fifty years."

Helena jerked around at the sound of wood scraping the floor, and saw her mother stifle a sob and stumble out the door. When she turned back, Kailani was staring at her.

Kailani licked her spoon clean, then filled it again with ice cream and waved the new spoonful under Helena's nose. "I think she needs you."

"I'm afraid it's more... complicated than that."

"Why? You mourn the same spirit, don't you?"

Jason tapped her on the shoulder and tilted his head toward the street. She looked out the storefront window at her mother huddled on a park bench in front of the village green, the statue of the soldier with the sabre at his side hovering over her as if standing guard.

Helena's throat began to tighten, and the words came out muffled. "I can't."

Kailani popped the ice cream into her mouth and let it roll across her tongue, then shoved the dish aside and reached for Helena's hand. "Yes you can. It's not so hard."

Helena at once understood what the pilgrims had discovered. Kailani's eyes were no longer the color of the ocean but the ocean itself, ageless and inviting. Anything seemed possible. When the Daughter stood and beckoned, people had to follow.

A few seconds later, the three of them stood over the bench.

"Martha?" Jason said, as if they were best friends. "Here's your only daughter, and this is your chance."

Kailani nodded and went back to finish her ice cream.

Panic-stricken, Helena glanced at Jason.

"You'll know what to do." He followed Kailani across the street.

When her mother looked up, her cheeks were moist with tears. "Oh, my girl, I'm so sorry."

"Is there space on that bench for me?"

"Come sit." Her mother brushed the seat next to her. "Please."

***

When Helena and her mother returned, Jason ordered them hot mulled ciders, the specialty of the house. As they blew across their steaming mugs and fumbled awkwardly for words, he decided to give them a little time to themselves.

"That cider looks too hot to drink," he said. "Why don't you let it cool for a while? I can take Kailani across the street to look at clothes."

Helena nodded, but her mother seemed skeptical. "Are you sure you'll know what to buy?"

"Of course not, but I can get her started. I promise not to buy anything without your approval."

With her reluctant agreement, he led Kailani across the street to Hal's Sporting Goods Mart, the largest building in town. The store appeared to stock everything: clothing, farm supplies, and equipment for every sport imaginable, especially those suited to the northern wilderness. Jason had counted on it keeping Kailani occupied, allowing the Brewster women a chance to review and reflect, but three steps into the doorway, Kailani stopped dead and yanked on his hand.

When he glanced down, he saw her eyes fixed on something overhead. Above them was a hunting trophy, the head of a fourteen-point buck. Its face was twisted in Kailani's direction, its mouth open and tongue lifted, its eyes curious, as if asking, "Why?"

Jason turned back to the girl. "It's a deer, Kailani. It's stuffed, not alive."

"What's it doing there? Was it killed by a motorized wagon?"

A knot formed in his stomach. No way out of this one. "It's a... trophy. That's all." Before she could ask, he added, "Hunters go into the woods and hunt. If they kill an animal, they use its body for food. Then, they keep the head to... show off their skill."

Kailani pulled away from him, took a step closer, and tilted her head as if to mimic the buck's expression. After a moment, she skipped over to the far wall, where rows of hunting rifles hung in racks. "And what are these?"

Jason sighed, already exhausted. He hadn't expected a sporting goods store to present such a challenge. "They're guns. They're used for hunting."

"Are they what killed the deer?"

"Probably. I think so."

After that discussion, he took her straight to the clothing section and the safety of dressing rooms and displays of winter coats. A friendly saleswoman was more than glad to measure Kailani and

THE DAUGHTER OF THE SEA AND THE SKY

recommend a wardrobe. With a tummy full of dessert and a stack of clothing to try on, the Daughter was at last content.

By the fifth coat, Jason was getting bored. As he stood to stretch his legs, he saw something that made him duck back out of sight. Through the racks of garments, he spotted Benjamin, who must've taken advantage of his absence to come into town. It wasn't just the little man's presence that concerned him.

Benjamin stood in front of the gun counter, making a purchase.

After Benjamin exited the store and was no longer visible through the front window, Jason he approached the clerk. "Could you tell me what that man was buying?"

"I'm sorry, sir. We're not allowed to discuss the purchases of other customers."

Jason forced a laugh. "It's all right. Benjamin and I work together at Glen Eagle Farm. Sebastian sent me here to place an order." He pulled out the small notepad he kept in his pocket in case a work idea struck him and flipped to the third page. "I wanted to make sure we didn't have the same items on our shopping list."

The clerk nodded. "Ah. No harm then, I guess. He was buying .308 caliber silvertips. Is that on your list?"

Jason ran down the invisible list with his finger.

"No it isn't. I should've known—Sebastian's always so organized."

Just then, the bell attached to the front door jingled, and Helena called to him. "What are you doing over there, and where's Kailani?"

"I was wandering around while I waited." He gestured toward the clothing section. "It seems the young lady likes clothing as much as sweets."

As Helena and Martha hurried over to shower squeals of approval on Kailani's wardrobe, Jason had other concerns. He glanced up at the deer and gazed into its glassy eyes, picturing the window of the quilting room and a squirrel scurrying across the lawn.

***

"I hate to nag, but... are you sure he's not a danger?" Jason slumped in the visitor chair, his long legs stretched out in front of him.

Sebastian paced back and forth behind his desk. "Of course not. I'm never sure of anything. I wasn't sure the old generator would hold out or that we'd have the wherewithal to replace it. What I do know is that it's unreasonable to punish people without proof."

DAVID LITWACK

"But why would he be buying ammunition?"

"I told you, Jason, we have several members who like to hunt, and Benjamin's the best of them. There's nothing wrong with hunting. I used to hunt myself until my bones couldn't take the cold anymore. You'll feel differently the first time you taste fresh venison."

"So you knew he had a gun?"

"Not a gun, Jason." Sebastian went to the file cabinet and withdrew a red folder. "It's a Browning Mark II Lightweight Stalker, an elegant weapon with a polished walnut stock. Modest recoil. I've fired it myself. Takes a .308 caliber charge, accurate within four hundred yards. Of course, Benjamin with his special scope can hit a target at double that distance."

Jason looked away, but Sebastian sailed on. "Would you like to know the serial number?"

He shook his head. "But why would he be buying ammunition now?"

"Come on, you're grasping at straws."

Sebastian went back to the file cabinet and pulled out a notice, which he slapped down on the desk. It read: *Northern Kingdom deer hunting season begins November 29.*

"Enough. I give up." He stared past Sebastian to the painting of the great house in winter, which he'd soon get to see as depicted, covered with snow. "Why do you do it, Sebastian?"

"Do what?"

"Put up with all of us. It seems like a thankless job."

"Thankless? Oh no." Sebastian looked genuinely surprised. "I used to run big projects with lots of employees, thought I was pretty important. This isn't that different. It's what I'm good at." He let his smile broaden until it nearly reached his earlobes. "How old do you think I am?"

Never a good question to answer. "Maybe sixty-five."

"Seventy-eight." He glanced to his right, at the teapot with the cherubs, and then out the bay window to the lawn. "I loved those projects, because I wanted to leave tracks like the little creatures in the morning. Not footprints, though. Brain prints. Let them know when I'm gone that I passed this way, that I was smart and hard-driving and competent. But it wasn't enough.

"When I came here after Lizzie died, I didn't plan to stay this long. Then I found they needed someone like me. I could leave tracks here

THE DAUGHTER OF THE SEA AND THE SKY

too, not just brain prints but something more—call them heart prints. To be useful, to be needed, to every so often make a difference in someone's life—that's enough for me."

He came out from behind the desk and pulled Jason by the elbow until he stood. Then he gave him a hard pat on the back. "Now in the name of reason, go worry about your job. Watch out for Helena and Kailani, and let me worry about the farm."

Jason slunk out of the office like a student who'd been scolded for a prank, but the scolding gave no closure. The prank, he feared, was yet to come.

Chapter 30

The Secretary of the Soulless

The Minister of Commerce studied the man across the table—imposing, obviously accustomed to power, and flanked by two burly guards. The minister tried not to be intimidated. After all, he'd met other high-ranking officials at the land bridge, but they'd been in charge of industry or education. This was the first one who commanded an army.

He shook off his doubts and focused on the man's face. The Secretary of the Department of Separation had small eyes nearly lost between cheek and brow, and a round, bald head with tufts of hair about the ears. Despite his imposing demeanor, he seemed neither disingenuous nor unkind.

Getting this meeting had been a struggle. Their business people were eager to work with him, lusting after the markets he represented. These defenders of reason were a different breed, more wary of the Blessed Lands. Contact this high up to find a little girl must have seemed frivolous.

Not to him. And not to the poetess.

THE DAUGHTER OF THE SEA AND THE SKY

The poetess had once described the land of her birth as a place where material prosperity dwelt side by side with inner emptiness, where everyone's companion was a sense of quiet despair.

He'd done business with many from there who worked for the good of others and tried their best, much as he did. Still, he sometimes wondered: was despair intrinsic to a society or an affliction of the human heart?

Though their life together had brought happiness, she tended to the darker moods. Now, she wandered their home like a wraith, refusing to hear about progress, the wound too painful to touch.

The progress was real, though. The message sent from the soulless confirmed that the daughter of the sea and the sky had landed and been found. If only he could get to the right people. Finally, after months of frustration, he took the step he dreaded most, begging the Supreme Leader to intervene.

He recalled sitting in the austere office, his government's seat of power, pleading his case and waiting for the Supreme Leader to respond.

***

"I myself have been searching," his mentor finally said, "for a way to reach out to the soulless."

The minister's heart beat faster, knowing how difficult such a step would be. The Supreme Leader was a virtuous man and had the welfare of his people at heart.

"But we must not approach the soulless from a position of weakness. We must maintain our dignity and honor. Never will I debase myself to them. So yes, I will reach out for you, but on one condition."

The minister bowed his head and closed his eyes, but his ears stayed open.

"That we withhold the truth from the soulless. That we invent a story, that we say she is a person of importance to our people, and we demand her return."

The minister opened his eyes and took in the dark wood paneling behind the desk, inlaid upon it the silver icon symbolizing their Lord — the great all-seeing eye staring out over the Blessed Lands.

"But how can any good come from the sin of falsehood?" he said.

193

The Supreme Leader came out from behind from the desk and rested a hand on the minister's shoulder. Despite the power of the man's office, he could feel its warmth.

"Lord Kanakunai will forgive, my friend, for such a worthy cause."

***

The secretary's voice interrupted his thoughts, bringing him back to the stark steel of the land bridge. "My sources tell me you're a reasonable man, that you've made positive changes in your country and are on the leading edge of a new generation that thinks differently about the world. Differently enough that, perhaps in the future, our peoples might be friends."

The minister waited while the secretary took a sip of water. His mind dwelled on the word "future." Of course. Such a high-level contact might start a process that could someday heal the wound that had split the world, precisely the opportunity the Supreme Leader had in mind. The minister would have done the same given the chance, though he cared nothing for politics now.

"But as to the present," the secretary resumed, "I and my organization will do what we can. I've sent out word. If she's anywhere in the Republic, she'll be found."

The minister turned away, pulled out his handkerchief, and wiped his brow. The poetess may have given up, but he'd continue the search to its end. He'd tell the poetess nothing yet, lest her despair weigh him down.

He couldn't allow himself to despair—not now, not when the search for the living had begun.

CHAPTER 31

A GOOD CIVIL SERVANT

Winter was nearly over and Carlson's retirement was approaching. From the barber's chair, he regarded himself in the mirror, feeling like a boy again. He scheduled his haircuts like clockwork for the third Tuesday of every month, an appointment his assistant knew to keep sacred. Once a month, just enough to keep the hair off his ears and the back of his neck clean.

The barbershop was a throwback, not one of the newer salons but more like the one his father had brought him to as a child. He breathed in the smell of shaving cream and musk oil, and exhaled a sigh of satisfaction. The zealots were right about one thing—there was something reassuring about tradition.

Even if he had to wait, he always insisted on the same barber, a plump-faced man named Charlie, who liked to chat mostly about sports. He'd raise a question, snip three times, and then provide the answer himself, punctuating each comment with a tsk-tsk if the local team had lost, or a chuckle if they'd won.

DAVID LITWACK

A glass case below the mirror held a photogram of three plump-faced boys, all dressed in uniforms. Behind them loomed a faded box of cereal with a picture of a star striker from twenty years ago. Next to it lay a retired whisk broom, its years of service done. Things were not discarded here, but honored for their memories.

Carlson relaxed as Charlie snipped. Soon would come the best part, the hum of the hot lather dispenser, the warmth as Charlie dabbed the lather on the back of his neck and around his ears. Then the stropping of the straight razor on the leather strap—no power trimmers here—and the razor so sharp, he'd hardly feel its touch. He noted the final flourish waiting on the counter, a shaker of ultrafine talc.

As Charlie completed his stropping, Carlson felt a vibration in his pocket. Charlie hesitated with the razor poised as Carlson pulled out his government-issued secure communicator and read the display.

"I'm sorry, Charlie. It's my assistant. She should know better than to bother me here."

He replaced the communicator in his pocket, tilted his head back, and relished the first stroke of the razor.

The buzzing started again. This time, a message displayed:

Call at once. Urgent.

The retirement clock on his desk was counting down. What was the number when he left? Twenty-nine days and an afternoon's worth of hours. He leaned back and tried one more time to relax, but before Charlie could resume, he tossed the striped cutting cape off and threw up his hands. The spell had been broken.

"This never happens, Charlie. I'm afraid we'll have to end it here. Just clean me up, please."

The barber unceremoniously wiped his ears and the back of his neck, then offered the talc as consolation.

Carlson waved it off. He was a half step out the door before he realized he'd forgotten to pay. He rushed back and handed Charlie his fee plus a generous tip.

In the privacy of his car, he contacted his assistant.

"I'm so glad you called," she said.

He waited a moment to let his irritation settle; no sense taking it out on her. "What's so urgent?"

"I'm sorry, I didn't know what else to do. It was the secretary himself."

"The secretary of what?"

196

THE DAUGHTER OF THE SEA AND THE SKY

"Of the department."

Carlson's mind raced. In his thirty-two years, a district manager had called him once. The notion that the secretary should call was absurd. "You can't possibly mean *that* secretary."

"Yes, that one." Her tone was clipped and tense. "He said he sent you a secure message for your eyes only. He left his personal number. You're to give him a response as soon as you've read it."

Carlson removed the communicator from his ear and stared at it, then set it back in place. "I'll be right there."

***

Back in the office, he hung his coat on the hook by the door and turned on his desktop communicator so it would warm up by the time he'd poured coffee. The screen flickered and firmed. Too many messages as usual, but the one he was seeking glared out in red—highest priority.

He resisted the urge to open it right away, instead taking two sips of coffee before sitting down. Then he clicked and read.

> *Security: Top Secret*
> *Priority: Most Urgent*
> *Subject: Seeking refugee from the land of the zealots*
>
> *We have reason to believe a child who traveled here from across the sea is loose in our midst. Timing matches your filing #201476 from Sept 1 of last year as well as your queries sent to the land bridge over the subsequent months. She is a special refugee and needs to be returned to department custody immediately. Priority cannot be overemphasized. If you recognize the girl in the attached image, notify the secretary at once.*

The secretary's personal comm code followed.

Carlson moved the pointer over the attachment. He kept telling himself the chance of a match was slim, a coincidence of timing. Despite claiming the sea and the sky as parents, Kailani hardly seemed important enough to move the head of this giant bureaucracy to find her.

He clicked.

The photogram opened. No, not a photogram but an image of a drawing. He reached into his pocket for a handkerchief and rubbed the

197

smudges off the screen. The girl in the image was younger, less pale, and more robust than the child he remembered—not a perfect match. Yet even from the screen, the ocean-blue eyes reached out to him, touching places in his heart he'd almost forgotten were there. He thought of Miriam and wondered what she was up to at this hour. He pictured his own daughter as a child curled up in his lap.

He'd been a good civil servant with an unblemished record for more than thirty-two years. The retirement clock read twenty-nine days, three hours, forty-one minutes and a steadily diminishing number of seconds. If he ignored the resemblance between the image on the screen and the child on the farm, perhaps his remaining time would pass without incident.

She was a distraught child, nothing more. Who knew what had scarred her in the land of the zealots, what had driven her to cross the ocean alone? Who knew what her government would do to her if she were sent back? Now she was in good hands, safe and secure, ready to grow up in the land of reason where she'd surely thrive. Everything was in order for her tribunal.

He glanced up and saw his ancestors glaring down at him from their brass frames. Disobedience was not in his genes. He dutifully scrolled to the secretary's private code....

...but his finger refused to call.

He knew as well as anyone how the bureaucracy could chew people up. With twenty-nine days, three hours, and forty-one minutes left, he couldn't bring himself to surrender Kailani. After all, it wasn't a perfect match. He could claim oversight on his part—ineptitude, not disobedience.

He set aside the government-issued secure communicator and typed a message instead:

No match found.

CHAPTER 32

A REFUGE FOR LOST SOULS

Winter fell harshly on the Northern Kingdom, harsher still for old folks whose bones felt the cold more intensely. Some days, Sebastian dreaded getting out of bed, afraid his knees might buckle and no longer support him. This morning, as he slogged through the slush to his office, the stiffness in his joints was least on his mind.

He stopped to take in the view. The spruce trees that lined the path had been coated overnight with a dusting of snow and looked like ladies-in-waiting to the great house. He inhaled the cold through his nose, savoring the aroma of the evergreens. The farm had become like a second wife to him, a soul mate — and his soul mate prospered.

The new generator hummed along, and the bank balance had grown large enough to contemplate renovating the great house. And why not? The grand dame deserved it, its sitting room host to a flow of pilgrims who'd provided the farm's newfound stability.

For the time being, Jason co-existed with Benjamin, Helena and her mother had reconciled, and Kailani seemed to be thriving. All that remained was for the tribunal to do the reasonable thing and turn permanent custody over to Jason and Helena. Perhaps, instead of going back to Albion Point, they'd raise her on the farm.

On the top step of the great house, Sebastian paused to kick the snow off his boots, and then gazed up, letting the sun warm his face. Monday, the first of March, a prelude to spring.

Once in his office, he set tea to brewing and settled into his high-backed chair. He'd just started skimming through the day's mail when his communicator buzzed.

"Good morning," he said.

There was a delay, as if the caller expected a more formal greeting. "Yes, may I speak to the person in charge?" The voice sounded tinny and official.

"That would be me. I'm Sebastian, managing director of the farm. Who's this?"

"My name is Henry Carlson. I'm a chief examiner for the Department of Separation."

Sebastian frowned. The next inspection wasn't until June and all the paperwork had been filed on time. The framed permits on his wall were current and in order. "What can I do for you, Mr. Carlson?"

"I have a matter I need to discuss. I'd like to set up a meeting."

"A meeting. Of course. We're always happy to meet with the department, but we're not due for an inspection for a few months. When would you like to meet?"

"I plan to come there tomorrow."

"Well, I don't think—"

"It has to be tomorrow."

"Very well, then." Sebastian hoped the chief examiner wouldn't notice the irritation in his voice. "Tomorrow it shall be. Could you give me some idea of—"

"It's about one of your residents."

"I'm sorry to hear that," he said, trying to buy time. "But can't we resolve it without meeting? We're a long way off the beaten path, and I'd love to save you the trip."

There was a pause, as if the chief examiner was tempted by the offer.

"No," he finally said. "I need to do this in person."

"Well, can you at least tell me which resident you're coming to visit?"

"I'm not coming for a visit."

Sebastian could hear a shuffling of papers, then anguish.

THE DAUGHTER OF THE SEA AND THE SKY

"It's about a girl you have staying there. Her name is... Kailani."

***

With the heel of his hand, Carlson rubbed the frost off the kitchen window of his tiny flat, the one he'd been exiled to after he and Miriam had divided the spoils. He peered through the cleared spot, checking the weather, then pulled on his driving gloves and headed out the door.

He settled into the seat of his sedan and arranged what he used to call the field trip essentials. He pulled a map from the storage compartment and folded it on the passenger seat so it displayed the first leg of his journey, then set his sunglasses on the dashboard in case the overcast burned off during the drive. He positioned his coffee in the center of the cup holder and started the engine. Before putting it into gear, he checked his communicator one last time.

Please let the trip be canceled.

No such luck. He groaned, yanked the shift lever, and pulled out of his designated space.

If all went well, four hours to go.

Less than ten miles from the city, he encountered a garden of cones on the highway, first blocking one lane and then another for no apparent reason.

Three hours passed before he finally came upon the first signs of country. In the old days, he'd often been sent north to provide security for diplomats meeting at the land bridge. He'd relished such trips back then, a diversion from the routine. Now that his retirement clock was ticking down, he preferred the routine.

His back ached whenever he had to drive for more than an hour. He arched his spine, stretching the muscles until his lower back stopped cramping, but there was no relief from the secretary's voice burning in his ears.

"How could you miss such an obvious resemblance, Carlson?"

"I'm sorry, Mr. Secretary. I thought it was a different girl."

"Aren't you people trained to look for details?"

"We are, but you gave so little information."

"The situation is sensitive."

"Yes, but—"

"No buts. You've been told all you need to know. Now get up there and bring the girl back. And if you screw up again, I swear I'll find reason to fire you for cause. Do I make myself clear?"

201

DAVID LITWACK

"I'll do my best—"

"Do I make myself clear?"

"Yes sir."

Fired for cause. Carlson knew what that meant—invalidation of his pension and loss of the peaceful retirement he'd earned after thirty-two years. All because he'd taken a risk to keep Kailani safe.

Yet given the chance, he'd do it again. It would have worked if not for the photogram.

The damned photogram.

How could Jason and Helena have allowed the child's image to be captured, much less posted on a public network? And the sanctimonious messages that accompanied it! What were they thinking? No wonder the department was all over Kailani—a blatant violation of her probation. Had he known, he would've made the trip to the farm just to reprimand them.

Now he had a better reason to go: not to save his pension, but for the little girl with the face of an angel. For whatever reason, the powers that be wanted her back. He needed to be with her for the handoff, to do what he could to ease her transition to the incarceration that likely awaited her.

If only the drive were shorter. If only his back didn't ache. If only the landscape he was heading into wasn't so bleak.

The road narrowed to two lanes and rolled with the terrain, forcing him to cut his speed in half. Beyond the mountains hung a gray and comfortless sky. The ribbon of black ahead showed little sign of life—no people, no wildlife, not so much as a sparrow on the power lines. The snow lay smooth on either side, with patches of blue ice where the wind had polished it clear, a sea of white and blue right to the edge of the pavement.

He passed a fenced-in field on the left that fronted a barn. A half dozen horses, a chestnut and five bays, stood out against the white background, their manes bobbing as they grazed where heat from the building had cleared a spot. Nearer the road, a dappled gray wandered in deep snow, almost invisible, stopping occasionally to paw at the ground, scratching away for a few blades of buried winter grass.

More fields, more barns, a shack in the woods, a shed filled with firewood, a post office, a fueling station, a general store, then repeat—passing like the days of his life.

THE DAUGHTER OF THE SEA AND THE SKY

He glanced at the map on the passenger seat, then back at the landscape, expecting to have reached Northweald by now. He tapped on the brake and checked his mirror before easing onto the shoulder and coming to a stop.

He opened the door and swung his legs around, letting the soles of his shoes land flat and dig into the snow. Then, careful not to slip, he stepped outside. It was cold—not January cold, but a more bearable March cold.

He extended his arms high over his head and yawned in a lungful of fresh air as he scanned the horizon. At the crest of the next hill, a plume of smoke rose. He slid reluctantly back into the driver's seat.

A minute later he turned into a fueling station nestled between two stands of trees.

A raw-boned boy in overalls sauntered out of the garage, wiping his hands on a greasy rag. "Fill 'er up, mister?"

Carlson eyed the gauge. "I think I'm okay. Can you tell me how to get to Glen Eagle Farm?"

The boy looked disappointed—no doubt customers were few and far between. "Glen Eagle. That's that place in Northweald."

"Yes, that's right."

"You coming from the south?"

He nodded.

"Overshot it by forty miles. The road to Glen Eagle takes a ninety degree turn at Westwood. Lots of people miss that turn."

Carlson grimaced. Forty miles, an hour's drive back.

The boy grinned at him, not condescending, just a friendly grin. "You going there to do artsy stuff?"

"Excuse me?"

"Heard it's an art colony. That what you do?"

He shook his head. "No, no, not me."

The boy finished wiping his hands, and studied his fingernails to check the results. "Didn't mean anything bad by it. I hear good things about that farm. They say sad folks go there and it seems to help somehow."

"I'm going on business."

"Business, huh? Well, maybe you'll get a chance to help someone too."

Carlson smiled. "Yes. Help someone. I may at that." He looked again at the gauge. "You know, on second thought, fill it up. You never can tell how many more wrong turns I'll make."

203

DAVID LITWACK

The boy grinned back at him. "Yes sir. Fill 'er up. Right away."

***

Sebastian had been waiting since lunch, leaving too much time to worry. He rechecked Kailani's papers—all in order. Perhaps the tribunal had been moved up. Or had the pilgrims bearing gifts violated some law? The department had become stricter and more secretive over the years, even as the threat from abroad waned. Who knew what crime they'd concocted for the girl from the enemy lands?

Finally, as the shadows began to lengthen, he received a call. Lots of traffic. A few wrong turns.

The chief examiner had sounded in no mood to be reasonable, so Sebastian kept the teapot with the cherubs hot, and himself in good humor while he paced the porch and waited. In the stillness of dusk, with no blanket of leaves to muffle the noise, he'd hear him coming a mile away.

Twilight was always his favorite time of day, but especially in winter, when the leaves were down and the mountains looked like picture-book cutouts in the crisp air. He stepped out from behind the plastic sheeting on the porch and moved to the edge of the lawn for a better view, as if getting closer would make the meeting occur sooner.

At last, the telltale sounds arrived: the car engine, the boards on the bridge, the tires squishing to a stop on the muddied parking lot.

Henry Carlson stepped out of the car, set his weathered briefcase down, and extended a hand. He was of similar height and build to Sebastian, but younger—they were all younger these days—and had weary eyes behind wire-rimmed bifocals. He looked unthreatening.

"You've had a long day," Sebastian said as he shook the man's hand.

"Such a long drive. I'm stiff and chilled to the bone."

"Would you like some tea? It'll help both the cold and the stiffness."

"I'd love some."

And so, following their perfunctory greeting in the parking lot, the two faced each other over tea in Sebastian's office.

Sebastian settled Mr. Carlson in one guest chair, while he took the other. No desk in between, a trick he'd learned from his business days. Use the desk to intimidate when they're looking for something from

THE DAUGHTER OF THE SEA AND THE SKY

you; otherwise, meet hat in hand as a supplicant. He was the supplicant this time and needed Mr. Carlson to be friendly, understanding, and to go away as quickly as possible.

A quick departure did not seem to be on the chief examiner's agenda. "I need to see the girl right away," he said.

"I'm afraid she's busy."

"Doing what?"

Sebastian spread his arms. "Working on crafts, heading to dinner. Something like that."

"I'm too tired for games, Sebastian."

"Games? You're the one who won't tell me what's going on. I'm responsible for her well-being and won't drag her in here without good reason."

The chief examiner broke off eye contact. "I also care... about her well-being."

Something odd seemed at work here, something Sebastian had never seen from an examiner: compassion.

He moderated his tone, suddenly unsure of the situation. "Then why don't you leave her be? She's doing so well here."

"I would if I could, but...." He took off his glasses and began cleaning them with a freshly pressed handkerchief, swirling the corners around each lens.

"But what?" After a long day of waiting, Sebastian's patience was wearing thin.

The examiner replaced the glasses and blinked twice. "But you denied me that option when you posted that photogram on the network."

Sebastian relaxed. "Ah, so that's it. Violated one of your rules. That photogram was the unauthorized act of one of our members. I'm sorry it happened, and I swear it won't happen again."

"I'm afraid this has gone well beyond apologies. I've been ordered to take her back."

Damn it. How could he let Kailani go back to prison because of Benjamin's quirk? "The photogram was published on my watch. Punish me if you have to. Levy a fine on the farm. But don't take Kailani away."

"I have no choice. Now this needn't be a problem. Just turn her over to me."

"She's not a problem, she's a child."

205

DAVID LITWACK

"I didn't mean to make this contentious, but you have to understand—"

"Understand what?"

The chief examiner took a sip of tea and winced when he realized it was still too hot. "That this problem—this child—is visible at the highest levels of the department."

Sebastian was primed for an argument, but the words made no sense. "You must be kidding."

"I'm afraid not."

"What could a child possibly have done to merit that kind of attention?"

Carlson looked away, focusing on the painting of the great house in winter as so many others had done when the discussion took an uncomfortable turn.

"I... don't... know," he said.

Sebastian stared at him. "You drove all the way up here to snatch the girl away and you don't know why?"

"I'm not high up enough to be privy to the whys of it, but I assure you the people involved are as high up as they come. They'll get what they want, one way or the other."

"What's that supposed to mean?"

"It means don't underestimate what they might do if you resist."

He slid to the edge of his seat. "Are you threatening my farm?"

Carlson's head snapped back. "Don't get feisty, Sebastian. I'm only here to take the child back and ease her transition. I have no interest in your refuge for lost souls."

Sebastian jumped up as fast as his cranky knees allowed. Neither of them were big men, but he did his best to loom over the seated examiner. "A refuge for lost souls, are we? How could I expect a bureaucrat like you to understand what we do here? But here's something you can understand, Chief Examiner Carlson: the child was sent to this refuge by the tribunal along with her legal guardian. You're here by my invitation and have no right to barge in and order me around without a warrant. I'm not going to turn my youngest resident over to you in the middle of winter, in the dark of night, when you can't even tell me why you're taking her."

He bent down until their noses were inches apart. "Do I make myself clear?"

"Perfectly." Carlson raised his voice for that single word. It sounded far off and yet loud, like a bullhorn in a windstorm.

206

He stood and put on his jacket, shaking his head all the while. With the tip of his finger, he shoved his bifocals higher up the bridge of his nose, then regarded Sebastian through them.

"I'm sorry we can't work this out. You're making it more painful than you know." He walked to the door, but stopped and turned in the frame. "Goodbye, Sebastian. Thank you for the tea."

He opened the door and left, letting a chill into the great house.

Sebastian followed him onto the porch.

The chief examiner walked down the steps and crossed the lawn to his car. He set his briefcase on the ground and took the handkerchief from his pocket, wiped his hands and dragged it across his mouth, then pulled one glove on and the other, stretching each finger to its tip.

"I'll be back tomorrow," he said without looking up, "with a warrant."

He picked up his briefcase, ducked into the sedan, and drove off across the parking lot to the dirt road in no rush. The car maneuvered over the old bridge and made its way up the hill. The taillights disappeared and the sound of the engine merged with the noise of the highway.

CHAPTER 33

A CALL TO ARMS

Helena was finishing dinner with Kailani when someone tapped on her shoulder. She twisted around in time to see Sebastian fold his finger back against his chest as if he'd never intended to touch her.

His face seemed pale, and his ears were twitching. "Hello, Helena."

She pointed to her mouth to show she was still chewing, then swallowed and took a drink before replying. "Hello, Sebastian."

"Lovely evening, isn't it?" His expression said otherwise.

She stared at him and then past him, searching for a reason for the visit.

He turned to Kailani. "And a good evening to you."

Kailani was chewing too but had no qualms about answering with her mouth full. She shifted the food to one cheek so it bulged like a chipmunk and said, "Hi, Mr. Sebastian."

"Would you mind if I borrow Helena for a few minutes?"

She shook her head and went back to her meal.

Helena blinked and glanced at him sideways.

THE DAUGHTER OF THE SEA AND THE SKY

He extended the unused finger and beckoned. "Let's talk in my office."

"Now?"

"Oh yes. Now."

She swung around in her seat, gave Kailani a pat on the head, and followed him out the door.

They weren't ten paces from the barn before she jumped in front to block his way. "What's going on, Sebastian?"

He lowered his eyes. In the light streaming from the barn windows, Helena recognized that look — the expression people have when they're about to deliver bad news.

He sighed and said, "They've come to take Kailani."

"Who?"

"The department. A Mr. Carslon was here and wants to take her back."

A wave of dread rushed through her as it had the day the doctor told her about her father. "When?"

"Right away. He'd have her now, but I sent him away."

"He can't do that. It's not yet time."

"He's getting a warrant from the tribunal. We'll have no choice."

Sebastian told her about Carlson's visit, how the department analysts had uncovered the photogram, and how the highest levels of the department were involved.

She ground her teeth and her eyes flared. She was tired of mourning. "They can't have her. I won't let them take her away."

"Be reasonable, Helena."

"I'm done being reasonable. I made a promise." She swept past him to the great house, but stopped and whirled around. "And I won't break it this time."

***

Helena knew where Jason would be. With all the work Benjamin piled on him during the day, he needed to eat fast at dinner and then dash off to meet his Polytech obligations. At least if he hoped to get some sleep.

She hesitated at the doorway to his office, reluctant to storm in and disrupt his life again. This time saving Kailani would take more than committing to the farm. She cleared her throat, hoping he'd turn, but he was as focused as ever. She stepped back and rapped on the door jamb.

209

He swiveled around and smiled when he saw her. "What brings you to my lair?"

She forced a nervous laugh, but the words came rushing out. "They want to take her. Right now. Tonight."

Jason squared his shoulders and gave his full attention. "Slow down. What are you talking about?"

She folded her arms and hugged herself. "Carlson was here. He came to take Kailani back to the department. Sebastian turned him away, but he said he'd be back in the morning with a warrant."

Jason clicked to save his work, then stood and came toward her, appearing to move so slowly she wasn't sure he was getting close until she felt his touch on her arms. He pulled and she gave in, resting her cheek against his chest. At once she was back on the cliffs, on that summer day with an onshore breeze that cooled but did not chill.

After four heartbeats, she drew away. "Oh, Jason, what are we going to do? He'll be back for her tomorrow."

"A warrant, you said? From the tribunal?"

She could hear her father's voice. *Be reasonable, Helena.* Then she pictured Kailani in the oversized prison uniform, wasting away in a cell. This was beyond reason.

"I won't turn her over," she said.

"What if he found her family? What if he's sending her home?"

"That's not what he said. He said she's wanted by the department at the highest levels."

"She's nine years old. What in the name of reason could the highest levels want with her?"

"They found the photogram."

Jason gazed off into the distance as if replaying the night of the Northern Lights in his mind. "Dressed like a priestess and praying."

"And all the followers and messages—"

"Calling it a miracle and mythmaking. Even so, why at the highest levels?"

Helena felt the panic surge like lava seething in the pit of her stomach. She recalled what Jason had told her. "You said Benjamin called her a prophet, and he was in the Blessed Lands."

"And she claimed she came to save the soulless."

"What if she's one of their priestesses, as important as she claims to be? Oh, Jason, what will we do?"

THE DAUGHTER OF THE SEA AND THE SKY

He fell back a step. Only two feet separated them, but it felt like a chasm.

"There's something else," he said. "A message. Anonymous. No subject. I didn't want to upset you."

"What did it say?"

"'Beware,'" he said as she held her breath. "'There are those who would do her harm.'"

***

Later that evening, Helena sat on the steps of their cabin, waiting for Jason. As she stared down the darkened path, the dim light played with her mind. Phantoms swirled in the dark as they had in her childhood home when she was five years old. When her breathing became quick and uneven, she closed her eyes and tried to picture the three of them at the Knob. She could almost smell the salt air, and feel the sea breeze on her cheeks.

Then the breeze turned into a gale. Jason became paper thin, like a kite, and sailed off with the next gust. She became her mother, holding on with all her might to a little girl who'd become translucent as well.

Footsteps on the path prompted her to open her eyes. She expected to find Jason, but Benjamin stood before her instead.

"Is something wrong, Helena?"

She stared at him as if seeing him for the first time. He made her uncomfortable, but what if...?

When she remained silent, he made his little bow, turned sideways, and slipped past her down the path.

"Benjamin," she called after him.

He stopped.

"They've come to take her."

He came back and rested a bony hand on her shoulder.

"Take a deep breath, Helena, and then tell me what you're trying to say."

"The department was here. They want to take Kailani away." The words spilled out before she could control them. "I don't know what you do to make people come here, but The Daughter needs you now."

Benjamin sucked in a lungful of air and lowered his head; for an instant she thought he was praying. When he looked up again, his eyes were ablaze.

"Have no fear, Helena. I shall help."

211

CHAPTER 34

ENEMIES

Wednesday. 11:00am. A caravan of cars rolled across the bridge and onto the sandy lot next to the lawn.

Sebastian was impressed. He'd figured they'd need at least a half day to get a warrant and muster the police.

Carlson led the procession in a bright new cruiser from Northweald. The other three cars were a mix from surrounding towns, some as far as twenty miles away, all they could gather in so little time. It might have been the biggest police action the Northern Kingdom had ever seen.

Carlson stepped out, followed by six burly policemen who formed a semicircle behind him, and waved the warrant. "Here it is, Sebastian, signed and sealed. Now I trust you'll cooperate and take us to the girl."

Sebastian blocked his path. "She'll need a few hours to get ready."

Carlson signaled to the policemen.

Sebastian called his bluff. "What are you going to do? Beat up an old man?"

Carlson ignored him. Two officers came forward, forming a wall while Carlson and the others passed around.

THE DAUGHTER OF THE SEA AND THE SKY

Sebastian tried to pry between them but it was like moving mountains. He sighed and stepped aside.

As the officers began to round the corner of the great house, Benjamin appeared leading seven young men with rakes and axes. They might've been a work detail but for their grim demeanor and the way they carried their tools, high up and threatening.

The lead policeman started toward them, but Carlson stepped in front and held up a hand. He turned to Sebastian, his brows asking the question.

Sebastian shrugged as if to say, "None of my doing."

Carlson glared at him. "I don't want trouble."

"Neither do I."

"Then in the name of reason, tell them to get out of the way."

Sebastian read the determination on Benjamin's face, a look he'd never seen before. His loyal assistant had disobeyed him only once. He suspected this would be the second time. "Let these officers pass, Benjamin. They have proper authorization."

The seven men fidgeted and shifted the farm implements from hand to hand, but not a one backed down.

Sebastian turned to the police detail. "Please, Mr. Carlson. No violence."

He watched the determination on Carlson's face evaporate. They stared at each other, mirror images, the same helpless look on both faces. After a minute, the chief examiner waved the officers back into their cruisers and they departed.

***

"If only I had more time, Mr. Secretary," Carlson pleaded into his communicator, the prior day's humiliation still fresh in his mind. "I know I can—"

"Time's not our friend, Carlson. You don't seem to appreciate the urgency of the situation."

"Perhaps, Mr. Secretary, if you shared more details about what's going on—"

"Enough! You don't have a need to know. Your job is to—" He was cut short by muffled voices in the background, as if someone had placed a hand over the transmitter. "Hold, Carlson. I have an incoming call from the President."

213

There was a click on the secure comm link, then music like something Carlson once heard in an elevator. He stretched the communicator as far from his ear as possible.

Following yesterday's confrontation, the secretary had rushed up a van full of field agents—the ones who dealt with terrorists, wore body armor, and carried automatic weapons. They arrived in the Northern Kingdom early Thursday morning. Carlson had urged them to keep a low profile, to stay out of sight and not incite the residents further, so they surveyed the farm from a distance, keeping watch through binoculars. They brought maps of the surrounding area, held meetings, and made marks on their maps.

He'd watched with horror as the planning progressed, exactly what he'd tried to avoid—taking Kailani by force. He imagined the frightened child being dragged from Helena's arms. The only chance to stop it was to plead his case to the secretary.

A second click. "Still there, Carlson? The heat is on. The President wants her turned over now. I have no choice but to—"

"But the girl!" Carlson brought the phone closer and gripped it so tightly his hand shook.

"Of course we'll do everything possible to protect the girl. She's the point of all this, but my men tell me there's been an influx of hooligans to the farm. We can't take any chances."

Carlson squeezed his eyes shut. The secretary was a political appointee, not a career professional. He'd lack sensitivity to the subtleties of the situation, focusing instead on the political ramifications. Carlson had never negotiated with someone so high up, but for Kailani's sake, he'd give it a try.

"If we act rashly, Mr. Secretary, the situation could easily escalate, causing an incident that might embarrass the President. I'm sure you wouldn't want that." He paused, letting the thought sink in. "I know the people involved. I can work with the managing director of the farm. If we give them time to think it over, this can be resolved peacefully. "

"What about the hooligans?"

"They're not hooligans, Mr. Secretary, just overeager young men trying to protect the girl. Our initial approach alarmed them and they overreacted."

Silence on the line. Carlson could hear asthmatic breathing on the other end. He waited.

THE DAUGHTER OF THE SEA AND THE SKY

"Very well, but you'd better not be screwing with me. You had a solid record before you messed up identifying the girl. I've always believed in trusting the man on the ground. I'll trust you... for now."

Carlson finally dared exhale.

The secretary wasn't finished. "Understand, my trust isn't open-ended. It's now Thursday, 6 p.m. Have her in department custody by Sunday noon. After that, we do it my way."

Click.

No further discussion. No music. The secure line had gone dead.

***

The day after Carlson had served the warrant was quiet, if Sebastian ignored the men in the trees who watched from a distance.

Then an influx of Benjamin's friends invaded. He'd permitted a few to enter as guests of the farm, but as their numbers increased, he tried to turn them away. There was no stopping them, as tents popped up on town conservation land to the east of the farm. They were within their rights. Besides, what could he do about it? Call the police?

The newcomers stood around and watched the men in the trees, who watched them back. It stirred memories that caused a tightening in his gut. He'd lived this scene before—a military encampment preparing for battle.

Friday morning, the situation worsened.

On his way to the office, he encountered a group of eight strangers, some carrying farm implements and others sports equipment—sticks and bats, anything that was hard and could be swung with force. The ragtag band seemed to be marching in a pattern, full of purpose.

"May I ask who you are and what you're doing on my farm?"

They stopped and shuffled their feet. The tallest, a gangly young man with a prominent Adam's apple, took a step forward. "We're a security patrol. Benjamin assigned us the eight-to-eleven shift."

"What eight-to-eleven shift?"

"Eight to eleven in the morning, eight to eleven at night."

"We drew lots," a second one said. "We're the lucky ones. Everyone else has to get up in the middle of the night."

"But why?"

DAVID LITWACK

They answered in a chorus. "To protect the Daughter."

***

As Helena led Kailani by the hand to breakfast—she always held her hand now whenever they were outdoors—she encountered a group of men marching in pairs from the great house to the barn.

When they caught sight of Kailani, they paused. Whispers passed among them with only two words audible: the Daughter. After a few seconds, they recovered their composure and made small, almost comical bows, then stepped off more smartly.

"Why are those men carrying rakes like that on their shoulders?" Kailani said.

"Just a work group to help clean up the farm."

"But what about the others, the ones carrying sticks?"

"Those aren't sticks. They're sports equipment like the kind you saw at Hal's."

"But what are they for?"

"To play games."

"And what do they do with them in the games?"

Helena wished Jason were there to take the next question. "They're used to hit balls."

"Why are they carrying them now?"

A deep sigh. There was no getting around it. "They're patrols Mr. Benjamin set up to keep you safe, to protect you from those men outside the gates."

"The men trying to hide in trees?"

"That's right."

Kailani looked down and began digging a little hole in the dirt with the tip of her shoe. "But why are the ones on the farm carrying equipment used to hit balls?"

"In case the people in the trees come inside."

"But what do sticks have to do with—"

Her ocean-blue eyes widened, and her mouth stayed open, unable to complete the thought. When Helena had no response, she yanked her hand away and dashed back to her cabin.

216

CHAPTER 35

ALLIES

It was hard to get away unnoticed, so Sebastian invented an excuse, telling everyone he was feeling ill and would be having dinner in his cabin. After a member of the kitchen crew brought food, and while most people were still at the barn, he put on his leather work boots and the parka with the fur-edged hood. Bundled up like that, he'd be hard to recognize in the dark. He considered bringing his walking staff, which might prove useful on this trek, but he decided against it—too distinctive a marker.

He snuck a look out the door to see if anyone was nearby, then stepped off down the path. At the statue of Grandmother Storyteller, he paused to adjust his clothing. He yanked the zipper of his parka higher so it nearly pinched the loose skin beneath his chin, and pulled his gloves tighter to make his wrists stop burning from the cold.

He jerked around as the sense of someone watching overwhelmed him. No one there. Just Grandmother Storyteller staring at him with her laughing eyes. A beautiful piece. He recalled Serena when she first came to the farm, the hole in her heart bare for all to see. He flashed a smile that mimicked Grandmother Storyteller's. All things of grace and beauty have their birth in pain.

The farm would have to survive.

Few residents knew the farm as he did. They came and went, but he remained, along with the old temple bell, the statues and the golden eagles, the constants of the farm. At the back of the pool, he shoved aside the branches of an overgrown bush and entered a back trail long unused, one Benjamin had stopped maintaining years before.

He tramped ahead across slush and frozen leaves and over an occasional downed tree, until he tripped on a twig, snapping it with a crack. He was able to keep himself upright only by grabbing a nearby sapling. He frowned, and his mouth inside the fur hood was set grimly. Foolish old man out alone in the dark; could've broken a hip and frozen to death.

Nearby, an owl flapped out of a tree, hooting its displeasure at being disturbed, leaving the bare treetop vibrating in the cold. The noise made him glance around at the world he would soon leave. He peered up at snatches of sky peeking through the branches and down at the ground sprinkled with frost. Then he watched the owl, following it until it flapped its way to the horizon and beyond.

A long time since he'd been down this trail, and in the intervening years his bones had become more brittle. Should've brought the staff. He proceeded now with more caution, stooping low to see the ground in the dim light, uncertain of each step. Maybe it was the cold, or maybe the circumstance.

At last, he came to the work road that ran along the adjoining horse farm. Fifty yards ahead, he could make out the outline of the chief examiner's sedan. As he emerged from the woods, the car door opened.

"I was worried you wouldn't come," Carlson said.

"I'm a little slower than I used to be."

"You look frozen. Come inside."

The car was cold. Carlson must've kept the engine off for fear of being discovered. At least Sebastian was out of the wind, and if they stayed long enough, their body heat would add a few degrees.

The cloud cover cleared just long enough for a moonbeam to pass through the windscreen and fall across the chief examiner's face. When Sebastian first met him, he'd violated one of his cardinal rules,

THE DAUGHTER OF THE SEA AND THE SKY

becoming angry at the situation and blaming the man. Now, he remembered Carlson's concern for Kailani and his reluctance to enforce the warrant. He may have misjudged him.

Carlson watched him shiver. "Should I turn on the engine?"

"No. Too risky."

"Better than getting pneumonia."

"I'll be okay."

Carlson fumbled with his briefcase, pulled out a quart-sized thermos and tilted it toward Sebastian. "Hot chocolate?"

"Thank you. That was thoughtful of you."

Carlson unscrewed the top and poured, peering over the plastic cup to check the level in the dim light. It made his bifocals steam.

Sebastian accepted the cup with both hands and sniffed the hot drink, recalling another night in a field long ago just prior to battle.

After securing the cover and tucking the thermos back into his briefcase, Carlson pulled out a woolen blanket, which he unfolded and laid over Sebastian's knees.

Sebastian pulled it to his chin and looked at the official from the department with fresh eyes. "Very thoughtful." He took two sips before speaking, placing an appropriate interval between manners and business. "Now, what can we do about this mess?"

Carlson glanced out the window as if checking for intruders, but more likely searching for words. When he spoke, his voice sounded pained. "When we first met, you said a bureaucrat like me could never understand what you do here. It made me angry and I misbehaved. I apologize. It's important to me that you know I care about Kailani. I'm the one who arranged for her to come to the farm."

He paused, waiting for a response. Sebastian nodded, but it didn't seem to satisfy him.

"I have... a daughter of my own," he said, his voice more urgent. "You have to believe I wouldn't wish Kailani harm."

"If that's true, we can be allies, because we want the same thing."

"It's true," the chief examiner said. "But it's important to me that you believe it."

Sebastian weighed his thoughts before replying. "I believe you." When the ensuing silence grew awkward, he added, "So what can we do to rescue her?"

"You have some hotheads, Sebastian, more every day. And my orders come from so high up, I can hardly conceive of it. They don't tell me much — no *need to know* — but I'm sure of one thing: Kailani will be returned to the department one way or another."

"Is that a threat?"

"No, it's a fact."

"But why?"

"It's way above my pay grade. They won't tell me anything more."

"If that's the case, how can you expect me to *do* more?"

"Sebastian, please."

"Not unless I know what they intend to do with her."

The chief examiner slumped in his seat, as if his head had become too heavy for his neck.

Sebastian began to sense the burden he carried. He watched the puffs of breath coming from their lips, fogging the car windows.

Carlson righted himself. "I can tell you what I think they'll do, based on more than thirty years at the department. As long as you understand it's only a guess."

"Go ahead."

The chief examiner took a deep breath, steeling himself like a soldier about to rush into battle. "Kailani will be sent to a rehabilitation center to be retrained. She's willful and old enough to have been indoctrinated by her countrymen — I'm sure you've seen that for yourself. It will take a while. During that time, she'll be well cared for. She won't be abused, but she'll stay there until she's assimilated to our ways."

"Assimilated how? In what way will they change her?"

"She'll stop believing in myths and learn to trust reason. In short, the sense of wonder that has... enchanted us all will diminish. She'll no longer believe she's the daughter of the sea and the sky."

"She's just a child, Carlson. How can they treat her that way?"

"I don't know. Maybe in our pursuit of reason, we've become as unreasonable as the other side."

Sebastian removed his gloves, rubbed his hands together, and blew into them. "I'm seventy-eight years old, and the older I get, the less impressed I am by reason."

"I may be starting to agree with you." Carlson puffed out three clouds of breath. "But I'm certain of one thing: she doesn't belong with your hotheads any more than she belongs with those troopers. Or worse, caught between the two. Please, Sebastian, hand her over to me before something terrible happens. Hand her over and I'll do my utmost to make sure she's treated well."

THE DAUGHTER OF THE SEA AND THE SKY

Sebastian raised the steaming cup, but stopped halfway to his lips and stared into it. Too little information, too much at stake. "That won't be easy."

"I didn't expect it would be, but consider the alternative."

He suddenly understood what the chief examiner had been trying to tell him. He shivered more from the conclusion than the cold. If Benjamin and his cohorts continued to resist, those higher up could shut down the farm.

"How long have you been at the farm?" Carlson said, as if he'd read his mind.

"Twelve years. Since my wife died."

"I'm sorry. I didn't know."

"It was a long time ago," he said, though it felt like yesterday. He raised the cup, took a sip, and swallowed. "Now all I have left is the farm. What can I... what can *we* do together to save the farm and make things easier for Kailani?"

"The problem is, we have only until Sunday noon. After that, it'll be out of my control. Can you cool down your hotheads by then?"

"I can try."

Carlson removed the glove from his right hand, fumbled in his pocket, and pulled out a card. "Here's my private number. Call me when you're able to transfer Kailani. I'll meet you here, same spot. Make sure it's after dark, and don't wait too close to the deadline."

Sebastian grimaced. "What if I can't?"

"Then you'll be dealing with the Secretary of the Department. He's a political appointee and heavy-handed. I'm afraid to think what he'll do, but if we work together, we can avoid that." Carlson extended his bare hand. "Agreed?"

Sebastian regarded Carlson, a good man beneath his official veneer, a decent man, not always right but doing his best. Like him.

He reached out with a firm grip and received the same in kind.

They were both guessing, trying to do what was right. The earth beneath him seemed suddenly insubstantial. Only one thing remained that he could rely on—the warmth of this handshake—but as he stared out the window at the moonlit field, he felt like the owl in the darkness, flying off to the horizon.

CHAPTER 36

TALK OF WAR

Friday morning, Helena clutched the arms of Sebastian's guest chair and tried to moderate her breathing. The light of dawn had barely flickered above the treetops when the managing director's sealed note had arrived. It said she and Jason needed to come right away, that the meeting was most urgent and they should tell no one. Jason had already left for his morning run, and she had to chase him down as he was doing stretches beneath the sentinel tree. He changed out of his running clothes, and they hurried arm in arm to the great house, clinging to each other as if afraid the meeting might split them apart.

Now Sebastian was going about his tea ritual with his usual maddening precision. He laid out three saucers in a row and tipped their cups upright, setting them softly in place as if he feared the least clink might make them shatter.

Helena made an effort to relax her grip and allow the blood to flow into her fingers. She'd been this way since childhood, too intense and ready to fight but always too cautious to pick a battle. This time, let caution be damned.

THE DAUGHTER OF THE SEA AND THE SKY

She glanced at Jason as he glared at Sebastian. His jaw was set, and his patience was wearing thin.

"What the hell's going on?" Jason finally said. His voice sounded high-pitched, like the strings of an instrument too tightly tuned.

What the hell, indeed. Benjamin's patrols were strutting about the farm while armed agents in camouflage spied on them from the trees. Now Sebastian had summoned the two of them for this meeting. What plot was he hatching?

Sebastian abandoned the tea cups and settled into his high-backed chair. His eyes sagged at the corners, and the weight of his years showed. "Truth is, I'm not sure what's going on. All I know is there are powerful people who want to take Kailani away, Benjamin's zealots who want to stop them, and a little girl caught in between."

"And?" Helena said.

"And the powerful people will win in the end... as they always do."

"Where will they take her?"

"I can't say for sure, but we're all people of reason and grounded in reality. We've watched Kailani these past few months, spouting mythmaker wisdom and breaking our laws. She's such a delightful child that we ignored the problem. After all, she was safe at our little farm, tucked away from the world. What harm could there be? But now the world has come to us. Where will they take her? I'm sure you can surmise."

Helena sucked air in between her teeth and grimaced at Jason. The warning he'd received resounded in her mind. *There are those who would do her harm.* "But we can't let them—"

"Doesn't matter, Helena. If the department wants her, the department will get her. These are people who control the law. These are people with armies. If we resist, there'll be trouble, not just for Kailani but for the farm." Sebastian made a steeple with his fingers and stared at them through it. "May I speak in confidence?"

"I thought you were already being honest with us," Jason said.

"Please, Jason, I can't do this without your help, but I need you to keep what I'm about to tell you secret. There are people around the farm who are... unpredictable. If word of what I'm about to tell you gets beyond that door—"

"It can't be *that* serious."

"Your generation has never been to war. I have. Trust me, it's that serious."

223

DAVID LITWACK

Helena suppressed a shudder. "What do you want from us?"

Sebastian told them about the plan he and Carlson had concocted to turn Kailani over. The chief examiner had promised to keep her safe and do whatever he could to ease her transition, but it required sneaking her away by Sunday noon.

While Helena listened in stunned silence, he tried to close the deal. "Can I count on you?"

She slumped in her chair. "I don't know who to trust anymore."

"I know how you feel, but at Sunday noon, control moves to a giant bureaucracy, built generations ago for a single purpose—to keep the Republic safe from zealots. In their great, all-seeing eye, Kailani is just another dangerous zealot who must be quarantined like a virus to keep the rest of us safe. I'm concerned for her and wish I could do more. I'm also worried we'll lose the farm. Most of all, I'm terrified someone will get killed. Trust me, there's no better choice. For reason's sake, help me let her go."

"How is it reasonable to send her to a fate she doesn't deserve?"

"You're being melodramatic. We're not savages. The rehabilitation center isn't a prison. It may be rough for a while, but in the end, she'll have a better life here than she'd have in the Blessed Lands."

"So you're asking us to not only trust you but the department? I can't do that, Sebastian. I made a promise to keep her from incarceration. I broke my promise to my father. I won't break this one."

Sebastian twiddled his fingers but kept his eyes locked on her. He was calculating, trying to find a way out.

Helena braced for his next onslaught.

"I understand," he finally said, "how much your father's death has grieved you. But with all respect, this is not about your father."

"Not about my father?" She leaned in and gripped the edge of the desk. "How could you know what I went through?"

"How could I...?" Sebastian's professional demeanor vanished. He blinked furiously and his hands began to shake. "Do you think you're the only one to watch someone die? I watched my Lizzie die for eight months, slipping from the woman I loved to a shell of herself. Near the end, I never left her but once—once, when she was too weak to call me from the next room. So I went to buy a bell—Lizzie's bell—but by the time I came back, she was hardly breathing. Then she took that one last gulp of air—"

He broke off eye contact and turned to the bay window instead, like he was hoping to see Lizzie come waltzing through the morning gloom.

THE DAUGHTER OF THE SEA AND THE SKY

Helena studied him in profile, the crumpled brow, the pale lips pressed tightly together as if to hold in the pain. The look of a mourner. He did know. He knew how strange a thing it is to watch someone die, to watch so long that death begins to make more sense than dying. And still, he stayed by her side.

When he looked back, his eyes pleaded with them. "For Kailani's sake, for you and Jason, for all those who have benefited from the farm... don't let your father's death cloud your reason. Nothing you can do will bring him back."

He was right. Nothing she could do would erase the fact of her father's death. Even so, that didn't mean....

She glanced past Sebastian to the narrow table and the flowerpot with the orchid growing in it. The face in the flower had changed. Now she saw a macabre clown, no longer laughing but mocking her: *Such a good girl, Helena, always doing what's expected of you, always being reasonable.*

Her mind recoiled. Sebastian had given up, but she'd find a way to save Kailani. If she had to be reasonable, she'd use reason to find that way.

"Let's say we agree," she said carefully. "How do you propose we get her out of the farm?"

"I need your help to slip her past Benjamin's men and take her to Grandmother Storyteller. Behind the statue, there's an overgrown path that leads to a dirt road heading north to the highway. Jason knows that road — it's where he runs."

Helena's heart began to race. *A path out of the farm? A road heading north?* She counted to three to slow herself down, and measured every word. "You win, Sebastian. It sounds like we have no choice. When's the latest we can hand her over? I want all the time I can get with her."

Jason turned, eyes questioning.

She cast a glance back, a look she knew he'd recognize, a secret code they'd used since childhood. *Trust me.*

"Before dawn Sunday," Sebastian said. "For safety's sake, she should be transferred in the dark. That'll give you tomorrow to make your goodbyes."

"How about an hour before sunrise?"

"An hour before sunrise, it is. I'll make the arrangements with Carlson."

Sebastian stood and went to the teapot, where he finally poured a cup for each of them. Then he reached for Lizzie's bell, a ritual to seal

225

the deal. He raised the bell, poised to ring it, but hesitated, regarding Helena curiously. After a second, he set it down, raised a cup instead, and took a sip of tea. His eyes never left hers.

When she could bear his stare no longer, she forced a nod. As she finished the gesture, she felt a prickling at the nape of her neck. Was that a door creaking? Surely she'd shut it when they came in.

She spun around. The door stood ajar, the narrowest of cracks showing.

No one there. Just her imagination running wild.

***

Jason remained quiet all the way back to the cabin, but Helena could tell his mind was churning.

Once inside, he stepped back from her and spoke. "What was that all about?"

She smiled at him, then closed the gap between them and pressed her lips to his. She felt her blood surge, the thrill of being close to him, the excitement of life reborn.

When they separated, he stared at her and wrinkled his brow. "What are you up to?"

"You know that adventure you were searching for when we were little? How you always told me to take a chance?"

He waited, and then nodded.

She lifted a hand to his cheek. "Now may be the time."

CHAPTER 37

A STATE OF SIEGE

When a knock came at the door, the secretary glanced up from his paperwork and scowled. He'd ordered his assistant to block all interruptions, hoping to finish by noon and make an early getaway for the weekend. The knocking became more insistent, a drumbeat impossible to ignore. He removed his glasses and checked the red numerals on the clock: 10:15 a.m. He grunted a response, and his aide barged in.

What now?

When the newly elected President had offered him the job, his first instinct was to decline. He'd put in his time, forty-two years starting at the bottom, building businesses the old-fashioned way with long hours, hard work and attention to detail. Now, at this stage of his life, he'd earned the right to take things easier. His interest in politics had always been self-serving, a way to protect his business interests, but the President was a hard man to turn down. He said the leadership of the department had become ceremonial, unlikely to be a burden. No crises had occurred in a generation.

Suddenly, the secretary had been thrust into the middle of an international incident, both crisis and opportunity. There'd been rumblings of change among the zealots, intelligence reports on the rise of a new generation of leaders. Limited contact had been made through back channels, and suddenly, Supreme Leader to President.

He'd been impressed by the Minister of Commerce, not what he'd expected from the other side, an educated man, earnest but practical. The story about this... daughter of the sea and the sky seemed farfetched, but in their meeting he'd recognized an impressive sincerity in the man across the table. He was either a great actor or telling the truth. No matter. The President's orders were clear: find the girl as discreetly as possible and return her to the Blessed Lands.

Simple enough—or so he thought. No one slipped though the borders anymore, and his department kept impeccable records. If the girl had landed, she'd be found, but he hadn't anticipated problems with his own people. Things were moving too slowly, and pressure from the President was building.

He sat up straight, reaching behind to adjust the custom-shaped pillow that supported his bad back, and accepted the folder from his aide. He scanned its contents. Progress had been made; a deal had been struck with the manager of the farm. The girl was to be turned over as demanded. Still, something smelled. Why wait till Sunday morning? Why not turn her over right away? Progress? Perhaps.

He hadn't succeeded in business for forty-two years by trusting his adversaries. He'd learned to take no chances.

He removed his reading glasses and glared at his aide. "Get me the director of internal security ASAP."

***

Friday, before dinner, as Sebastian finished up in his office he heard a ruckus coming from in front of the great house. He went to the foyer and approached the door, reached for the knob but stayed his hand. Instead, he brushed aside the lace curtain and peeked through the window.

Several dozen of Benjamin's friends had gathered on the lawn, gawking at a scene across the bridge. At the far side, the entrance to the farm had been blocked by a phalanx of department agents in riot gear. They looked like modern-day gladiators, muscular and menacing with

THE DAUGHTER OF THE SEA AND THE SKY

black shields, black flak jackets, and black helmets barely visible in the dim light of dusk. Only their faceplates reflected the setting sun, creating the illusion of floating heads—a hundred or more. Behind them stood a squadron of armored vehicles with domed turrets on top, their guns pointing at the great house.

How had it come to this? Strangers everywhere, troopers readying for battle, zealots eager to fight for their cause, and all the good people who'd benefited from the farm. Would it all be lost?

He staggered back to the office. The scheme he'd concocted with Carlson was on shaky ground, and he feared Helena might hatch some schemes of her own, unaware of the consequences of her choice. What if she refused to go along? The unreasonable show of force confirmed what Carlson had suspected: the secretary would be granting no reprieve.

He groped for alternatives, running through the litany that had served him so well over the years: gather data, lay out options, plan ahead. All that came to mind was a more ominous maxim: be prepared for the worst.

He stared out the bay window at the events swirling out of control. He was too old for this. His was an age when an unpleasant surprise meant a call to attend the funeral of an old friend—he even had a dark suit and a pair of dress shoes set aside for the occasion. He'd dutifully follow the hearse to the cemetery, stand over the open grave, and watch the casket lowered into the ground. Increasingly, as he smelled the moist earth and listened to the thud of shovelfuls of dirt landing on the coffin, he'd dwell on his own mortality, how one day soon these very thoughts would vanish from the world, apparently forever.

After Lizzie died, he'd dabbled with religious beliefs. Now, much closer to his death than his birth, it seemed like the Spirit should be foremost in his mind. Yet he clung to this world even more. Each morning, as he stepped from his cabin to discover he was still alive, the taste of the cold seemed sweeter, the smell of the pines much stronger. Each successive sunset seemed more spectacular, the texture of its colors more vivid. He studied the faces of farm members more closely, recounting their stories in his mind. Most of all, he wondered if the farm would survive.

He turned away from the scene outside to look at the more peaceful portrait of the great house in winter. He couldn't take his eyes off it, afraid of what new surprise he might find if he looked away.

He'd bounced back from the edge of despair twice before, following the war and after Lizzie died. He was too old to bounce back again.

CHAPTER 38

LOST AND FOUND

After dinner Friday evening, Jason tried to focus on his work, but was distracted by Benjamin's men shouting catcalls at the armed horde on the far side of the lawn. There'd be no respite from the crisis. Sunday's deadline loomed and with it, the need for a decision on Helena's plan.

He recalled Kailani thrashing about in the icy waters off Albion Point. At that moment, as he towed her back to shore, he thought he'd do anything to save her. When he was younger, he'd been a risk taker, always ready for an adventure. Why not now?

His thoughts were interrupted by the roar of a generator starting up, followed by a pale light streaming through the hallway. The catcalls grew louder. He rose from his chair and went to the front door to see what was going on. No surprise. As darkness settled in, the besieging force had illuminated the lawn, creating a brightly lit no man's land. Without the cover of darkness, Benjamin's men had retreated to the front steps of the great house to continue their chants.

THE DAUGHTER OF THE SEA AND THE SKY

Jason stomped back to the office, unable to watch anymore. When he arrived at his desk, he found a new message waiting on the encomm screen. It glared at him in bold letters bordered in red. Highest priority.

Jason-Adams. Comply with the Department of Separation and surrender the girl. Failure to comply will result in immediate termination.

Apparently, the department's reach extended even to Polytech management. The powers of reason were all aligned against them.

Helena's plan was irrational. If they were caught, Kailani would be imprisoned, and the two of them as well.

"Madness," he muttered as he grabbed the pointer to delete the message.

"Why are you talking to the screen, Jason?"

His hand froze. He spun around to Kailani standing in the doorway, still as the air before a storm and just as somber. He turned back long enough to hide the message and darken the screen.

"How long have you been there?"

"Long enough," she said.

"What are you doing here? Where's Helena?"

"I snuck away." She twirled a strand of hair around her finger. "Helena's been acting strange lately, and she won't tell me what's going on. Will you tell me, Jason?"

He took a runner's breath and invited her in.

She came at once and settled on his lap.

"How'd you get away?"

"It's a secret."

"You can tell me. I won't let anybody know besides Helena."

"Promise?"

"Promise."

"There's a window over my bed. No one thinks of it because it's so small, but I can fit through. That is... if I have any place to go." She glanced down, studying his knee.

"Are you all right, Kailani?"

She released the strand of hair and looked at him with her ocean-blue eyes.

"First, I was happy here. Then Mr. Benjamin told me you'd be destroyed if I didn't talk to the people who came. So when the people came, I talked to them. It seemed to make them feel better, and that made me feel good. Then the men with guns came and Mr. Benjamin's friends started

231

marching around with sticks. Now Helena won't let me play in the labyrinth or go anywhere by myself—and she squeezes my hand too hard."

"She's trying to keep you safe."

"Safe? Is that why those men are here? To hurt me?"

"No. They're not—"

"Then why are they here?"

He hesitated to tell her, but she had a right to know. "They're here to take you back."

"Back where? To the Blessed Lands? I can't go back yet."

"Why not?"

"I haven't finished my penance."

"It doesn't matter. I don't think it's to the Blessed Lands."

"Then where? Not the...."

She reached for the encomm screen and let her fingertips glide over its surface, then grasped the pointer and shook it. When the screen brightened, she clicked here, there, everywhere as if trying to find the hidden message.

Gently, he took the pointer out of her hand.

She spoke without looking at him. "What does termination mean, and why were you mad at the screen?"

The answer stuck in Jason's throat. He waited, listening, irrationally hoping for advice from on high. All he heard was the heater fan kicking on, muffling the shouts coming from the porch.

Then a new sound: footsteps thumping down the hallway, coming fast. A sound like booted troopers running. He was relieved when Helena and her mother burst in.

"Here you are," Helena said.

Kailani pressed closer to him. "It's all right. I came to visit Jason."

"Don't you ever run off like that again. Do you have any idea how much you scared us?"

Kailani slipped off his lap and went to her, but stopped an arm's length away. "Jason will be terminated if you don't send me back."

"Who told you that?"

"I saw it on the screen."

Helena's lips stretched into a thin, bloodless line. After a moment, she turned to her mother. "Please take Kailani to her cabin. Jason and I need to talk."

Martha placed an arm around Kailani's shoulder and began to lead her away.

THE DAUGHTER OF THE SEA AND THE SKY

Before they reached the hallway, Helena called out to them. "Kailani?"

"Yes."

"Would you like to go back to the Blessed Lands?"

The little girl stared at her shoe tops. "Only if my penance is complete."

Jason came forward and knelt close to her. With one finger, he lifted her chin until their eyes met. "Why do you need to do penance before you go home?"

Her ocean-blue eyes glistened. "Because... I've done something terribly wrong."

Then she grasped Martha Brewster's hand and led her out of the great house.

Chapter 39

As Simple as Stones

Saturday dawned, and despite the swirl of events, Jason stayed committed to his morning run. It gave him time alone, away from things too complex to understand. He pressed his hands against the bark of the sentinel tree, leaned forward and stretched. As he came closer to the ground, he could make out tracks left in the frost by Sebastian's little creatures—bird claws and rabbit paws and a larger set of markings that might have been a raccoon.

When a wedge of light spread across the tracks, he turned to find its source and caught the curtains of Kailani's window being pushed aside. *What's she doing up so early?*

Two of Benjamin's guards dozed under blankets on the steps by her locked door.

Jason switched to his hamstring stretch, spreading his legs and lowering his palms until they brushed the frost. This time he shifted his position to watch the back wall of Kailani's cabin, the wall with a window only a child could slip through.

THE DAUGHTER OF THE SEA AND THE SKY

As he stretched, hidden in the shadows, he saw the window swing outward.

A moment later, Kailani slipped through and dropped to the ground.

What is she up to?

She'd sailed a boat alone across the ocean and nearly drowned herself in the tide. Was it possible she'd try to run off alone through the wilderness?

He gave her time to get a bit ahead, and then followed.

She turned down the familiar path, not toward the farm's entrance where the department agents awaited, but toward Grandmother Storyteller, the labyrinth and the Spirit Hill. She made no apparent effort to be stealthy but made almost no sound. Separated by no more than a hundred yards, she seemed weightless before him, her footfalls whispering across the frozen ground.

She stopped at the rock with the word "Reflection" carved in it, traced the letters with her finger, and entered the shelter. Jason turned sideways behind a tree trunk and watched as she pulled something from her pocket, a message attached to a string, and stretched as high as she could to hang it from one of the saplings.

She stared at it until it stopped spinning, then strolled back down the path with more spring to her step. He followed until she climbed back into the window of her cabin and the light inside blinked out.

He took off at a sprint, now running with a purpose. He'd come to know the hole in Helena's heart and had found his own as well. But what about Kailani? Was she just a salve for everyone else's wounds, or did she have a wound of her own? In a fraction of the time it had taken to follow her, he arrived back at the shelter.

Above his head hung totems—colored beads, a cheesecloth bag of spices, a paper plate painted with a face in its center, the old foam cup, and anything that could bear a message. He fumbled through the notes, most of them crinkly and dog-eared, searching lower down for a fresh one at the height a nine-year-old could reach.

As he groped about in the gray morning light, a feather grazed his cheek—Kailani's eagle feather, its quill stuck through the top of a note. He steadied the paper, twisting it until it faced the sunrise and he could read the words.

To the wind. I miss you. I'd go where you dwell, take your place if I could, so you can return to the sea and the sky. But you're gone for good. And now the sea and the sky have forsaken me.

DAVID LITWACK

*To the sea. I'm sorry I'm such a disappointment to you. Maybe
you expected too much, saw more in me than I was. Forgive me.*
*And to the sky. If only I could heal your pain so you could find
a way to love me again.*

The note slipped from Jason's fingers, paper and feather fluttering
in the breeze like a butterfly on a string.

***

After leaving the Reflection shelter, Jason went for a long run. He
jogged down the path to the horse farm and followed the dirt road,
farther than he'd ever gone before. At its end, he stayed in the shadows
until a truck lumbered by, then crossed the highway and explored the
far side. He searched until he caught a break in the trees, the poorly
marked start of a trail.

When he'd seen enough, he turned back and took off, sprinting
until his calves ached and his lungs burned, until exhaustion drove
thought from his mind. As he ran along the road, he saw only the edges
of the trees, their outlines blurred as though at the point of dissolving.
He heard only his own breathing and the pounding of his shoes on the
path. As far as his eyes and ears could tell, the rest of the world had
vanished without leaving a shadow or whisper behind.

***

Later that afternoon, he sat at his desk and stared at the screen,
accomplishing nothing. Finally he logged off and headed back toward
Kailani's cabin.

It was dinner time. He watched as Benjamin's guards brought
trays, and waited until the trays were removed. By that time, the sun
had dipped low on the horizon, scattering rays of light between the
branches. He hesitated, uncertain. Then at once, he leapt to the porch,
taking all three stairs in a single stride.

He announced his presence with knocks so hard, his knuckles
stung from the cold.

Helena opened the door.

"Come with me," he said.

She glanced back to where Kailani sat slumped on her bed. "Now?"

"These men can watch her."

THE DAUGHTER OF THE SEA AND THE SKY

She checked with Kailani, grabbed a warm jacket, and followed him out the door.

He led her down the path past Grandmother Storyteller, with no word or touch between them until they reached the stone that marked the entrance to the Reflection shelter.

"This way," he said, and she followed him inside.

She read the note, once, twice, three times, but said nothing.

From there, they tramped along in the near dusk to the trail between the knee-high boulders, and hiked up the path to the Spirit Hill.

All about them lay the ravages of winter, broken branches and debris and at one point, a dead tree that had fallen across the path. Jason offered to help her over, but she declined. Finally, when they were halfway up and the steepness had increased, she reached out and grasped his hand.

By the time they reached the top, the orange ball of the March sun was a thumb's width from the horizon. They had just settled on the bench with the lion face on top when Helena stood up as if she'd forgotten something. She fumbled on the ground until she found three stones, and then placed them in a row between them.

"For you," she said as she set the first stone. "For Kailani, and for me."

Jason gazed out, trying to think where to begin. Beyond the woods, the mountains stretched out, row upon row, dark blue fading into grays and then merging with the haze of the sky.

After a minute, he turned to her. "If only it were as simple as stones."

"It *is* simple," she said. "We both know what to do."

"Are you sure you're ready to embrace blind faith in the Spirit?

"As ready as I've been to have blind faith in reason. What if both sides make myths? They make myths of their god. We make a god of reason. Most of us are just trying to find our way in life, and that's hard enough. Does it matter so much where we live? Not as long as Kailani's safe, and you and I are together."

"What if they're all like Benjamin?"

"They won't be."

"How do you know?"

"Because *they* sent him back. More likely they'll be like Kailani." She took his hands in hers and squeezed. "The hell with reason, Jason.

237

My father taught me to do what was right, not what was simple. What's right is to take her home."

He stood and wandered to the edge of the trees, as if walking into the setting sun. Helena came up behind and rested a hand on his shoulder, and together they stared down the trail they'd climbed just moments before. In the waning light of dusk, it looked like a tunnel with only darkness at its end.

He turned to face her. "We should go. It's getting hard to see."

"Not until we decide. The deadline's tomorrow."

A gust of wind kicked up, rattling tree limbs and twigs on the ground, a bleak and lonely sound. Jason pressed his eyelids shut and tried to sort through the images flowing through his mind, sketches of memories past.

He saw himself as a young boy, walking Helena home along the cliffs. He saw the classroom where they'd first met, recreating the scene in detail. Helena sat by the open window, back straight, eyes trained on the teacher. He could still trace the curve of her neck as he watched, hoping she'd turn for an instant and notice him.

He saw the blackboard in front with its partially erased text and the broken pieces of chalk on its ledge. He could smell the chalk dust and the scent of flowers in the vase on the teacher's podium. He could see the world map behind the podium showing the land bridge, with the asylum gate and the statue of the Lady of Reason blown out in exaggerated size.

The image flickered and changed. A different one formed in his mind, the poster of a firefly newly set free, a young girl holding an empty jar, one arm extended, fingers parted as if to recapture possibilities lost.

He grasped Helena by the arms.

Her brows lifted, and she stood balanced in the moment. One hand stretched out to touch him, the fingertips almost reaching to his cheek.

He nodded, a quick okay. Then he took her hand and led her down the darkened path back to Kailani's cabin.

CHAPTER 40

A TRAILER IN THE WOODS

The Minister of Commerce paced the confines of the trailer. The government of the soulless had sent it here, to this cold and faraway spot near the land bridge, a place to await Kailani's return. The trailer was wide enough for a bed and a desk, with a two-foot walkway in between. A recreational vehicle, they called it, but he enjoyed no recreation in it, just the constant pacing and a mood swinging between hope and despair.

They'd provided him with pen and paper, and a courier waiting outside, so he could transact business and keep occupied.

And send for the poetess when he was sure of the child's return.

Now, at last, the word had come. She was safe and would be on her way, but there was some delay, a procedural matter. He'd complained bitterly. To be so close — why did he have to wait? The diplomats assured him she'd be returned no later than Sunday. Still, the question remained: was it time to tell the poetess?

How shattered she'd looked the evening before he left, hunched over the railing of their lanai, leaning out over the valley as if trying to touch the desert below.

DAVID LITWACK

She kept her back to him as she spoke. "It's my fault she's gone."

"Moving to the mainland was *our* decision. We couldn't know how she'd respond." He touched her on the arm, trying to make her face him.

She pulled away. "That's not why she ran off."

"You mustn't—"

She silenced him with a slash of her hand. "We had words the night before. I told her it was time to take responsibility and move on, forgetting she was a child and that her pain was as great as mine. I added my misery to hers."

"You're being too harsh on yourself."

"Too harsh?" She turned, her face pale and drawn. "She'd always been strong-willed, needing the last word, but that night, she said nothing and walked away. Now she's gone, maybe forever."

Gone forever? Not if the leaders of the soulless were true to their word. He crossed the final steps to the desk and stared at the blank sheet of paper waiting for him. Beside it lay an envelope, addressed and ready to go. He pressed his palms together in front of his chest as if praying, then gradually raised them until his fingertips brushed his lips. He could feel the warm whisper of his breath.

He backed away and strode past the desk to the door, thought to go out into the chill air to clear his head, but stopped when he remembered the guards posted there. He was no prisoner, but he'd need to explain himself to their officials. How would he tell these strangers that he wanted to be alone in the snow-crusted woods, to feel the wind on his face, to envision a face surrounded by golden hair—two faces really, one young and one older—to remember it all, the joy and the pain. How to explain that?

He stepped back to the desk and with a single motion, graceful for a man his size, slid the chair back and sat down.

He should have anticipated how they'd respond. Their bureaucracy was no different from his own. They knew he was a top official from the other side, a progressive, sympathetic with their thinking, close to the Supreme Leader.

And demanding the return of a person of importance.

They'd never let such a request pass, as they said in this country, "below the radar." As his own government would have done, they overreacted and sent an army.

For some reason he could not fathom, the people of this settlement in the wilderness were reluctant to let her go. According to the

240

diplomats, the residents of the farm loved her and were trying to protect her until they were sure she'd be treated well. Three generations after the treaty, they remained suspicious.

Having been instrumental in breaking the impasse between worlds, he understood.

Now, men with body armor and guns surrounded the settlement, and though their diplomats said the situation was under control, he worried. Would his sin of falsehood come back to haunt his dreams?

Time to tell the poetess? She wanted certainty, but some risk remained. He was certain of only two things: Kailani was alive, and not far away.

He grabbed the pen and let his thick hand hover over the paper. He waited, picturing the two faces, one young and one older, both beloved by him.

He began to write, forming each letter in his well-practiced script.

My dearest poetess.

CHAPTER 41

CONFRONTATION

The mall was brightly lit, but Sebastian could sense the darkness descending through the skylights overhead. He'd picked this mall because it was nearby, and he didn't want to leave Lizzie for long, but he had no idea what kind of store would carry a bell.

He wandered through the aisles, past sales clerks, purveyors of perfume and cosmetics. Late in the day, the crowds had thinned. Occasional young couples goggled at pasty mannequins, dreaming of their future lives and of things they could ill afford. The mannequins' fingers waved at them and at the empty air.

Desperate to get back, he stopped at each counter for directions. "I'm looking for a bell for my wife."

"Sorry. Try housewares."

"Anything will do, but I'd prefer something with a loop for her finger."

"We have nothing but egg timers. Try jewelry and accessories."

"A strong tone, perhaps, with engravings on its sides."

THE DAUGHTER OF THE SEA AND THE SKY

"Nothing but crystal here. Try the music store. Try the gift shop. Try...."

A bell pealed in his head, tolling the hours — Lizzie's dying.

***

Lizzie was gone. Why was the bell still ringing? And why was its tolling so much deeper than he remembered?

His mind cleared and he opened his eyes.

Sunday had arrived at Glen Eagle Farm — the deadline. The weak light of dawn streamed through the clerestory, sending dust motes dancing above his bed. His smile widened. By now the plan should be complete. Kailani would have been turned over to Carlson.

So why the tolling of the bell?

He struggled to connect the clanging with the circumstance. He'd heard this bell before — a less frantic ringing calling farm members to meals, or a more joyous sound, rung by an exuberant artist to celebrate the completion of a painting, but never had he heard the temple bell rung with anger.

His smile turned to a frown. A tumult rose outside, loud voices, the stamp of running feet, and suddenly, a pounding on his door.

He threw off the blankets and swung his feet to the floor, but before standing he paused to let his joints remember how to move. He'd be of no use to anyone if he fell and broke a hip.

He stood, unfolding his body like cardboard that had been crumpled for trash day and stubbornly insisted on returning to its original form. Then he tottered, flexing his knees and letting his brain recall how to balance. Once he was stable, he thrust his feet into the worn slippers, pulled on the purple terry cloth robe, and opened the door.

Out of breath and angry, the blood drained from Carlson's face.

"I waited an hour," he said. "They never came."

Sebastian grabbed his walking staff and followed him out the door.

Though a frost lay on the ground, the March air had warmed enough to raise a fog. As they rushed toward Kailani's cabin, wisps of white swirled round his ankles and streamed off his staff, giving the four faces white moustaches. He moved as fast as the floppy slippers allowed, and tried to think.

He remembered the temperament of troopers left with nothing to do, far from home and in a harsh climate. Does dry tinder lie near fire for long before bursting into flames? The commander must have been itching to act. The secretary probably never trusted Carlson and suspected some subterfuge. If they'd decided to take Kailani by force, what better time than in the dim light before dawn?

When he rounded the corner, he was unprepared for what he found. Bleary-eyed farm members in various stages of undress were emerging from their cabins to watch. Benjamin's men stood off to one side, stripped of their sticks and rakes and corralled by a dozen armed guards. A disciplined column of troopers poured through the pergola toward Kailani's cabin.

Sebastian raced toward the sentinel tree to block them, slippers slapping at his heels and the untied belt of his robe flapping in the breeze. "Where do you think you're going?"

"Out of the way," the commander of the column barked, "or you'll be arrested for obstruction."

Carlson raced up beside him. "But we had a deal."

"Too late," the commander said. "I have orders, direct from the secretary."

Sebastian held his ground, fool that he was. He raised his staff, not like a weapon, but like a wizard's wand trying to cast a spell that would hold back the tide.

The commander signaled his column forward.

At the last moment, Carlson grabbed Sebastian's arm and yanked him out of the way.

The commander mounted the steps of Kailani's cabin and tried the door; locked from the inside. At his signal, two sturdy men dragged forward a steel tube with handles on top. The commander stepped aside as the two men approached the door.

The nightmare unfolded before Sebastian, just what he'd hoped to avoid.

Carlson cried out, his voice a screech of despair. "Have pity on the child."

The commander gave a hand signal, and the men swung the steel tube.

Thud! Metal smashed into wood.

The child. A voice in Sebastian's head cried out from a place he'd nearly forgotten was there.

Smash! Splinters flew.

The dear, dear child.

Crack! The door swung wide, and Sebastian felt a wrenching in his heart as if Lizzie were dying again.

THE DAUGHTER OF THE SEA AND THE SKY

The advance guard rushed in with their body armor and their helmets with the faceplates and their weapons at the ready.

Sebastian waited for a cry of fright.

Nothing.

A moment later, the lead trooper stepped smartly out the door and approached his commander.

"No one there," he said as if it was another day at the office. "She's gone."

***

Benjamin crouched behind a row of gawking farm members, hidden from the troopers, one of the few benefits of being slight of stature. At the far side, in front of the sentinel tree, the commander had formed his men in a column and was preparing them for action. Beams from the spotlights reflected off the plastic face guards and made them gleam.

His Lemurians stood off to the side, subdued and silent. When the troopers had begun their advance, the Lemurians had crumbled like dry leaves, their faith so much weaker than his own.

The farm members had gathered to his right and left. Faces twitched with strain; eyes forgot to blink.

A voice near him whispered. "Will they attack?"

"What will happen to the girl if they do?" another said.

The commander shouted an order and the line began its march toward the Daughter's cabin.

There was a flash of purple terry cloth—Sebastian bursting forward to block the way. At once, he was a dervish, slippers flapping as he dashed toward them waving his staff.

In their helmets and boots, the troopers looked like giants next to him, a foot taller and twice his girth.

Foolish old man, though he showed more courage than the Lemurians.

To no avail. The column surged forward.

Benjamin listened to the thump of boots on the stairs, the crash of steel on wood. Then the door splintered and gave way.

An odd silence, and then a trooper re-emerged. His words seemed amplified by the fog. "No one there. She's gone."

245

DAVID LITWACK

Benjamin raised his eyes to the heavens, and they filled with tears. A miracle at last, and where there was one, others might follow.

***

The troopers searched every cabin, including Benjamin's, but found nothing.

He knew they'd come someday and had concealed his necessities in a carefully constructed compartment behind the wall.

Now, with their anger spent, the department men had retreated from the raw cold to their vans. Their commander had withdrawn to the great house to report back to his master and await further orders.

When Benjamin was certain they were gone, he returned to his cabin and locked the door behind him. He slid the bed aside and released the latch to the hidden store. From it he withdrew the pack, always ready with fresh supplies, the camouflage-colored hunting gear, and the Lightweight Stalker.

He'd trained for this mission his whole life. He finally understood the divine plan—why he'd been buried away at the farm for ten long years, why his faith had been tested, his soul tempered like steel. The time was at hand; the Lord would point His great finger at him and in a voice booming from the clouds, call his name. He was ready.

He peeked out the door into the gloom. Certain no one was watching, he gathered up his gear and headed out on a path he'd traveled once before, to Grandmother Storyteller and beyond.

CHAPTER 42

IN THE LAND OF THE STRANGER

Jason set a frantic pace, insisting they get as far from the farm as possible before sunup. Kailani pranced along behind him as if she were on an outing to the Knob.

Helena brought up the rear. Her calves burned, and the improvised pack she'd made out of bed sheets and kerchiefs tugged at her shoulders, but they had only a few hours of darkness left before the department learned of their escape. She willed herself not to tire as the minutes and miles passed, refusing to slow them down. This was, after all, her plan.

How foolish she'd been to worry about Kailani. Afraid to frighten the child, she'd concocted a story.

***

"We're going on an excursion, far from the men with the sticks and the guns. It will be a long walk, much of it in the dark, and we'll have to camp in the woods overnight. Think of it as an adventure. Maybe we'll find the ocean."

"The ocean?" Kainali said, bouncing on her toes as if ready to leave that minute.

"Uh-huh, but only if you keep it a secret between the three of us, and you do exactly as I say."

Her blue eyes widened and her brows became question marks. "What will I have to do?"

"Go back to your cabin and lock the door behind you. Then get some sleep. Shortly after midnight, I'll wake you by knocking on the common wall, a distinct knock you can recognize. Three taps, then two, then three more. Can you remember that?"

Kailani nodded, engrossed in the game. "Three, then two, then three." She went to the desk, bunched her tiny fingers into a fist, and rapped on its wooden top. "Like this?"

"Yes. You respond with four taps of your own, so I'll know you heard. Then count slowly to a hundred to give Jason and me a head start. We can leave out the front door, and no one will follow, but they'll be watching you. So you'll need to climb out the window, and then go down the path to Grandmother Storyteller. Go as quick and as quiet as you can. No need to bring anything with you. Jason and I will be there to meet you and take care of the rest."

Later that night, Kailani arrived at Grandmother Storyteller only moments behind them, apparently too excited to count to a hundred. She disobeyed in one other way too: she bore a small bundle under her arm, wrapped in a pillowcase. When Helena asked what was in it, she grasped the bundle tighter and whispered, "It's a secret. I can't tell you now."

Helena let it go. No time to dawdle.

From Grandmother Storyteller, Jason carried Kailani across the bramble to the dirt road that ran along the horse farm. Then he set her down, and they took off at a jog. Any concern Helena had that the child would have trouble keeping up quickly evaporated; she danced along as if lighter than air.

Half an hour later, they crossed the deserted highway and entered a narrow trail, barely visible in the moonlight. Soon thereafter they began to climb. Their pace slowed as the night deepened.

Jason trudged ahead, poking at the path with a stick he'd found in the brush, swinging it to the left and right in small arcs to probe for wayward stumps and rocks.

Kailani kept her eyes glued to his shadowy back, and Helena followed the child's golden hair like a beacon in the dark.

248

THE DAUGHTER OF THE SEA AND THE SKY

After a few more hours of forced march, Jason brought the column to a halt. He found a downed tree, tested it with his stick for rot, and plopped down on top. As Helena and Kailani straggled over to join him, he broke out the water bottles.

Helena pulled out a bag of dried figs from her makeshift pack and distributed them to the others.

Once everyone had quenched their thirst and more or less sated their hunger, she turned her attention to Kailani. The euphoria of their escape had vanished, replaced by exhaustion. All three were tired, but Kailani's shoulders drooped in a way she'd never seen before.

Helena draped an arm around her. "Are you all right?"

"Uh-huh."

"Can I see what's inside your pillowcase now?" She reached for the bundle tucked between the girl's knees.

Kailani yanked it away, hugging it to her chest, but after a moment, she gave in.

Helena untied the knot and peeked through the opening, then groped inside to confirm her finding. Neatly folded at the bottom were the chiffon dress her mother had made and the red ribbon with the bow. Nestled on top was the string of aquamarine stars.

She gaped at Kailani. "You figured out where we're going?"

"No, but I knew we were never coming back. I didn't want to leave these behind."

"I'm sorry, Kailani. We had no choice. Tomorrow they were coming to take you away, back to the department."

Helena felt a tremor run through the child. She wanted to draw her close but knew the question was coming.

Kailani faced her, eyes on fire as if lit from within. "Tell me, Helena, where *are* we going?"

She glanced at Jason, but this was no time for taking turns. This question was hers to answer. "To the land bridge."

Kailani stood and stared off to the north as if trying to see all the way to the journey's end. She stayed like that for what seemed forever, legs apart and back arched. The only evidence she was among the living was the blink of her lashes and the puffs of breath bursting from her lips.

Then she began to sing.

"In the land of the stranger I rise or I fall."

"What does that mean?" Helena asked.

DAVID LITWACK

"It's a song the sky used to sing to me. It's from the Holy Book. I should've known. The land bridge is where my penance will end, one way or the other."

Helena waited, watching.

Standing there in the dark, the child seemed like a phantom engulfed in a mirage.

"Why there?" she said so softly she could hardly hear her own words.

"Because," Kailani said, "that's where the sea met the sky."

***

Jason paused to check on his fellow travelers.

Helena staggered along as if driven by will alone, and Kailani was barely awake on her feet.

He couldn't let them rest until they were close to the asylum gate—close enough that when they awoke before dawn, they could still make the final dash under the cover of darkness.

He glanced back up the mountain, trying to gauge how far they'd come.

The first stretch had been as expected—the dirt road he'd jogged down the day before. He had a sense of the trail through the woods, at least before it began to climb, but the hike up the mountain had been steeper than expected, a lung-busting ascent to the top of the ridge. For a time, the path became so cluttered with fallen trees and dead branches that navigating in the dark became a matter of faith.

By the time it crested, the sun had come up. From the summit, he could see an embankment of fog rolling into the valley below. It looked suitably spiritual, a scene he could imagine some god conjuring in one of his lesser miracles, a barrier between worlds.

From there, downslope and daylight had made for steady progress.

Now twilight approached and the sun faded to a pale glimmer through the mist. Moisture clung to everything, beading on his skin and dampening his clothes. The temperature was dropping.

"Where are we?" Kailani said.

He bent down and brushed back a lock of damp hair matted across her cheek. "You're doing great. This was harder than I thought, but we're almost there. See the tops of the trees?"

She nodded.

"They're not sloping downhill anymore. That means we're near the bottom, and at the foot of the mountain—the land bridge."

250

THE DAUGHTER OF THE SEA AND THE SKY

"But when will we be there?"

"Not tonight. We'll get some sleep here in the woods and go there just before dawn. First I have to make sure we're close."

He eased his arms free of the pack and let it slip off, then searched for a tree with branches low to the ground and easy to climb. He found one nearby. Fighting the ache in his limbs, he scrambled up high enough to see.

The light was fading but a glow on the horizon remained. Using the setting sun as a guide, he turned to the north. Not far ahead, the forest ended and a stark hill took its place, a circle of brown earth perfect in its perimeter, as if measured by a surveyor. An imposing wrought iron fence surrounded it, broken on the near side by a gate.

He breathed a sigh. *Now to find a safe place to camp for the night.*

He shifted his gaze to the south. From that vantage, he could make out gashes in the mountainside where runoff from melting snow had formed brooks. He followed them to where they merged into a larger stream. A hundred yards along the stream lay a natural clearing, not far from where he stood and out of sight of the trail.

He started to climb down, but stopped at the scrape of sliding scree. He peered into the distance.

High up on the trail, he spotted what appeared to be a solitary man walking toward them, moving with the gait of a hunter.

Jason shook his head, knowing how the light of dusk could play tricks. He rubbed his eyes with the heel of his hand, blinked twice, and then looked again.

Nothing. If someone had been there, he'd either vanished or blended in with the trees.

***

Helena rested on the pine needle-strewn ground, huddled beneath the blankets she'd taken from their cabin. She squeezed her eyelids shut and tried to calm herself, her customary ritual when preparing for sleep.

Jason snored softly beside her, and at the far side of the clearing, Kailani lay still.

She should be sleeping as well, but though exhausted from the trek, no sleep came. She worried about the upcoming dash to the land bridge and their acceptance into the Blessed Lands, but strangely, she suffered little anxiety about leaving the land of her

DAVID LITWACK

birth. Tomorrow a new day would dawn, and though her life would change forever, she was unfazed.

Growing up, she'd always had a sense of living someone else's life in a place she didn't belong. The months on the farm had confused her more. Gods and spirits, reason and logic—all had merged into a blur.

She drew in a breath too intense for sleep, and let it out slowly as every citizen in the Republic had been taught, to quiet her passions and see her situation through the clear lens of reason. As her breathing slowed, reason faded, replaced by an unreasonable calm, a feeling that she was about to find her place in the world. Maybe this was what Benjamin had been trying to tell her. Maybe at the center of that calm was what she'd sought all along—her own spirit, and with it a connection to everyone else who had ever lived, to Jason, to Kailani, and to her father.

She breathed in and out again and stretched her mind to reach for the eternal. She could sense something larger than herself, but whether it was the Spirit or the soughing of the wind through the trees, she couldn't tell. Would she find what she was missing in the Blessed Lands, that final leap of faith? She may never know, but of one thing she was certain: once she crossed the land bridge, she'd no longer be the Helena her father had envisioned.

That version would vanish like a ghost. *Poof* and she'd be gone, despite all their reason.

She startled to a tap on her shoulder and turned to find Kailani pressing a finger to her lips. Her own lips parted, but at the child's urging, she stayed silent. Then the finger curled into a gesture of beckoning. Helena rolled onto one side and stood. Her feet were bare, and the ground rocky and uneven. It scraped at her toes and the edges of her heels as she let Kailani lead her to the far side of the clearing.

"I could tell you weren't asleep," Kailani whispered, "and I didn't want to wake Jason."

The child shivered, so Helena fetched a blanket and wrapped it around her.

"Were you having trouble sleeping like me?" she said.

"Uh-huh. I kept praying for the Spirit to tell me whether to go or not, but on this night, of all nights, the Spirit was silent."

"Oh, Kailani, you have to go. If you stay, it's back to the cell."

"But what will happen when we get there?"

"We'll be together, you and me and Jason."

"What about the sea and the sky?"

THE DAUGHTER OF THE SEA AND THE SKY

Helena gave her a piercing look. "If there's a better place for you to go, we'll take you there. If not, we'll settle in together."

"Helena?"

"Yes."

"Do you think they've forgiven me?"

"Who?"

"The sea and the sky."

Helena gazed at Kailani, the picture of innocence. "Why wouldn't they forgive you?"

"Because I haven't completed my penance yet. Mr. Benjamin said I needed to do penance for a long time, maybe for the rest of my life."

"Mr. Benjamin!" Helena blurted out, almost loud enough to wake Jason. "Forget what he said. All he cares about is what's right for Mr. Benjamin."

She knelt down so her knees nestled on the carpet of pine needles, and leaned in close enough to read Kailani's eyes in the dim light. "If you need permission to end your penance, ask me. I'll grant it to you. You've done enough already."

"But how will I know if I'm forgiven?" Her voice quivered, a mournful sound.

How will I know if I'm forgiven? A question Helena might have asked herself.

"I don't know. You haven't told us anything about the sea or the sky or what you've done to need forgiveness. But I do know that sometimes we take on more blame than we deserve, and it's not for others to forgive us, but ourselves."

She waited for a response, but none came. She grasped Kailani by the arms. Almost lost in the blanket, she seemed not the daughter of the sea and the sky but a waif alone in a foreign land. Helena no longer cared whether the Spirit existed or not. There was only this poor, dear child weighed down by an unknown burden.

She turned Kailani until a sliver of moonlight crept across her face. The pale light spread, revealing a flush that had blossomed on the child's cheeks.

And there it was, her expression plain to see, almost like Benjamin's in the beam of the sentinel tree floodlights, but hers was not the look of an aspiring saint. Hers was the look of a child. It showed a different kind of longing, a simpler kind of hope.

Kailani wanted to go home.

253

CHAPTER 43

A SCENE FROM THE APOCALYPSE

Benjamin crouched in the brush, as he had so often when stalking a sad-eyed doe, but this time he hunted different prey. It had been a long night, and he'd used the time for prayer and reflection. In the wee hours of the morning, when the moon had set and the hint of sunlight had not yet shimmered through the trees, he was rewarded with a revelation.

Judgment day was at hand.

He could hear it in the pre-dawn with the woods coming alive, with the chattering of the birds and the rustling of a thousand leaves. He could see it, the universe beginning to converge, the stars above swirling in a giant spiral to form a new heaven, a home where only the faithful would be welcome. He could smell it on the breeze

Now, at last, he understood the divine plan. He knew why, on those cold and dreary mornings, his father had dragged him out and schooled him in the art of hunting; why he'd been taught to track, to read broken twigs on a branch and scuff marks in the mud; why he'd learned the craft of concealment, to hide unnoticed even until kingdom come.

THE DAUGHTER OF THE SEA AND THE SKY

Sure, he'd been burdened with adversity, his small stature, his offensive appearance, the high-pitched whine of his voice. He'd also been blessed with patience and an enduring faith, and something more—the ability to go for days without sleep.

Now he spied on the stream. They'd have to come for water, and the one who woke first would come alone. He knew who she would be. Why? Because he'd branded the curse of penance on her heart—penance a lever on the soul. That unfulfilled responsibility would haunt her dreams.

Things had been going well. For a time, the front lawn of the farm had been transformed into a morality play, good against evil, a scene from the apocalypse. Now it was nearing the final act.

He startled to the sound of footsteps whispering through the pine needles, footsteps too light to be those of the nonbelievers.

There she was, walking alone, a blanket draped around her shoulders, its fringes grazing the ground and brushing her bare feet. In her eyes, the pallor of a troubled sleep.

She approached the stream, let the blanket fall to the ground, and knelt. She stayed still for a long time, staring at her reflection in the water.

Now, to accost her without alerting the others.

As she bent down to splash water on her face, a wind kicked up. With the rush of the stream and the gust of the wind, she'd never hear his approach.

He slipped from the brush, moving stealthily, heel to toe as he'd been taught.

She sensed his presence too late; he clapped a hand over her mouth and held her tight.

"Daughter of the Sea and the Sky," he whispered. "Don't be afraid. I come in the name of our Lord. I can help you, but you mustn't wake the others. Promise to be quiet and I'll release you. Nod if you understand."

He waited, measuring her heartbeat as it sped up and then calmed.

Her body went limp, and she nodded.

He let go.

She turned and faced him. "Mr. Benjamin, you frightened me."

"I'm sorry, but I had no choice. The others would never understand."

"Why are you here?"

DAVID LITWACK

"To take you back."

"But they'll put me in the cell."

"No they won't. I can protect you."

"We're going to the Blessed Lands."

"You can't go yet. It's not time."

She drew in a breath. A momentary doubt clouded her face. "Helena told me my penance is done, that I can forgive myself."

"Forgive? Only the Lord can forgive." His voice rose and he struggled to temper its tone. "I've had a vision from Lord Kanakunai himself, and He has appointed me master of your penance. You are blessed, Kailani, chosen to be the center of a new beginning, a reprieve for the world, but you must stay among the soulless until the apocalypse."

Her back stiffened, and she lifted her chin. "I won't go with you."

"If you don't, you'll be denying your destiny." He moved closer, close enough so she'd feel the heat of his breath. His voice became a hiss. "Your soul will be damned, condemned to wander for eternity."

She stared at him, the ocean-blue eyes narrowing. Slowly, she began to shake her head, speeding up until the golden hair swished about her shoulders. Then, before he could grab her, she slipped away and ran back down the trail.

He watched her go, making no effort to follow. It must be the will of the Lord.

So near the apocalypse. I'll not be denied.

CHAPTER 44

THE ASYLUM GATE

Helena dreamed she was standing at the asylum gate, waiting to be admitted into the Blessed Lands. A high bench made of rosewood with angels carved into its center blocked her way. One of Kailani's senkyosei, a withered old zealot with fierce eyes and his head covered by a hood the color of dirt, was judging her.

In a booming voice that belied his size, the preacher kept asking the same question. "What right did *you* have to forgive the Daughter?"

Each time she tried to answer, the beat of a drum—*ka-thoom, ka-thoom*—drowned out her words.

The sound was curiously familiar. She glanced to her right and to her left, hoping to identify its source. *Ka-thoom.* It seemed to be coming from where she stood. She was breathing too fast and tried to calm herself—after all, it was only a dream. As her breathing slowed, the drumming slowed as well. Then she knew: the sound was the beating of her heart.

Jason called her name, his voice distant and hollow as if coming through a tunnel. He wanted her to do something, to go someplace, but where? Then he touched her, stroking her arm.

She opened her eyes and let them adjust to the light.

Nearly dawn.

As soon as the fog in her mind lifted, she checked on Kailani, but the spot where she'd slept was bare. Before Helena could ask the question, Jason gestured toward the entrance to the clearing.

The child stood there, dressed and ready to go, clutching her pillowcase bundle to her chest and hugging herself. She seemed to be glaring at the horizon as if daring the future to come.

"She's been like that since I woke up," Jason said. "No matter. It's time for us to go."

He'd instructed them to pack the night before, all but the blankets and the clothes on their backs, so they were ready to go.

With Jason in the lead, they bushwhacked to the trail and took off at a trot. He'd assured them it wasn't far. Sure enough, in what seemed little more than a hundred strides, a break in the trees appeared.

Beyond the trees the path lay exposed, a naked ribbon of earth leading to a wrought-iron gate. Words sculpted into the overhead arch read, "Leaving the Republic." To the right of the gate was a two-story structure, where guards were barracked and refugees processed. Opposite the barracks and facing the gate stood the statue she'd seen on posters since childhood—a larger-than-life, robed woman perched on a ten-foot-high pedestal, her right hand holding a flaming torch high above her head—the Lady of Reason welcoming asylum seekers to their new life.

Jason extended an arm and pointed, as he'd done that day on the ride to the farm, when he'd caught sight of the deer.

Next to the gate stood a small guardhouse. A trooper slumped inside, awake but not fully alert.

Helena took a deep breath, grasped Kailani by the hand, and took off.

In the morning gloom, the guard didn't immediately spot them emerging from the woods. But as soon as he saw them, he sounded the alarm.

Now they were in full sprint, tossing stealth to the winds.

Thirty yards to go....

The guard had taken too long to alert the others, precious seconds lost.

Twenty yards....

He quickly regrouped.

THE DAUGHTER OF THE SEA AND THE SKY

Ten....

Jason swerved suddenly and shoved the startled guard out of the way. They were almost to the gate.

Kailani stumbled and fell.

Helena cried out to Jason, who pivoted and swept the girl up with one arm, barely breaking stride. The troops from the barracks were on their heels.

And then they were through.

As they paused to admire what they'd accomplished, they were startled to see a squad of troopers hidden behind the fence on what was supposed to be neutral ground. Instantly, they were surrounded.

"Asylum!" Helena cried.

The commander moved forward from behind his men. He was unarmed, and his face bore a look not of combat but of concern.

He held out a hand. "Come with me, please."

"But you can't arrest us. We're inside the gate."

He smiled. "You're not under arrest, Ms. Brewster. Someone wants to speak with you. That's all."

He stepped aside and waved for them to pass.

The cordon of troopers parted. Behind them, previously hidden by the bulk of the armored men, stood Sebastian and Carlson.

***

"We made a terrible mistake," Sebastian said.

Jason glared at the managing director, then shifted his ire to Carlson, who was lining up paperclips he'd discovered on the military-issue desk.

When he noticed Jason's glare, he withdrew his hand and winced. "The department and its secrecy," he said. "When they refused to tell me anything, I assumed the worst. Given the photogram and all the preaching she'd done, a return to incarceration seemed like the logical conclusion. Fifty-two years of bad blood will do that to you. Perhaps we're not as rational as we think."

Jason glanced around the commander's office, a small room with little space for much more than the desk and some chairs. At the commander's insistence, he'd been seated in the big chair behind the desk—a peace offering, he presumed. The other two sat opposite him on canvas folding chairs, under orders from the commander to apologize and explain. Both began speaking at once, and his weary mind tried to follow. Fragments of phrases filtered through.

"A high-ranking zealot. Claims Kailani's a person of importance to the Blessed Lands. Moved heaven and earth to get her back."

His mind began to clear, though what they said made little sense.

"Unprecedented diplomacy. Supreme Leader to President."

Kailani, the object of this international intrigue, huddled with Helena in the commander's quarters next door. They needed answers, to understand the department's intentions without alarming the child further, and Helena had volunteered to stay with her while he found out more.

He stared at the naked light bulb above the desk and tried to put his fears into words. "A person of importance. Is that good or bad? How do we know what the zealots will do with her? How can we be sure they won't use her like Benjamin did?"

"The secretary has guaranteed her safety," Carlson said.

"But how do we know we can trust him? How do we know what deals he's made at Kailani's expense?"

"Be reasonable," Sebastian said. "After this mess we've made—" He waved his arm broadly as if to encompass the land bridge, the military encampment, and all that had transpired on the farm. "—you think he'd lie to us?"

Jason refused to back down. Sebastian had been wrong about Benjamin; he could be wrong again. "Kailani ran away for a reason."

"Why not ask her?" Carlson said.

"No. Thanks to you, she's too frightened to tell us anything."

"They could just take her."

"Is that what you want?"

"Then what do you propose?"

Jason wanted to stomp out of the room and leave the two behind, but with so much at stake, he needed to think it through, to be reasonable one last time.

He fixed his eyes on Carlson. "Let me meet with this high-ranking zealot."

Carlson's hands shook, making the paperclips flee in disarray. "Do you realize what you're asking? It would be like requesting an audience with the secretary himself."

"We could be risking Kailani's life. Do you trust him *that* much?"

"I... don't know." Carlson abandoned the paperclips and faced him. "They haven't let me near him."

THE DAUGHTER OF THE SEA AND THE SKY

"Then how do you expect *me* to trust him?"

"Because you have no choice. The secretary's frustrated enough. One more delay and he'll have the troops drag her off screaming."

Jason looked from Carlson to Sebastian. The muscles of his jaw stiffened. "No meeting, no Kailani."

Carlson heaved a sigh and rose to go. "I'll ask, but I make no promises."

Jason followed him out the door and watched him navigate the narrow corridor to make the call. After he was out of sight, Jason turned to find Sebastian regarding him with concern.

"Are you sure you know what you're doing?" Sebastian said.

"I'm sure."

"At some point, you're going to have to take a leap of faith. This whole reason thing is overrated. You may never know the truth."

"I'll know."

"What we see as sincerity may be something different for zealots. Even if this so-called minister swears on his immortal soul that he'll treat her well, how can you be sure? Even Benjamin would claim he had her best interests at heart."

As usual, Sebastian was being too analytical. The pragmatism that had made them kindred spirits was useless now.

Jason smiled for the first time that day, as if he'd discovered something new about himself. "I'll know. I have no idea how, but I'll know."

Five minutes later, Carlson returned. "The meeting's been approved."

Jason relaxed, but tensed again when the chief examiner had more to say.

"But to get this meeting, I had to agree to their terms. The secretary feels the minister will lose face otherwise."

Sebastian arched his brows. "What does that mean?"

"It means no more sneaking around. No dirt roads in a field or trails through the woods. It means a formal ceremony for the whole world to see, press and all, and it has to take place before sunset."

"And if not?" Sebastian said.

"If not?" The chief examiner's face contorted in pain. "Then they'll take her by force, Jason and Helena will go to prison for obstruction, and your farm will be shut down for good."

CHAPTER 45

A MEETING OF WORLDS

The commander had granted Jason ten minutes to brief Helena so she'd have time to prepare Kailani for the handoff. He sat across from her, their knees touching as he explained the plan. He assured her he'd return with proof of the zealot's intent, and stressed the need to act before something dire happened.

He waited for her response.

Sunshine filtering through the window flickered across her face, highlighting the intensity in her eyes. Dark shadows beneath them made the sockets seem sunken, as if she hadn't slept in weeks.

"How can you be sure," she said "that they'll do her no harm?"

"I'll know when I meet him."

"How?"

"I just will."

Her intensity eased into a smile. "You're making it up, aren't you, going on how you feel?"

"Sometimes, it's the best you can do."

"Jason Adams, mythmaker."

THE DAUGHTER OF THE SEA AND THE SKY

He smiled back. "I must've learned it from you."

She touched his cheek and gave him a kiss. "Then I hope you're right."

Next, Carlson led him out the gate to where an unmarked black vehicle awaited. Two armed guards stood nearby, along with a man in a blue suit, who Carlson introduced as a protocol officer from the Department of Foreign Affairs.

One guard opened the back door and prompted Jason to enter. The protocol officer slid in beside him and closed the door, while the guards took up posts on either side.

The officer delivered the briefing in rapid fire; Jason's role was to listen and nod.

"You'll be driven to a trailer on the far side of the land bridge, where you'll meet the Minister of Commerce from the Blessed Lands. Always, always refer to his home as the Blessed Lands. Never use the words *zealot* or *mythmaker*.

"Before entering, you'll be subjected to a search. Agents from the Republic will scan you for metal objects, and guardsmen from the Blessed Lands will pat you down. Come with pockets empty, no wallet, no watch, no keys.

"Once inside the trailer, I'll introduce you to the minister. You should bow to him as a sign of respect." The protocol officer demonstrated, squaring his shoulders and pressing both palms together, then dipping his head. "Always keep your eyes on the other man. When you bend, observe the minister's bow. You are of lower station and younger, so you must bow more deeply than him. Never, ever turn your back on him, and refer to him only as Excellency.

"Never speak first. Answer only when spoken to. Allow the minister to initiate every topic."

Then the biggest surprise.

"Per the request of the minister, you and he are to be left alone — no guards, no Carlson, no protocol officer.

"Do you understand?"

Jason nodded, expecting to sign a form at the end, but instead the officer rapped on the window and the two guards entered the front.

The driver started the engine, and the car began rolling along so slowly that only the bumps in the road made Jason aware they were moving.

Three minutes later, they parked. In front of them, guarded by a dozen men with automatic weapons, stood a large blue and white trailer.

***

Jason sat with his hands folded and his eyes fixed on the zealot minister. With the curtains pulled tight, the light in the trailer was muted, but he could still take stock of the man. Most noticeable was his size—a bear of a man, as tall as Jason but broader in every aspect, big shoulders and a barrel chest with thick forearms and hands. The sort of man who might move two governments to retrieve a single child.

Why did he want her so much?

The minister remained silent, sizing him up, and Jason waited as he'd been instructed.

When the minister finally spoke, his voice was hardly official and barely under control. "I've been told... that you are the one who rescued Kailani from drowning."

Jason nodded.

"In that case, I'm in your debt. May Lord Kanakunai be gracious unto you for your act of kindness." He followed with a small bow, more a dip of the head, and waited, a clear indication that he expected a response.

All the protocols rattled through Jason's mind, and he made a deeper bow back. "I did what anyone would've done in my place, Excellency."

"Nevertheless, it was you who saved her. We are grateful. You know Kailani well, I'm told. Such a special child." He reached for a glass of water and took a sip, then withdrew a large handkerchief and wiped his mouth. "I don't understand why there's been such a delay. I don't know why all these armed men are necessary. I don't care. All I want is to have her back. Now, Mister... Jason, I've been informed that you'll return her to me by the end of the day, but you've requested this meeting first. What is it you wish from me? A reward?"

Jason blinked and struggled to temper his response. "No, nothing. Nothing at all, Excellency. Anything I... *we* have done was for Kailani's sake."

The minister looked puzzled. "Then why this meeting?"

Jason recalled the admonitions of the protocol officer, but this was his moment. He drew in a breath and released it, aware he was

THE DAUGHTER OF THE SEA AND THE SKY

surrounded by guardsmen with weapons. "We want to know your intentions. Her happiness is of utmost importance to us."

"Ah." The minister paused as if buying time to reorient his thoughts. "That's a sentiment that seems more appropriate in the Blessed Lands, not the land of profit and loss. I'm moved by your concern, but I assure you, she'll be treated well."

If only that were true. "If I may ask, sir... Excellency...."

For the first time, the minister smiled. "I see you've been briefed by the protocol officer. Please, you saved Kailani and we are in your debt. You've earned the right to ask anything you wish."

"If I may, Excellency, excuse me for saying this but... why does this girl matter so much to the people of the Blessed Lands?"

The minister stared at him for what seemed like an eternity. "Now I understand why you asked for this meeting. You're worried there may be some deception, some zealot subterfuge."

Jason blanched, but retained his poise. "As you said, she's a special child. We'd like to be more comfortable before turning her over."

The minister pressed his thick hands on the desktop. "You would withhold her from me?"

"Only if—"

"You fear I would do her harm?" His voice was rising.

Jason pictured Kailani sobbing at the reflection shelter, and held his ground. "Excellency, I don't know what you'd do. I don't understand you or your people or the way you live in the Blessed Lands, or how you might use a child. Here's what I do know: Kailani is dear to us, and we'll fight to our last breath to keep her safe."

Jason readied for rage, but instead, the man from the Blessed Lands closed his eyes and became still—deeply still, the way Jason imagined someone devout would appear in prayer.

Finally, the minister opened his eyes and said, "Lord, forgive me."

Jason's mouth opened, but no words came out. He gaped at the minister, waiting for more.

"I made a promise to my leader," the minister said, "to save face for my people, and so, for the sake of national pride, I hid the truth from the soulless. The result of my folly? You've made up myths of your own. It's time for both of us to set myths aside. Why do I seek Kailani? Not for my people or my country. I seek her for my wife, and for the love of a father for his child."

265

Jason studied the minister anew. His hair was black, his skin olive. His eyes were almond-shaped, deep and brown, more the color of the earth than the ocean.

"But how can she be your daughter? You look nothing like her and... you seem too old to be the father of a nine-year-old."

The minister touched two fingers to his heart in the same way Kailani did.

"I'm moved by your concern and will explain. I married late in life, only after I found someone whose spirit I could share. She was from your land, a transmigrant, younger than me and fair. She has porcelain skin and golden hair with eyes the color of the ocean. She gave birth to an angel in her own image."

Jason watched as the powerful minister's face melted into tenderness at the thought of his wife and child. It sounded plausible, but plausible wasn't good enough. "Can you tell me, Excellency, how she refers to herself?"

The minister looked taken aback, then laughed, a laughter as deep as the stillness had been. "I see you still doubt me, but I know everything a father should know. Kailani never stops asking questions, loves sweets, and she calls herself the daughter of the sea and the sky."

Jason held his gaze. "And why, Excellency, does she call herself that?"

He braced for another outburst, but the minister was strangely composed.

"My beautiful, willful daughter. She'd inherited her mother's appearance and my stubborn disposition, even as a newborn. We named her after the both of us, a melding of spirits. My given name is Kai, which in our language means the sea. When her mother transmigrated, she took on a name more appropriate to our land, calling herself Lani, which means the sky. From the time Kailani was an infant, we called her the daughter of the sea and the sky. As she got older, she realized she was different from the other children and began using that name to show she was special."

Sebastian had been wrong: things strongly felt could be known for sure. Now he felt sure this was Kailani's father. But still.... "Then why, Excellency, if she was so loved, did she run away?"

The minister finally flared. "Don't you know that with a single word, I could have those armed men take her and bring her to me?"

Jason stared, unflinching. "Is that what you want?"

The minister's deep-set eyes began to glisten. "Forgive me. It's been such a long search, such a painful time."

THE DAUGHTER OF THE SEA AND THE SKY

He took another sip of water. "A few years after Kailani was born, my wife conceived again, this time a daughter who looked more like my people, and we became a family of four. In the next few years, demands on my time increased. The more I accomplished, the less time I had with my family. Still, I tried to be with them every moment I could—my two daughters, my greatest joy."

His words softened now. "Life was too good. Perhaps I'd been guilty of vanity or of not appreciating my lot. Our youngest daughter was lost nine months ago in an accident at our island home, a drowning. Kailani was alone with her on the beach. I'd been away on business and arrived barely in time to see her placed in the ground. My wife was distraught, afraid the ocean might take Kailani as well, and insisted we move to the mainland, inland and far from the sea. Kailani thought we were punishing her, no matter how much we reassured her. I believe she went to her mother's homeland as a misguided attempt to do penance."

A reason at last, though not absolute proof. Helena would have to take his word. Time to thank the minister for his patience, to back away, bowing as he went, never taking his eyes off the man until he was out the door.

But one last thought gnawed at Jason. "Excellency, if I may ask, what was your other daughter's name?"

The minister went pale. "The lost one? The one whose name I've been unable to utter since her death?"

Jason shook his head, appalled at what he'd done. *Enough.* The man before him loved Kailani more than any of them, the love only a father could have. "I'm sorry, Excellency. I didn't mean to—"

The high-ranking official from the Blessed Lands waved him off. The name emerged weak and hoarse—the voice of a man in pain. "Makani."

"And," Jason said, "what does that mean in your language?"

"It means," he replied, "the wind."

CHAPTER 46

THE APOCALYPSE AT HAND

Helena sat on the cot in the commander's quarters, trying to pay attention as Jason warmed her hands between his and told the story. The commander had lent them this room so they could have a place to rest after their ordeal and talk in private, out of ear shot of the nearby office where Carlson and Sebastian were keeping Kailani occupied.

The quarters were military stark, furnished only with the cot, a chair, and a plain wooden bureau. On the bureau sat a picture of the commander's family, his wife sporting an officer's cap worn askew with his two daughters at her side. Opposite the cot, a single window hung open to let in the fresh air from what had become a mild spring day.

Jason explained why Kailani had sailed across the ocean, how at last she could be returned to the family she'd left behind. He told her how the minister was grateful for what they'd done and how, if they still wished to transmigrate, he'd facilitate their request, even find jobs for them in the Ministry of Commerce. But if not, he'd understand and ensure all charges against them were dropped.

All good news.

THE DAUGHTER OF THE SEA AND THE SKY

The breeze blowing through the window kept distracting her. She stared out past the barren landscape surrounding the barracks to the forest beyond, mesmerized by the swaying of the treetops, all so different—cedars and firs, spruces and pines—but moving together in harmony. The rustling of their branches carried on the breeze like a song.

Jason finished and waited for her reaction.

She nodded and smiled, her mood lightening with each breath. She knew the reason why.

Kailani's wind had been set free and was singing to her.

***

Helena watched Kailani closely. While Jason told about his meeting with her father, the child covered her mouth with one hand as if to keep the words from spilling out.

Finally, the hand dropped away, and she let out a squeal. "He's here? At the land bridge?"

Jason nodded.

Her brows crinkled into a knot. "Then why hasn't he come to see me?"

"If it were up to him," Jason said, "he'd have come the instant you arrived, but your father's an important man. With so much at stake between our peoples, they want to return you to him in an official ceremony, a peace offering for the whole world to see."

Kailani wandered over to the cot and sat so lightly, the mattress barely sagged. "What do you think I should do, Helena?"

Seeing her there made Helena recall the cot in the department cell. Then the images flowed: Kailani newly dredged from the sea; sipping tea at Molly's; sobbing at the Reflection shelter; summoning the wind on the Spirit Hill; and believing she'd been blessed by the Northern Lights.

Much less than the Daughter of the Sea and the Sky. And so much more.

"My father's gone," Helena said, "but yours is here, and he's not unfathomable like the sea or unreachable like the sky. He's real and he wants to take you home."

"But what if my penance wasn't enough?"

Helena settled on the bed and wrapped an arm around her. "We have lots in common, you and I, more than I knew when we first met by

269

DAVID LITWACK

the cliffs. I lost a father at nearly the same time you lost a sister. We both tried so hard to save them, even after they were gone. When we failed, we blamed ourselves. We were wrong."

Kailani stared up at her, the ocean-blue eyes hungering for more.

"Now I have Jason and you have your parents. I don't know whether the Spirit exists or not, but I'm sure of one thing: the best we can do for those who are gone is to pass our love on to the living."

Kailani's tension eased, and she buried her face in Helena's breast.

Jason checked his watch. "It's getting to be time."

"Give her a minute." Helena grasped Kailani by the shoulders and looked into her eyes. "Are you ready?"

Kailani considered no more than a second, and then reached inside her pillowcase to pull out the white dress with the red ribbon. "Is it okay if I wear this to the ceremony?"

"Of course."

"And one more thing." She delved deeper into the makeshift pack. When she withdrew her hand, her tiny fist was clenched as if hiding a secret. "Will you help me with these?"

Her fingers uncurled to reveal the aquamarine stars.

***

At Helena's request, Jason went ahead to check out the arrangements. Everything appeared to be in order, as negotiated with the minister, the protocol officer, the commander, and a representative of the media.

Most of the troops had returned to the barracks but stayed mustered by the doorway at the ready. Two dozen others had been selected to participate in the ceremony. They were fitted out in dress uniforms with lots of polished brass, but unarmed, deployed as an honor guard on either side of the path to the steel hut.

Media members were allowed to observe from behind.

The transfer would occur at five o'clock, late enough to give the press time to arrive but leaving enough daylight to get good pictures for the news.

Jason checked his watch: five minutes to go.

He scanned the area and studied the faces around him before signaling to fetch Kailani. A few seconds later, she emerged from the barracks.

The honor guard snapped to attention, and cameras flashed.

THE DAUGHTER OF THE SEA AND THE SKY

She looked radiant in her white dress, with the red bow in front and the aquamarine stars in her hair.

While most of the onlookers were fixed on Kailani, Jason watched Helena, who walked alongside holding her hand, but lightly now. At the gate, they embraced and said their goodbyes.

Kailani began the walk up the hill, her eyes focused on the hut where her father waited, but when she passed Jason, she strayed from the path and stepped toward him. She crooked her finger and gestured for him to bend low. Then she draped her arms around his neck in a hug.

As she did so, she whispered in his ear. "Mr. Benjamin was wrong. My soul will be saved, and my penance will end today."

Jason smiled, nodded, and then grimaced as a thought struck him. "When did you last speak to Benjamin?"

"By the stream near our campsite this morning."

Jason spun toward the tree line and was instantly blinded by the low afternoon sun. As he looked away, letting his eyes readjust, he calculated: accurate at eight hundred yards. The woods were no more than fifty.

Benjamin could be hiding anywhere.

He thought of a squirrel scampering across the lawn in front of the great house and heard Benjamin's high-pitched whine.

I'd hit it every time.

Instead of letting Kailani go, he scooped her up by the waist so he was between her and the trees, and began running toward the shelter of the barracks.

A shot rang out, kicking up gravel inches from where the girl had stood.

He changed direction, zigzagging now as he calculated how long it would take to seat a new round. Then a second shot, faster than he'd expected. He stumbled and fell to one knee, almost dropping Kailani. Through blurred vision, he saw Helena race toward him, pointing to his lower pant leg where a red blotch had begun to spread.

"Take her," he said with little air.

"But what—"

"Benjamin."

Helena froze, her eyes darting around uncertainly, but only for an instant. She grabbed the child and took off for the barracks.

By now, troopers were rushing everywhere, the honor guard sprinting for weapons, while their comrades mustered outside, helmets

271

and rifles clattering ominously. One helped Jason to his feet and brought him over to the commander.

As Jason briefed him, Sebastian joined in, leaning heavily on his walking staff and showing all of his seventy-eight years.

"I was wrong again, Jason. And now...." Sebastian grabbed the commander's arm. "Let me go with you."

"You'd only slow us down."

"He has a long-range rifle with a scope and is an expert marksman. You'll have to approach cautiously. I can go that fast. I've known him for years. He might listen to me."

The commander nodded and signaled for his lieutenant to bring him along.

With the aid of the trooper, Jason limped back to the barracks to find Helena huddled with Kailani in a corner on the floor.

"Your leg," she said. "I'll get a first-aid kit."

He winced as she rolled up his pant leg, but once she washed off the blood, the damage didn't look too bad. He'd been lucky; only a glancing blow from a .308 caliber silvertip intended for Kailani.

While she gingerly bandaged his leg, he squinted into the afternoon sun and pondered what their escape had done—transformed the worshipper into the hunter.

***

Jason sat on a stool and assessed the situation. Benjamin was a stalker, trained to skulk in the woods. The troopers were boys, most of them younger than him, and with no war fought in their lifetimes, he wondered at their experience. Could a squad of heavily armed boys find Benjamin?

Behind him, Helena sat with Kailani, holding the frightened girl's hand and stroking her hair.

Carlson had gone off to report to his superiors, something hardly necessary since the media had broadcast the attack.

Ten minutes of infuriating silence followed. Jason waited as the throbbing in his leg subsided, studying the tree line and hoping for a hint of what was happening.

He startled at a burst of gunfire. A violent end for Benjamin? Not likely. These new shots were close by and had come from the south, far from where the patrol was searching.

THE DAUGHTER OF THE SEA AND THE SKY

A nearby radio crackled to life, followed by a sharp command. Half a squad was ordered to remain, while the others were dispatched in the new direction. They too soon disappeared into the woods.

Jason stood and tested his leg. It had stiffened but would sustain his weight. He hobbled to the doorway to check outside, taking measure of the men who remained.

They were fingering the safeties on their weapons and nervously scanning the trees. All so young.

But something was wrong.

He'd heard shots but no ricochets. There were no gashes in the ground, no shards of the building ripped away. Benjamin was too good a marksman to be that far off.

He held his breath and listened.

A well-placed round kicked up dust at the squad leader's feet, a challenge rather than a threat to kill. The troopers scrambled for cover. The squad leader redeployed his men, one to the sentry house by the gate, the others behind trees at the edge of the forest.

Jason tried to follow, but the squad leader stopped him with a hand to his chest. "Stay here." He pointed to Helena and Kailani. "Stay with them."

For the next few minutes, Jason tried to gauge the sounds — shouts to the east, cries to the south, but no more gunfire. Then, from beyond the doorway, a clunk and a thud.

He glanced around; only one way in. Anyone trying to get to Kailani would have to pass through him. He lurched down the stairs, trying to tread lightly on his injured leg, and peered past the end of the barracks. By the guardhouse, he saw the soles of boots on the ground. The sentry was down.

A runner's breath. He was not alone.

Despite the squad leader's orders, he staggered outside. Benjamin was armed, and he was not. He needed the sentry's gun, but as he neared the guardhouse, a crunch of gravel from the Lady of Reason made him turn.

Benjamin slipped out from behind the statue's pedestal, the Browning Mark II Stalker nestled in his arms. "Hello, Jason." His voice was calm, as if they were planning for another day pulling weeds.

Jason inched toward him, but before he could come within an arm's length, Benjamin leveled the weapon at his chest.

"I did everything to warn you, Jason. I even learned to send an anonymous message. Bewaaare." He dragged out the last syllable and

273

punctuated it with a cackle. The barrel of the rifle dipped, but before Jason could take advantage, Benjamin regained focus. "I knew all along you'd never understand. Now out of my way. The apocalypse is at hand."

Jason's heart thumped as blood forced its way through his veins. He thought of Helena, of Kailani, of a cause worth dying for. He held his ground.

Benjamin squeezed the trigger, taking up slack.

A cry from behind. "No!"

Jason followed Benjamin's eyes to see Helena emerge from the barracks.

***

Helena had no need to slow her breathing. It had become strangely measured as she watched the two of them standing there—Jason alone and unarmed, Benjamin with rifle in hand. A sense of loss washed over her, so profound she felt as if her father were dying again. A voice inside her shouted: *Not this time.* Reason and spirit mixed into an elixir called courage, and the voice became sound.

"No." She stepped in front of Jason and confronted Benjamin, her eyes unblinking. "You mustn't do this, Benjamin. It's not the way of the Spirit."

The little man bared his teeth and glared at her. "And how would a nonbeliever know the way of the Spirit?"

"Because I *am* a believer now, thanks to you. You taught me, Benjamin, and what I've learned is that the way of the Spirit is the way of life."

Out of the corner of her eye, she caught troopers emerging from the woods. One of them had his weapon aimed at Benjamin's heart.

"The way of life, Benjamin. For all of us. For Jason and Kailani. For me and for you." She held out a hand, palm up, as if expecting him to hand over the rifle.

At the tree line, more troopers appeared. A dozen safeties clicked off.

One last, deep breath, and what? A prayer? "Time to choose, Benjamin. To choose life."

Benjamin glanced at the troopers, now an army with every weapon trained on him. Then he gazed skyward and closed his eyes.

THE DAUGHTER OF THE SEA AND THE SKY

The lightweight Stalker slipped from his hands and fell to the ground.

***

Helena surveyed the scene, trying to absorb what had happened. The commander had agreed to withdraw most of the troopers back to their barracks, though he insisted on an extra dozen in the honor guard. The media were thrilled with the turn of events—a better story—but wanted to hurry the ceremony along so it would finish before the light faded.

The sky had begun to darken, but a band of blue had opened between the edge of the clouds and the mountains. As the sun sank low enough to find the gap, it lit up the no man's land.

Time for goodbyes. Helena and Jason knelt side by side so Kailani could reach them both. The child lingered, leaning in and touching her forehead to each of theirs. Then a quick hug, and she was gone.

Helena watched her float up the hill, neither turning nor pausing until she neared the steel hut at the peak of the land bridge.

A cry, this time from the entrance to the hut. A dark-skinned bear of a man burst through with open arms, thick and broad like the branches of the sentinel tree, and behind him a woman with golden hair and eyes the color of the ocean.

As the sunlight flickered off the stars in her hair, their daughter rushed toward them, not stopping until she basked in the glow of the sea and the sky.

EPILOGUE

The sun had warmed enough to overwhelm the fog and break through, sending its rays across the Freedom Ocean. Helena's eyes narrowed as she tried to read the message. Too much glare. She half-squatted and shifted her chair until the shadow of an umbrella fell across the screen.

Better.

At the top of the message, she selected the attached video, the latest enhancement from Jason's team at the Polytech.

After a moment, Kailani appeared, no longer a child but a gangly young woman of fourteen. The hair was still golden and the eyes the color of the ocean, but her features had elongated, some not quite in proportion. Adolescent awkwardness had replaced childlike grace, the self-consciousness of a growing body. No matter. Time would make adjustments and she'd blossom.

The video began to play. Kailani's voice was only slightly less dreamy than it had been five years before, when she'd arrived in her small boat. Her father, she said, was working on an agreement with the Republic that would allow for an exchange of students. She hoped someday to go to university there, maybe even to the Polytechnic

Institute to study science like Helena and help make a better world. She hoped she could stay at the house on the cliffs with them.

Of course she could, now that it was a happier place.

On the grass before Helena, Juliana crawled to the picket fence, as she'd done earlier that morning when her daddy was watching. She grabbed hold and pulled with all her eleven-month-old might, almost rising to her feet before plopping back down again.

Helena sniffed the salt air and listened to the sounds of the cliffs — the lapping of the waves against the rocks, the sigh of the breeze in the birches. She glanced out at the expanse of ocean her daughter had yet to discover and smiled. Juliana would succeed soon enough, maybe tomorrow or the next day.

After all, it was in the nature of the Spirit to rise up and walk.

ABOUT THE AUTHOR

The urge to write first struck David at age sixteen when working on a newsletter at a youth encampment in the woods of northern Maine. It may have been the wild night when lightning flashed at sunset, followed by the northern lights rippling after dark, or maybe it was the newsletter's editor, a girl with eyes the color of the ocean, but he was inspired to write about the blurry line between reality and the fantastic.

Using two fingers and lots of white-out, he religiously typed five pages a day throughout college and well into his twenties. Then life intervened. When he found time again to daydream, the urge to write returned.

David now lives in the Great Northwest and anywhere else that catches his fancy. He no longer limits himself to five pages a day, and is thankful every keystroke for the invention of the word processor.

For more, please visit his website at www.DavidLitwack.com.

MORE FROM EVOLVED PUBLISHING

We offer great books across multiple genres, featuring high-quality editing (which we believe is second-to-none) and fantastic covers.

As a hybrid small press, your support as loyal readers is so important to us, and we have strived, with tireless dedication and sheer determination, to deliver on the promise of our motto:
QUALITY IS PRIORITY #1!

Please check out all of our great books, which you can find at this link:
www.EvolvedPub.com/Catalog/

Thank you!